ALSO BY ANNA QUINDLEN

Living Out Loud

Object

Lessons

Object Lessons

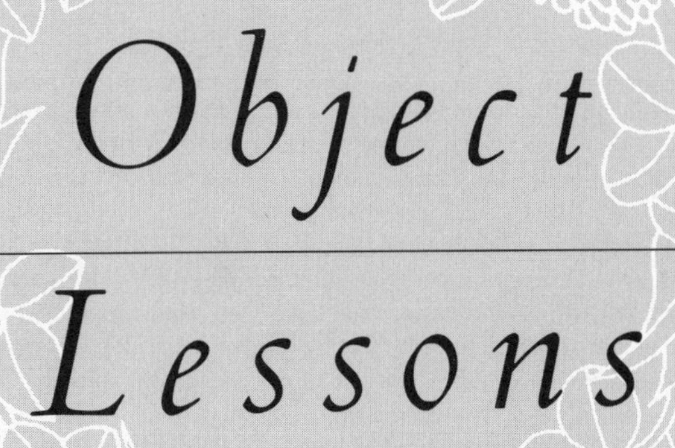

Anna Quindlen

Random House / New York

 Published in the United States by Random House, Inc., New York and simultaneously in Canada by Random House of Canada Limited, Toronto.

Grateful acknowledgment is made to Cherio Corporation for permission to reprint excerpts from "Daddy's Little Girl," words and music by Bobby Burke and Horace Gerlach.

Library of Congress Cataloging-in-Publication Data
Quindlen, Anna.
Object lessons / by Anna Quindlen.
p. cm.
ISBN 0-394-56965-2
I. Title.
PS3567.U336B54 1991
813'.54—dc20 90-48656

This is a work of fiction. Names, characters, places and incidents are the product of the author's imagination or are used fictitiously. Any resemblance to actual events, locales or persons, living or dead, is entirely coincidental.

Manufactured in the United States of America
9 8 7 6 5 4 3 2
First Edition

Book design by Jo Anne Metsch

For my mother and my father

Object

Lessons

1

EVER AFTER, WHENEVER SHE SMELLED the peculiar odor of new construction, of pine planking and plastic plumbing pipes, she would think of that summer, think of it as the time of changes. She would never be an imprecise thinker, Maggie Scanlan; she would always see the trees as well as the forest. It would have been most like her to think of that summer as the summer her grandfather had the stroke, or the summer her mother learned to drive, or the summer Helen moved away, or the summer she and Debbie and Bruce and Richard became so beguiled by danger in the broad fields behind Maggie's down-at-heel old house, or the summer she and Debbie stopped being friends.

All those things would be in her mind when she remembered that time later on. But they always came together, making her think of that summer as a time apart, a time which could never be forgotten but was terrible to remember: the time when her whole life changed, and when she changed, too. When she thought of herself and of her family, and of the town in which they lived, she thought of them torn in two—as they were before and as they were afterward, as though there had been a great rift in the earth of their existence, separating one piece of ground from the other. Her grandfather Scanlan always referred to life on earth and the life to come as *here* and *hereafter*: "You've got your here, and you've got your hereafter, little girl," he had said to her more than once. "Take care of the first, and the second will take care of itself." Sometimes Maggie remembered those words when she remembered that summer. Afterward, all the rest of her life would seem to her a hereafter. Here and hereafter, and in between was that summer, the time of changes.

Perhaps she saw it all whole because of so many years of listening to her grandfather create labels, calling everything from bare legs in church to the Mass performed in English "the Vatican follies," lumping all the bullets and the bombs and the bloodshed in his native Ireland under the heading of "the Troubles." Or perhaps it was because Maggie needed to find a common thread in the things that happened, all the things that turned that summer into the moat which separated her childhood from what came after, and which began to turn her into the person she would eventually become. "Change comes slowly," Sister Anastasia, her history teacher, had written on the blackboard when Maggie was in seventh grade. But after that summer, the summer she turned thirteen, Maggie knew that, like so much else the nuns had taught her, this was untrue.

Sometimes change came all at once, with a sound like a fire taking hold of dry wood and paper, with a roar that rose around you so you couldn't hear yourself think. And then, when the roar died down, even when the fires were damped, everything was different. People came to realize, when they talked about those years, that they were years which set one sort of America apart from another. Twenty years later they would speak of that time as beginning with the war, or the sexual revolution, or Woodstock. But Maggie knew it right away; she believed it began with the sound of a bulldozer moving dirt in her own backyard.

For that was the summer they began building the development behind the Scanlan house. That was the beginning.

On a June morning, a week after school let out, Maggie came down to breakfast and found her father standing at the window over the sink with a cup of coffee in his hand, watching an earth mover the color of a pumpkin heave great scoops of dirt crowned with reeds and grass into the air and onto a pile just beyond the creek. Maggie stood beside him and pushed up on her skinny forearms to look outside, but all she could see was the shovel when it reached its highest point and changed gears with a powerful grinding that seemed to make her bones go cold.

"Son of a bitch," Tommy Scanlan said with an air of wonder.

"Tom," said Maggie's mother, just "Tom," but what it meant was, don't swear in front of the children. Maggie's father didn't turn around or even seem to hear his wife. He just drank his coffee, making a little sibilant sound, and watched the earth mover lumber back and forth, back and forth, its shovel going up and down and over and up and down and over again.

A sign announcing the development had stood in the fields behind the house for four years, since before the fourth Scanlan baby had been born. It started out white with green letters. "On this site," the sign read: COMING SOON. TENNYSON PARK. A COMMUNITY OF HOMES FROM $39,500. "Ha," said Maggie's grandfather Scanlan, who knew the price of everything.

Two men with a post digger had come and put the sign up at the end of the cul-de-sac behind Park Street. After the sign went up, the older children in the neighborhood waited for something to happen, but it never did. For years it seemed to stand as a testimonial to the fact that everything was fine just the way it was, that everyone in Kenwood knew one another and was happy in the knowledge that all their neighbors were people like themselves: Irish, Catholic, well enough off not to be anxious about much except the slow, inexorable encroachment of those who were not their kind. The sign got older and the paint got duller and someone carved a cross into the back of it with a knife and all the excitement about new construction and new people died down. One Halloween the sign got pelted with eggs, and the eggs just stayed there through that winter, yellow rivulets that froze on the white and green.

Mrs. Kelly, who lived in the house at the end of the cul-de-sac and whose driveway was nearest the sign, was by turns enraged and terrified at the prospect of the development. She said that they had built a development near her sister in New Jersey, split-levels and ranch houses, and the next thing they knew there had to be a traffic light at the end of the street because of all the cars. But Mrs. Kelly's husband died of emphysema three years after the sign went up, and Mrs. Kelly went to live with her sister in New Jersey, and there was still no development, just the sign.

Maggie sprang up onto the kitchen counter and sat there, swinging her legs. "Get down," Connie Scanlan said, feeding Joseph scrambled eggs, although Joseph was really old enough to feed himself. Maggie stayed put, knowing her mother couldn't concentrate on more than one child at a time, and Connie went back to pushing the eggs into Joseph's mouth and wiping his little red chin with a napkin after each spoonful, the bowl of egg balanced in her lap. "You heard your mother," Tommy Scanlan added, but he continued to look out the window.

"Is that it?"

"What?"

"Tennyson Park," Maggie said.

Her father looked over at her and put down his cup. "Get down," he said, and turning to his wife, his hands in the pockets of his pants, he said, "That's the best-kept secret in construction. They're digging foundations, you've gotta figure cement within the month, you've gotta figure actual construction in two. My father hasn't said anything, my brothers haven't said anything, and I haven't heard a word from any of the union guys. But they're out there today with an earth mover, they'll have cement trucks by next week."

Without looking up, Connie Scanlan said, "Your father doesn't know everything, Tom."

"You're right my father doesn't know everything, but he happens to know what's going on in construction," Tommy said. "And this is the kind of thing he usually hears about. And being in the cement business you'd think I'd have heard about it, and I haven't."

"Maggie usually hears because she listens to everything," Damien said in his squeaky cartoon voice.

Tommy looked down at the second of his three sons, a skinny little boy as angular and jumpy as a grasshopper. Suddenly Tommy grinned, the easy grin that lit his face every once in a while and made him look half his thirty-three years.

"We'll keep that in mind, Dame," Tommy said, as Maggie glared at her brother across the kitchen table, and then he looked out the window again. "Jesus, am I going to catch hell," he said, and the grin faded to a grim line. "The old man will be on me about this for six months."

"I don't know why everybody calls Grandpop that," said Maggie. "He's not that old. Sixty-five's old, but not that old." She hopped down from the counter. "Daddy, will you drive me to Debbie's?" she said, as her father took his white shirt off a hanger bent to hang on top of the kitchen door.

"What happened to the president's physical fitness program?" Tommy asked. "She lives just up the street, for Christ's sake."

"Tom," said his wife, as the baby grabbed at the last spoonful of eggs.

"The president died," said Maggie. "There's no more fitness program. It's really hot, and Debbie's mother always drives me places."

"You'll walk," said her father, knotting a brown tie. "I'm late." He went into the hallway and took his jacket from over the banister.

" 'Bye," Connie said, but the click of the door sounded over her voice.

" 'Bye," Maggie said.

The Scanlans had lived in Kenwood, a small town on the Westchester border of the Bronx, since Maggie was a year old. It was not really a town, just one in a string of suburbs which had grown up around the city like a too-tight collar. The houses had been built right after the First World War, adequate houses, not grand ones, with a few flourishes—a stained-glass window on a landing here, a fanlight there. There were some center-hall Colonials, some mock Tudors, and a few boxy Cape Cods. Kenwood was no more than a dozen streets surrounding a spurious downtown: a dry cleaner; a drugstore with an attached medical-supply business with bedpans and laced corsets in the window; a real estate office with photographs of houses pinned to a cork bulletin board just inside the door; a hobby shop; and a stop on the railroad line into New York City.

Maggie's father helped run a cement company in the Bronx. His office was underneath an elevated subway line and next to the big wholesale vegetable depot. Unlike most of the fathers, who could be found at 7:00 A.M. reading the newspaper at the train station, Tom Scanlan drove into the city every day.

The pitch of their driveway was too steep, ever since a friend of Tommy's from high school had done an asphalt job on it, and whenever Tom backed out, his rear bumper bounced up off the street. As Maggie left the house that morning her father was just pulling out of the driveway, and she could see his mouth form the words "son of a bitch" as the back of his car hit the road and then bounced up level again.

It was hot in the June sun, and bright as a bare light bulb, but Maggie felt cool beneath the maple trees that lined the street, their leaves so green they looked almost black. Their branches hung over all but the center line of the street; in springtime the whirligigs that held their seeds floated down in tiny spirals, and they fell so thickly that the sidewalks were sticky with them, and the lawns grew untidy with seedlings. The trees were so large now, and cast such an indelible shade, that shrubs only grew in the backyards of the houses in Kenwood, except for the leggy rhododendrons that were planted on either side of the front doors of almost every home. Occasionally there would be talk about cutting down some trees to give the azaleas or forsythia a fighting chance, but most of the adults in the neighborhood had been city kids, and they found themselves incapable of cutting down trees. They tended their lawns with reverence, buying rotating sprinklers and hoses with holes along their lengths so that the water made little arcs of diamonds in the sunshine.

Maggie felt at peace here, on these quiet streets. She did not think of loving Kenwood, just as it did not occur to her to think about loving her parents, or her brothers Terence and Damien and little Joseph. It was simply her place, the place where she did not have to think twice about how to get where she was going and what to do when she got there. She remembered vaguely that when she was little her house had been that sort of place, too, but it seemed a long time ago. Now her house felt too crowded, too public. Once Maggie had heard her mother say that it was impossible for two women to share the same kitchen. Connie Scanlan had been talking about living in a beach house for a month with her sister-in-law, but the words had stayed with Maggie because she thought they applied to her and her mother as well. The house belonged to Connie. Kenwood, with its scuffed baseball field and its narrow creek and its ring of tousled fields, was Maggie's home. As she listened to the sound of the earth movers grinding away behind her, a faint shudder shook her shoulders, the feeling her aunt Celeste once told her signified someone walking over your grave.

She glanced back at her own house, but it looked empty and still, the two white pillars on either side of the doorway grubby with fingerprints. When they had first moved to Kenwood from a two-family house in the northeast Bronx that belonged to Connie's aunt and uncle, Tommy Scanlan had repainted the pillars every six months or so. But he was tired when he got home from work these days; he worked most Saturdays during good weather, and keeping up with the dirt the children left behind now seemed futile. He was the only one of his friends who had lived in the suburbs before he was married; his parents still lived there, in a big fieldstone house with a gazebo and a fountain in the backyard, in a section of Westchester County a little north of Kenwood, where the houses were so far apart that the neighbors' windows were only an occasional glint of sunlight through the trees. Tommy had lived there from the time he was fifteen until he got married at the age of twenty. Aunt Celeste had once told Maggie's mother, when the two of them were drinking beer on the front steps one night, that she suspected the pillars made Tommy feel he had come down in the world.

"Paint 'em black," John Scanlan said with a great guffaw on one of the rare visits he and his wife, Mary Frances, had made to the home of their middle son. Maggie noticed sometimes that when her father passed the columns a little white scar above his eyebrow jumped and writhed like one of the tiny white worms that sucked the life from her grandfather Mazza's tomato plants, and she supposed he was remembering John Scanlan's words.

That was what impressed Maggie most about her grandfather Scanlan: not that he dispensed down payments, tuition money, doctor's fees, with nothing in return except everyone knowing that he'd bought and paid for your house, your children's school, your wife's single room on the maternity floor. It was that he could, almost magically, make his children bob and move and sway like marionettes. Tommy's scar was the least of his accomplishments. His other four sons could be made to nod, pale, blush, shift in their chairs, pace on his Oriental rugs, simply by the words and looks John Scanlan could turn upon them. Maggie's grandmother sometimes seemed seized with St. Vitus's dance when her husband was angry. Only Sister John of the Cross, Maggie's aunt Margaret, John Scanlan's only living daughter, could sit motionless, expressionless, in her father's presence. Maggie sometimes thought her grandfather would have stuck a pin in Margaret if he could have been assured it would make her jump. She had paid a heavy price for her composure. "Hiding behind the skirts of Jesus, Sister?" John Scanlan would sometimes say, and then Margaret would smile slowly, without mirth, and so would John, because they both knew he had put his finger on it.

Maggie's mother managed to remain calm when she was around her father-in-law, too, although John Scanlan would have been delighted to hear how Connie railed against his machinations in the privacy of her own small kitchen. Sometimes Maggie felt that no one ever talked about what was really going on in her father's family, although everyone seemed to talk all the time. But she had heard enough from her aunt Celeste and her cousin Monica, and even occasionally—when Maggie was eavesdropping—from her own mother, to know that her mother's place amidst the Scanlans was not a comfortable one.

And she had only to look at the family gathered around John Scanlan's mahogany dining table at any holiday dinner to know which of his grandchildren were different from the rest. All of Maggie's many cousins looked a good deal alike—fair, even colorless, with placid faces. The children of Tommy Scanlan did not conform. Maggie herself was olive-skinned, with thick, heavy hair and curiously opaque green eyes, catlike and surprising. She had realized some time ago that no one would ever call her cute. She was thin—not slim and graceful but lanky on its way to being something else, caught in that uncomfortable place between childhood and maturity. Sometimes she felt as if her whole family was caught in some middle ground, too. If she heard that she was her mother's daughter one more time, she was sure she would start to scream.

Three blocks from her own house, over the railroad tracks, Maggie's closest friend, Debbie Malone, lived with her seven brothers and sisters in a large center-hall Colonial. Mrs. Malone was pregnant again, her muscular little legs sticking out of brown maternity shorts beneath the great cantilevered thrust of her belly. In the afternoons she lay on a yellow chaise longue made of strips of rubber that was set out beneath a maple tree in the Malones' backyard. Her calves and arms stuck to the rubber in the heat, and as the children eddied around her, demanding money for ice cream, complaining about one another, asking permission to do things they had never been permitted to do and would not be permitted to do now, she lay perspiring in the shade, staring up at the motionless leaves. Mrs. Malone was a good-humored woman who liked sports, but the heat got her down. One of her favorite activities had always been shoveling the snow off the long cement walk that led up to her front door. Her children slipped out of her as easily as if she were a water slide into the crowded pool of their household.

Maggie never knocked when she went to the Malones; she just walked around back and let herself into the kitchen through the screen door. Mrs. Malone treated her as if she were a member of the family, which was strange considering that she had more than enough family to go round. But Maggie loved the easy feeling, and responded by being more solicitous and communicative than the Malone children, who, with the exception of Helen, the eldest, were simple machines. Mrs. Malone, Maggie supposed, was a simple machine, too. She seemed to like her family, her husband, and her house with a kind of straightforward good humor. Maggie threw herself right into this; she was constantly struck by what a welcome change it was from her own family, in which she felt as if she were moving through a carnival fun house, waiting for a skeleton to leap out from behind a closed door. Mr. and Mrs. Malone had met in the fifth grade at St. Cyril's School in an Irish section of Manhattan, and when they were together they seemed more like brother and sister than husband and wife, at least from Maggie's experience of married people.

"Doesn't all that hair make you hot, Pee Wee?" Mrs. Malone said, as she turned from the sink and looked Maggie up and down. "Nope," said Maggie, the way she always did when she was asked that question, and she threw her hair over her shoulder, pushed her damp bangs back with the flat of her hand and sat down at the redwood picnic table in the kitchen.

"Can we go swimming?" she asked.

"Did you bring your suit?"

"I left it here the last time."

"Is that red one yours?" Mrs. Malone said, rinsing some forks. "I was wondering where that came from. I asked Aggie and she said it wasn't hers, but I put it in her underwear drawer anyway. Go up and get it and get your partner in crime and we'll all go."

"Are you going swimming too?"

"No I am not," said Mrs. Malone, wiping her hands on a dirty dishtowel. "I'll sit by the pool and put my feet in and wish it was a month from now and I was twenty pounds lighter."

The pool was in the next town, at what was called the Kenwoodie Club. It was really nothing more than a swimming pool and a nine-hole golf course surrounded by a chain-link fence, with an entrance gate where a guard checked laminated membership cards. Nearly all the people Maggie went to school with spent the day there, doing cannonballs off the diving board or spitting in the baby pool.

Helen Malone had become famous at the Kenwoodie Club after a trip to California the summer before, when she had emerged from the locker room one day in the closest thing the club had ever seen to a bikini. It was an abbreviated two-piece with push-up cups, and a bottom half that rode a full two inches below her navel. Mrs. Malone had been asked to see that the suit stayed at home next time. "If they think I can control Helen Malone," she had muttered in the car on the way home that day, "they've got another think coming."

Even her own mother talked about Helen Malone in the third person, as though she were someone none of them knew. Maggie thought that the only person who truly acted as if she knew Helen Malone was Helen herself. Her legend was considerable. At Sacred Heart Academy all anyone needed to do was mention Helen Malone's name and the girls became stern and watchful. She was known to be terribly sophisticated, and perhaps even something more than that. But what really riveted all of them, all the freckled, pleasant, ordinary girls with whom Helen shared study hall and Bible history and glee club, were two things. The first was that Helen was beautiful. This was never agreed upon, of course; there were girls who said she was odd-looking, that her nose was thin and pointed. But they never said this in front of the boys they knew. Helen's eyes were a clear blue, and her nose straight and small, but her lips were full, as though they'd been inflated, and her hair was full, too, full and glossy. Mrs. Malone sometimes said that at the hospital they'd given her Liz Taylor's baby by mistake.

But, more important, her beauty seemed to stand for something inside her, a kind of apartness, and a feeling that she knew exactly where she was going and how she was going to get there, and that she would go, happily, alone. She rarely spoke, never gossiped, was never silly, and had never seemed young. She was grown up, and had been for as long as anyone could remember. Perhaps this was what obsessed Maggie and Debbie about her most. They rifled through her drawers constantly, trying on her old prom dresses and tossing her underwear back and forth as though they were playing hot potato, embarrassed by their curiosity but compelled by it, too. There were always letters from boys they had never heard of, and some of them wrote poems. "I long to peel you like a ripe peach," someone named Edward with an address at Cornell University had written, and Debbie had read it over and over. "What does that mean?" she said, her freckled cheeks scarlet.

"You don't even peel peaches," Maggie said, and Debbie looked at her pityingly. "What do you want him to say, that he wants to peel her like an orange?" Maggie stared at the envelope. "The stamp is upside down for love," she said.

Last year, Maggie remembered, Sister Regina Marie had asked them to write down, without thinking, the answer to the question: Who are you? It was the only time in her school career Maggie could remember not knowing an answer. It had been a kind of psychological trick, really; Sister didn't even ask them to hand the papers in, just told them to put the answers in their pockets and think about what they had found to say about themselves.

"What did you write, Mag?" Debbie had asked on the playground, blinking her blue eyes, like Helen's but paler, smoothing back her black hair, like Helen's but kinky. In fact Debbie looked like a blurred version of Helen, angles blunted, colors muted. "I put that I am still becoming who I am," Maggie said. "God," Debbie sighed. "That's why you get As and I get stupid Cs." And she took a piece of paper out of her pocket and handed it to Maggie. In Debbie's rounded writing, with the circles dotting the i's, was written, "I am Helen Malone's sister."

Afterward, when she was in her own room, Maggie had taken her own paper from her blazer pocket, unfolded it and put it on her bureau. It was blank.

Helen was the only Malone child with a room of her own. On its door was a small blackboard for messages. It was always full. Maggie passed it now on her way to Debbie's room, up beneath the slanting roof of the third floor. "In by 11!" Mrs. Malone had written at the top in capital letters, and below "John Kelly called—will call again" and "Can I wear your white eyelet blouse tonight? Aggie (I'll wash it)." Underneath the second was written neatly in blue chalk "NO." Her neat penmanship on the blackboard and a glass in the sink were often the only signs of Helen in the Malone house for days at a time.

Debbie was lying on her bed staring at the ceiling, still wearing her nightgown. "Summer's just started and I'm bored already," she said as Maggie came in.

Maggie sat on the edge of the bed, silent. Debbie shut her eyes. Her nose was sunburned. "Today she got a dozen red roses," she said finally.

"Really?" said Maggie. "From who?"

"Who knows?" Debbie said. "Some guy. She stuck the card down the front of her shirt."

"Can we see?"

"They're in the living room. She said she'd put them where the whole family could enjoy them. I think that means they're from somebody she doesn't like that much."

Maggie sighed. "Amazing." The two girls stared into space. Maggie bit a cuticle. "Your mother said she'll drive us to the club," she said.

"Same old thing," said Debbie. "Boring, boring, boring." But she got up and started to put on her clothes just the same. "I'd better get boobs soon," she said, her voice muffled as she dressed beneath the tent of her nightgown, but Maggie just said "Shut up" and started to look through Aggie's underwear drawer for her old red bathing suit.

"Sometimes you're such a baby, Mag," said Debbie listlessly.

"Shut up," Maggie said again, taking her suit and heading downstairs.

2

I N LATE AFTERNOON, WHEN THE HUmidity had begun to ebb somewhat and the sheen of perspiration on all the children to fade, Connie Scanlan sat down crosslegged on the floor of her dining room to look at her good dishes. She always waited until she was alone to do this, for she thought that if anyone saw her they would surely say to themselves, "Well, she's finally lost her mind."

Her pale knees glimmered amid the china spread out in front of her, as though they, too, were porcelain. Twelve dinner plates, twelve saucers, twelve cups, twelve dessert plates, a tureen, three serving dishes, a coffee pot, a creamer, and a sugar bowl. They were all a pale, pale cream color, with purple and red flowers painted around the edge and a gilded rim, and each dish, each cup, came with its own gray chamois bag, as though they were pieces of jewelry. The china seemed to Connie the only vestige of some foolish feeling she had once had about what her adult life would be like. Day after day she washed the plastic bowls in the sink, and now and then she thought of these others, shining beneath their little shrouds, too good for everyday, for meatloaf and macaroni and cheese.

It had turned out that her life was an everyday sort of thing, too. She did not know why she had expected something different. Perhaps it was that her own family life had been so dark and peculiar, her elderly parents rarely exchanging a word, herself the only child, that she had easily fallen prey to the images of bright domesticity conjured up by popular songs and movies. Perhaps it was that, daring as the union between Connie Mazza and Tommy Scanlan had been, flying in the face of John Scanlan and his family, it had started off as the stuff of grand opera, and she had expected it to go on being so. The bitter taste in Connie's mouth was the residue of disillusionment.

Her marriage was to have been her entry to a normal life, the life she imagined everyone else lived when she looked at the world from within the gates of Calvary Cemetery. She had supposed that a husband and children would teach her to be one of the group, but instead she felt more and more alone among more and more people, a woman whose universe was contained beneath her own sternum. Sometimes she wondered if the cemetery gates had grown inside her as well, closing her off from a world naturally communal and gregarious.

Her aunt Rose had always told her that children would be the joy of her life, and even though Connie felt she had been the bane of her own mother's existence, she had believed what Rose said. And sometimes, when the children were small, still attached to their mother by the umbilical cord of weakness and primitive need, she felt that this was true, that with a baby on her hip she was not alone. Looking at each one in the bassinet, the little fingers splayed like small pink starfish on the crib sheets, she imagined what they would become, to the world and to her. In this, too, she sometimes felt that being an only child served her poorly, and that her imaginings came from books and women's magazine articles and movies. The eldest boy would be her helpmate and protector. The youngest would be slightly sentimental, a little mischievous, always allied with his mother. Perhaps the picture in her mind had been most vivid for the first daughter. "Now you will have someone to do things with," everyone told her after Maggie was born, and that was what she had thought she had given birth to: her closest friend, her soulmate. Her imaginings had turned out to be as useless as her wedding china. Connie's need and her children's maturity combined to cause bitter disappointment, for as the children grew and moved away, from her and her dreams of them, they seemed to her strangers, Scanlans.

She remembered the day her father-in-law had first met Maggie. He had found her playing on his lawn with her aunt Margaret four years after Connie and Tommy's wedding. Connie had thought that the child was at the convent until she saw the little hand, still dimpled at the knuckle, clutching a hundred-dollar bill.

"I'm sorry, Con," Margaret had said. "They took to each other like fish to water." Connie's narrow chest had gone cold. A year later her daughter was in private school, her tuition paid for by her grandfather. Connie had never felt the same about her since.

After that she had waited for the vultures to circle her marriage, but with the exception of a few obligatory holiday dinners and the occasional party, she and Tommy had somehow managed to stay outside her father-in-law's grip. She supposed that, with the exception of Maggie, he found them all beneath his notice.

John Scanlan had gotten his son James named chief of his department at Christ Hospital by giving them new X-ray equipment, and he had chosen a house for Mark and Gail, not far from his own. His younger sons had come to work for him and without a whimper had become completely dependent on their father's industry, and his whims.

Only Margaret had escaped for a time, sent to study philosophy at Tulane while living in a New Orleans convent covered with wisteria and wrought iron. She had written home about a doctoral degree and the fiery food, and had bloomed in the heat.

And then John Scanlan had taken the Mother Superior to lunch in a steak house, given her a check for ten thousand dollars for a new chapel for the order's retreat house, and Margaret had been reassigned to a school not five miles from the house she had left for the convent. She taught first grade and read Kierkegaard on the sly. Sometimes Connie looked at all of them, gathered around the big table in John and Mary Frances Scanlan's dining room, and thought they all were covered with blood except for her.

Slowly she stacked the plates and placed them on the bottom shelves of the breakfront. From outside she could hear a peculiar noise, and looked out the dining-room window to watch Maggie come up the street, moving toward home, flat-footed and slow. It struck her again that Maggie walked a little like Connie's own mother had, head down, shoulders thrust forward. "The weight of the world on her shoulders," someone had once said to Connie of her mother, and it was true of her daughter, too. Otherwise, she knew, the two couldn't have been more different.

Anna Mazza had been built like a cardboard box, and Connie had often thought she had all the sensitivity of one. Maggie was always thinking, thinking, thinking, keeping silent only so she could figure out what made the world work. Connie didn't feel qualified to tell her; she was still trying to figure it out herself. And so the two of them had sunk into silence just around the time that both had noticed that Maggie would soon be taller than Connie.

Her cousin Celeste had assured Connie that this was the way it was with girls, that they should be put in the deep freeze until they were twenty-one, that every mother was made to feel she was a palpable insult by a daughter of a certain age. But all Connie could remember was how much she had loved Maggie as a baby, how the nurses would hold her up at the nursery window and perfect strangers on the other side would say "oh" with such conviction that small spots of fog would appear on the glass.

Maggie had had a great furry head of black hair, navy eyes that seemed bottomless, a moon face, and two small violet bruises where the forceps had reached in and pulled her out. She had weighed an even ten pounds, and Connie, small and wan in her satin bed jacket, had felt that Maggie was her great accomplishment, the finest thing she had ever done. But the connection between herself and her daughter had slowly disappeared, until there were only memories of warm curves, of a little pink mouth working against her skin. When Connie had asked the last week of school whether she should order next year's uniform blouses with darts in them, Maggie had seethed for three days, leaving the house for hours on end, discernible when she was around by the way she made the closing of a door or the placing of a glass on a table sound like something between profanity and physical violence. "You know why they call them growing pains?" Connie had said to Celeste, who sometimes seemed to be the only person she could talk to. "It's because I'm going to kill her."

From the window Connie could see the length of the street, could see Maggie coming slowly toward the house and realized that the noise she had heard was the slapping of Maggie's rubber flip-flops hitting the pavement. From this distance Connie was struck anew by the way in which Maggie favored Tommy, who was skinny, with one of those bony Irish-boy bodies that hang from the shoulders as though their shirts were still on hangers. Maggie was thin and bony, too, the moon face of babyhood now squared off at the jaw. She insisted on wearing last year's bathing suit, even though it was too short for her lengthening torso and she spent all her time yanking it down to cover her butt. Connie thought of Joseph up in his crib, pink and wet in the heat, his mouth open, silver slug trails of saliva on the sheets. An hour ago she had stood over him and thought that the rift would come soon. Now he was her little love, warm and sweet, always ready to wrap his arms around her middle and lay his head on the pillow of her breastbone. Soon he would change, develop edges to his character that would come to cut the connection between them. It had happened with each of his brothers. She supposed the boys were down at the ball field, Damien trailing after Terence forlornly, although Damien hated athletics nearly as much as Connie did. The odd couple, their mother had thought as she watched them go, the elder boy dark, stolid, and so attached to his baseball mitt that he cradled it in bed at night, the younger as high-strung and uncoordinated as a colt.

Connie put her hand up to touch her hair. She realized that she had gone all day without once looking into a mirror, and she wondered if there would be no reflection in the glass, as if she were a vampire. In the house in which Connie had grown up, there had been only one mirror, over the sink, and its silver was scarred and grubby. In her own house there were many more mirrors, but somewhere along the line she had stopped looking into them. The silence pressed in upon her like a damp hand.

Connie Scanlan had been raised in the Bronx, and had never been able to adjust to what she considered the sneaky sounds of the suburbs, the hissing of the sprinklers, the hum of the occasional car, the children's voices calling to one another, carrying so clearly that they had learned to whisper anything important. The city sounds had a primary color: horns, screams, the solid *thwack* of a broomstick connecting with a hard ball, the *clunk* of the ball coming down into the leather glove. The section of the Bronx where her family lived was considered a kind of suburb by them all, not like the Lower East Side or Little Italy. But it still smelled and sounded of the city. In Kenwood sometimes, particularly on summer afternoons, the street would be so still that she would be tempted to put *South Pacific* or some Sinatra album on the stereo and turn it up loud enough to drown the quiet out. But she was always afraid someone would hear; she didn't want to give them one more reason to talk about her behind her back.

She was sure they did already, in this homogenous place where the second generation Dohertys and O'Briens and Kellys lived after they married one another's sisters, cousins, friends, and left the city behind. Only a few had muddied the blood lines with outsiders, and often those brave or foolish ones had done it to spit in the face of their families. Connie had not believed this was the case when Tommy had proposed to her, even when Celeste, big and bold as a helium balloon in bridesmaids' blue taffeta, had said at the wedding, "This is a pretty elaborate way to make sure your old man never talks to you again. You sure you want to play Cinderella the rest of your life, kid?" Instead of fading with time, experience had intensified those words in Connie's memory.

The back door slammed as Maggie came in and dumped her damp towel on the counter. Her wet hair had made a big spot on the back of her blouse, and for some reason this made Connie angry.

"Don't they make you wear a bathing cap at that pool?"

"Yeah, but it doesn't work with my hair," Maggie said, drinking water at the sink. "It's hard for me to get it all inside the cap."

"So it gets wet anyway."

"No it doesn't. I wear the cap and then I take it off when we're ready to go, and I go under to get my hair wet."

"Let me get this straight," Connie said. "You wear the cap to keep your hair dry and then at the end you take the cap off and get your hair wet? Does that make sense?"

"You don't understand because you don't know how to swim," said Maggie. "Everybody does it."

"If everybody jumped off the Brooklyn Bridge, would you do that too?" Connie said, without even thinking.

"You always say that."

"Hang this on the line before you leave," Connie said, unrolling the towel with a snap. The red suit fell on the floor, and with it a flutter of damp dirty paper. Connie stooped down. It was a twenty-dollar bill. She picked it up between two fingers as though it was a bug. "How is your grandfather Scanlan?" Connie said.

Maggie took the money and her wet things and turned away. "He said we're all going to the house on Sunday. How come?"

"On Sunday I am cleaning the linen closet," Connie said, turning toward the sink. "Go hang up your suit."

From the window she watched her daughter fumble with the clothespins and slip the money into her pocket. It enraged her that even without being present John Scanlan could ruin her day. "Don't you wake your brother up," Connie hissed, as her daughter came back through the kitchen on her way upstairs.

She looked at the sink filled with cereal bowls, coffee cups, Mickey Mouse glasses with low tidelines of orange pulp. Upstairs she could hear Joseph humming to himself. "Damn it," she said, spraying detergent onto a sponge.

A thousand times Tommy had told her she was doing it wrong, that you were supposed to fill the sink with water and let the dishes soak. A thousand times she had shut her mouth and done it her way. She'd been doing dishes since she was seven years old, standing on the red leatherette seat of a stepstool, when there had been only her own plate and glass to wash. She'd washed her own cereal bowl before school and her own plates after dinner, while her father and her mother worked. Nobody was going to tell her how to do a dish.

Suddenly there was a stultifying silence, oppressive as the heat, as the last earth mover working in the fields behind the house quieted, rumbled once like a death rattle and was still.

Connie was a short woman, low to the ground, and even if she stood on tiptoe, she could not quite make out how much work had been done, except that there seemed to be great gashes in the reedlike weeds, and here and there a massive pile of fresh brown earth. A half dozen of the big machines stood at rest. For the first time Connie noticed that someone had placed two portable toilets at the far end of the field. The man who had been driving the last earth mover was almost at the back door before she realized he was coming to her house. Connie noticed that his gray undershirt was stained black beneath the arms with huge half-moons of perspiration. He peered through the screen at her, blinded by the dim indoors after the glare of the day.

"Hello?" he said.

"Yes?" Connie's voice was cold.

"Could I trouble you to use the phone?" he asked, still peering through the screen.

Connie opened the door a bit. The man had glossy hair, like an animal's pelt, and eyebrows so thick that they looked like an amateur theatrical effect. He looked at Connie and Connie looked at him; for a moment they just gaped at one another, and then both started to laugh.

"Connie Mazza," he said, smoothing back his hair.

"Oh," she said, snapping her fingers. "Don't tell me, I'll get it. Don't tell me."

He laughed again. "Martinelli," he said.

"I knew *that* part."

"Joe," he added.

"Joey. Joey Martinelli. I would have had it in a minute. Come in. Use the phone. Do you want a beer?" She started to laugh again. "It's nice to see a familiar face."

"I knew you lived in the neighborhood," he said, "but I swear to God I didn't know this was your house."

"You're working on this project?"

"I'm the foreman. But we're in such a big hurry that I'm driving the backhoe part time. We did six foundations today. I swear I thought somebody was going to have a stroke in this heat."

"You dug foundations for six houses today?"

He nodded. "And we're supposed to do six tomorrow. The people are in some kind of a rush."

"I don't know why," said Connie. "They've been planning this for years." She pointed to the phone. "Go ahead."

She watched him as he dialed. He had the sort of muscles men developed from heavy lifting, and he stood awkwardly when he stood still. She remembered that he had been one of the good athletes when she was a girl, one of the nice boys in the neighborhood who always held the door if you left the drugstore when they did. She hadn't known him well, although she had gone out with his younger brother a few times.

She heard him talking on the phone about dinner. "Your wife?" she said after he hung up.

"My mother," he said ruefully.

"How 'bout a beer?" she said, even though it felt strange to be alone in the house with a man. A noise from above made her start; she hadn't counted the children, or even remembered them for a moment.

"Thanks, but I gotta finish up and get home. We're supposed to be done here by the end of the year. Nice houses, too. Laundry chutes. Disposals. Carpet. Not like these old ones, but nice houses."

"An old house is a lot of work," Connie said.

"Yeah." He looked down at his shoes and at the grime he was leaving on the speckled linoleum. "Oh, boy, I'm sorry. My mother would kill me if she could see this."

"You're right," said Connie, and they both laughed again. As she watched him cross the fields she remembered that his father had died in the excavation of a subway tunnel somewhere deep beneath the surface of the borough of Queens. Perhaps that was why she was surprised to find him in this line of work. Or perhaps it was that she vaguely remembered he had been smarter than that, one of the boys likely to break free of the Italian immigrant tradition of dirt beneath the fingernails. His brother had worn aftershave that smelled like peppermint. And Joey had delivered papers to earn pocket money; he had brought the *News* to her father every morning. It was odd what you remembered, like her remembering those bruises on Maggie's head after all these years. It was interesting to find that one short conversation with an almost-stranger had improved her mood immeasurably.

Hot as it was, she stretched up to get the big bowl from the top shelf of the kitchen cabinets, and humming to herself, began to make a cake.

3

TOMMY SCANLAN STARED OUT THE WINdow of his office in the gray-green cinderblock building that was the home of First Concrete. Below him was the lot where he and the other men parked their cars, and behind the chain-link fence was another, larger lot where they kept the cement mixers, great clanking beasts incongruously painted in red-and-white candy-cane stripes. At the moment there was a single cement mixer there, its hood up, its enormous greasy motor exposed like the entrails of a big animal, and next to the cement mixer was a black Lincoln Continental with a high-gloss shine.

"Ah, shit," Tommy said aloud, looking down at the big car. There was a faint tapping at his office door, and Tommy switched off the radio atop his filing cabinet. "Ah, shit," he said again, going to open it.

One of the mechanics, a squat, swarthy man named Gino, whose wavy hair looked like the ocean on a rough day, stood at the door in his red-and-white striped First Concrete shirt. All the men hated the shirts, but Gino was the shop steward and he never showed up at First Concrete out of uniform.

"The old man is downstairs," Gino said. The men never used a salutation when they addressed Tommy in the office; they weren't sure whether to call him Mr. Scanlan or not.

Tommy had failed to notice this particular semantic dilemma, but he appreciated the fact that they always said "the old man" and not "your old man." It made Tom feel small to be reminded of his father's power.

"Did you tell him I was here?" Tommy asked, looking out the window.

"Downstairs they told him they weren't sure where you were," Gino said. "I don't think he's coming up. He's got us changing the oil in his car. Your brother's with him."

Tommy could see his father standing in one of his gray suits, in the maintenance lot, looking at the disabled cement mixer. The old man turned and said something to the mechanic working on his car, and the man handed him a rag. John Scanlan wiped the striped side of the cement mixer, then shook his head. "Oh, hell," Tommy muttered, lighting a cigarette.

The stripes on the trucks had been Tommy's father's idea of free advertising; no one, John Scanlan had reasoned, would ever be able to mistake a First Concrete cement mixer for the cement mixers of Reliable, or Gatto Brothers, or Bronx River Cement. On the other hand, no one ever made fun of those other cement mixers, either. Sometimes, when Tommy handed his card to a developer, or a factory owner, or someone from the city who was looking for a couple hundred dollars in exchange for a contract to lay some sidewalks or pour the foundation for a school gymnasium, he would see a look of discovery pass over the guy's face. No matter how often it happened, Tommy's chest would tighten at that moment. "The ones with the stripes, right?" the customer would say. "The red-and-white stripes?" And the look of discovery would be replaced by a big grin. "Can't miss those babies."

Tommy was in charge of keeping the trucks looking good, but he hated the stripes so much that he would let them go until they'd faded to pale pink and dirty gray. It wasn't the ridicule; it was the reminder. "Look at me!" the stripes seemed to shout, just as John Scanlan always did. If Tommy had had his way, the trucks would have been gray. They would have looked like what they were: trucks that carried cement, not big pieces of peppermint candy on wheels. But Tommy never had his way. Sooner or later his father would see one of the trucks, on one of his trips around the city to have lunch in some parish rectory or another—"good booze at Queen of Peace," he might say to Tom the next time he saw him, or "one more plate of corned beef and cabbage and I'm not going back to St. Teresa's"—and the old man would be on the phone complaining that the trucks needed a fresh coat of paint.

He never called Tommy directly. Buddy Phelan, who was the president of First Concrete and, not coincidentally, the godson of the monsignor who handled purchasing for the biggest suburban diocese in the metropolitan area, would come into Tommy's office with a bemused grin on his face, and say, "Hey, Tom. Time to give the trucks a going over, whattaya say?" And Tommy would know that his father had called that morning to suggest that the man who owned one hundred percent of First Concrete, and who had the right to hire and fire those who worked there, did not like his clever subliminal advertising gimmick compromised by a failure of upkeep and a heavy layer of city grime.

Buddy Phelan always assumed that Tommy hated him, but this was not true. In his heart of hearts Tommy hated no one, except occasionally himself, and he was pleased to be vice president of operations at First Concrete, a big title for a mundane job. If he had been the "big boss," as the men who drove the trucks called Buddy, he would not have been able to chat with the workers so effortlessly when they came in at the end of the day, smelly and glad to talk without the roar of the mixer or the road in their ears. He would have felt constrained from going into Sal's at lunchtime and sitting at the bar with a sandwich and a draft beer, putting in his two cents about the Yankees, the weather, or the coloreds. It would have been impossible for him to join the pick-up basketball games that took place across the street most afternoons, when he felt free and young and extraordinarily competent: dribble downcourt, push off from the knees, send the orange ball sailing with a motion of his wrist that had become second nature in Catholic school gyms, watch it sink with only that slight lisp of a sound that had given the shot the name "swish." Basketball made him feel simultaneously like a man and a boy. Everyone nodded to Buddy Phelan when he left for the night, climbing into his Olds 98, but no one ever asked him to join them for a beer, except Tommy, when he had nothing better to do. He felt sorry for the guy.

When he turned from the window, Gino was gone and his brother Mark was just coming up the stairs. Mark was flushed bright pink in the heat, but his tie was still tied tight, while Tommy's was at half-mast. They looked like brothers, both mostly beige: beige hair, faded from the tow they'd had as boys, beige freckles, darker beige eyes. But where Tommy was long and rangy, Mark was solid and short. It was only after Mark had married that he had been able to convince his family to stop calling him "Squirt," although John Scanlan, who was an even six feet tall, still felt compelled to make comments about his son's height from time to time.

"We're going to have to paint the trucks next week," Tommy said.

"I don't know why you fight him on that," Mark said. "You know who wins."

The two stood silent, sweating. Tommy took a great deal of satisfaction out of the fact that he didn't work directly for his father, and Mark resented him for it, thinking that depending on John Scanlan's largesse once removed was worse than simply facing facts and going to work for Scanlan & Co. "We're all in the family business," their sister Margaret always said with a grin. Mark could not understand how this could apply to obstetrics or a religious vocation, but Margaret said that was simply because he was always too literal.

In fact Tommy would have preferred not to work for any Scanlan enterprise. When he and Connie had first married they had talked of moving to California, of living where it was always warm and no one had ever heard of John Scanlan, where they didn't care if you were Italian as long as you weren't Mexican. But their own fecundity had laid waste to that dream. During the first five years of their marriage, when they had heard not a word from Tommy's parents, they had learned how difficult it was to pay the bills on a working man's salary. Then John Scanlan had taken an interest in Maggie, and Tommy had been hired, after a perfunctory interview, as a vice president at First

Concrete. His wife had barely spoken to him for nearly two months after he took the job. The words she had used to break the silence were "I'm pregnant again."

There were only two reasons why Tommy preferred being an executive to being one of the men carrying and shoveling cement. The first was that he needed the money. He and Connie had practiced rhythm since Maggie was born, and they had three sons to show for it, and a suspicion of another on the way. Saddle shoes alone ran him two hundred dollars a year. The other thing he loved about his job was his office. As offices went, it was on the small side, with a window that looked over the parking lot to the basketball court and playground across the street, and the red-brick public school building beyond that. When two trains passed going in opposite directions on the elevated line, his office shivered like a child with a high fever. Sometimes in the summer the Sanitation Department would not be quick enough about picking up the garbage, and the wholesale fruit market across the road would give off an overripe sweet smell. But Tommy had a gray desk, a gray file cabinet, a gray table that held an adding machine and stood beneath a wall displaying a full-color map of the city of New York, with pins in it for job locations, which made Tommy feel a little like a general. He kept his framed Fordham diploma, the result of two years of full-time studies and four years of nights after Maggie and Terence were born, in the big bottom drawer of his desk, along with a bottle of Four Roses and a sweatshirt to change into for basketball games. He also had a studio photograph of Connie on her wedding day, her eyes so big and black amid the whites and grays of the picture that it looked as if they'd been made with the end of a lighted cigarette. When certain clients, mainly the big boys, came to see him, he put the picture on the filing cabinet, but most of the time he kept it in the drawer. His brother Mark had noticed this once, and had gone home to report to his wife that things in Tom and Connie's marriage were even worse than they'd imagined. In truth the picture had been put away for exactly the opposite reason; while most men considered it simply part of their office equipment, like a stapler or a striped tie, Tommy Scanlan believed that the photograph would tell the world a private thing: that he was crazy about his wife.

Like so many of their friends, Connie Mazza and Tommy Scanlan had gotten married because they were expecting a baby. It had come as a great surprise to both of them. Connie's sole exposure to sex education had been the day before her twelfth birthday, when her aunt Rose had given her a box of sanitary napkins almost a year too late. Tommy found out afterward that it had never occurred to Connie that the surge of heat and compulsion and the aftermath of embarrassment she had felt on weekend nights in his car could result in the conception of a child.

Tommy had known better, but he had been similarly dim in not realizing that it was impossible that the answer to "Is this a safe time?" could be "Yes" every Friday and Saturday night. It was not until after they were married that he discovered that Connie had supposed he was asking only about the chances of someone catching him under her long skirts and net petticoats. Maggie had been born six months after their wedding, and Tommy's explanation of her prematurity was for many years a great joke among his brothers, given the fact that the infant was the biggest baby in the nursery. Connie said nothing. By the time she had her baby, she did not care what anyone thought.

Even all these years later, when Tommy Scanlan looked across the kitchen table after a couple of beers and wondered who the hell this woman was, he knew that if they had not gotten caught he would have married her just the same. When they met at the YMCA jitterbug contest he had been going with someone else, a lively girl named Mary Roe, who had freckles and wild auburn curls and was a friend of his sister. He had danced with Connie only because the two winning couples in the contest had been asked to switch partners after the trophies had been given out. Connie was so small she had come only to his shoulder, her back as narrow as a child's. She had black hair waved off her face, and black eyes so big and blank that he almost felt he could see inside her head. Her skin was white and her lipstick a pure clear red. She looked like a painting to him. She spoke not one word during the entire dance—the song had been "Moonlight Serenade," and he thought he could very faintly hear, or perhaps feel, her humming—but as the music stopped she said "Thank you" and did not step away. He felt as though he'd been punched in the chest.

When the music started again, he simply held on to her and began to dance some more. That was the way it was for the rest of the night, as Mary Roe watched from the sidelines and finally went out to a car with Mark Scanlan and let him do everything she had never let a boy do to her before.

Connie went home that night with Jimmy Martinelli, the boy who had brought her to the dance in the first place. He drove her in silence to the cemetery where the Mazzas lived, leaned across her to open the door from inside, said "Good luck" and drove away.

Most people assumed that Tommy had fallen in love with Connie because of the way she looked. The fashion of their adolescence had been for pink-skinned blondes with small noses and soft mouths, and so Connie had never believed anyone, including Tommy, when they said that she was beautiful. Tommy remembered their first Christmas, when she had brought home two boxes of cards to send to their friends and families, the message "Blessed Christmas" inside on cream-colored paper and a Renaissance painting of the Virgin Mary on the front. Connie had picked the cards because she thought they would go over well with various Scanlans, but when Tommy had seen the painting he had burst out laughing. "I've heard of people who send out pictures of themselves on their cards, but nobody who sends out paintings," he said. And in truth the serenely beautiful Madonna, with her slightly sallow skin, dark hair, prominent nose and full lips looked very much like Connie. Tommy had turned over the card and read the fine print. "Giotto," he said. "Did you pose for this?"

"For your information, we invented the Renaissance," Connie had said in a huff, going up to their room until he came and kissed the frown from between her eyebrows.

But it was not her looks that had so compelled him. Tommy had never been able to put it into words, but it was the blankness of her he was so mesmerized by, the feeling of an empty bottle waiting to be filled, and filled by him. He had been waiting for so long for someone to take him seriously, to listen to him. Looking at her great bottomless eyes he got the feeling that that was what she was doing, although as the years went by he would sometimes wonder if it was simply that nobody was home in there. He could never get a word in edgewise with his family, and he was a little afraid of both his parents, his mother with her patently false patina of elegance and control, his father with his seemingly effortless ability to rise in the world and his disdain for those who did not. It had not escaped Tommy's notice that Connie Mazza would rise in the world simply by moving to a place where people lived, instead of one where they were buried. He was also sexually enthralled by her. When she would lean forward to tune the car radio and he would get a whiff of her, his blood felt as if it would burst from his body.

He had suspected that there would be trouble when, after a highly public breakdown by Mary Roe in the ladies' room at Sacred Heart Academy, his sister Margaret had come home and asked him, meaning no harm, whether he was really going with a Puerto Rican girl from Spanish Harlem. But there was little talk of the affair until, six weeks after they had begun dating, and five weeks after Tommy decided he meant to marry Connie, he had brought her home for Sunday dinner.

Connie had shopped for a week and had spent all the money she had saved from her secretarial job on a red satin dress with a sweetheart neckline and a tiny tight waist from which her bust loomed like a stretch of cream crepe de Chine. As they drove up the long driveway to the Scanlan house and saw Tommy's sister and one of her friends sitting on the steps in navy-blue skirts and pale-blue sweater sets, Connie had known she had made a dreadful mistake.

At dinner no one spoke to her except Mary Frances, who handed dishes across the table and said "Peas?" and "Potatoes?" as though she and Connie were characters in *The Philadelphia Story*. After Tommy had driven Connie home, he had come back to find his father sitting in the living room in the dark, his cigar burned to the nub at one end and chewed to the nub at the other. "If you think I busted my ass so you could marry some goddamn guinea from the Bronx, you've got another think coming," said Mr. Scanlan, who was quite drunk. Tommy went upstairs while his father continued to talk; the only other word Tommy caught was "wop." The following Friday Connie told him that her period was late.

And that had been that. They had gotten caught, and Tommy had felt that the ties had tightened with each of the babies, each of them unplanned, each of them making the ties more fast, each of them keeping them from—what? He did not know. His feeling about what their lives might have been were as vague as his feelings about Connie, formed of odd, intense, momentary yearnings. He sometimes wondered what they would have been like as a couple, what life would have been like had they not instantly become a family, had not his empty vessel been filled year after year with the babies she loved so much and watched grow so sadly. Sometimes he would wake in the morning, the sky blue-gray as a dolphin's back, and for just a few moments he would wonder who this was in bed beside him, and whether he was going to be late for his nine o'clock class. It would come to him slowly that the house was filled with people, created by him, connected to him for life, and he would be weak with incredulity and fear. He knew what it meant to be a father; it meant being sure, outspoken, critical, bold, controlled. It meant being John Scanlan. This life of his was a masquerade.

Then he would roll over, embrace his wife, lift her frilled nightgown and straddle her narrow body, as he had this morning. And he would be all right again, throwing off the sheets afterward, pulling on his shorts, going to the bathroom, thinking only for a moment of another baby next year, wondering if it was a safe time, putting on his T-shirt and his suit pants and going down to breakfast.

"So I hear you and your boss drove a half hour out of your way to get his oil changed," Tommy said to Mark, running his hand along his damp forehead. "What did I screw up now?"

"Is it a possibility that the owner of this company just might want to stop in occasionally and see how things are going?" said Mark, who had flushed at the words "your boss."

"Is it a possibility that he wanted to see how things are going? No," said Tommy. "Is it a possibility that he wants to give me a hard time about something? You know it. What'd I do this time, except let the goddamned candy canes get dirty?"

"He says you and Connie and the kids should come to the house

Sunday," Mark said, running his finger around the inside of his collar.

"Why?"

"Would he tell me?" said Mark. "I'm just carrying the message. He was smiling when he said it."

"That's the worst news I've heard all day," Tommy said. "That means something's up. Maybe he finally got my marriage annulled."

Looking out the window again, his back to his brother, Tommy watched his father climb into the cab of the cement mixer. There was a low rumble as the engine turned over, and then John Scanlan began to drive the thing around the lot in circles, like a child with a new bicycle.

Tommy began to examine his conscience. Before confession you were supposed to consider your sins; as a boy, Tommy had tried to do this, and come back time and time again to petty theft, disobedience, and self-abuse. But when he had to face his father there always seemed to be an infinite number of sins to consider, although lately he had felt as if he might be in a state of grace. First Concrete was not losing money. Maggie had justified John Scanlan's investment in her school tuition by getting the highest average in her class. Connie had actually agreed to attend a card party with the other Scanlan wives. He was trying to figure out why his father wanted to see all of them at once when Mark added, "He said something about some new construction behind your house. I think he's pissed we didn't get any of the contracts. Particularly cement."

"I didn't know a thing about it until all hell broke loose this morning," said Tommy. "The company's in the Bronx. Who says we have to get work in Westchester? We're plenty busy with city work."

"Come to the house on Sunday," said Mark. "What's the harm? The kids can play outside. Maybe he's just trying to be sociable."

"Get real."

"We don't see you enough, anyhow. Gail never sees Connie. She asked her over for bridge last Thursday but she said she couldn't come."

"Connie's not feeling too well."

Mark's mouth narrowed into a bitter line, making him look as if he was trying to hold his teeth in. "What, again?" he finally said.

"Maybe, maybe not. It's too soon to tell."

Below them the cement mixer was still circling the lot. John Scanlan narrowly missed taking the passenger side off his own freshly waxed car as a mechanic backed the Lincoln out of one of the bays. The old man laid on the horn, which gave off a deep throaty honk, like some big water bird.

"I have to go," Mark said. "I'll see you Sunday."

Tommy did not reply. He watched his father climb down from the cement mixer. The old man stopped to talk for a moment to the mechanic, and Tommy saw the man begin to grin and bob his head.

So many people were drawn to John Scanlan—drawn by his power, and by his personality, too; by the big voice, the vigor, the gift he had for colorful language, the sheer force of the man. On the wall behind his desk at Scanlan & Co., he had hung a framed copy of a quotation about Teddy Roosevelt: "The baby at every christening, the bride at every wedding, the corpse at every funeral." No one who knew John Scanlan had to ask what it meant. Anyone who had ever been to a christening, a wedding, a funeral he attended knew he outshone the baby, the bride, the corpse. He could inspire love in an instant from anyone who happened to be in his good graces. It was just that so few people ever were.

Tommy could not remember a time when he had ever been in his father's good graces. As he watched, Mark loped across the parking lot and got into his father's car.

Tommy turned the radio back on. Sinatra was singing "A Foggy Day in London Town," Tommy's favorite song. He closed his office door and sat down at his desk. From his file drawer he took out the photograph of his wife and placed it on one corner of the desk. Another baby. More saddle shoes. Another place at the table to be filled. His stomach had turned sour and his head hurt.

In a half hour, he would go over to Sal's for lunch. He could think things over. Not whether he would go to his father's or not; he'd be there, and he'd have Connie with him, even if it meant another argument. It was a question of what he'd do when he got there. He looked at the photograph, at those beautiful eyes. Another baby. He could only push his father so far. The last time he'd taken him on had been the now unimaginable night when he'd won his wife. Tommy would always think of that as his greatest triumph.

"Shit, what can it be now?" he said, as the strings swelled and Sinatra finished singing.

4

"NAME THE SEVEN DEADLY SINS," JOHN Scanlan said absently as he stood in the kitchen of his house mixing martinis.

"Sloth," Maggie said. "Gluttony, envy." She stuck her finger into a jar of olives, trying to coax out the three remaining in the bottom. "Avarice," she added. "Lust."

"The twelve apostles."

"John," Maggie began, as she always did.

Her grandfather had something on his mind. She had known it as soon as she'd seen him that morning, his blue eyes dim, as though turned within. For just a moment, when he saw Connie and Tommy enter the house together, Maggie's father's hand held protectively at the small of Connie's back, John's eyes had brightened, blazed, danced. Now he seemed preoccupied.

Maggie had been able to recite the deadly sins since first grade. The apostles were a throwaway question. Most recently her grandfather had asked her to recite from memory the Passion According to St. Mark, and Maggie had been amazed when she had learned it successfully. She was even more amazed to be corrected by her grandfather on two small phrases. When she got home and looked at the New Testament, she had seen that he had been right. She wondered who had made him memorize the Passion; she couldn't imagine anyone making her grandfather do anything.

John filled the glasses from a silver shaker with his initials on it which his wife had purchased because she thought it might make a good heirloom someday. He picked up the matching silver tray and turned to Maggie. "Come into the living room for the entertainment," he said, and his eyes glistened, his wide mouth creased into a humorless tight-lipped grin.

"What entertainment?" Maggie was still going after the olives.

"Ha!" her grandfather said, pushing through the swinging door.

Maggie heard a little stage cough behind her and knew that her cousin Monica had entered the room. She was wearing the moiré taffeta dress with the high waist and enormous puffed sleeves she had worn the week before for her high school graduation. In it she looked beautiful and virginal, her honey-colored hair flipping up on her shoulders, her nails polished the same color as the add-a-pearl necklace her parents had completed as a graduation gift. When Maggie had stopped after the commencement ceremony to congratulate Helen Malone, who had been in the same graduating class as Monica, Helen had smiled slowly and said, "Your cousin wins the award for best disguise." Looking over her shoulder at Monica now, Maggie thought she knew exactly what Helen meant. With her pretty face and her curved smile, Monica looked kind and sweet. She stared at Maggie with the cool, direct look she did so well. Then she looked pointedly at Maggie's fingers in the olive jar. "How attractive," she said, and Maggie withdrew her hand so quickly that the jar toppled over onto the counter, and brine splattered onto her flowered skirt and the linoleum floor. "Most attractive," Monica said, leaving Maggie to clean up the mess and wish she was back home in her shorts.

On Sundays, when Maggie went to her grandparents' house, it was usually with her father. Her mother stayed home with the younger children. Maggie had known everything she needed to know about her mother and her father's family when she had started to page through Tommy and Connie's big white leatherette wedding album when she was four years old. She could never understand what had moved the photographer to go up into the choir loft, look down, and take a picture of the congregation, which showed a great massing of relations on the bride's side of the church and no one behind the groom except his brothers, the ushers, who had appeared in their cutaways in defiance of their father's wishes. She could never understand why her mother chose to put that picture in the album. "It's a sad picture, Mommy," Maggie had said once when she was young, before she had begun quietly to take sides.

"It shows something," her mother had said, her lips closing like a red metal zipper. Maggie supposed that whatever the something was, it was long-lived, for her mother came to her in-laws' home only when a special invitation was issued.

Maggie was there often. She liked the order, the cleanliness and the smell of polish, smells that were absent from her everyday life. In her grandmother's living room there was a baby grand piano, a painting of flowers over the fireplace, a corner cabinet filled with china statues of characters from Shakespeare, and enormous quantities of brocade in a color her grandmother called mauve. There was a big kitchen with geraniums on the wallpaper, and curtains that matched, and a pantry with glass-fronted cabinets. All the food behind the glass was arranged in alphabetical order; the family joke was that Mary Frances Scanlan never served mixed vegetables, because she wouldn't know whether to file the cans under M or V.

It was the house of people who had money. "Mag, are you rich?" Debbie had asked her once when they had ridden up the long driveway on their bicycles, the lawn stretching away on either side. Maggie had answered, honest as always, "They are. We aren't."

Now the brocade furniture in the living room was full of people. Her mother was sitting in the corner of the couch, Joseph slumped against her, his eyes half closed as he sucked his middle fingers. Next to her mother was her aunt Cass, Monica's mother. Uncle James was sitting next to his wife.

"Delivered twins last night, Concetta," James said with a grin.

"Oh, God," Connie said, her stomach fighting the martini her father-in-law had pressed upon her. "That poor woman."

"No, no," said James, waving his left hand, his wedding band sunk a little into the flesh of his finger, "Very easy delivery. Just popped right out, one after another."

"For God's sake," said Mary Frances Scanlan, putting her drink down on a coaster on the coffee table. "It's bad enough, shop talk, but your shop talk is the worst, Jimmy."

"Sorry," said James pleasantly. "All part of life, Mother. No sense denying it."

"No sense discussing it," said Mary Frances as Maggie came in with another tray of drinks. "Maggie, here's your cherry. Come quick or I'll give it to one of your brothers."

Her grandmother held a maraschino cherry by the stem, dangling it, dripping, over her whiskey sour. Maggie always ate the cherry from her grandmother's drink, trying not to feel the bite of the liquor before she got to the syrupy taste of the fruit. Like so many other customs in her family, it had continued long past the time that those involved enjoyed it. In fact, Maggie could not remember that she had ever enjoyed it; it had simply become tradition and could not be tampered with. By the time she had eaten the thing, the back of her tongue was usually numb. For a moment she thought of refusing, but instead she took the cherry and held it over her cupped hand, hoping for a chance to throw it away. She looked across the room and saw Monica smiling at her, and she opened her mouth and popped the whole thing in, stem and all. When she wiped her hands on her skirt, Monica laughed.

"Well, gentlemen," said her grandfather, coming up behind Maggie and lifting his Scotch from amid the martinis on the tray, "The Roman Catholic church is going to hell in a handbasket." John Scanlan had a tendency to choose phrases and stick with them. "Hell in a handbasket" was one of his favorites.

"Shop talk," said Mary Frances, crossing her legs and pulling at a stray thread on the brocade chair with her index finger and thumb.

"It's shop talk that pays for this house," her husband said. "It's shop talk that pays for that Lincoln Continental and the private schools for all these children."

Maggie heard a sigh from the hallway. Monica had moved back into the shadows.

"And for your orthodontia, miss," John Scanlan said without turning around to look at Monica, whose teeth as a child, before she became perfect, had been as crooked as the tombstones in an old cemetery.

John Scanlan said it nice and evenly, the way he said almost everything else. The oldtimers at the factory always said that it took a man a couple of hours after he'd been fired to take it all in, because John Scanlan said "You're fired" in the afternoon in exactly the voice in which he said "Good morning" each morning. Maggie had noticed lately that it was a good bit like the voice in which she answered catechism questions: Why did God make me? God made me to know Him, to love Him, and to serve Him in this world and to be happy with Him forever in the next.

"Today in church I see four women without hats," he continued. "Without anything on their heads. Never mind those flimsy little black veils that all you girls are wearing"—her grandfather looked over at Maggie, whose rayon mantilla was sitting on top of her little patent handbag on the hall telephone table—"now we've got women bareheaded. Bareheaded! As though they were going to Coney Island instead of the House of the Lord of Hosts.

"This is all because of that woman," he added, meaning the president's widow, who had begun wearing the mantilla to Mass on summer Sundays several years before, "who has probably never given a thought to the millinery industry in her life.

"Similarly, Johnnie, who runs the hat shop on Main Street, tells me that business is bad. Men are not wearing hats anymore, he tells me. Now whose fault is that?"

They all knew the answer. Mary Frances, who was her husband's straight man as well as his wife, sipped her drink, put it down, folded her hands in her lap, and said obediently, "The president."

"Exactly!" John Scanlan slammed his broad flat hand down on the table next to him.

From behind her Maggie could hear Monica sigh again. She looked over at her mother, whose eyes were shiny from alcohol. Connie looked as though she had left her consciousness at home in Kenwood and sent her body on to the Scanlans without her. Maggie realized that that was how her mother always looked when she was around Tommy's family. She also realized that her parents never sat together when they were at John and Mary Frances's house. Maggie's father was sitting on the piano bench across the room.

Variations of this conversation took place every Sunday at the Scanlan house. John hated the Kennedys, whom he saw as a bunch of second-rate Scanlans with too much hair. And he hated what was happening to the Catholic church because of Pope John XXIII, not because, like his contemporaries, he thought the changes were blasphemous, but because he thought they were bad for business. "The two Johns," he called the men he thought responsible for unnecessary change in America, although both were now dead: the boy president and the populist pope.

While all around him in Our Lady of Lourdes people slowly, painfully adapted themselves to the Mass in English, John Scanlan whispered the Latin. It was disconcerting to share a pew with him. The priest would intone "The Lord be with you," and from John's seat would come a sound, like a snake exhaling, the carrying sibilants of "Dominus vobiscum." Occasionally when they were together her grandfather, a tall handsome man with yellowing white hair, would turn to Maggie and inquire, "Confiteor deo?" and Maggie would be expected to answer "omnipotenti," or, on occasion, to finish the entire prayer. "A plus," Monica sometimes called her, and, like everything else Monica said, the tone was pleasant, the smile ubiquitous, and the meaning mean as hell.

John Scanlan had started manufacturing communion hosts when he was twenty-one, a newlywed with two years of college, eleven younger siblings, and a mother dying of the same lung cancer that had killed her husband ten years before. For a week after he quit school John had thought about growth industries and then he had rented a pressing machine and space in a garage on a back street in the South Bronx and begun to stamp out little wafers of unleavened bread. The Jews who rented him the place thought he was crazy. Two years later he had his own factory and twenty-two employees.

He began to make holy cards, vestments, and assorted communion veils and confirmation robes, and the three sons who worked in the business knew how to market them all: buy from a Catholic. It was as simple as that. John Scanlan's only real competitor had been a company in Illinois owned by a Methodist; the year Maggie was born it had gone out of business, only six months after its founder had gotten drunk at a convention and made a joke about Scanlan & Co., the Irish, and booze.

John Scanlan now had a plant in Manila doing machine embroidery on vestments and altar cloths, a plant in White Plains that employed 160 people, and a not-so-hidden interest in three construction companies, two garment factories, and the cement company for which Tommy worked. He was very, very rich.

He was rich enough to retire and be rich for the rest of his life, but he had no wish to. All he wanted to do was to manage the lives of his children, and to be left alone so he could become richer still. Already there were a few parishes in progressive suburbs which were simplifying their altars and the rites that took place upon them. John Scanlan predicted that by the year 2000 priests would be saying Mass in Bermuda shorts, handing out kaiser rolls at communion, and Scanlan & Co. would be bankrupt.

"Now he'll say 'Then, good-by easy street,' " Maggie thought, looking down at her skirt.

"Then, good-by easy street," said John Scanlan, picking up his drink.

"Pop," said Mark, "we can diversify. We can modify. If the Church decides to simplify the vestments, change the altar cloths, it would take us three days to change the machines over from the old lamb motif to a simple plain cross. The church changes, we change with it."

"We are not talking about embroidery. We are talking about disaster."

"Jesus, why do I bother?" Uncle Mark said, refilling his glass from the cocktail shaker.

"I often wonder the same thing," his father said flatly.

Maggie's father pumped the piano pedals and stayed out of the way. His glass was empty but he made no move to refill it. Connie's glass was still half full. She had a sheen of sweat on her upper lip, which even for early July seemed a bit extravagant.

"Concetta?" said Mary Frances, leaning forward with a pleasant smile, like a woman in a magazine. "Another?"

"No. Thank you. Really," said Maggie's mother, who had never been able to think of a term of address for her mother-in-law and so for thirteen years had called her nothing at all.

"Well, let's talk about Tom here," Mr. Scanlan said, without looking at his middle son. "They're ripping Tom's backyard up. Making a shantytown. I have knowledge of this only secondhand, because no one saw fit to give us any of the contracts for this development. Be that as it may, it will be all over in that part of the world by next year."

"They dug six foundations in one day," Maggie said.

"Good girl," said her grandfather. "Six foundations. Soon it'll be thirty-six. They're planning seventy-two houses for that site, and not houses I'd want to live in. That plasterboard stuff you can put your elbow right through. Maybe even septic tanks. Cheap kitchens. You know the idea: Come live where the other half lives."

"Maybe the development will bring property values up," Tommy said. "Nice new development behind the old houses. Lots of people think those houses are better than the old ones."

"I think they'll be beautiful," said Connie. "I heard they're going to have laundry chutes and garbage disposals in the kitchens. And sunken living rooms and patios."

There was a long silence. Maggie picked at a cuticle and avoided looking at her mother. It was a canon of the Scanlan household that old things were better than new ones. It was not to be argued with, like eating the cherry. Maggie chewed her little finger.

"The first thing a man looks at is your hands," Mary Frances said softly to Maggie, pulling at her granddaughter's fingers, frowning at the dried blood in the corner of each bitten nail.

"I heard they're very nice houses," Connie added, and Maggie could hear the anger in her voice.

"No such thing, little girl. When you see them you'll tell me different. Half basements. Wall-to-wall on slab. Property values over there will land in the toilet. Sheenies to the right of you. Sheenies to the left of you." John took a big sip of his martini and smiled, a smile Maggie noticed was oddly like Monica's. Maggie thought her grandfather's eyes looked like the sapphires in her grandmother's big sapphire-and-diamond earrings. She remembered when she was a little girl thinking that she could see through the blue of her grandfather's eyes into his head, see wheels and cogs and clicking things, like the inside of a watch. She could almost hear the clicking now.

"But you two won't have to worry about all that," John said, pulling something from his pants pocket, tossing it with a grin into Connie's lap, where it made a little metallic sound as it hit her engagement and wedding rings. Maggie turned to her father, but he was looking down at the piano keys. The room was very still.

"Congratulations," Mary Frances said brightly, but still Connie had not lifted her hands from her lap. Joseph murmured softly in his sleep and turned to tuck his head into his mother's side. Finally James said, "Those look like keys to me."

"Oh, brilliant," John said under his breath, and aloud he said, "And the door they open is oak, four inches thick with a mullioned window in it, and the rooms inside, none of them are smaller than twenty by fifteen, not even the kitchen. Six bedrooms, four baths, a fireplace you could stand in in the living room. The prettiest azaleas on the block."

"Remember the Ryans, Tom?" Mary Frances said brightly. "They've moved to Florida. Only three houses down from us. Maggie could walk up the hill to have Saturday lunch with your father."

"We could never afford that house, Mother," Tommy said quietly, and Maggie looked down at her patent-leather shoes, luminous in the half light.

"Bought and paid for," John Scanlan said. "Bought and paid for." Connie raised her head, and Maggie thought her mother's hair looked like patent leather, too, and Connie's voice sounded soft and warm.

"What took you so long?" she said, and she stared right into John Scanlan's eyes, and the room was quiet. Maggie saw her grandfather look right back at Connie, as though there were only the two of them in the room, as though he loved her. "Ah, little girl," he said, "I have the gift of perfect timing."

"We're not moving, Pop," Tommy said, but his father did not look at him.

"We'll discuss it another time," John said, but he still looked deep into Connie's eyes, and he still smiled.

"No," she said, but no one seemed to hear her. Suddenly, as though of one accord, the various Scanlans by birth and by marriage rose and began to gather up their handbags and call to their children. It was as though they had come for something and now it was accomplished. Only Connie remained sitting, staring over at her husband on the piano stool.

"Tom, bring the glasses into the kitchen," Mary Frances said as she walked into the hallway, and Tommy stood up and lifted the tray, his wife watching him silently.

Maggie could hear the sounds of departure and cleaning up as she went upstairs to the bathroom. She heard the front door slam and knew her parents would be waiting for her out in the car, not speaking, the boys bouncing in the back seat.

Monica was in the bedroom at the top of the stairs, looking carefully at her face in one of the mirrors. The room had two single beds with pink spreads, two dressing tables with pink-and-white ruffled skirts, two bureaus, two bride dolls. It was always called the girls' room, but only Maggie's aunt Margaret had ever used it. The other girl was Elizabeth Ann, the Scanlan baby who had died at birth. Sometimes Mary Frances would come up to this room and sit on the bed that was never used, the better one, the one by the window, and she would stare out over the big lawn and the shrubbery like a person struck blind, holding a pillow to her chest. And if Maggie came upon her on those occasions she would beckon her to the bed, and stroke her hair until Maggie's head started to feel numb and her shoulders to cramp. All the time Mary Frances looked far, far away, staring without seeing a thing.

It was just like Monica, Maggie thought, to seat herself carelessly on that bed now, pulling the carefully arranged spread a little awry.

On those few nights when Maggie had slept in this room, she had always been careful not to sleep in, even to sit on, Elizabeth Ann's bed.

"So you're moving," Monica said.

"You heard my mother," Maggie said.

"I heard your mother, and I heard our grandfather. 'Oil and water,' my mother once called them. The oil part was absolutely right for your mother, but I'm not sure about water for Grandpop. I guess your parents are oil and water, too. I guess that's what happens when you meet, get engaged, and get married all in a couple of weeks. Oil and water."

"Shut up, Monica," Maggie said.

Monica turned back to the mirror. "Just think," she said, studying her face. "We'll have a whole week to catch up on things when we go to the beach with Grandmom. My last year going, too, now that I'm out of school." She locked eyes with Maggie in the mirror. "I have so much to tell you. Just the other day, Richard Joseph's older sister was telling me how her brother and all his friends call you a carpenter's dream—flat as a board. I didn't know he was your boyfriend."

Maggie looked down at her skirt. On one side was an olive juice stain, on the other a wet mark made by gin. She sniffed and realized that she smelled strange. Then her head snapped back. She did not want Monica to think she was crying. She started downstairs.

"I can't wait to see your new bathing suit," Monica called after her in her pleasantest voice. "Or your new house."

When Maggie got to the bottom of the stairs, her grandfather was standing in the doorway, looking out upon the great sweep of his lawn, and at the station wagon in the driveway. Maggie stood next to him for a moment, trying to see it as he did. She hoped her mother couldn't see her.

"Your grandmother's right, for once," John Scanlan said, putting his big hand atop her head. "You and I can have lunch together. You've got a lot to learn, little girl. This whole kit and caboodle is going to be what they call an object lesson for you. For some other people, too."

"I don't really want to move, Grandpop," Maggie said.

"Not a question of want, miss. We're talking about a question of need." He put his hand into his pants pocket and took out the keys he had thrown into Connie's lap. "Your mother left these on the couch," he said with a grin. "Give 'em to her."

"I'll give them to my dad."

"Your mother," John Scanlan said. "You heard me. Go on."

5

HE NEXT MORNING MAGGIE WENT TO the Bronx to see her grandfather—her grandfather Mazza, not her grandfather Scanlan. Her grandfather Scanlan tried to stay as far away as possible from New York City, although he had grown up there; he had moved his business to White Plains when he bought the big house in Westchester County, and he always referred to the Bronx as "the godforsaken Bronx." (Brooklyn was "the slum," and Manhattan "that hellhole." Queens, for some odd reason, was "the home of mental midgets." John Scanlan never spoke of Staten Island.) Maggie's grandfather Mazza, on the other hand, had not been out of the Bronx for almost ten years.

Maggie was supposed to take the train to his house, but she usually rode her bicycle, getting off to run beside it as she sprinted across the highways that took people from New York City to New England. She brought her grandfather groceries, and put the brown paper bag, still warm from the sun and the metal mesh of her bicycle basket, on the red table in the middle of the kitchen. Then she put all the groceries away, except for the tomatoes, which she left on the kitchen counter. Once she had forgotten to put the groceries away, and when she came back a week later they were still there, the meat and vegetables giving off a sweet dead smell, the milk and butter high as Gorgonzola cheese. It seemed safer and more proper to dump all the stuff in the can at the end of the drive than to ask her grandfather for an explanation. She knew of no monosyllabic explanation for such a thing, and was sure no polysyllabic explanation would be forthcoming. Her grandfather Mazza preferred contemplation to conversation.

In fact her two grandfathers would have been a perfect match—one a talker, the other a listener—except that they would have had complete disdain for each other's background, work, family and character. No one seemed to find it odd that they had never met.

Angelo Mazza was a small man, very elegant, who always wore a white shirt buttoned to the top button and a pair of beige or pale gray pants tailored by his brother-in-law, a pants maker. When he had arrived from Italy after the First World War, one of his cousins, who had come over earlier, had found him a position as the caretaker of Calvary Cemetery, a Catholic cemetery nearly on the border of Westchester County and the Bronx. Angelo had taken the job until something better came along, but nothing ever did. The job paid a very small salary, and provided him with a tiny stone cottage just within the cemetery gates: a living room, a small dining room, a kitchen, one bedroom downstairs and a very small one upstairs under the eaves. To make ends meet, his wife had taken the subway to the city, as they called Manhattan, to the garment district, where she had been a finisher for ladies' lingerie.

There were some in his family who had thought Angelo would stay single all his life. He was a very private man, the eldest of five, all the other children girls; he had always had his own room, and his mother, who had been a widow almost as long as he could remember, treated him like a prince. But as soon as he had been old enough to grow a mustache his female relatives had been on him constantly, bringing this girl and that girl to the house, the poor young women turning red as they listened to the phony excuses about why they had shown up at this or that particular time. He was forty years old when he finally married. At a party at his sister Rose's he had sat next to a young woman with fat black plaits crossed over her head and a face and shape both bovine. She spoke no English and knew no one at the party; she was a niece visiting a woman down the street, who had been invited merely from politeness because she was a young widow whose husband and two children had died in a flu epidemic in the countryside outside Milan. Angelo had been so moved by the widow's discomfort and fear that he had sat beside her, not talking much, all afternoon, and had gone to her aunt's to have coffee the next day. Three months later they were married.

His only child had once turned to him, after yet another quarrel with her mother about her clothes, her manner, her schoolwork, herself, and asked tearfully, "Why did you marry her?" Angelo had turned away, begun wiping the kitchen counter, then suddenly had turned back and, lifting his silvery head, said in Italian, "Because she needed someone." "Why you?" Connie had screamed back, weeping, the tears falling onto the hands she held against her cheeks. "She needed someone like me," said Angelo, and went outside to his rosebushes while his daughter sat at the head of the kitchen table and sobbed.

Maggie usually found her grandfather by the rosebushes, kneeling on a square of cotton fabric he kept in his tool closet especially for that purpose. He believed those who tried to tend plants standing up were doomed to failure. He would cultivate carefully around the roots, mix a handful of peat moss in the black topsoil, and occasionally allow his only granddaughter to help him. It saddened him that Maggie's brothers did not seem interested, but secretly he thought of them as Irish children, children with no ties to the earth at all. Maggie he thought of as one of his people.

He never called her Maggie, always Maria Goretti, which was her full name, after the young Italian girl who had been canonized because she fought off a rapist and died rather than capitulate and live. Angelo had always thought Concetta's decision to name the first child so flagrantly was a rebellion against her husband's enormous, ebullient family, but if it had been, then the nickname given her by her grandmother Scanlan had effectively muted the protest. Not even the nuns at school called Maggie by her given name, except when they called her up to get her report card.

"Hi, Grandpop," she said, as she sat on the ground next to him.

"You catch cold," he said.

"Grandpop, it's July. It's too hot to catch cold. The ground is dry. Can I work?"

"You get your tools."

When she came back from the supply closet she went for a moment inside the house to go to the bathroom. As always she opened the door of the medicine cabinet and peered inside, at the small cake of black mascara and the disc of rouge left behind by her mother. In the small bedroom, its ceiling sloped with the roof line, there was also her mother's high school yearbook and a closet full of old clothes: a black suit, a red satin dress with a low neck, a checked dirndl, a peasant blouse. It was stifling on the top floor, and Maggie did not stop to look again at the yearbook picture. She knew it by heart: Concetta Anna Mazza, Chorus, 2, 3, 4; Dance Club 4. And beneath that, in italics, the quotation: "She walks in beauty, like the night."

Outside, over the low stone wall just behind the rose garden, was the neighborhood—blocks of clapboard row houses shining clean and quiet in the sun, like so many others in the North Bronx, the backyards filled with tomato plants and the ornamental urns filled with hydrangeas. No one had ever suggested, however, that there was another cemetery like her grandfather's anywhere else. When Angelo Mazza had taken over the place it had seemed half empty, tombstones only on one side, although a good many of the other plots had been purchased by families moving into the area around it. It had looked a little like a golf course, satisfyingly green and yet a bit austere, with its great metal gates crowned with one enormous cross flanked by two smaller ones. Angelo had gone to work.

On either side of the gates he had planted pink azaleas, and along the fence that separated the cemetery from a back alley and a block of backyards he had put a wisteria, a stick of a thing with three skinny tendrils. Along the fieldstone wall he had planted orange lilies he had found beside a creek one day in Westchester Country, growing wild in mats of green foliage. He put violets around his own front door, which duplicated themselves as fast as field mice, and around back he put the rose garden and a vegetable garden and herb patch. When

Concetta was a little girl he had sometimes taken her upstate for picnics on Sundays, when there were few funerals and her mother liked to rest, and he would dig up wildflowers and roll them in damp sheets of newspaper and plant them when they arrived back home. Angelo had been doing this for nearly forty years, and the result was that in Calvary Cemetery in July there were flowers everywhere. People said it was more wonderful than the Botanical Garden, and once, before Maggie was born, the curator there had even come to talk to him. Her grandfather always told Maggie that the man actually knew surprisingly little about the proper care of plants.

When Maggie knelt down next to him he was working coffee grounds into the soil with his hands. Beside him was a bowl with soap, water, and a sponge, to clean the aphids from the rose bushes. The roses he liked best were white with an edging of bright pink along the petals. There were three bushes behind the house and two on either side of Maggie's grandmother's grave, grown so thick in the three years since the headstone had been put in and the bushes had been planted that only MAZZA in capital letters was visible, the "Anna 1890–1963" and "Angelo 1880–" hidden beneath the leaves of the plants. The grave was in the back, near the wall, and today there was a tan canvas tent not far from it. Paul Fogarty and his mongoloid brother, Leonard, had just finished digging and were standing, sweating, leaning on shovels.

"Who's getting buried?" Maggie said.

"Mrs. Romano," her grandfather said. "She died in her sleep."

"Her daughter was a friend of Mommy's."

"Her niece," Angelo Mazza said, running the sponge down one long green stem, the paler green bugs leaping before him. "This one, only boys."

They worked together under the hot sun for half an hour, but Maggie was restless and her hair kept falling into her eyes. She went inside to wash her hands and pull her hair back from her face with a rubber band, but instead of returning to the plants she began to wander around the cemetery grounds. The older graves were in the back, the pale gray headstones blackening where the letters were cut and the roses were sculpted in the granite. Maggie's landmark had always been an angel on a pedestal, blank-eyed as a blind man, a spray of flowers slanting over one arm as if the angel was a beauty queen, to mark the grave of a woman who had died forty years before. Her grandfather had planted azaleas around its base, but they lasted only through the beginning of May; their white flowers turned mocha-colored, then curled and dropped to the ground. The green leaves of the plants looked as though they were perspiring in the July heat. A man squatted by a monument against the back wall.

"Hello, sweetheart," said Mr. Gennaro, who carved the inscriptions in the stones. "You're getting big. Bigger than your mama, I bet, by now."

"Two inches," said Maggie. "She says I'm a Scanlan."

"Never mind that crap," the old man said, unstrapping his leather tool belt and placing it at the foot of a square pink marble stone with nothing on it but the name JESSUP in capital letters. Maggie remembered that when she was first learning to spell she thought this was the place where Jesus was buried, and she was punished in school for insisting that the Holy Sepulchre was in the Bronx and wasn't half as big as Joe the greengrocer's mausoleum.

"Who's Jessup?" she said.

"Old guy lived a couple blocks up the avenue, over his office. A lawyer. Nice man, no family, did house closings and things during the day, upstairs in three rooms at night. About ten years back the doctor told him he was sick and he came here and picked out a plot. Your grandpop found the guy a nice space. The stone went up about five years ago. I'm doing name, date of birth."

"He's not dead yet?"

"Nah. You know doctors. He wasn't really that sick."

Mr. Gennaro squatted down and began to measure the stone. He pulled a wax pencil from behind one ear, hairy as a coconut, and made a mark here and there. Maggie jiggled her legs.

"You look more like a Mazza than a Scanlan to me," he said after a while, outlining letters with his pencil. "You look a lot like your mama did when she was your age. She was smaller than you are and she didn't have so much hair. But your faces look alike."

"You've been around here a long time," said Maggie, squinting in a shaft of sun that had suddenly cut through the trees, trying to think about a girl her age, looking like her, hanging around the cemetery, jiggling her legs in the light.

"God, yeah," Mr. Gennaro said. "I know your grandfather almost my whole life. Your grandmother, too, may she rest in peace. She was a tough cookie. And your mother. I remember the day she was married. There was a funeral coming in and your mama coming out of the house in her dress, some shiny stuff with all kinds of lace, and she almost got in the wrong limo. You think they look at you funny, a kid in the cemetery, you should have seen the people in that limo when they saw your mother all dressed up like that. Ten o'clock in the morning and they thought they were seeing ghosts. Jesus, she looked beautiful, but so little, like some little bird. I told your grandfather, never mind that the boy's not Italian, that he's an American boy, he's a nice boy, he'll be good to her."

"What did Grandpop say?"

"Jesus," said Mr. Gennaro, letting his rear fall back on his heels, wiping sweat from his forehead with his arm. "I don't remember. Nothing, probably. Your father was a nice boy. I remember one day he was out back with the old man, trying to help with the tomatoes, but your grandpop didn't want nothing to do with him. So your father was talking to me. God, that boy got red in the sun. I thought he was going to have a stroke. And all of a sudden he says to me, 'Mr. Gennaro, I love her with all my heart.' Well, what the hell could you say. It was beautiful. So what if he was an American boy? All you see are Italian names here," he added, his eyes searching the cemetery for an exception and finally coming back to JESSUP. "But you have a lot of Italian boys here married to American girls."

"We're all American," said Maggie a little primly.

"Yeah, well, that's one way of looking at it," said Mr. Gennaro, digging into the marble with his chisel. "Anyway, your parents were a match. Look at all you kids. How's your dad, anyway?"

"Fine, I think," Maggie said. "I think we're moving."

"How come?"

"How come I think it or how come we're doing it?"

"Jesus," said Mr. Gennaro with a grin, "you are some philosopher. Answer both and let's see what happens."

"I think it because my grandfather said we were, and we're doing it because he wants us to."

Mr. Gennaro's smile faded. "Your other grandfather." Maggie nodded. "People aren't always right, and people don't always get their way," he said, looking off into the distance.

"He's not people," Maggie said, but Mr. Gennaro didn't reply.

Maggie watched him work for a minute more and then wandered down Consolation Way, her hands behind her back. It had never occurred to her to think of her parents as human beings before, and particularly as human beings with some secret and tenuous connection to one another. When they danced together, as they had last night, or when occasionally they touched, she had always felt that she was watching something artificial and far away, as though they were in a movie, acting the parts of husband and wife. Until now she had always thought of them in much the same way she thought of the house, as something that allowed her to live.

The night before, she and her brothers had wandered through the field after dinner, counting the holes the construction crew had made, looking into them with a flashlight. Tommy and Connie were sitting on lawn chairs on the patio, and looking back in the darkness Maggie could see them, and see deep into the lighted kitchen of the house, could even see the little trivet over the stove from the Pennsylvania Dutch country that said: No matter where I feed my guests, it seems they like my kitchen best. The bulk of the house was a gray-black shadow, the yellow rectangles of windows floating within its vague borders. Maggie could see twin specks of red near the ground, the tips of her parents' cigarettes, and occasionally the soft murmur of their voices would stop and her father would say loudly, "Be careful out there. I don't want to drive to the emergency room tonight."

Damien had the flashlight, although both Terence and Maggie tried to take it from him; crickets leapt up from beneath his sneakers, and his thin legs flashed in the beam, as though disembodied. "Here's another one," he said, as he came to the edge of another hole; as his brother and sister edged nearer, afraid of falling in, he let the light rove around the sides.

"They're not that big," said Maggie. "I thought they'd be a lot bigger than this."

"Grandpop said they're only half basements and the rest is on slab," said Terence.

"They're still not that big," Maggie said.

"There are five of them," Damien said.

"The man in the kitchen said six."

"There was a man in the kitchen?" said Terence.

"Talking to Mom."

"Are you sure?" Terence said. "A man we don't know?"

"I saw him, stupid," said Maggie, running away without thinking of the holes pocking the fields.

From the back of the street at nighttime you could see into all the houses, see the blue light of the television and the heads of the people as they moved about inside. Maggie roamed the perimeter slowly, the reeds stabbing at her legs, not as a Peeping Tom might, but like someone looking at pictures in a museum. Other summers, at this time of day, she would have been cooling off after a game of Kick the Can or Monkey in the Middle on the street, or catching lightning bugs in an old mayonnaise jar, or sleeping over at Debbie's house in Mr. Malone's army issue pup tent pitched in the backyard. All of these things suddenly seemed dull, but she did not know what else to do with herself. She sometimes went to the day camp at the park, weaving key rings out of strips of plastic and making mosaic ashtrays, but after five years of day camp she was sick to death of key rings and ash trays. At night she had taken to wandering in the fields, seeing an argument here, a kiss there. She liked the way the houses looked from the outside staring in. The air was fresher at night, even though the heat did not let up much; it felt as though the day was shaking itself out after the still stuffiness of the afternoon.

Through a side window of her own house she could see that her parents had moved into the living room. They were standing face to face, and as she drew nearer she could hear music playing. She recognized the song and the singer: Frank Sinatra, "Here's that Rainy Day." Tommy Scanlan loved music, and Maggie got a quarter from her father every time she could identify a song after only the opening notes, before anyone sang a word. "Here's that Rainy Day" was her father's second favorite song, after "A Foggy Day in London Town."

Maggie realized her parents were dancing. Their heads turned slowly, and she could see their shoulders swaying in time to the music. Sometimes her father would pull Maggie off the floor to dance with him, but she would stumble and step on his feet and he would become impatient after only a few turns. "You're leading," he would say, and Maggie would say "Who cares?" and leave the room. But Tommy and Connie had met at a dance contest, and they were perfectly partnered. He led effortlessly, and she followed easily. It seemed hard to imagine that the man and woman gliding around the living room were the same two people who often stepped sullenly around each other in the kitchen, bickering over who had forgotten to buy breakfast cereal and whether the screens needed to be washed. Maggie wondered if everyone was really more than one person, like Jekyll and Hyde or the woman in *The Three Faces of Eve*, who changed from one personality into another. She thought that perhaps there was more to the Malones than met the eye, and to her aunt Margaret, and certainly to her cousin Monica, whose manners were flawless as long as anyone over the age of thirty was around. The only people she was sure were exactly what they seemed were her aunt Celeste and Helen Malone. She had often suspected that her parents were not entirely what she saw at the dinner table, particularly since she had learned what it had required for them to conceive four children. Two very different people from the ones she knew would have had to be involved in that. She watched carefully as they spun silently to the music. She suspected she was watching those two people now, and the blood rose up into her sweaty face, heat upon heat.

Behind her Damien and Terence were approaching, making much too much noise. "Shut up," she whispered, all consonants, and they did, peering over her shoulder. "I think Mom is prettier than aunt Celeste," said Damien, who still sometimes liked to climb into Connie's lap and wordlessly touch her hair and face. "I do, too," said Maggie, and the boys looked surprised, for Maggie was critical of everyone, particularly those she knew best.

"They're kissing," said Terence softly, his *sss* whistling in a quiet lull in the music.

"They're not kissing, they're dancing," Maggie said.

"They're allowed to kiss," said Damien loudly, turning the flashlight on and shining it in Maggie's face. "They're married."

Maggie knocked the light from his hands and both boys scrambled out into the backyard to grab it. "Maggie," Damien whined, "it's gone." "Shut up," Maggie said. The music stopped and suddenly the buzz of the crickets sounded very loud and harsh, as though they were somehow predatory. Maggie heard her father mumble something, and then Connie replied loudly, "Tell me, please, that I'm not hearing what I think I'm hearing."

"Maggie," Damien whined again, his voice faint, calling from the end of the yard. Maggie leaned closer to the screen. "Over my dead body," Connie said, pulling away, but Maggie saw her father's stringy forearms tighten and hold her fast. Connie beat her little fists against his chest, and he laid his sandy head on her dark one.

Damien and Terence were behind Maggie. "You broke the flashlight," Damien said sadly, pushing the switch back and forth with his thumb, which was red and chapped from his incessant sucking. "It's time to go in," Maggie said, and as she moved to the screen door and opened it, the boys could see their parents move apart, their mother smooth her hair. Their father walked through to the kitchen. "Tell your brothers to come in," he said to Maggie as he opened the refrigerator. In its white glow his pale skin was mottled pink. He reached for a beer and held the bottle against his forehead. Terence and Damien stood outside the screen door peering in, seeing him through the wire mesh as though he was on television. "Don't just stand there," Tommy said impatiently as he looked over and saw them, Terence's mouth a little open, Damien's fair skin flushed pinker than his own. "Come on in and go to bed."

When Maggie went into the living room it was empty, and she wondered where her mother had gone. She had not wondered what her parents had been talking about; a distance, filled by the charged electricity of married people on the verge of a fight, had been between them in the car all the way home on Sunday. For the first time Maggie realized it was sensible for her mother to stay away from the Scanlans. Her grandfather Scanlan's house was always full of discord. Her grandfather Mazza's was the most peaceful place in the world. But her mother never came here, either. Maggie supposed that, like other people, Connie saw a cemetery only as a place of death.

As Maggie went back and knelt beside her grandfather, a hearse, familiar as a station wagon, swung past the house and down Nazareth Way to the back plots. Behind it was the flower car, piled high with gladiolus. Angelo Mazza's eyelids drooped. He hated cut flowers, but his emotions were always just a flicker across his face. From inside the lead limousine someone lifted a hand to him. Maggie made the sign of the cross.

"Not so many cars for the old people," Angelo said, as a dozen cars followed, their headlights shining faintly in the bright sunshine.

"What about Mrs. Romano's boys?"

"Two killed in the war, one a heart attack at Mass five years ago. One left, he lives far away."

Across the stretch of lawn Maggie could see people begin to emerge from their cars, the view interrupted only by the DiGenova family's obelisk and the mausoleum with the Good Shepherd stained-glass window in which the Lisa family were buried. A priest, she could not tell which one, took his place and opened his black leatherbound missal, a purple stole slung round his hunched shoulders. "In the name of the Father and of the Son and of the Holy Spirit," he said, and everyone made the sign of the cross in unison.

Two men in dark-gray suits stood apart from the mourners. They turned and looked across at the Mazza house, their hands folded in front of them. ". . . Gives me the creeps," Maggie heard one say, and knew they were talking about her again, and about the unseemliness of children in cemeteries.

"Why did the Romanos go to the O'Neal's funeral home to get buried?" she asked.

"No Italian funeral homes," her grandfather said.

One of the men, the older, balder one, walked across to the road and down it toward them. He wore on his face a carefully arranged smile of welcome. "Angelo," he said, in the voice of a professional greeter, oily and loud, pulling a breath mint from his pocket and popping it into his mouth as he towered over Maggie and her grandfather.

"Hi, Mr. O'Neal," Maggie said. "How's Cathy?"

"She's fine, honey, fine," Matthew O'Neal said, lowering his voice so he couldn't be heard by the group under the tent. "Misses the girls at Sacred Heart, that's for sure."

"Does she like her new school? Mrs. Malone told me there's a pool and tennis."

"There is, there is," he said, sucking on the mint.

"Tell her I said hi," said Maggie, although she disliked Cathy O'Neal, who was chubby and wore her hair in sausage curls and who told patently fantastic stories about the goings-on in the preparation room on the third floor of the O'Neal Home for Funerals.

"I will," said Mr. O'Neal. "And my best to your grandfather," he added, meaning her grandfather Scanlan.

Turning to her other grandfather, who was still kneeling in front of the roses, he said, "Mrs. Romano's son was very concerned about the vines behind his mother's grave. He thinks they really may come right over the stone."

"I will prune," Angelo said flatly.

"The plants are bothersome to quite a lot of people," said Mr. O'Neal. "It's the idea of them." Maggie knew what he meant. People hated to think about what went on underground in a cemetery. When people looked at the lush growth and strong colors of Angelo's plants, they could conclude only one thing.

"Good soil," said Maggie's grandfather, echoing her thoughts, his eyes gleaming in the sunlight.

"Yes." Mr. O'Neal clasped his hands behind him, then in front again. He sighed. He and Angelo had had this discussion before.

The fact was that there were very few of his customers who complained about the luxuriant growth in Calvary Cemetery, just as he had been exaggerating when he had told Angelo years before that people didn't like to see Maggie hanging around, chewing on the ends of her braids, popping up from behind tombstones like an apparition in a gingham blouse and shorts. He was the one bothered by these things. He always thought that the child's odd behavior, her air of watchfulness, was an object lesson in what happened when you mixed blood that wasn't meant to be mixed, although no one could deny that she'd gotten the Scanlan brains, walking away with all the honors in her class year after year. But Matthew O'Neal knew his business, even if his daughter couldn't master fractions, and he knew that cemeteries were not supposed to be turned into gardens, nor children permitted there. Once at a Friendly Sons of St. Patrick testimonial he had made some comments to John Scanlan about how pleasant it was to see Maria Goretti around Calvary and what a change of pace it made. But John had only chewed purposefully at the end of a large cigar and looked at him narrowly, as though he knew that the tone did not match the message. When Matthew O'Neal moved off to refill his drink, he heard John Scanlan say in the sudden silence, "Goddamn ghoul," and then the low murmur of conversation began again.

"Give my best to your grandfather, Maggie," Mr. O'Neal said, as he turned to walk back to the group at the graveside, who were passing their rosaries through their fingers. Without answering him, grandfather and granddaughter bent again over the black soil, the rims of their fingernails edged with earth.

6

HE CHILDREN WERE ALL AT THE TABLE, its mottled red Formica dense with cereal bowls and Fred Flintstone cups, when Connie went out into the backyard to watch the construction crew begin their work. She could sense rather than hear Maggie and Terence squabbling, and she heard the clatter at the sink as Tommy went rooting around on the counter for a spoon for his coffee. She was holding her own cup, cradling it in her hands as though to keep herself warm. The sun was still climbing the horizon behind her, and her knees and elbows felt cool in her plaid shorts and white shirt.

Little by little over the years she had begun to dress more like Tommy's sister and sisters-in-law, more like a Catholic private school girl and less like a girl from a tough public school where the Italian boys wore shirts so starched they could stand up by themselves. Only in her evening dresses and her evening makeup, both always black or red, did she look like her old self. A man waved, circling closer on a big tractor: it was Joey, wearing work clothes and a hard hat, protective plastic glasses on a strip of elastic dangling around his neck. Connie waved back and then turned and went into the house, shivering a little, stumbling on the stones and weeds that gave way to the feeble grass of their backyard. She was still smiling as she came in.

"That's Joey Martinelli," she said to Tommy, dropping into her seat next to Joseph's chair. "Jimmy Martinelli's older brother. I knew him in school. He's the supervisor on this construction project."

"Mommy says he's a friend of ours," Maggie said.

"Not mine," said Tom.

"He says they expect to have the models by the first week in September," Connie added.

"He's nuts," Tommy said, pouring coffee.

"Just three models," said Connie. "There's one that's a ranch house and another that's a split-level and another that's a Colonial like this."

"Not like this," Tommy said.

"Please, Tom," Connie said, "I don't want to listen again to how terrible new houses are. I just thought you would want to know."

"How did he know we live here?" Tommy said.

"He didn't. He came up to use the phone one day and picked our house out of a clear blue sky. I saw him out back before, and went over to say hello and take him a cup of coffee."

Tommy's own mug was half full. "There wasn't enough goddamn coffee for me," he said.

"Tom."

"Don't 'Tom' me," he shouted over the noise from the construction site. "I don't eat any goddamn breakfast. I have one cup of coffee in the morning. I want my one cup of coffee."

"I'll make another pot," Connie said.

Tommy walked to the swinging kitchen door. Then he went out to the hall, took his jacket and tie off the banister, and was gone. The half-cup of coffee sat untasted on the table. The children could not even hear the door slam, although Maggie was sure it had. "Grandpop's right," she said. "Those things are really loud."

Connie did not say anything. She was looking out the kitchen window and washing the coffee pot, but her shoulders rose and fell as though she sighed. She stood there for a long time as the children disappeared one by one, Maggie to the Malones, Terence and Damien to the ballfield, Joseph into the dining room, where he put a ball of crumpled paper into a plastic cup and took it out again.

Connie was tired. She had finally gotten the curtains she liked on the kitchen windows, and now she was afraid she was going to have to pick up and move to some house she had never seen before, a house even farther away from its neighbors than the one she lived in now, even more mired in silence. She would never have enough furniture for a house that size, and she pictured little excursions to furniture stores with Mary Frances, the two of them holding swatches of brocade, her mother-in-law arguing about price.

She realized she had been standing at the sink a long time, washing dishes mechanically, only when the earth movers stopped and the cement trucks arrived outside. Connie could tell by the insignia on the side of their doors that they were from an Italian firm that was one of Tommy's biggest competitors. He always contended that they were owned by the Mafia, as though murder and extortion were the only way Italians could make money, and this enraged Connie, although her uncle Frank said they were Mafia, too. A truck had pulled a long low trailer to one end of the field, and the workmen gathered around it, unscrewing the lids of their thermoses, faint plumes of steam rising from the openings. One passed around a white cardboard box. She could hear the sound of their voices but not their words. Coffee break. She plugged in the percolator and started another pot.

She had tried to talk to Tommy about the new house, but it had been useless. When he was home the children were there, and when the children were asleep Connie had usually fallen asleep, too, her eyes running wild beneath their translucent lids in the fitful sleep of the exhausted.

Celeste had always told her that she had gotten out of her own marriage just in time, even though it had lasted only a year; she had gotten out when they were still talking to one another, even though most of the talking was yelling. It had taken Connie a while to understand what her cousin meant, but now she thought she did. Occasionally in the car she would look over and see another couple in the next lane, sharing the front seat, both of them staring through the windshield, looking straight ahead, saying nothing. Until recently she had not noticed that she and Tommy were doing the same.

It was not that she did not love him. It was just that she felt as if they were in separate cars, metal and glass surrounding them, oblivious to each other's sounds. She assumed they had the same destination, but it seemed futile now even to ask. So much had been left unspoken in their marriage, and now they were speechless. She thought that if they moved to the house her father-in-law had bought, they would never hear each other speak again.

She reached out to touch her curtains. "I'm staying here," she said, as though saying it aloud would make it so, and she felt a surge of rage so great that it seemed ready to cripple her. "Goddamnit," she said softly, and then she repeated it, louder. "Goddamnit. *I am staying here.* I don't care where the rest of them go. I am staying here." Tears began to run down her face, the hot tears of rage. She pictured her husband, her children, the chairs and beds and sheets and towels, carted off to the big new house, and she there, alone, in the empty rooms. It was better than imagining herself in those other rooms, none of them smaller than twenty by fifteen, held hostage by John Scanlan.

After a few minutes Joey Martinelli emerged from the trailer and began to walk across the fields. The workmen stared at his back, and fell silent. Even if she had not seen the coffee mug hanging by its handle on his index finger, Connie would have known he was coming to her house. As he got closer he looked up and smiled at her.

"You didn't have to bring it back right away," Connie said, opening the back screen door and standing aside to let him in.

"I figured you might want it," he said, holding out the mug. "I know you girls. My mother has a row of little hooks inside the cabinets to hang the cups. If one hook is empty, it drives her crazy."

Connie wished her life was that orderly. She could not remember the last time she had bothered to hang the coffee mugs from the little hooks inside her cabinets. "I always liked your mother," Connie said. "She used to bring cake at Christmas."

"She still brings it to your father," Joey said. "She's convinced he's starving to death. She used to bring him over little things, gravy, chicken, whatever. One of her girlfriends passed some remark about how she was trying to catch another husband, so she stopped doing it. She says your girl takes care of him anyway."

"Maria Goretti."

"The skinny kid, right? With all the hair? She looks something like you but not too much."

"I don't know who they look like," Connie said. "Come on in and have a roll."

"I just ate," he said, "but I'll take some more coffee."

He sat down at the Formica table and Connie was sorry to see that it still had rings on it from breakfast. She poured coffee into the mug he had returned and put a doughnut on the plate.

"Your husband is in construction?" Joe said.

"Tommy," said Connie. "He runs a company called First Concrete."

"With the striped trucks. They're pretty good. Expensive. His old man owns it."

"I didn't know everybody knew that," Connie said, sitting down opposite him.

"His old man owns everything," said Joe, wrapping his hands around his coffee cup, and when he saw her face, he added, "Sorry."

"No, it's all right," Connie said. "Tommy's sort of the black sheep. You know. Because of me."

"No, really?" said Joe, who knew that this was true because everyone in his mother's neighborhood said so. He flexed his fingers and studied them as he added, "He got the prize. I know some of the other wives, from dances and stuff. Real Irish girls. Freckles, piano legs, no chest. He got the prize."

Connie felt the flush begin on her throat. Her lips buzzed with the blood inside them. Finally Joey looked right at her and added, "You were always so pretty," as though he dared her to contradict him.

"Your brother Jimmy have kids?" Connie finally said, when her breath came back.

"Three," said Joe, and as if on cue Joseph toddled in from the dining room. "Bear," he shouted, holding his tattered brown bear aloft.

"Thanks," Joe said, reaching for the toy, but the baby pulled it back. "No, no," he said, and Connie lifted him up and kissed his head. "Bear is his security blanket," she said. "He can't go anywhere without Bear. Are you ready for a nap, JoJo?" she added.

"No," Joseph said.

"I gotta go anyhow," Joey Martinelli said, standing and putting his cup in the sink. "When am I going to teach you to drive?"

"You don't have to do that," Connie said. "I wouldn't have told you I didn't know how if I knew you were going to think you had to give me driving lessons."

"No, really, it'll be fun. I taught my brother. I taught my cousins. We'll find a parking lot somewhere and you can drive around in circles. I don't know, we might have to find you a phone book to sit on, but I can have you driving in a couple of weeks if you want."

Connie was surprised at herself as she said, "Okay, if you don't mind. I'd really like to get out more. Just do my own shopping, take the kids places, go and see my cousin."

"So tomorrow at four I'll come and we can start. We'll put the baby in the back seat. Deal?"

Connie smiled. "Deal." He stuck out his hand and they shook, the little boy between them. It was an oddly comforting gesture. "Jeez," he said, looking down, "you have the littlest hands of any girl I ever knew." He opened his big fist and there it was, lying on his palm as though, Connie thought, it was displayed on a pillow. She pulled her hand away and thrust it deep into the pocket of her shorts.

"Tomorrow," Joey said, as he let himself out the back door.

When he was gone Connie hung all the coffee cups on their hooks in the cabinet, and then took Joseph upstairs for his nap. In the upstairs hallway she stood on tiptoe to look at herself in the mirror. All the mirrors were hung at Tommy's height, so that the bottom half of her own face, her mouth and chin, were always invisible. She thought perhaps she should get her hair cut. "I'm staying right here," she said to herself, only half aloud, and wondered as she went downstairs what it would be like to know how to drive, to go wherever you wanted to go whenever you wanted to go there.

7

N WEDNESDAY MORNING MAGGIE WAS sitting on the front steps when her aunt Celeste arrived. Damien had collected cicadas in a shoe box, surrounding them with tiny tufts of grass and a collection of sticks, and now he wanted to name them. Once he had used up Matthew, Mark, Luke, John, Mickey, Donald and Pluto, he had come to Maggie for help. The two of them argued; she suggested some girls' names and Damien was sure that all cicadas were boys. When Celeste pulled up in front of the house in her red car, the one with the pleated silver fins, Damien appealed to her for support. She took one look at the bugs, their iridescent backs gleaming in the sun, their squat bullet bodies motionless amid the grass and sticks, and said, "Those are male animals." Then she opened the screen door and let herself in. Maggie left Damien talking to the bugs and went inside.

Celeste was not really Maggie's aunt, but her mother's first cousin and closest friend; the two women had been like sisters growing up, the only sister Connie was likely to get, the closest person to her as she grew older. Celeste came once a week in the summer, when business was slow. She brought a shopping bag filled with clothes and costume jewelry for her cousin Connie ("poor Connie," she always said with a sigh) and play makeup for Maggie, which Connie took away and hid on the top shelf of her closet, between the douche bag and the copy of *Tropic of Cancer*. "This is the new you," Celeste would announce, pulling Capri pants and a blouse with low ruffled shoulders out of the bag. Then she would force Connie to put on the clothes and a pair of hoop earrings and walk around the living room until they both would laugh so hard Celeste would cry, "I'm going to pee myself," and run off to the bathroom, little rivulets of mascara running into the lines around her eyes. Maggie never saw her mother wear the clothes Celeste brought after the first time she tried them on; they stayed in her bottom drawer, smelling of sizing. They were not Scanlan clothes.

"What do you think, Mag?" Connie said, twirling around on her tiny feet, forgetting herself.

"I don't know," Maggie said glumly, which was half the truth, the other half being that Connie looked lovely in an odd, eccentric way, like a Gypsy princess.

"Oh, don't be such an old woman," her mother said. "Ce, come here. Your goddaughter disapproves of me."

"Oh my God," Celeste said, smoothing down her skirt as she returned from the bathroom. "My poor bladder. You girls."

Celeste was the only person Maggie knew who was divorced. She had gotten married the year before Connie and Tommy, to a school friend of Tommy's named Charlie Black, who drank. It wasn't the drinking that had made her finally leave, although that was a convenient excuse; it wasn't even the fact that all Celeste's Max Factor pancake could not conceal her bruises on Sunday mornings at Mass. Maggie had heard her once tell Connie that what got to her was the basic boredom of it all, the sameness of sitting around every evening watching Charlie drink beer in his leatherette recliner, his hair flopping over his forehead, his T-shirt yellow beneath the armpits. Every morning Celeste would clean her house, do her laundry, start dinner, talk to her mother on the telephone, walk the poodle, take off her nail polish, put on a different color, watch her little stories on television, and be finished and bored to tears by three in the afternoon. She knew she should have figured this out beforehand; when she thought about it, she had told Connie, she realized that the beginning of life was one great event after another, your first bra and first date and first kiss, your proms and dances and finally your wedding, and then suddenly there was nothing to do for the rest of your life. In the beginning she always went to see Connie in the afternoon, particularly when Connie and Tommy were living in Celeste's mother's house, in Celeste's old room. But after the baby was born Connie was too busy to talk.

Six months after Maggie arrived, Celeste got on the train one day, without a clue as to where she was going, and got off at Times Square. She entered four office buildings, filled out four job applications, and was hired immediately as a secretary. When she got home and told Charlie, he knocked out her right front incisor and threw the poodle out the second-story window. Without a word (she told Connie she couldn't really talk because of the tooth) she packed her vanity case and went home to her old room. Tommy and Connie had moved the month before to Westchester.

Celeste still lived at home, in a kind of extended adolescence in which she spent all her salary on clothes and makeup and spent a lot of time criticizing her mother's cooking. Like Connie, she was a showy combination of black and white, dark hair and white skin, but she was big and getting bigger, a big hefty woman with a big shelf of a bust. When she walked through the garment district to her current job as executive secretary to the president of a blouse company, the Puerto Rican boys who pushed the racks of clothes from building to building would smack their lips and call her "Mama." She pretended not to notice, but she really didn't mind.

"So I think I'm getting married again," Celeste said, settling back in a chair with a cup of coffee.

"Uh huh," Connie said. "Tell me another."

"Honest to God," she said, staring down at the large pear-shaped diamond, yellow as an egg yolk, which she now wore on her right hand and which was the only memento of her last engagement. Maggie had heard one of her Scanlan aunts say that Celeste had the largest collection of yellow diamonds in the world, and when Maggie asked her mother if this was true, Connie only said "That bitch" and slammed out of the room.

"Why do you want to get married? You have everything. You make a good living, have a nice house, privacy, freedom. You've got everything you had in high school except you're old enough to enjoy it. Besides, you hated being married."

"I don't have kids."

"Kids," said Connie. "You're a kid. Besides, it would kill your mother. Can you imagine your mother if you had to be married by a judge or something? Or a rabbi? She'd have a stroke."

Celeste's current boyfriend was a Jew. All of her boyfriends since her divorce had been Jewish. She said it was a well-known fact that Jews did not hit women.

"I know a nice Italian guy I could fix you up with."

"You? Who? Get out."

"Really. Remember Jimmy Martinelli that I used to date? Remember—you were in class with his cousin Anna Maria?"

"The one with the glasses? And the nose?"

"Well, his brother Joseph is working on this construction they're doing here, on the development—"

"Oh Jesus, Con," Celeste said, lighting a cigarette. "My mother is always trying to fix me up with that guy. He's never been married, right? So what's wrong with him? He's like me—can't live with them, can't live without them."

"I think he's shy," Connie said, reaching over and taking Celeste's cigarette and using it to light her own, a gesture Maggie thought was the height of sophistication. She leaned forward to watch her mother pull in on the cigarette, her cheeks filling and deflating like those of a little animal. Connie looked up and saw Maggie staring at her. "Aren't you going swimming?" she said.

"I guess," said Maggie.

"Well, have a good time."

Maggie did not move.

"Vamoose, kid," said Celeste. "I hope you like your lip pomade." She put her cheek out for a continental kiss. "You smell good," Maggie said. "Tabu," said Celeste. "That's what Monica wears," Maggie said. "Shit," answered her aunt. "Celeste!" said Connie.

Maggie went upstairs to get her bathing suit and towel. Her face still smelled like perfume on one side; whenever she turned her head she got a whiff of it, making her feel grown-up and a little bad.

Her room was the nicest one in the house. It had gingham curtains at the window and a gingham spread on the canopy bed, a bulletin board over the desk, and a little dressing table with a gingham skirt. It was like a magazine photograph of a little girl's room; in fact her mother had painstakingly copied it out of a magazine when Maggie was still young enough to be sleeping in a crib. On the floor next to her bed was an old yellow-and-brown striped suitcase filled with the clothes she was taking to the beach. In the middle of July each summer, Mary Frances took all her female grandchildren of a certain age to a seaside town called South Beach. She thought of this as a great excursion they would remember the rest of their lives. Maggie thought of it as sharing a bedroom with Monica for a week. She remembered that there had been times when she was very young when the trip had actually been fun—the restaurant meals, the hotel sheets smelling of starch, the long days jumping breakers on the beach. Now all she could think of was Monica looking her up and down with that smile.

She heard heavy footsteps on the stairs and started to close her door when she saw it was Celeste. Her aunt was carrying a brown bag and grinning. She slipped inside and closed the door. "Santa Claus is coming to town," she said, picking a piece of tobacco from her smile with the end of one long fingernail. She reached inside the bag and pulled out a jumble of green-and-orange print fabric and spread it on the bed. It was a two-piece bathing suit, the top strapless, with small arcs of bone inside so that it looked as if there was a bust in it, even lying there on the bed. Celeste turned the bottom over. The back was covered with row upon row of tiny ruffles. It was the showiest bathing suit Maggie had ever seen, and she could tell by looking at it that it was just her size.

Celeste suddenly seemed embarrassed by her own audacity. She winked at Maggie. "Can't go to the beach looking like Shirley Temple when you're really Lana Turner," she said, while Maggie tried to remember which one Lana Turner was. She looked down at the suitcase open on the floor. "That's the bag your mother took on her honeymoon," Celeste said. "I remember because I filled it with rice. God, she just about killed me. She told me she pulled out her peignoir that first night and the place looked like a Chinese restaurant." Celeste's eyes grew thoughtful. "Anyhow, wear this in good health, kiddo. I'm not sure it's the kind of suit you want to do the breaststroke in. For one thing, you might lose the top. But I can guarantee that everybody will look twice at it." She kissed Maggie on the cheek and moved to the door, crumpling the bag as she went. "Go easy on your old mom," she said. "She's having a tough time these days."

"Why?" said Maggie, holding the suit against her chest.

"One thing and another."

"Grandpop says she has to get on board," Maggie said.

"Sometimes I wish somebody would squish your grandfather like one of those bugs your brother's got outside," Celeste said. "He thinks he can run everybody's life."

"He does run everybody's life," Maggie said.

"I'd like to see him try that shit with me," Celeste said. "Do me a favor—don't tell your mother I said shit, don't tell her we had this discussion, and don't listen to everything your grandfather says." Celeste licked her finger and patted down one of her spit curls. "I'll leave you alone so you can try that thing on."

When she was gone Maggie closed the door again and slipped out of her shorts and shirt. With her back to the mirror she put on the bathing suit, tugging the top into place, exhaling exaggeratedly to find out if it would stay up without effort. Finally she turned toward the mirror. The suit was a perfect fit. The green turned her eyes the color of lime LifeSavers; the ruffles made her look as if she had hips, and the bones in the bodice made her look as if she had a bust. She looked down. If she was careful, no one would be able to tell that there were two inches of open space between the top and her own chest. She held her arms out and twirled in front of the mirror.

Downstairs she heard Damien calling, "Maggie." She ran to the door and threw her back against it. "Go away, Dame," she called, and after a minute she could hear the staccato sound of his sneakers running outside. She went back to the mirror and put her hands on her hips.

From below her bedroom window she heard voices, and looking out she saw her mother standing in the grass, her arms crossed on her chest. She seemed very small, and Maggie felt as if she were looking at her through the wrong end of a telescope. She realized that these days she was always seeing her mother from a distance, as if in pictures—framed in a window, frozen in some pose, her face revealed in some essential way. Just yesterday she had come silently into the dining room on bare feet and seen Connie through the door leading to the kitchen, leaning back against the counter, flushed and radiant. Maggie had suddenly thought that her mother looked beautiful, young, more wondrous than Helen Malone. For a moment she had been stunned by her mother's likeness to someone she could not quite place. And then she had realized that the resemblance was to the picture on her grandfather Mazza's bureau, in the gold frame next to the clothed statue of the Infant Jesus of Prague, the picture of Concetta Mazza at her high school graduation, with black fabric draped round her bare shoulders and a self-conscious happy look on her face, walking in beauty like the night.

Then Maggie had moved, and her mother had moved, and the moment had been over. That was when she saw the man in the kitchen.

"Here's the big girl," he had said, in a false voice. "I'm Mr. Martinelli. I know your grandfather."

"Which one?" Maggie had said, as she sat down at the table and pushed away the coffee cups.

"The Italian one," he said in Italian, and Connie turned and said in the same language, "She can't speak it. You know, they forget. She never hears it." Maggie understood most of what they were saying, but she just sat with her head down, her hair falling around her face.

"I'm going to teach your mother to drive," the man said in the same false voice, smiling at Maggie again, his fingers tapping on a key lying near the edge of the kitchen table.

"Why?" Maggie longed to grab hold of his eyebrows and pull, and reddened at the thought.

"Why not?" Connie said, and Maggie shrugged. She knew that she had cast a pall over the kitchen, but she did not care. "Aren't you finished work?" Maggie said to Mr. Martinelli, suddenly aware that it was quiet out back as Connie began gathering up the dishes.

"I'm leaving," he said. "But I'll see you again."

"I'm going to the beach next week," said Maggie defiantly, but when she looked up and saw his face she realized he had been talking to her mother.

"Is he the one you went to the dance with?" Maggie said after he had gone out the back door, and Connie turned and asked "Who told you about that?"

"Celeste."

"Aunt Celeste. No, it was his brother. Joe was too old. Four years older than me."

"He's really old," said Maggie.

Her mother made a sound like a snort and continued to wash the cups. Joseph shrieked from the playpen on the patio and Maggie went outside to see him. "JoJo, JoJo," she crooned, and the baby grabbed her long hair and stuck it into his mouth. She carried him in on her hip. "He's hungry," she said, putting him in his high chair, and then she saw that her mother was being sick in the sink, and she stood and stared and then got a banana and began to mash it in a bowl for the baby. After Connie had wiped her mouth and taken a drink, Maggie said, "Does Daddy know?"

Connie's eyes looked enormous. "What?" she said.

"That you're going to learn to drive."

"Oh. That. No, I think I'll make it a surprise."

Maggie had looked up from feeding Joseph. "It'll be a surprise, all right," she had said. "When are we moving?"

"What?"

"When are we moving into the new house?"

"We're not moving. This is our house." Connie's face was very pale and there were gray circles beneath her eyes. "I don't know where you got the idea that we're moving."

"Grandpop bought us a bigger house. He gave you keys and everything. He says it has a basketball hoop and a little room over the garage I can have for myself."

Connie dried her hands on a dishtowel. "Whose side are you on?"

Maggie felt she was going to be sick, too, and wondered if it was just the sharp vinegar smell lingering in the kitchen. "I didn't know there were sides," she said.

"Never mind," Connie said. "I shouldn't have said that. We're not moving."

"Are you sure?" Maggie said.

"We are not moving," said Connie in a trembling voice, and Maggie had taken Joseph out of his chair and back to the patio.

Out on the patio now, Celeste stepped into the sun, a Pall Mall glowing white against the blood red of her lacquered nails. She followed Connie onto the lawn, off balance because the heels of her shoes had sunk into the dirt. They had their backs to her, but Maggie could hear snatches of what they were saying. Celeste threw back her head and, her mouth working like a fish out of water, blew a chain of smoke rings into the still air. Suddenly she turned to Connie and said loudly, "We've all gotta grow up sometime, Con."

"So when is it your turn?"

"I'm as grown as I'm gonna get. Here's the God's truth—you're more of a kid than I am, never mind the husband and the four kids and the house. You need to start acting like the mother of a growing girl, not just living in a dream world."

"I was never a kid, Cece. How come I was never a kid? It's not fair."

"You're right," Celeste said. "But you got no choice now, sweetheart. You gotta hold this family together."

"I thought the man held the family together."

Celeste blew more smoke rings. "There's only one thing men hold, and that's when they got to go to the bathroom. All right, sorry,"

Celeste added, seeing her cousin's face. "But sometimes I think you watch too many movies. Your daughter needs you now."

"She doesn't like me, Ce."

"Get out," Celeste said, dropping her cigarette into the grass and rubbing it out with the pointed toe of her shoe. "What's to like? You're her mother. Did you like your mother? Do I like my mother? You need to show her things. Remember how old Rose slapped me when I first got the curse? Boom! 'It's an old Italian custom,' she says. I should have thanked her for preparing me for Charlie."

Connie did not answer. She had her arms wrapped around herself as though she was holding her body together. Maggie could see the construction crew on their lunch break; the two women gave them a little wave, and the men waved back. Maggie moved away from the screen, afraid someone would see her. Celeste put her arm around Connie's shoulder, and they stood that way for what seemed like a long time: Celeste holding Connie, Connie's head of black curls on her shoulder, Maggie holding back the sheer white curtains beneath the pink gingham ones. Then one of the men yelled "Back to the grind!" and the women turned and went indoors. Maggie saw that her mother's face was wet and her long nose a little shiny, and she heard her say softly, her voice breaking, "They're gonna win, Cece. I can feel it. Ten years from now I'll be living in one of their houses, sitting on their furniture, wearing their clothes, and my kids will be their kids. She's already one of them."

"Don't overreact, sweetheart," Celeste said. "You got the ace in the hole. If your husband has to chose between you and them, he'd choose you every time. He already did it when it mattered."

"And what if my daughter has to choose between me and them, Cece? It's not as simple as Cinderella anymore."

"Hey, honey," Celeste said. "This isn't like you. You having your friend, or what? The curse upon you? You and me, we always were on the same schedule."

Maggie heard her mother laugh, high and a little shaky, and saw Celeste smooth her hair.

"I wish," Connie said, with an odd shrillness in her voice.

"Oh, shit," Celeste said, stopping and looking down at her cousin. "Not again. Can't you count?" Maggie wondered what they were talking about, and as she looked down at her mother her eyes began to brim with tears, for no reason she could figure out except that her mother was crying, too.

8

N THE FOURTH DAY OF THEIR ANNUAL trip to the beach, the Scanlan women had their photograph taken at Cap'n Jim's restaurant. Maggie knew that as surely as her grandmother would disapprove of her bathing suit, and her cousin Teresa would get sunburned so badly she would smell like Noxzema for a month, on the fourth day they would have their picture taken to testify that they were having a wonderful time and were part of a supremely happy family.

While the photographer set up his tripod, Maggie looked around to see what he would see: Monica laughing, her hair shining in the lights; Teresa, who was the same age as Maggie, her eyes pale blue as eucalyptus mints, her face a little vacant; and the twins, a matching patina of pale pink over their faces and arms, staring down self-consciously at their shrimp cocktails. Mary Frances had gone to the ladies' room to freshen her lipstick, which had come off on the rim of her whiskey-sour glass. The picture would cost five dollars, and when it was sent to her at home, Mary Frances would put it in the silver frame that held last year's picture. Maggie had taken the velvet back off that frame one day, and had found seven photographs of the group, starting back when she was six years old, her lips drawn down in an awkward smile to hide the fact that her two front teeth were missing. Monica was eleven in that first picture, and looked, Maggie had been sad to see, much as she looked today, except that there had been the glint of her braces. On Monica, even braces looked good, as if she had jewelry on her teeth.

"Congratulations, Maggie," Monica said now, readjusting the bow holding back her hair. "My father says that your mother is going to have another baby." Monica made the word "another" last a long, long time.

"So what?" Maggie said.

"Really? When? Ooooh," said Teresa, picking up the last shrimp with her stubby freckled fingers. "I hope it's a girl this time."

They were eating by a plate-glass window in the restaurant. It was actually a refurbished tugboat, big and square, with graceless utilitarian lines, which picked diners up at 6:00 and 8:30 from a pier on the bay side of the town of South Beach and sailed along the shore while they ate. Mary Frances took the girls to dinner at Cap'n Jim's each year because she assumed they liked the novelty of it, and each year they mimed excitement and delight, convinced that it was Mary Frances's favorite restaurant. In fact after years of Friday night meatless suppers, Mary Frances hated fish, and she had no stomach for the sea; she usually ate little and drank a good deal. Maggie was like her in this; she usually drank so much soda during these meals that she had to go to the bathroom at least twice, each time thinking of what happened after she flushed the toilet this far from land.

"What are you girls giggling about?" Mary Frances said pleasantly as she came back to the table, although the only one giggling was Teresa. Mary Frances sat down in the middle, between Monica and Maggie, and the photographer fiddled with some dials on his camera. "What a handsome group," he said, and Mary Frances smiled, and the shutter clicked. "All sisters, I presume," he said, and Mary Frances laughed, and the shutter clicked again. It was the same photographer as always, wearing a captain's hat and smoking a cigar. He said the same things every year.

They had spent the day on the beach, where the sound of the sea and the strength of the sun had lulled them all into afternoon naps, even Mary Frances in her rented beach chair. Her magazine would fall open on her lap, her mouth would goggle a bit, and she would doze, waking suddenly, embarrassed, to say, "My, but it's warm." Mary Frances was not entirely comfortable with her granddaughters—she had been the youngest of nine children, and was accustomed to being the baby herself—and she did her best to hide it by playing the role of grandmother the way she expected Billie Burke or Spring Byington would. She affected a sort of breezy elegance, which usually consisted of wide eyes, a half-smile, and the phrase "Well, girls?" all accompanied with a slight sideways tilt of the head. Maggie had once seen a movie starring Greer Garson and had become indignant at the way Greer Garson had imitated her grandmother. It was only in the last year or so that she had realized that Mary Frances herself was doing the imitating.

On the beach, Maggie had listened to the radio and lain on her back on a towel. The air was white with unalloyed sunlight, and her lips tasted like salt from the sea, and from her own sweat. Around her were girls sparkling with baby oil, their hands always busy with their hair, their eyes moving back and forth along the horizon for some boy or another, their nipped-in waists the perfect counterpoint to their bosoms and their hips.

And then there were the littler girls, the ones Maggie had been like the summer before, shrill and jumpy, smelling of Coppertone, wet white T-shirts over their cotton suits to keep them from burning, their plastic buckets beside them on their blankets. And the middle-sized ones, like her cousin Teresa, still digging for sand crabs at the water's edge, still wearing her shapeless nylon tank suit, although she had to slump to keep her nipples from poking its navy-blue surface. Maggie felt as if she belonged nowhere, and to none of them. "Roll over, roll over," the deejay sang every hour, parroting the children's song to warn his listeners to tan evenly, but Maggie stayed on her back, afraid that if she lay on her stomach she would dent the top part of her bathing suit.

Monica was sitting under an umbrella; she tanned only an hour a day because she had read in *Seventeen* that too much sun gave you wrinkles. Occasionally she got up to stroll down the beach, her pink eyelet suit hugging her body, and Maggie would watch her stop at the lifeguard stand and talk to the two young men who sat there, their zinc-oxided noses two white flags on the horizon. Other boys would stop by, and Monica would swivel from one to another. Finally she came back to lie under the umbrella.

In midafternoon, when Maggie was falling asleep, the voice on the radio said, "I've got a special request here from the guys in the sophomore sports club at Fordham. This one goes out to the beautiful, the untouchable, the incredible Helen. No last names, please." Then he played a song Maggie had never heard before, by Johnny Mathis, whose voice kept breaking on the high notes. When Maggie looked up at her cousin, Monica was staring out to sea, her eyes narrowed. "Untouchable my ass," she muttered.

"What, dear?" Mary Frances said pleasantly.

"Nothing, Grandmom," said Monica, and she got slowly to her feet and walked back to the lifeguard stand.

When Monica was gone, Maggie gingerly turned over onto her stomach. She lay flat for a minute, the sand shifting slightly beneath her cheek, and then she propped herself up on her elbows and looked down. Sure enough, her convex top was now concave.

"Oooh," she moaned.

"What, dear?"

"Nothing, Grandmom," Maggie said, pushing out the cups with her finger.

"I love your bathing suit, Maggie," Teresa said with a giggle. "You look like a cancan dancer."

"Watch your mouth, dear," said Mary Frances.

When they were not at the beach, they strolled along the boardwalk, played miniature golf while Mary Frances watched, ate surf and turf at restaurants with imitation fishnets on the walls. Mary Frances told the same stories every year, and over the years Maggie had begun to think there was something sad about them, as though what Mary Frances didn't discuss was somehow different and darker than these pat anecdotes.

Maggie knew very little about her grandmother's past life, except that Mary Frances still mourned Elizabeth Ann, the baby who had died, and Maggie sometimes wondered whether being surrounded by her granddaughters reminded her of her loss. Her aunt Margaret had told Maggie that Mary Frances herself had been born two months after her father had died of tuberculosis and that when she was little she had thought her name was "posthumous child" because so many people called her that. Inevitably the children Mary Frances felt most drawn to were the vulnerable ones. Maggie knew that her grandmother was fondest of Tommy, and she tried not to think about what that meant, for her father and for her. Maggie knew that her grandmother loved her, too, although the rest of the family thought of Maggie as John Scanlan's pet.

After they had had their picture taken, a full moon rose outside the window of Cap'n Jim's, and they looked at the man in the moon as they had cheesecake for dessert. The boat was approaching the pier, and the girls gathered up their white patent handbags and began to follow their grandmother to the door. The guesthouse where they always stayed—"patronized," Mary Frances said, as though she was somehow condescending to the place—was right across the street from the pier. It was a squat, rather pretty white building with white pebbles instead of a lawn, big pots of geraniums flanking the path to the front door, and a porch that ran around three sides where they spent the evening looking over the sea and rocking in their rocking chairs.

"Grandmom, I have cramps," Monica said, as they crossed the road in single file, looking, Maggie thought, like a row of ducks in their yellow and white summer dresses and their shiny white summer dress shoes. "Can I go in and lie down?"

"There's no need to be so explicit," said Mary Frances. "Just go ahead. The rest of us will be out here."

They sat down, facing the ocean, the sounds dying down as the diners moved away from the boat, the sounds dying down to the slow, rhythmical *boom-boom* of the surf, occasionally shot through with a trill of high laughter from the beach.

Maggie mulled over the news about a new baby, which was not

really news after the day she had seen her mother being sick in the sink. One of her most enduring images of her mother was of a headless person, a small torso bent double, making strangled heaving sounds over the sink. For a long time it was the only way she thought of her mother, on those rare occasions when she did think of her when they were apart, although now sometimes there would appear unwanted in her mind the picture of her mother looking like that high school photograph, her face alight, not like a mother at all.

Maggie knew that soon it would be time for Mary Frances to tell stories. Usually when they were at the beach Mary Frances told the story about how she had met John Scanlan. She had been small and pretty, with soft brown hair and hazel eyes, and John Scanlan had looked down at her and said, "You're going to marry me whether you like it or not." It was a great family story, the epitome of what they all liked to think of as the Scanlan directness and determination, character traits that in fact only John and Maggie's aunt Margaret, Sister John of the Cross, happened to possess. But Maggie realized now that the fact that her grandfather had gotten his way said as much about Mary Frances as it did about John Scanlan. For that was how it had happened, really, and even now Maggie could hear it in her grandmother's voice: Mary Frances had not known whether she liked it or not, whether she liked *him* or not; she only knew that John had taken charge of the situation, and that had been that.

And that had been that ever since. In the first ten years she had had seven children, while her husband had become grand, feared and fawned upon by nearly everyone he met. And somehow, over those years, she had come to love him. Maggie could see that it pained her that John let the world know he thought she was silly and childish, although Connie had once said that that was part of the reason John had married Mary Frances, so that he could think she was silly and childish and manage her. Somehow the "whether you like it or not" story always made Maggie feel sad.

"Tell about the lifeguard," Maggie said, looking sideways at her grandmother, who was staring fixedly toward the black void of the horizon.

"Oh, that old story," her grandmother said.

"I love that story," said Teresa.

"Well, as you all know I'm not much of a swimmer," said Mary Frances, whose grandchildren had never seen her do anything in a bathing suit except sit on the beach. "I was with my friend Ruthie Corrigan and we were at the Alden, a guest house down the street here, I think it's called the Grande now. We had a room on the top floor with those dormer windows and just barely room enough for two. Seven dollars a week it was, which may seem cheap to you, but was dear then, I can tell you, especially for me. Not that we were poor. But there wasn't money to burn."

"And you went swimming," said Maggie.

"And we went swimming," Mary Frances continued. "There was a dreadful undertow, one of those where you can just barely stand up. It was dragging us around, but Ruthie was a bigger girl than me, a very big girl, with great big bones and feet, I think they were tens, if you can imagine, and she was staying put and I was all over the place out there. And I was trying to be calm, but finally I said 'Ruthie, I'm drowning, say your prayers and I'll say mine.' And she hollered, oh, did she holler. And before I knew what had happened there was this young man pulling me out by the hair."

Mary Frances stopped to catch her breath, her face as pink as the embroidery on her pocket handkerchief.

"He was as handsome as Francis X. Bushman—"

"Who's Francis X. Bushmer?" said Teresa, who had a mind, John Scanlan always said, "like a sieve."

"Shut up," said Maggie. "An actor. Pay attention."

"He was as handsome as Francis X. Bushman," Mary Frances said, "with beautiful wavy hair and the prettiest teeth. I was all right when he got me up on the beach, only out of breath and a little scared, but Ruthie was screaming like a banshee and finally I had to tell her to be quiet so he could tell me his name. Roderick. Can you beat that? Roderick. Like a duke, I said to Ruthie. And right there on the beach he said, 'May I take you to dinner tonight?' And me still trying to catch my breath, so I just nodded. 'May I take you?' Like a duke, I said to Ruthie."

"But you didn't go," said Maggie.

"I didn't go, no," said Mary Frances with a slight clicking noise, her mouth dry from the whiskey sours. "That afternoon I met your grandfather. And that was that."

Maggie waited.

"He swept me off my feet," Mary Frances said with a sigh.

It suddenly seemed very quiet and the noise of the ocean seemed loud. "I have to go to the bathroom," said one of the twins softly, as though she was a toddler who needed to be taken and helped. "Well, go then, dear, don't discuss it," Mary Frances said impatiently.

"Grandmom, can I go for a walk on the beach?" Maggie asked, as her cousin slipped away.

"In your stockings?"

"I didn't wear them tonight."

"I wish I'd known that. I would have sent you back upstairs. Well, go ahead then."

Maggie handed Teresa her white patent pumps and ran down the stairs. The road that separated the guesthouse from the beach was empty and the sand felt surprisingly cold. The night was so black that Maggie knew she had reached the water's edge only when she felt the sea run over her feet. When she looked for the moon she realized that it must be hidden behind the clouds, and she wondered if it would rain, and what they would all do if it did, stuck together at the beach on a rainy day. To one side she could hear an odd whirring sound, and dimly in the dark she made out the silhouette of someone surf-casting. She began to walk in the opposite direction.

She felt at home walking on the beach. The lonely, empty feeling in her stomach, which seemed out of place in everyday life—at the pool, playing softball, at school, with her brothers—felt suitable at the beach. She walked for what seemed like a long time, and then turned at one of the stone jetties and walked back again, looking for the lights of the guesthouse beyond the dunes. She saw them from some distance away and began to climb to the middle of the beach.

She was perhaps a block away from the house when she almost stepped on a half-naked couple sprawled on a blanket. She drew back and then squinted in the darkness, able to make out the curve of the boy's bare buttocks and the ridiculous welter of clothes gathered around his ankles. "Oh my god," he kept repeating, moving up and down. "Oh my god." Beneath him a girl seemed to be staring blankly at the sky overhead, the whites of her eyes visible even in the darkness. Maggie realized that the girl was staring at her, and that it was her cousin Monica, looking expressionless, grim, her fingernails sparkling on the boy's shoulder as the moon momentarily emerged from the clouds. "Oh my God," he said again, and Maggie drew back and ran across the sand to the break in the dunes.

She kept on running across the street, up onto the porch of the guesthouse; then she sat there hugging her knees for a few minutes before she went upstairs to the room she and Monica shared. One of the twin beds was lumpy with what Maggie knew would be an artful arrangement of pillows. She pulled out her own pillow and turned on her side, feigning sleep when she heard footfalls an hour later. She spent all night wondering what to do, but the matter was settled for her the next morning, as she and Monica walked to the beach together several steps behind their grandmother. Monica gave her a level look, not unlike the one she had given her the night before on the beach, and said quietly, "Who'd believe you? Grandpop says you have an overactive imagination." Then she walked ahead, her carefully oiled calves shining in the sun, talking to Mary Frances.

Maggie lagged behind, and so it was she that Mrs. Polisky, the owner of the guesthouse, reached first as she came trotting up behind them, her fat face red. "Tell your grandmother you've got to come into the house," she gasped. "You've got to go home. Your grandfather's had an accident."

9

OHN SCANLAN LAY IN THE HOSPITAL bed, the left side of his face looking as though it was melting into his shoulder, a thick line of saliva edging his jawline. "Wipe his mouth," Mark said to one of the nurses, but as soon as she had done so the spittle crept down again.

Except for the fact that his family stood behind a sheet of glass, kept out of the intensive care unit by regulations that even now her uncle James was appealing, Maggie thought that it looked like one of the deathbed scenes of the British royal family in her book about Queen Victoria. Her grandfather did not look dead; he looked ruined, as though he would have to be renovated from top to bottom to regain any semblance of his former self. Mary Frances was sitting beside his bed, stroking his hand and clutching the cord to the intravenous feed.

"Will he die?" Maggie asked, the only one of the grandchildren left there, the twins having been sent home by cab, Teresa sent to the cafeteria in hysterics, and Monica left in the waiting room with some of the aunts, reading an old copy of *Vogue*.

"What kind of question is that?" Mark asked. "Jesus. Of course not."

Maggie noticed that a tube running from underneath the covers down the side of the bed was bright yellow, and she began to feel sick. She had been in a hospital only twice before, once for stitches in her knee, once to visit her mother when Joseph was born, her father sneaking her in past the nurses' stations, but it had not been like this. Even the smell was different; there was still the odor of disinfectant, but it was overlaid with that of rubber and dirty clothes. She went outside into the waiting area, where her father was talking on the pay phone.

"Did you find her?" Monica was asking him.

"Mind your own business," Tommy Scanlan said, dropping in another coin.

"Maggie, honey, do you have any idea where your mother could be?" Aunt Cass asked.

"At home."

"No, she's not."

"At Celeste's?"

"Your brothers are there, thank God. But Celeste doesn't know where your mother went."

Tommy slammed down the pay phone and said, "She can't even drive, for Christ's sake. She hates the train. Where is she?"

"Did you call Grandpop?" asked Maggie, who thought it was probably a bad time to mention that her mother might be able to drive after all.

"He said he'd find her. How's he going to find her? The closest Angelo Mazza's ever come to driving is riding shotgun in the flower car at a funeral."

"Perhaps she's visiting a friend in the neighborhood," Aunt Cass said.

"She doesn't have any friends," Tommy said, and Maggie flinched. "She has Celeste," she said quietly.

Maggie went back inside and stared through the glass partition. Looking at her grandfather was like looking at the babies in the nursery. Occasionally she would see her grandmother's mouth moving, but no sound traveled through the thick glass, which was crisscrossed with narrow silver ribbons of wire.

Her aunt Margaret was fingering the big black rosary beads that always hung around her waist, although whether it was a prayerful gesture or a nervous one Maggie could not tell. Maggie leaned up against her, something she would not have done with any other nun, or with any of her other aunts for that matter. "Pumpkin, pumpkin," said Margaret, squeezing her around the waist. "Life is tough, isn't it? You know what someone once said? 'Life is a comedy for those who think and a tragedy for those who feel.' " Margaret squeezed her again and Maggie felt the tears fill her eyes, coaxed out by her aunt's warm hand.

"I don't know how anyone could ever think this was a comedy," Maggie said.

Her aunt pulled two butterscotch drops from one of her seemingly bottomless nun's pockets, handed one to Maggie, and sucked on the other herself. Maggie thought her aunt was being companionable, but she also knew from experience that in times of stress Aunt Margaret relied heavily on sweets. She had once told Maggie that she sucked lemon drops whenever she had to teach arithmetic, which was her weakest subject.

Maggie could hear her father out in the waiting room, swearing. "For a religious family, we sure take the Lord's name in vain a lot," her aunt said.

"Do you think Grandpop's going to die?"

"It doesn't look good, does it, sweetie? I don't know, lots of people have strokes and get better. Lots of them don't die. But they're paralyzed, or they can't talk, or something like that."

"Grandpop would really hate that," Maggie said, and she began to feel the pressure behind her nose and eyes that meant she might start to cry.

"I know," said her aunt, turning the big wooden crucifix at the end of her rosary over and over in her hands.

"Do you think that crucifix is too large?" Mark suddenly asked his sister.

"What?"

"The crucifix. Is it too large? We're thinking of scaling it down. I think it's too large. I'd even like to remove the Christ figure and keep a simple wooden cross, which seems more in keeping with Vatican II to me. But Dad says he thinks the nuns wouldn't stand for it. We could cut a good bit off the manufacturing cost of each one if we made the cross half again as big."

"Mark, are we actually having this conversation, here, at this moment?" said his sister, staring at him with her big blue Irish eyes, nearly the same navy as a parochial school uniform. She was wearing what Maggie's father always called her "For Chrissake, boys" look, and Maggie thought she looked very young and pretty.

Her uncle Mark was always saying it was such a shame that Margaret had joined the convent. Once Maggie had asked, very seriously, when she was in one of her religious phases, how her aunt had known that she had had the call from God. "That's a complicated question, sweetheart," her aunt had answered. But Maggie had heard her father say that the call from God was a lot of nonsense, and that when he had asked Margaret why she was ruining her life, his sister had answered a little sadly, "It's quiet, and they'll send me to college."

"So it was your father's fault?" Connie had said, and Tommy had sighed and said, "Yes, Concetta. The flood. The plagues of Egypt. The Second World War. My sister taking the veil. John Scanlan caused them all."

Maggie remembered that she had not been quite sure whether her father was teasing or not.

The door to the hospital room opened and Uncle James came in, wearing his white coat. "They won't let anyone but Mother and I inside," he said, sounding testy. "The director said he didn't care if our name was Kennedy."

"Don't let Daddy hear that," Margaret said. "He'd have another stroke."

"I don't find that funny, Sister," said James, who had called Margaret "Sister" even before she entered the convent. "This is serious."

The door opened again and Connie slipped in. She was wearing shorts and sneakers, and she seemed out of breath. The fluorescent lights overhead turned her the color of skim milk, blue and sickly;

looking around, Maggie realized they all looked that way, except for Uncle Mark, who cultivated a tan while playing golf and had only paled to a light coffee color. "Hi, Con," said Margaret, who liked her sister-in-law.

"Oh, God," said Connie, who had just caught sight of the figure behind the glass.

"Where have you been? Your husband has been worried sick," said Uncle James, putting his hands on his narrow hips.

"Is he going to be all right?" Connie asked, pressed up against the glass, and for just a moment Maggie thought she was asking about Tommy. Mary Frances caught a glimpse of Connie and waved weakly. Maggie realized that her grandmother, who had made good posture her life's work, was slumping in the straight chair. That, combined with the pathetic little whiffle of her fingers at the daughter-in-law she seemed to like least, and the helplessness of John Scanlan in the bed beside her, made it seem as though Mary Frances had suddenly been rendered old and powerless too.

Maggie had spent the ride home from the beach staring at Monica in the seat in front of her, looking for something, anything—a bruise, a shadow beneath her wide, amber-colored eyes, a look on her face—to testify to what she had seen on the beach the night before. Now she began to wonder if her uneventful life had suddenly taken a turn for the worse and would become one impossible scene after another, leaving her, as she was today, so tired she could hardly stand.

"It happened overnight," Margaret said to Connie. "He called James but James didn't realize who it was."

"I thought it was a crank call," said James. "All I could hear was breathing and moaning."

"Oh God," Connie said.

Tommy came in behind his wife, and clutched her shoulders as though he would lift her off the ground. He spun her around. "Where the hell have you been?" he said, his eyes wild. "Where? Everyone was here except for you. You disappeared off the face of the earth." He was speaking so loudly that Mary Frances turned toward them. "He could have died. Where the hell were you?"

"Tom," Connie said, trying to wriggle out from under his hands.

"Where *were* you? I got scared."

"Stop it."

"Tell me."

"I went for a walk."

"A *walk?* Who walks in our neighborhood? Who? Even people with dogs don't walk."

"I wanted to be by myself."

"You've been by yourself your whole life. Now suddenly you like being by yourself? Then be by yourself." He let go of her and she stumbled backward, falling against Maggie. Connie looked down at her daughter, as though she was seeing her for the first time. "You're back," she said, and Maggie began to cry.

"Stop it, Tom," Margaret said, stooping to cradle Maggie in her black gabardine arms.

"She shouldn't be in here," said Connie, and she took Maggie's hand and moved away from her husband, turning toward the door. "This is no place for children."

"Where else should she be?" Tommy said. "Her grandfather's dying."

The tears had started to run down Maggie's face, soaking the neck of her cotton shirt. She looked through the glass again and saw that what her father said was true. Mary Frances was staring at all of them, her eyes enormous, but Maggie couldn't tell whether it was because of the dumb show of anger and grief she could see before her, or because of some dumb show of her own playing itself out inside her head.

"Send Maggie out to sit with Monica," Uncle James said.

"No," Maggie said. "I want to stay here."

Connie dropped her daughter's hand and sat down heavily in a straight chair.

"Ah, to hell with it," Tommy said, all the heat and anger gone from his voice, and he leaned his head against the glass and began to cry. Maggie could see Mary Frances's mouth behind the glass forming the word "Tom" over and over again, but there was no sound except that of Tommy sobbing. Finally Connie went over to him and put her hand gently on his arm, his arm with its pale down and tiny freckles.

"Go home, Concetta," he said in a small voice, and then he moved away.

10

"HOW DO I SMELL?" DEBBIE ASKED.

Outside, the crickets were so loud they sounded like construction machines; the air was heavy with the heat and the cologne the two girls had put on before they left the Malone house. Debbie had been able to find only her mother's Chanel No. 5, a full bottle Mrs. Malone had gotten for Christmas once and never used; Maggie thought she smelled like a grandmother going to church. Maggie was wearing Tabu, from a little sample bottle belonging to her aunt Celeste. Every time she moved she thought of Monica, and the white flash of bare buttocks on the beach, and she felt hot and then cold, as though she had the flu.

"You smell sophisticated," Maggie said, and she could tell by the look on Debbie's face, with its saddle of freckles and snub nose, that she'd said just the right thing.

The development behind Maggie's house had grown rapidly from nothing into something, more rapidly than Maggie's mother could turn being sick in the sink into another baby. The skeletons of the houses were ranged around the fields, stretching far into the woods at the end of their street. The construction crew had framed in at least two dozen buildings, carved streets in red mud out of the gray-brown earth, left packing crates full of bathtubs and hot-water heaters scattered here and there. The noise was no longer deafening—all the foundations had been dug—but it was persistent and annoying, like the little circular clouds of gnats out back in the late afternoon.

The children had been strictly forbidden to play there, which was one of several reasons why it had become the focus of neighborhood activity after dark. As soon as dinner was over and the sounds of hammering and basso conversation had ceased, anyone over the age of six would slink down the street and around through the woods and swarm over the insides of the skeleton structures, chasing one another up half-completed staircases, looking at the stars through roofs that were nothing more than two-by-fours every two feet, sitting against the concrete in the cool basements and pitching bent nails at one another's ankles. For the first time in their lives they became occupants of houses that were theirs alone.

That first night after Maggie got back from the beach, Debbie had taken her to a split-level house near the edge of the development. It had space for a picture window that would look from the kitchen into the front yard. There was no glass in the windows, and sometimes the lightning bugs and the mosquitoes flew through the rooms and then out again. The little things that lived in the fields had moved back to the edges where the tractors had not yet gone, the rabbits and the field mice and the occasional raccoon that foraged through the garbage cans, only to be taken away in a trap after someone called the ASPCA. The butterflies were still there, but they seemed to be just passing through, settling on a stack of sheetrock and then moving on in a flurry of black-and-yellow ruffles. Only the stream had stayed the same, a narrow sluice of water that ran through Kenwood and into the next town, threading its way beneath the stone abutments of the railroad trestle. Debbie and Maggie had wandered its edges for years, playing with the clay that shone blue-gray in pockets around its banks, lifting rocks and grabbing for the crayfish as they shot out in explosions of silt and water, searching for newts to put in jelly jars, their suction pads pressed to the glass.

The split-level seemed like a big doll's house without furniture, as they sat crosslegged in the master bedroom, a yellow summer moon shining through the square where the window would be. They were waiting for the boys to arrive—the infamous Richard Joseph, and Bruce Stroud, who always went every place with Richard, a kind of Robin to his friend's Batman. The Ouija was balanced on their bony knees and a flashlight lay between them, its beam illuminating the little table from beneath, and sending the heart-shaped shadow of the pointer slanting steeply across the sawdust and the nails lying scattered about the plywood. The air smelled like Christmas trees.

"What is the name of the man I will marry?" Maggie asked darkly, and Debbie giggled. Deep in her heart Maggie had always known that the Ouija only worked if someone pushed it, although at pajama parties she insisted she believed in its magic. Now she wondered why neither of them had decided to push it around to spell out the name of some imaginary future husband.

"Maybe you're not going to get married," Debbie finally said. Maggie lifted her hands and then asked what the future would bring for her parents. "Dumb question," said Debbie, wrinkling her nose and pulling her hands away. "Who cares about the future of parents?"

"I care about the future of your parents. I like your parents," Maggie said.

"I like my parents okay," said Debbie, "but, it's like, they're all taken care of. They know what their future is, who they're married to, how many kids they're going to have, what they wore to the prom. They're sort of finished."

"Something could happen."

"Like what?" said Debbie, and she sounded so doubtful that Maggie could not bring herself to say, What if they start to hate each other? What if one of them starts to love someone else? What if they never talked to each other, or to you? Debbie's life seemed so simple to Maggie; how could she tell her friend that she and her mother didn't even belong to the same family?

They were silent for a minute, the sounds of distant television sets carrying to them faintly through the development, and then Debbie said, "Want to go to Bridget's tomorrow? She's got a Princess phone."

Bridget Hearn was fourteen and lived next door to the Malones. She had taken Debbie up in a desultory fashion in the first weeks of summer vacation, because her own best friend was at the shore until Labor Day, and because she wanted a chance to go through Helen's drawers.

"No."

"She called Richard the other day and asked if he had Prince Albert in a can."

Maggie groaned. "You have to call a store to do that joke."

"But wait, wait, guess what he said? She goes 'Excuse me, but do you have Prince Albert in a can?' And Richard says, 'No, I already let him out.' " He said the perfect thing without even knowing she was going to call."

"She's stupid," said Maggie. "She only cares about boys and clothes. And Helen."

"Her parents go out a lot," Debbie said. "She had Richard and Bruce over one night until midnight. She went down the basement with Richard for an hour and Bruce had to sit upstairs and watch television alone."

"And?"

"And how do I know? She didn't tell me." In the silence, they could hear someone laughing nearby. Finally Debbie said, "She said Richard tried to French-kiss with her."

"And?" said Maggie.

"She said she didn't let him."

"What a lie," said Maggie, whose parents had told her she couldn't hang around with Bridget Hearn after seeing her one day at Mass with a Band-Aid incompletely covering a hickey on her neck. Maggie thought of Monica again. "Do you think Helen has done it?" she asked.

"God, Mag, are you crazy? She's not married."

"So. People who aren't married must do it sometimes."

"Yeah, and wind up like that girl two years ago, what was her name? Who had to go to a home and then her parents moved away? Forget it."

"Maybe doing it is better than we think it is. Our parents do it."

"Because they have to."

"Maybe they want to," Maggie said.

"You're nuts," Debbie said, flicking off the flashlight. Maggie put her hands back on the Ouija. "Let's ask if I'm really moving," she said.

"Doesn't your grandfather say that you're moving?" Debbie picked idly at a scab on her knee.

"He bought us a house but my mother says we're not going to move into it. My father says no, too. Anyway, my grandfather's sick now."

"Sick or not, if your grandfather bought you a house, then you're moving," Debbie said.

Maggie wondered why everyone else in the world suddenly seemed so sure of themselves, and only she felt that every answer was the wrong answer, every situation a strange one. That morning, remembering the scene at the hospital the night before, she had thought about going to see her grandfather Mazza at the cemetery. But she thought of her set of tools, her square of fabric, and they seemed to belong to someone she had once been friendly with but who had since moved away, or gone to another school. This morning she had even felt out of place on the familiar streets of Kenwood. The air had been filled with the buzz of bulldozers, and the familiar curb where she and Debbie had written their initials in wet cement when they were nine had been crushed to pebbles by the wheels of the dump trucks pulling in between two houses. When she finally arrived at the Malones, the front door stood open, as though the place had been abandoned.

On the way over, scuffing her sneakers along the cement, she had begun to think of the summer before, when she and Debbie had lain in sleeping bags in the Malone backyard and listed the things they no longer believed in. They had decided they no longer believed that if you held a Milky Way in front of the open mouth of someone with a tapeworm, the tapeworm would leap out. They no longer believed that someone with four children had done it four times. ("Or someone with six children six times," Maggie had added, not wanting her parents to appear to be the only sex maniacs in Kenwood.) They no longer believed that heaven was in the sky, or that nuns had crewcuts. (Maggie had seen her aunt Margaret's hair one day when they were both in the bathroom at her grandfather's house.)

Maggie had been thinking of that night as she dragged along in the heat, because she was no longer sure what she believed in. She had dreamed about the hospital room, and the plastic tubes winding round and round the bed like the forest of thorns in *Sleeping Beauty*. In the dream Monica was lying there instead of John Scanlan, and her eyes were staring straight ahead; she looked as if she was dead, except that she was smiling. When Maggie drifted up from the dream, the light hazy through her gingham curtains, she wondered how much of what happened yesterday had really happened, and how much was the dream, or something she'd seen on television, or read in a book. She knew the fight between her parents was real because she could still remember how good it felt when she held her mother's hand, and how long it had seemed since that had happened. She remembered her fear and disappointment when Connie let her go.

But when she tried to think of telling Debbie about everything, about her cousin lying on the beach beneath a boy and the moon, about her grandfather lying there drooling, about her mother disappearing and her father fogging up the intensive care waiting-room glass as he sobbed, she could not think of a way to make any of it sound like part of the life they had both known up until then. And she could not bear to think of a different kind of life, a life where things went bad and fell apart all the time, in which people stepped over, trampled really, all the lines she had counted on to give order and shape to every day. She wondered how much of what she felt was her imagination. On the way to the Malones she stared into the sun, as though to burn up what was in her brain; she wondered if she had, as her grandfather Scanlan often said, "spun a bit of a yarn into a sweater."

But when she saw the open front door of the Malone's house, she knew that the one place she had counted on always to stay sane had gone crazy, too.

In the center of the hallway, where someone could trip over them and break a leg if they weren't careful, were two pale blue Samsonite suitcases and a box of books.

Maggie peered into the box: the top two books were *Wuthering Heights* and something Maggie had never heard of called *The Prophet*. The suitcases smelled like new plastic, like Christmas morning, and had the gold initials HAM stamped on the combination locks. Anyone but Helen Malone would have faced ridicule about those initials, but she never even seemed to notice them. Debbie's initials were DAM, of which she was rather proud. With all the rest she had to do, Mrs. Malone could not be bothered dreaming up middle names: all the girls got Ann, and all the boys Robert.

Maggie stood in the hallway for several minutes, alone, wondering whether she should go around and come in the back door as usual, when suddenly Mrs. Malone came running down the stairs. Her face looked bleached in the morning light, and she moved so quickly that her belly bounced and swayed separately from the rest of her body. She scowled at the sight of the suitcases. "The hell of it is," she said, "that I bought her those damn suitcases for a graduation present. I should have bought her the desk lamp instead." She noticed Maggie standing there. "You're back early," she said. "Miss Debbie is upstairs. Ask her if she's flying to Paris this afternoon."

"Helen's moving out," Debbie said, as soon as Maggie opened the door to her bedroom.

While she was at the beach Maggie had missed the two most exciting days in the history of the Malone household. On Monday afternoon, on their way home from the Kenwoodie Club, a striped towel draped around her long neck, Helen had informed Mrs. Malone that she had gotten an apartment of her own. Mrs. Malone had never been considered a stupid woman, but it took her a full five minutes to puzzle out what Helen meant.

It turned out that when Helen had taken a special English literature enrichment course at Fordham that spring, she had met a student who had rented an apartment in Manhattan, near Columbia University. The girl had offered Helen one of the bedrooms in return for half the rent. Helen had cleaned out her savings account and packed her clothes before anyone knew what was happening; her closet was empty except for her Sacred Heart uniform and the long dotted-swiss dress she had worn three weeks before for her graduation. She had given Aggie her jewelry box, and Debbie her dictionary.

"I asked for the bikini but she just laughed," Debbie said.

Mrs. Malone had been wild. For two days, she had slammed around the kitchen late into the night, cleaning the refrigerator, her flip-flops slapping the linoleum as though she was spanking it. Even now Maggie could hear intermittent ranting from downstairs, part of a monologue about how people didn't know when they had it good, how they always wanted what they didn't have, how they would have to learn the hard way. Mr. Malone had found the decision complicated by the fact that the other girl was the daughter of a judge with whom he had long wanted to be on speaking terms. The two men had met at the apartment, turned on the faucets to check the water pressure, talked sternly to the superintendent, and agreed that they would put up with this nonsense until the girls' money ran out, which was expected to happen just in time for the Christmas holidays.

"She's coming," Debbie said suddenly, in the middle of describing all this to Maggie, and they heard the sound of footsteps walking down the hall from Helen's room. The two girls followed her soundlessly, watching her back as she trotted downstairs. Mrs. Malone stood in the hallway next to the suitcases, her hands on her hips.

"Did you take my blue blouse?" she asked.

Maggie stood at the top of the stairs and heard Helen laugh, and behind Helen, through the open door, Maggie could see sunlight. At the curb was a car as blue as the sky. Helen put her arms around her mother's shoulders. She towered over Mrs. Malone.

"Your blue blouse is safe upstairs. I will be safe at 113th Street and Broadway. I will come home soon. I will call every day."

"I don't want to talk to you every day."

Helen laughed again. "I know," she said, "but I'll do it anyway." She looked up to the head of the stairs, and her face glowed pink, as though she'd been running.

"You're back early," she said to Maggie. "What happened—did Monica drown?"

"No such luck," said Maggie.

"Come see me," Helen said, and Maggie wondered if she meant

it. "I'll teach you two how to smoke cigarettes." Mrs. Malone hit Helen on the shoulder and then she started to laugh herself. Maggie could see tears in the eyes of both mother and daughter.

"Oh, you," Mrs. Malone said.

The car at the curb beeped its horn twice, and Helen picked up the suitcases. "Debbie, could you get the box?" she called, and Debbie sailed downstairs, away from Maggie, into the midst of it all. As Helen started to walk out, Mrs. Malone turned and went into the kitchen, her head down. Debbie was already out the door.

Helen turned in the doorway, the sun lighting her black hair. "I left you something in my top drawer," she said to Maggie, and then she was gone.

Maggie ran back upstairs to the bedroom at the end of the hall. On the blackboard Helen had written À BIENTÔT, which Maggie knew was French for something. The single bed had been stripped down to its naked mattress, and the top of the bureau, which had always been a welter of bracelets and postcards and ribbons, was swept clean.

Maggie opened the top drawer. Inside was the California bikini. She held it to her face and smelled the sharp chlorine smell. The color was faded, and the underwire in one of the cups was bent. Maggie felt to the back of the drawer to see if Helen could possibly have meant something else, but that was the only thing left in there. Then she heard the front door close, and feet on the stairs, and without thinking she slipped into Debbie's room and shoved the suit to the bottom of her beach bag, under her towel.

She thought of something Helen had said once about Maggie and Debbie, who had been best friends since first grade, although Maggie was thoughtful and serious and studious and Debbie was often called "pea brain" by the members of her own family: "Debbie likes Maggie because Maggie makes her feel special, and Maggie likes Debbie because Debbie makes her feel normal."

She had thought of that all the rest of the day, and now, as she and Debbie sat in the development house, waiting for the boys to come, it kept running through her head: Debbie normal, Maggie special. She took a deep breath.

She hated the air this time of the summer, the thick heavy air of

July, like something woolly twisted around your head, clogging your nose, making it hard to breathe. Her hair felt like wet wash on the back of her neck. During the afternoon she had made a clover chain and had forgotten to take it off her head. The flowers were browning now, and brittle. Debbie's hair had been cut into a funny kind of pageboy, and each night she took pink foam rollers and rolled the ends over them, so that each morning her hair all around turned under like the curve of a comma, although by night the curve was gone.

"This must be what Helen will do all the time," Maggie said. "She'll just call a bunch of guys and say, 'Come over, we'll watch television. If I like you, you can stay. If not, I'll kick you out. It's my house, I run things. You're not my husband. I do what I want.' "

Debbie looked doubtful. "I don't think even Helen would kick Richard out," she said.

Richard Joseph was the coolest boy in Kenwood. Everyone said so. He was fourteen, but sixteen-year-old girls were interested in him. He was tall and had blond hair and blue eyes and hair on the back of his hands, and a smile that started slowly at the corner of his mouth and then moved to the middle.

"I don't know how Mary Joseph ever came to have that boy with the bedroom eyes," Mrs. Malone had once said about him.

Richard Joseph played bass guitar in a garage band. He had mooned a table of mothers from the high dive at the Kenwoodie Club and managed to convince the manager that the elastic in his trunks had snapped. And once, at a party during Christmas vacation, he had asked Maggie to dance. She was the youngest girl he'd ever noticed, and most of the girls at Sacred Heart thought he had done it just to embarrass her.

So did Maggie. She did not know what to expect from the evening. It seemed as though meeting boys, alone, here, on the second floor, was completely different from seeing them at the swimming pool, or in the rec room of somebody's house. Debbie had told her father she was staying at Maggie's, and Maggie had left a note saying she was staying at the Malones.

"They're coming," Debbie said in a whisper, which seemed unnecessary, since the two boys were singing "She Loves You" in not particularly close harmony, the flats and sharps carrying like trumpet blasts through the still night. Maggie saw a light go on in a house not far from her own.

"SSShhhhh," Debbie hissed, leaning out the window in a great cloud of Chanel No. 5. "Yeah, yeah, yeah, yeah," the two boys sang, playing imaginary guitars on the front of their madras shorts, paying no attention. In a minute their heads came into view at the top of the crude ladder the construction men had nailed into place until they were ready to put in the stairs. "Cool," said Richard, his wavy yellow hair bright even in the dark. "Really cool," said Bruce, who was Richard's permanent audience, a thin boy with spiky light hair and long legs who reminded Maggie of pictures she'd seen of her father at that age.

"We could get in a lot of trouble if they found us out here," Maggie said.

"Jesus, you sound like a nun, you know?" Richard said. "Everybody's out here. The Kelly twins are out here with a couple of girls from Sacred Heart named Kathy or Kelly or something—"

"The two Kathys," said Debbie. "Gross. They do everything together. They get back-to-back appointments to get their hair cut."

"So do the Kellys," said Richard.

"That's true," said Bruce, but no one seemed to hear him.

"Everybody comes out here now. Wait until they turn the water on," Richard added. "I'm going to come out here and take a shower."

"Gross," said Debbie.

"My dad says they'll have to hire a guard soon," Maggie said.

"I like your dad," said Richard. "He's a good guy. You ever seen his jump shot? He has a mean jump shot."

"I like your mother, Maggie," Bruce said.

"Your mother is a babe and a half," Richard said.

"Her mother?" said Debbie. "God! Her *mother?*"

"Monica, too," said Richard. "She's a babe and a half. My brother is friends with her boyfriend."

"She has a boyfriend around here?" Maggie asked.

"What do you mean, around here?" Richard said. "Where else would she have one? I think his name's Donald but everybody calls him Duck. He goes to college with my brother."

Maggie slid down against the wall until she was sitting with her knees in front of her nose. Richard came over and sat down next to her. "Your parents were dancing in your living room just now."

"You peeked in the windows?" Maggie asked, and without knowing why, it made her angry, afraid of what Richard might have seen or heard.

"I don't peek, I look," Richard said, slipping his arm around Maggie's shoulders as though to reassure her. "I look in everybody's windows."

"That's true," said Bruce, staring ruefully at the arm in the half light of the half moon.

"Great perfume," said Richard.

"I can't believe you peeked in our windows," said Maggie, pulling away from the arm, standing up and starting down the ladder, thinking that she was leaving because of the invasion of privacy but knowing she was going for some other, deeper reason that she could not explain.

"Hey," said Richard.

"God, Maggie," Debbie said. She leaned out the window and watched her friend come out of the door of the house. "Maggie," she said again, but there was no answer.

"Maggie," said Bruce, scrambling down the stairs.

"Hey, forget it," said Richard. "I'm not going to go chasing after her." But Bruce's head had already disappeared down the ladder.

"Bridget Hearn was just saying the other day how strange Maggie acts sometimes," Debbie said.

Maggie could hear Bruce calling her as she stumbled across the clumps of dirt and debris that made up the lawn. She walked with her head down, and twice she almost fell, swerving around a framed-in house. "Maggie," she heard him call behind her. "Yo—Maggie. Stop." When she came to a big stack of two-by-fours she sat down on it, her chin in her hands. She kept her head down because she knew there were tears in her eyes.

Bruce came up and sat down next to her, but not too close. For a minute he cracked his knuckles, and finally he said, the timbre of his voice shaky, "He didn't really do it. Look in the windows, I mean. Not really. He always says stuff like that so that people will think he's cool."

Maggie looked up. She could tell immediately that Bruce was lying, trying to be nice.

"It's all right," she said. "I don't know why I did that. Everything's sort of messed up. I can't really explain."

"That's okay," said Bruce. "I feel that way all the time."

"Really?"

"Yeah."

"I never felt that way until a little while ago. Now I feel like everything's crazy."

"I know," Bruce said. He began cracking his knuckles again. "Richard likes you," he finally said. "He told me he really likes you. He said you'll be a babe and a half someday."

"Right," said Maggie sarcastically.

"No, really. He told me."

"I don't see why he's your friend," Maggie said.

"Why is Debbie your friend?" Bruce asked, and Maggie remembered Helen again. Bruce made Richard feel normal and Richard made Bruce feel special. Maybe that was the key to every relationship.

"She just is," Maggie said.

Bruce smiled. Maggie noticed in the dim illumination from the streetlights on the next block that he had hair on his legs. He was looking at the dirt, and, as she watched, he picked up an old nail and tossed it in front of them into the darkness.

He picked up another one, silvery against the tan of his palm, and rolled it around. Wordlessly Bruce handed her the nail. "That looks pretty," he said after a moment.

"What?"

He pointed to her head and Maggie put a hand up and felt the wreath of clover. She started to pull it off. "Don't take it off," he said. "It looks nice. My mother made those things for my sister when she was little."

Maggie lowered her head again. Bruce's mother had died when they were in fifth grade. She felt terrible because she suddenly remembered why Bruce would feel the world was topsy-turvy. "Who cooks dinner in your house?" Maggie finally said, without meaning to.

"The housekeeper," Bruce said. "She cooks dinner and then she leaves. She's not too good a cook. She makes hamburgers a lot."

"I don't know why I asked you that."

"It's okay. Everybody asks me stuff like that. I think people can't figure out what it would be like to have a family that's not like anybody else's family."

"I can," Maggie said, and again she felt as though the words had slipped out.

"Why? You have the normalest family in the world. How would you feel if every time you went to church you could tell that people were pointing at you and saying 'There's the ones with no mother.' "

Maggie didn't know what to say. Bruce picked up another nail. Maggie thought she had never been involved in a conversation with so many silences, except for the ones she had with her grandfather Mazza. Finally Bruce cleared his throat and said, "I remember when you came to my mother's funeral. You had on a black dress with a red tie around the collar. You sent a Mass card. That was really nice."

"The whole class sent flowers."

"I know. That was nice, too. I just hated the way everybody looked at me when I went back to school. Like I was sick or something."

They sat there for a long time, the small night noises clear in the darkness. Maggie suddenly sniffed the air.

"They're smoking cigarettes," Bruce said. "Richard stole a pack of his mother's Salems."

There was a funny clicking sound from inside the development house, and then a little scream. Maggie saw Debbie stick her head out the window. "Come here," she hissed.

"Leave me alone," Maggie said, and her voice sounded loud in the still air.

"It's important," Debbie said, and suddenly behind her there was a flash of orange, like the sun over the horizon of the beach first thing in the morning.

"Oh, hell," Bruce said.

"What?"

Silently he took her hand and pulled her to her feet, and they began to run across the field, leaping over the bigger clods of earth. Maggie stumbled a little. She knew she should concentrate on where she was going, but all she could think of was his hand holding hers.

Inside the development house the smell of smoke was stronger, and a glow was coming from the open square at the top of the ladder. They scrambled up. In one corner a pile of cardboard boxes was burning brightly, the flames hugging a corner of the wall and blackening the two-by-fours of the ceiling. A stray breeze seemed to lift the center of the blaze and send it higher, and in the orange light Maggie could see that Debbie's eyes were dazzled, and Richard was smiling faintly and running his long fingers through his hair.

"Jesus," Bruce whispered.

"I'll get some water," Maggie said, but Richard reached for her arm and held her there, turned toward the fire.

"Don't be a jerk," he said.

"You're crazy," Maggie said. "You're really crazy."

"You're crazy," Richard said, mocking her in a high voice, twisting her arm a little.

"We're going to burn the whole place down," Debbie whispered, but even as she spoke the flames began to shrink, the boxes collapsing into a pile of rose-gray ash, the wood concave where the heat had eaten it away. The four of them stood and stared until finally there was only a great cloud of gray smoke.

"Damn," Richard said. "The wood must be damp."

"You did that on purpose?" Maggie said.

"Wasn't it cool?" Debbie said. "You should have seen it at first. It just went *woosh* like a wave. It almost caught our hair."

"Lighter fluid," said Richard.

"You could have burned the whole house down," Maggie said.

"Jesus," said Richard, "are you always like this? It's not a house. Nobody lives here. Nobody got hurt. Don't you want something to do? Can't you stand a little excitement?" Richard twisted her arm some more. "I give excitement lessons free."

Debbie giggled.

"You're all crazy," said Maggie. She started down the ladder again. "God, is she always like that?" she heard Richard say again.

"I'll walk you home," said Bruce, coming up behind her.

"I know how to get to my own house."

"I want to." They walked together in silence, not looking back, until finally Maggie said, "I wish I could figure out what's going on with people."

"He's easy to figure out. He gets bored."

"That can't be the only reason why people do the things they do. It's got to be more complicated than that."

"I think it's pretty simple."

Maggie could feel the nail in the pocket of her shorts. They walked along in silence until they got to her backyard and then Maggie ran ahead, across the lawn. She thought she heard a small voice call "good-by"; then there was no sound except the crickets. But when she got upstairs to her bedroom, before she turned on the light, she looked out and she could see Bruce still standing at the edge of the yard. She thought he'd seen her, too, because as soon as she'd looked out the window he'd turned and walked back into the development, his head down.

Her door opened, and her mother was standing in the doorway. The light from the hallway fell through the pale folds of her nylon nightgown, and Maggie looked away.

"I thought you were staying at the Malones," Connie said.

"I changed my mind."

"I could hear your voice outside," Connie said, still standing in the half-dark. "Were you with some boy out there?"

"I was talking to a boy I know. Bruce."

"That poor boy whose mother died?"

Maggie winced. Connie added, "Aren't you a little young to be hanging out at night with boys?"

"How old is old enough to be hanging out at night with boys?"

Connie shrugged. She looked tired. The lines from her nose to her mouth seemed deeper than usual. "I don't know. I'm asking you."

"Don't ask me. You're the mother."

"Then I think you're too young."

"I'm getting older," Maggie said, wanting to say much more. "I'm getting a lot older." She expected her mother to ask her what she meant by that, but instead she just sighed. "Yes," Connie said, "I know." She sniffed and Maggie was afraid she could smell the smoke, then realized it must be the Tabu. Connie turned on the bedside lamp and looked at Maggie sadly. Then she smiled. "That's pretty," she said, pointing to Maggie's head.

Maggie took the clover chain off and held it, limp and dying, in her hand. "Where did you get that?" Connie said.

"I made it," Maggie said. "It's easy. You just tie them together. Mrs. Malone taught us. Don't you know how?"

Connie shook her head.

"Your mother didn't teach you?"

Connie shook her head again. "I don't know whether she didn't know how or she just didn't want to teach me."

"I think if she didn't do it, it was probably because she didn't know how. If she could have, she would have."

"Maybe," said Connie. "Go to sleep." Then she ran her hand along Maggie's upper arm. "What did you do?" she asked, and Maggie looked down to see the marks of fingers purpling on the tan skin above her elbow.

"I fell," she said, drawing back. Her mother looked at her for a long minute, and then turned and left, closing the door behind her.

When her mother was gone Maggie stared at herself in the mirror. She looked at the bruises and put the nail from her pocket into her jewelry box, the red leather one Celeste had given her for her birthday. She lay in bed, the moon casting a silver shaft of cold light across the ceiling, and wondered whether in the morning she would be saddled with another dreamlike memory, half real, half incredible. For a long time she kept her eyes open wide in the darkness, and finally, still smelling smoke, she fell asleep.

11

JOHN SCANLAN'S HOSPITAL ROOM looked like a committee meeting of the Friendly Sons of St. Patrick. A half dozen men, sleek and florid in their sharkskin and seersucker suits, came in after work to pump his good hand and make jokes about pinching the nurses. Tommy stayed out in the hall, wandering around the nurses' station, buying a bag of M & M's from the vending machine and eating them in the stairwell, reading the newspaper. It was cool in the hospital, and after ten days the nurses were accustomed to seeing the Scanlan family and didn't take much notice of them.

The day before, a student nurse had seen Tommy looking through some papers near her desk and had snatched them from him, her little freckled face as agitated as an infant's. "Mr. Scanlan," she had said, the white cotton curving over the shelf of her bosom, which vibrated with indignation, "that is your father's chart." "Damn straight," Tommy had replied. The doctor had a horrible scrawl—not a Catholic boy, that's for sure, no wonder only the Jews were doctors, the nuns would have their rulers out over this stuff—and the only part Tommy could make out appeared again and again, day after day: "No improvement."

Tommy had been having trouble sleeping. There was a bend in the street just in front of the house, and when a car came by he would watch the diamond-shaped patterns of the lights roll across the ceiling and over the top of Connie's head, like a searchlight. He had black dreams that he could remember only in bits, a rodent face here, a free fall there, a chase, a pursuit, a knife, a gun, but no tale to wrap around them. He would wake with adrenaline throbbing in his chest and look over at his wife, who slept with her hands folded on her chest, her hair fanning out on the pillow. He wondered what was in her dreams.

He was not willing to connect his nightmares to the sight of his father in the hospital bed. He was not even willing to concede that the man was very sick. John Scanlan had turned his hospital room into an office, with piles of invoices and correspondence on the window sill. His former secretary, a square and silent woman named Dorothy O'Haire, who had faded blond hair and dark eyes, came for three hours each day to help him keep up and to read him the newspapers. Tommy knew that Dorothy was there a great deal, but somehow he never managed to see her when he was at the hospital. She had stopped working for John Scanlan nine years ago, when her daughter had been born, but when she heard of the stroke she had volunteered to come back and help. John had told the chief of staff that they would never see another penny of Scanlan money if they didn't discharge him at the end of the week, but the doctors had steadfastly refused to let him go home, and the best the old man had been able to do was to bully them into letting Dorothy in outside visiting hours. "I have my ways," he told his son when he asked about the arrangment. "Mind your own business."

When Tommy was at the hospital, his father seemed much as usual, except that he wore striped pajamas especially bought for the hospital stay. ("Goddamn pansy clothes," he said, when they brought them in. "Sixty-five years and I never wore a pair of these things until now.") During the day, he was at his best: swearing at the staff, demanding more pillows, making the nurse take the crucifix down from the wall so he could determine the model and estimate how much the hospital was paying for its religious articles, bullying Dorothy while she stared at him fixedly.

Tommy never saw his father at night, when he seemed almost as ill as he had been at the beginning, when the corner of his mouth hung low so that his face looked like the masks of both comedy and tragedy; when, although his mother had been dead for nearly half a century, he talked to her about the beginnings of his business and James's whooping cough; when he cried like a baby against the pleated dress front of some night nurse and said, "I don't know, I don't know" over and over again. Even John did not fully remember those times.

Tommy could tell his father was thinking about the more distant past, carrying it with him like a bad taste in his mouth. Occasionally John would lie back on the pillows, his shoulders slipping into the two comfortable narrow grooves worn in the mattress, and then Tommy knew his father was remembering all the others who had dreamed their lives away in taverns, slept them away on sofas in small front rooms, all the men from his boyhood in the tenement buildings who had squandered their lives sitting on stoops, taking their time, telling their stories, being "That Jack, now what a fine fellow he is" and "That Joe, you can't beat him for a good yarn," wasting away from lack of ambition until they were only death's-heads with a lifetime of jokes to their credit. Sometimes John Scanlan thought he owed them everything, because they had haunted him every day of his life, his own old man among them, putting in his time at the Department of Public Works, leaving a life insurance policy just large enough to cover the two-night wake and the plot at St. Ann's. In the hospital they danced in his head whenever he rested, and he would sit up suddenly and begin to add up columns of figures as though possessed, as indeed he always had been. Tommy could tell when his father had been having these spells because John would look at his middle son suspiciously, noticing his resemblance to those hail-fellows-well-met of years gone by.

Tommy came to the hospital every day, apologizing for Connie's absence, saying she was sick, which was true but not the problem. She said she hated hospitals, although she did well enough in them when she was having the kids. She said sometimes that it was a good thing that her own mother had died suddenly, turning a lavender blue one evening at the kitchen table and sliding to the linoleum floor, dead somewhere between the edge of the table and the legs of the chair, because Connie could not have borne being with her in the hospital. Connie could not have borne being with her anyway, Tommy thought.

Margaret was there most afternoons, too, and after a while it occurred to Tommy to wonder how she had so much time on her hands. "It's summer," his sister had said, but that didn't seem reason enough. She had taken to carrying a book with her whenever she came to the hospital, and for the first few days Tommy thought it was the New Testament. Waiting out in the hall for his father's room to empty of visitors, he had looked at the title: *Jane Eyre, An Autobiography*.

"How come you're reading *Jane Eyre*?" Maggie asked her aunt, peeking over her father's shoulder.

"Just for fun," Margaret said.

"You've never read it before?" said Maggie. "It's a great book."

"Is it religious?" Tommy asked.

Margaret laughed. "Tom, honey, underneath this habit—it's me. Average girl. Good dancer. I'm allowed to read books that aren't necessarily religious, or even edifying." Tommy looked skeptical.

"Inside every nun is a woman," she added.

"Do me a favor, Peg," Tommy replied, using her old childhood nickname. "Don't tell Dad that. He's had one stroke already."

After the men had left, all the men who did business with John Scanlan, and all the ones who wanted to, the ones who owned the cement and construction and candle and casket companies, Tommy went into his father's room, his daughter and his sister behind him. Buddy Phelan had brought a fruit basket, which was still wrapped in its tinted plastic. There was a bottle of Canadian Club and two cans of ginger ale on the bedside table.

"That Monica was in here an hour ago," John said to Maggie, "sweet as can be. More there than meets the eye, I bet. She said all you girls were having a grand time at the seashore before I gave you such a scare. What's your problem down there, little girl?"

"I'm tying my shoe," said Maggie, who did not want him to see her face.

"You shouldn't be coming to see me here wearing those sneakers, like you're going to play basketball instead of going to call on your grandfather. You girls don't have good sense. Your cousin Teresa was here yesterday, wearing a scapular under her little shirt. Can you beat that? The Sacred Heart shining through the white of her blouse, like a big stain. The girl's an imbecile."

"She has Sister Luke. She's very religious. She loves stuff like that."

"Nuns," John Scanlan snorted, and Margaret laughed. "The only one I've ever known with the sense God gave her is your aunt. Don't be a nun, girl. Give me your word."

"I don't know, Grandpop," Maggie said, thinking of the scene at the Malones, and the flames licking the corner of the development house. "It sounds kind of peaceful."

"Ha," her grandfather said. "Peaceful. Who gives a damn about peaceful. That makes for a dull life, girl. Remember that. How's your brother?"

"Which one?"

"All of them, for Christ's sake. How the hell am I supposed to keep track of all these children?" He reached into the bottom drawer of the bedside table and drew out a Mason jar that glowed amber in the hospital lights. "They would have killed me days ago if it wasn't for the Scotch," he said. He poured two fingers' worth into a plastic cup and added water from a pitcher. "Don't tell on me," he said to Maggie, as though his children were not there, and drank it down.

"You better watch the booze, Pop," Margaret said.

"You watch your mouth, Sister," John Scanlan said. "I'm still your father even if you are a bride of Christ. I need some time alone with your brother here. Take your niece to the cafeteria and buy her a chocolate bar."

When they were gone the old man leaned back and closed his eyes.

"Jesus, Dad, you're killing yourself," Tommy said, moving empty glasses to the windowsill, but his father just lay there and looked at him, his eyes dull. With the departure of his daughter and his granddaughter, John Scanlan seemed to shrink and grow gray. Tommy sat down in the visitor's chair and waited for some sort of tirade.

"I don't know, Tommy," John finally said, sounding half asleep. "I don't know what the hell to think. I'm tired of this damn hospital. Father McLeod came in here today to talk to me. Scots-Irish, for God's sake. Who the hell ordained him? He says I've had a rare treat in devoting my business life to the business of God. He'd been practicing that one all the way over in the black Buick, right?" The brogue was beginning to creep into his father's voice and Tommy inhaled deeply. The room felt close and smelled of Clorox. "I said 'There's my problem, Father. I should have been devoting my business life to the business of making money.' Now I've got your brother in here, wants to have one of the Manila factories making little blouses for girls. Says that down there in the city the girls are dressing up like fortunetellers and buying embroidered blouses. Big market. I said 'Jesus Christ, Mark, why don't we just change over to dresses?' He thought I was serious. Told me he wanted to discuss that next. Jesus Christ. I've wasted my life."

"Stop," Tommy said.

"The priest asks me if I want the last rites. He said there's nothing to be afraid of, that he knows I know the rewards of life eternal. Life eternal, shit." The old man's face was beginning to redden, his long fingers on the sheets to shake. Tommy came over to the bed. He thought about taking his father's hand, but instead held onto the button that summoned the nurse. "I don't give a good goddamn about life eternal, I told him. I got everything in my life the way I wanted it, everything all lined up right, and I want it to stay that way. Everything. It's not the dying I mind, it's the changing. You see what I mean." He looked up at Tommy, and the younger man began to cry at the terrible light in his father's eyes, as though John Scanlan was seeing visions. "Everything the way I want it. After all this time. You want to keep it just the way it is. Right? Right?"

"I don't know, Dad," Tommy said.

The big head fell, the silver hair looking greasy and gray. John Scanlan reached over for a jelly glass on the bedside table and sipped slowly. "Stop whimpering," he said without looking up. "Your daughter's a funny girl. Takes things too seriously. Always stewing over something. Not like that Monica. She's a slick one, that Monica. She's not pulling anything over on me. I knew a girl just like her once. Went off to Hollywood and took a screen test. Married a man old enough to be her father who owned half of Los Angeles. What was I telling you?"

"Connie apologizes for not—"

"Ah, don't give me that crap, Tommy," said the old man, waving his hand. "Where's your mother?"

"She's coming over later with a piece of pie. Rhubarb pie that your sister Anne made."

"Oh Jesus. The kids must really think the end is near, they're sending me pie." John Scanlan always called his younger brothers and sisters "the kids." He saw them once a year, at a party he held in the reception room of Scanlan & Co. Last year his youngest brother had gotten so drunk that he had approached John, jabbed him in his red boutonniere with his index finger, and said, "I hate your guts." "I know, Jamie, I know," the elder man had said, putting his arm around his brother's shoulder. "And well you should."

"And your mother, too, carting pie from Annie over here," John said now, sipping his drink. "She must be scared."

"Stop," said Tom again.

"Do me a favor," John Scanlan said suddenly, his eyes narrow, shrewd as a predatory bird's. "Help us out in the business or your brother will be pushing ladies' lingerie with the sheenies down on 38th Street. I don't think he knows his ass from his elbow."

"I'll think about it," Tommy said.

"How's the building going, out by you?"

"They're working fast."

"The men are coming this week to clean out your new house. Your mother has them waxing the floors and washing down the walls."

Tommy squared his shoulders, and all the sympathy he had felt evaporated, as though the blood was draining from his body. He was cold with the emptiness of his antagonism and his fear, and he knew how scared he was when he began to wonder if his father's despair and weakness had all been a ploy to lead to this moment.

"We don't want the house," he said. "We're fine where we are. Really. Give it to Joe. He and Annette will be thrilled."

John Scanlan closed his eyes, and Tommy wondered if he had drifted off to sleep. Then slowly the heavy lids came up, and Tommy saw that his father's eyes were like blue bullets, aimed straight to the heart.

"No mortgage payments," he said.

"I can handle my mortgage payments," Tommy said.

"Not without a job you can't," John Scanlan said, and Tommy heard in his voice the word "Checkmate."

"What the hell is that supposed to mean?"

"You figure it out, buddy boy. I've done my part. I gave you a good job at that concrete company, and I'll give you a better one over to the factory, and I bought you and your wife a house fit for a king and queen. I've done my part. It's time you did yours."

"Why are you doing this? I'm a grown man. I run my own life."

John Scanlan let out a great snort, and then began to cough, a cough so long and hacking that Tommy thought he would never catch his breath. For a minute Tommy thought he'd like to just let him choke to death, and then he poured his father a glass of water and handed it to him. Finally John was quiet again, his chest heaving. The two men stared at each other. Tommy knew that his father was going to die, and he knew that John Scanlan had set himself a task before he did so and that that task was to see that the last of the Scanlan boys was exactly where he wanted him to be. He knew, too, that the family would gather round, waiting, waiting, for Tommy to do this one small thing for a dying man, and that if he did it, that which made him who he was would be lost forever, and he would become what he had so often been called: one of the Scanlan boys. One of the old man's sons. A fight to the finish, they called it in cowboy movies, and so it was, and Tommy knew he would lose. Suddenly John Scanlan smiled at him, and Tommy knew that they had both been thinking the same thing.

"This won't work," Tommy said.

"You want to bet?" John said. "I'll bet you a baby grand piano for that new living room."

Tommy stood up. He could hear his mother outside, talking to the nurse. "Why?" he said again.

"I owe it to you, son," John said. "You'd only make a mess of it yourself."

"No."

"Tom," the old man said when Tommy was at the door, "your wife's expecting again, James said."

Tommy nodded.

"Good," said John Scanlan. "I'm happy to hear that."

There was a long silence. Tommy could hear his father's breathing, a rumbling trapped inside the sunken chest. His father's eyes narrowed, and the breathing become more labored. "This one last thing," the old man said, his hand over his heart.

"Jesus," Tommy said, "you're really doing it. Pat O'Brien and the deathbed scene. The old Irish dad and his last request."

"I'm more alive than you are, sonny boy," John Scanlan said.

"Go to hell."

"Listen, Tommy. Let me let you in on a secret. There is no hell. There's no heaven, either. There's only this. You have to make the best of it. I'm going to make the best of it for you. You and your pretty wife."

"No."

"Yes," John Scanlan said. "Now send your mother in. And give your brother a hand before he drives the whole kit and caboodle into the goddamn ground."

12

ONNIE LAY BACK AGAINST THE SEAT OF her brother-in-law Mark's new car and thought that it smelled like the inside of an expensive purse. It looked like the inside of a purse, too, come to think of it, or at least like the inside of Mark's wife's purse. Connie remembered one evening going into Gail's black clutch bag to get some aspirin and discovering that aside from a wallet that looked brand new, a set of keys, a lipstick, and a comb, there was nothing inside, not even a stray bobby pin. Just for a moment it had crossed her mind that the reason Gail was unable to have children was because she didn't leave any crumbs, or pennies, or used tissues floating around in the bottom of her purse. She knew it was a mean thought, and reflexively, the way her aunt Rose had taught her to do when she was small, she had made the sign of the cross.

Gail was driving her home from the party because Connie felt sick. She felt sick all the time now. It was a struggle to breathe in the heavy hot July air, the cannonball of her womb lodged just below her ribs, crowding her lungs. She stared out the window, knowing she must represent some kind of reproach to her childless sister-in-law.

The road was edged with black-eyed Susans; Connie could remember she and her father digging them up not far from here one long-ago Sunday. It had been the summer she was twelve, when Anna Mazza was spending most of her time in Brooklyn. The aunt who had taken Anna in when she came to America was old and sick, her belly grown big and blue from cancer. Connie had been left alone with her father, working with him in the garden for the first time. It had begun with a hollyhock covered in black bugs, its tall stem dirty and withered. It had ended when her mother came home, scowling her disapproval at the grass stains on Connie's clothes. Or perhaps it had been when Celeste came back from the shore, walking up the drive and through the gates, her swelling behind encased in a kind of playsuit in a shiny blue-and-red synthetic print of cowboys and Indians. "Movie star," Connie had said a little disdainfully, kneeling in front of the tomatoes. "Who are you, Lana Turner?"

"Rita Hayworth," said Celeste, who actually did resemble Rita Hayworth, and then she gave her uncle Angelo a big kiss. He drew back as though she had bitten him on the nose, and he looked her full figure up and down with an expression of shock and horror. And then he turned and stared at his daughter and that expression was still there, the kind of look Connie imagined God must have given Eve in the Garden of Eden.

"You all dirty," was all he said.

It was many years later that she had realized that that was the day her father discovered she was female. She had never felt close to him again, and she was convinced that he had never felt close to her.

She thought she saw a shadow of that same look pass over his face when he saw her in her wedding dress, coming down the stairs with her bouquet in one hand. She remembered what she had thought at the time: he's just a man, an ordinary man.

She had thought that, too, when she first saw John Scanlan in the hospital, a vulnerable, ordinary, shrunken man surrounded by white cotton. She even sometimes thought it of Tommy, when she lay beside him at night, although it did not make her angry at him the way it did with his father, and her own. It only awakened her sympathy. When her father had first given her that look, it had made her feel ashamed; now she merely thought that men were somehow afraid of the things they loved best, that they were the real children of the world, without bringing with them any of the joys you had with children, at least for a time.

She knew the contours of her bedroom in the dark as well as she knew anything; the shadow of the two-pronged light fixture like the letter W on the ceiling, the pale-yellow light through the drape of the curtains from the streetlight across the lawn, the odd blotches, like old faces, made by the cabbage roses on the wallpaper, the sliding shadows of the six-paned windows as a car came up and around the street, its engine wheezing in the still night air. Against the wall was a composite picture of her three oldest children: Maggie holding Terence holding Damien, ages seven, six, and one, and then individual portraits of each, the baby a little spastic propped on a platform, the other two wearing fixed, forced smiles. Between the first two and the next two she had had two miscarriages, surges of odd clots that had made her think she was being punished for not loving her children enough, for not believing they were what she had always thought they would be to her. The pregnancies were always difficult, too, kneeling on the bathroom floor, staring into the water in the toilet bowl. The first time she had thought she was dying, or would have a retarded child, a baby with no fingers, or seven fingers, or a mongoloid like Leonard Fogarty. "Listen, kid," Celeste had said, "everybody throws up when they're in the family way. That's how you know you are." Like almost everything her cousin said, it sounded improbable; like almost everything she said, it turned out to be right.

Connie had never had a pregnancy test. One night soon after Maggie was born she had eaten a bad clam at a Coney Island clam bar and had spent the next week wondering how they would afford another baby. It had seemed sort of ridiculous until two months later, when she was sick again and it turned out that she was pregnant with Terence.

Her sisters-in-law were never ill when they were pregnant. Joe's wife, Annette, had played tennis up until the week before she had the twins, although everyone had made such a fuss about it that Connie was more amazed by her ability to withstand the criticism than to rush the net. James's wife had admitted to "a little gas," but quietly and with a guilty manner, as though she thought it might be seen as some reflection on her husband's professional skill.

This afternoon Connie had been at a card party with all of them, at one of the boys' schools just north of Kenwood, a big Gothic building with a Latin inscription over the double doors, and they had all exchanged glances when she had leapt up to find the one women's bathroom in the whole cavernous place. "She really has a hard time, doesn't she?" Jack's wife, Maureen, had said, with an air of assumed sympathy, and they all nodded and thought to themselves: God, the fuss.

But their eyes all seemed to meet in the vicinity of Gail's long, faintly equine face. Then they looked at the cards in their hands, which they busily rearranged. "She certainly does," Gail said, looking around. She often felt that she was unfairly lumped with Connie, that because she had been born Protestant and converted to marry Mark she too was considered an outsider. She made every attempt to show that this was not the case.

"Are you all right?" Annette had asked when Connie came back to the table, her face newly powdered, fresh lipstick dark against the white. She had not been able to find the right bathroom, and had thrown up in a stainless steel sink in the chemistry lab.

"Fine. I'm used to it."

"What about some tea with milk?" Cass had said.

"Nothing. I think I'd better go."

The women had looked around at one another. One of them would have to drive Connie home, and the petits fours had not even come around yet, nor the door prize been announced. The prize was a black cashmere sweater with a dyed mink collar, and everyone had exclaimed over it except for Mrs. O'Neal, who said she already had one, and Mrs. Malone, who said she'd give it away if she got it. "You could give it to Helen," someone said. "It's just the color of her hair." Everyone was quiet for a moment. "Helen's lost her mind," Mrs. Malone said drily, "but I haven't."

Finally Connie said, "Gail, could you give me a lift?"

"Of course," her sister-in-law said, and the others had leaned back and looked at their cards as the two women gathered up their pocketbooks and their white summer gloves. "Tommy looks tired these days," Cass said, as she watched them walk away and they began to play cards again.

"Tommy looks tired these days," said Gail as they drove along in her black sedan, Connie thinking to herself that Gail really did not know how to negotiate a corner properly.

"He *is* tired," Connie said. "He works hard all day and he goes to the hospital a lot in the evening."

"How does he think Dad looks?" Gail asked.

"Like hell." There was silence for several blocks, then Connie said. "Tell Mark to get John to leave him alone. He's driving him nuts with all this about the house and the company. Tom feels bad enough about his father. It's not fair to be holding him up on this now."

Gail touched her barrettes and smoothed back her hair. She had never heard Connie say so much before. "I think Tommy should talk to Mark about it. I don't get involved in his business."

"Oh bullshit, Gail," Connie said, plucking at the fingers of her gloves. She realized it was the first time she had ever said the word out loud, and she liked the feel of it in her mouth, the sound of it, like a powerful and disdainful sneeze. "Everybody's business is everybody else's business in this family. Nobody's made a decision on their own in all the years I've been around."

"That may be how you feel—"

"Who picked out your house, Gail?"

Her sister-in-law's narrow lips tightened. "I did."

"John Scanlan did. He heard it was for sale the day after the old man who lived in it died and Mark bought it that afternoon. So don't tell me about keeping your business private. If you hadn't bought it, he would have tried to get Tommy to buy it. If not Tommy, Joe. Margaret gets passed over because of the convent. Pull over."

"Excuse me?"

"Pull over," Connie said, "or I'm going to throw up on your upholstery."

When she was finished and they had pulled away from the curb, they were both silent again. Finally Connie reached out tentatively and touched her sister-in-law's arm.

"I'm sorry," she said. "I just don't want Tommy to worry. He worries all the time."

"He has to take some responsibility for the family, Connie," Gail said primly.

"Why? Why does he have to? They're all adults. He takes enough responsibility in his heart."

They turned onto Park Street and the trees arched over them, a tunnel lined with brick and stucco façades, closed doors with impenetrable screens. From somewhere they could hear children yelling, and the sound of bulldozers. As they pulled into the driveway, the windows of the car a blur of reflected sunlight and tree branches, Connie thought she saw Terence sitting on the steps of the house, his big shaggy head hanging heavy between his knees. But as he looked up she realized it was Joey Martinelli, and she swung open the car door fast, feeling for the ground with her patent-leather high heels, still a little faint. "I've been waiting for you," he called, not moving.

"Thanks for the ride," Connie said.

"Is that—?" said Gail, and stopped.

"Is that who, Gail?"

"Mark said that you were—friendly with one of the—workers at the construction sight." Gail got the words out as though she was speaking English as a second language, and Connie smiled.

"Now, I managed to figure out that *workers* meant greasy dagos but I'm not quite sure about *friendly*. Does friendly mean I talk to him in the kitchen when he comes over for a drink of water, or does friendly mean I'm meeting him in my slip behind the bulldozers?"

Gail inhaled audibly. "I don't know why you have to be like this," she said. "No one means anything by what they say and yet you take everything as an insult. Any other woman would be thrilled to have her in-laws buy her a big house. It's much bigger than any of the rest of us have, but I don't begrudge it, with all these children. But to have a family that takes an interest, and then to be so critical—I just don't understand it. At the smallest thing you take offense, you assume that somehow you are being insulted, you . . ."

"What does my illicit relationship with the Carpenters' Union have to do with a big house I don't want or need?"

"It's the principle of the thing," Gail said, her face unpleasantly mottled with emotion. "Everything with you is a struggle. What would be just part of life for other people has to be some sort of big complicated thing with you. You isolate Tommy from his family, you make it clear you have contempt for all of us—"

"I have contempt for you? That's a good one."

"No one cares about ethnic differences any longer, Connie. No one thinks about those things."

"How come John says my oldest son has guinea eyebrows?"

"You see, that's just the point. He makes a little joke—"

As Connie climbed out of the car, a favorite expression of Celeste's popped into her head, and without thinking she said, "Button it, Gail." She walked over to Joey as her sister-in-law backed out of the driveway. "Sorry," he said as she approached, pale beneath her powder, her nose beginning to shine. "It's okay," she said, sitting down beside him.

"You're going to get your dress all dirty. Plus your lady friend is still watching you."

Connie looked up and waved at Gail, then put her elbows on her knees and her chin in her hands. It occurred to her suddenly that her heart was beating fast, and that she was having a good time. It was difficult to tell whether it was because of Gail, or because of Joey. When she looked at him she could see herself in his eyes. "I don't know what's come over me," she said, talking almost to herself. "Why were you waiting for me?" she added.

"Time for another lesson."

"I'm not sure I can right now. Are the kids inside?"

"Not so I can tell."

Connie eased her pumps off and stretched her legs in front of her. "My sisters-in-law aren't bad people. They just don't like me," she said.

"I can understand that," Joey said.

"Thanks," Connie said.

"It's an old thing, isn't it?" he said. "Women don't get on with a good-looking woman." Then, as though he'd realized what he said, he ducked his glossy head. "You know what I mean. I even remember my mother and her friends talking about you, how you were the best-looking girl any of them had ever seen." He laughed. "Except that no one would ever notice it because you were a midget princess held prisoner in a deep, dark cemetery."

Connie laughed, too, but she could tell she was still pink and flustered by the compliment. "Your mother's nice," she said, not knowing what else to say.

"I think she always hoped my brother would marry you. She was mad as hell when she found out you were going to marry Scanlan. She said you were just making trouble for yourself." For a moment the two of them looked at each other, and then Connie sighed.

"Let's go in," she finally said.

Inside, the house was perfectly still and smelled faintly of tuna fish. She dropped her shoes on the living-room floor and stood barefoot at the bottom of the stairs. "Maggie?" she called, but there was no answer.

Outside a car stopped, idled, died. Connie opened the door to see Celeste getting out. For some reason she was wearing a picture hat with fake flowers around the brim. She waved, and wobbled up the steps on a pair of stiletto heels, white patent leather with black scuff marks. "Damn," she said, looking down, wetting her finger and balancing on one foot like a flamingo to raise the other and try to wipe away the marks. Connie laughed and held the door open for her. At least Gail had missed this.

"Sorry to bust in," Celeste said. "I got you a blouse on sale." Celeste looked at Connie's navy-blue linen sheath with the white piping. "Don't tell me—let me guess. Lunch with your mother-in-law."

"Very good, Ce, very good. Card party with my sisters-in-law."

"All of them?"

"All of them."

Celeste screamed, clutched her breast, fell to the couch. Then she reached inside her shopping bag. "Next time, wear this," she said. "It's a size four. You're the only person in the world who could wear it." Celeste held up a white lace blouse. Connie could see daylight through it. Joey appeared in the doorway, holding a glass of water. "Who's that for?" he said, his big eyebrows raised.

"Whoops," said Celeste.

"How you doing, Celeste?" Joey Martinelli said. "You remember me?"

"Now that I see you I do," said Celeste, handing her cousin the blouse. "You used to hang out with Bobby, who lived around the block. The one who's a cop now? With the brother who's a cop?"

"Giambone. Bobby Giambone. Yeah, I met you at his house once. You were maybe sixteen, seventeen. I think you were engaged."

Celeste sighed. "I was engaged all the time then. So how come I don't see you around any more?"

"Ah, I don't know. You know how it is—we're all grown-up now. No more parties, no more dances. I never see anybody. I work, I go home, fall asleep. That's about it."

"You ever see Bobby?"

"He moved out of the city. He has a nice place with one of those above-ground pools out on the Island. He hates the city. All the cops, they hate the city."

Celeste reached out for his water glass and sipped from it thoughtfully, leaving a lip print on it the color of bubble gum. "So how's it coming?" she said, jerking her head toward the window, the flowers on her hat moving as though a thunderstorm was coming up.

"Okay. We're having a little bit of trouble with the kids out there. A lot of them are bored with vacation and vandalizing the place in their spare time. They set us back some."

"Kids'll be kids," Celeste said.

"Yeah, well some of them are being a little more than kids. Somebody set fire to one of the models two nights ago. Thank God it didn't do too much damage."

"Which night?" Connie asked, narrowing her eyes.

"Night before last. If it happens again, we got a real problem."

"So you're not done yet," Celeste said.

"We'll be done the models soon. A lot of the others will be finished by October, the rest in November. We sold the first one two days ago."

"You sold one?" Connie said.

"Yeah, to a young couple who live in Queens. He's in business.

They have one kid, a little girl, must be adopted. She's Korean. I think they're Jewish."

Celeste started to laugh, and the flowers on the hat went wild. "What's so funny?" Joey Martinelli said.

"She's thinking about my husband's father," Connie said, and she began to smile.

Celeste let out a whoop. "Bring the old man over here in an ambulance," she said, gasping for breath. "Jews with a Chink kid. Oh my god. He'll move to another state."

"My father-in-law isn't crazy about all this," Connie said. "He's ready to move us to a better neighborhood."

"Hey, I'm always for that," said Joey, grinning.

"So *you* move," Connie said. "I like picking my own neighborhood."

"I love that guy," said Celeste. "He's perfect. My mother says to me last week, 'Father O'Hearn over to Holy Redeemer gave the damnedest sermon yesterday. It was about Jesus and golf.' I said 'Ma, do me a favor. Call the hospital and tell Mr. Scanlan.' "

Joey Martinelli smiled. "That's some hat you got," he said, but his eyes were on Connie, who was stretching her legs in front of her, wiggling her toes, cramped from their afternoon in her good pumps. Her skirt had crept up her legs, and the curve of her thighs shone in nylon stockings. "I like that blouse," Joey said to no one in particular, and Connie crumpled it up in her fist, an edge of white lace falling from between her fingers. Celeste looked from Joey's face to that of her cousin, and then back again. "Fix me a seven-and-seven, Con," she said, her eyes narrowed, and she patted the couch beside her. "Joe," she said, "you come sit here next to me."

13

SAL'S WAS A TAVERN A BLOCK AWAY from First Concrete. Its door was set on a diagonal at the corner of two busy streets and thrown into perpetual shade by the elevated subway line. It looked like any tavern in America at the time, with neon beer signs in the window and red plastic seats in the booths and gangly bar stools ranged around a long, long bar filled with old men in the afternoons and working men at night. Above the register hung the first dollar Sal's ever took in, nineteen years earlier. The only thing worth mentioning about Sal's was that they made a spectacular hamburger out of good-grade chuck that Sal D'Alessandro got from a cop who got it as part of his payoff from a wholesale butcher in the wholesale meat market. All the cops ate and drank free at Sal's, and if any of their wives called, Sal always said their husbands had just been there and been called out on some emergency. Tommy usually ate lunch at Sal's. He liked the company and the food.

He took Mark there when, during the last week in July, his brother asked him to lunch. "Jesus, look at this place," Mark said, staring at the retired guys with gray stubble on their faces watching *As the World Turns* on the television. Sal came over after they got their beers, a bar towel hanging from the waistband of his pants. He shook hands with Mark officiously, like the maître d' in a bad French restaurant, and said that Mark looked like his mother. "When was Mom ever in this place?" Mark said, leaning across the table after Sal had left. "You got me," Tommy said. "Dad used to come here for lunch when he was still down the street, but I can't imagine him bringing Mom here." Mark looked around again and said, "Well, she sure as hell didn't come here by herself."

Tommy liked being with his brothers like this, alone, one on one, and he particularly liked being with Mark, who was only a year older than he was, and for whom he felt the slightly condescending sympathy that a man who easily fathers children feels for a man who has been incapable of doing so. ("Maybe it's him," Connie had said one night when they were talking about why Gail hadn't produced a child. "My ass," Tommy had replied, looking like his father.) Not having a family had set Mark apart. Combined with his height, it had diminished him in the family's eyes, and so he was reduced to asserting himself by arguing with his father over the color of embroidery on cassocks. Tommy knew that given a choice between his own position of black sheep and his brother's of barren issue, he'd stick with his own any time.

Gail had once talked about adoption, but John Scanlan had put the lid on that one. "It's not the same," he had said flatly. "You don't know what in the hell you're getting." Then his pale blue eyes had roved over his own family, ranged in their habitual postures of attention and apprehension in his living room. "I don't know," he had added, "maybe you never know."

Tommy had known something was up when he and his brother had met outside their father's hospital room two nights ago and Mark had suggested they get together. "Mark asked you to lunch?" Connie had said, one black eyebrow arched, like some exotic form of punctuation. "What's up?" Of course she knew what was up; it was either the company, the house, or her.

Every year or so someone in his family sat down and talked to Tommy about his wife, as though she was a car that needed a paint job. There was never a question of a trade-in—Mary Frances still asked Celeste how her husband was, even though Celeste had been divorced far longer than she'd been married. "Soused," Celeste always answered with good humor. It was only that they all wanted Connie to run more smoothly, to mix in, to blend in, to be more like them. The worst moment of Tommy's life had been a tenth anniversary dinner Mark had given them three years before, at which Connie had become rather high on fruity whiskey sours, the taste of the liquor lost amidst all the pineapple. There had been a cake with a little bride and groom, and toasts, and Connie had turned to all of them, the bride and groom in her hand, and had said in an odd squeaky voice, "Where were all of you on my wedding day?" And she had said it staring straight at John Scanlan, who stared right back. The effect had been blunted a bit by the fact that Connie had suddenly put her hand over her mouth, and run to the bathroom. Tommy went after her, and when they returned, his parents were gone from the table. "How long has that been going on?" James had said in a professional tone of voice to Connie, whose face was gray-white, and Tommy had said, "Jesus, James, she drank too much." But James had been right after all; she was expecting Joseph at the time, although neither of them had known it.

Now, sitting in Sal's with Tom, Mark said, "So your wife's pregnant again," and the remark lay on the table between them. Then Mark's eyes emptied and he added, "Look, Tom, you're going to need that new house no matter what you say. You'll have five. You need more room."

"We have plenty of room," Tommy said, rubbing the back of his neck. "Let's not start with the house. I don't want to move."

"Your wife doesn't want to move."

"Her too."

"You know she told Gail she wants to live in one of those development houses they're building?"

"Mark, she says those things to get you people aggravated. She's tired of having people make decisions about her life."

Sal arrived with the hamburgers. "Mr. Scanlan, medium," he said, putting the one with the blue stick in its bun in front of Tommy. "Mr.

Scanlan, medium rare," he added, putting the one with the red stick in front of Mark. Tommy wondered where he'd found the little sticks, and how special the occasion needed to be for Sal to use them. Tommy had been ordering hamburgers at Sal's for years and had never had a stick in his before.

Both men ate in silence, ketchup dripping onto their plates. Then Mark said, his mouth full, "People are talking about your wife."

"I don't want to hear this," Tommy said.

"Joe says he went over to St. Pius School to drop off a case of votive candles and he sees her out back with some guy playing hopscotch. She's jumping around like a kid with some big guinea—"

"Hey!" Tommy said, so loudly that two of the men at the bar turned.

"Sorry, sorry, sorry. Anyhow, she waves at Joe like it's the most natural thing in the world for her to be there with some guy. Now, Joe sees her, he makes allowances. Other people are going to wonder what the hell is going on."

Tommy was wondering the same thing himself, but he was damned if he would say anything to Mark. His brother went on talking. "She's always out with those guys who are building those houses," he said. "That's where she was when Pop went into the hospital that day. People have been seeing her out their windows talking to those guys."

Tommy put down his hamburger, wiped his hands on a paper napkin, and sat back in the booth. "She knows the guy who's running the project. He's from her old neighborhood. He's a nice person. She knows his mother. She went out with his brother." He picked up his hamburger. "We're not talking about this anymore. You're all against her. All of you. Always have been."

Tommy was angry and perplexed. That morning he had noticed that the valleys of Connie's face were lavender, the peaks yellow, her eyes as bright as black marbles. She was always ill when she was pregnant, as though it was an early warning. Joseph was beginning to talk in sentences; in a few years he would be saying things she neither liked nor understood. This was the way it was for her, being a mother: a sickness and then a cleaving to her heart, a time of pure love and then the horrible moving away. Sometimes the only way she could love them was to remember them when they were small, pressing her face into the box of flannel receiving blankets in the linen closet, nappy and soft as a baby's head.

Several nights ago, Tommy had been watching the ball game on television, yelling insults at the Yankees pitching staff, throwing pillows at the screen, when he had noticed that Connie was not in the house. Neither were the older children; he was alone with Joseph, who was snoring through a stuffed-up nose in his crib, the night light throwing strange shadows across his fat face. There had been no one on the streets outside, no sound except for the soft murmur of people several houses down talking on their front steps. But in the backyard, just past the dusty bare spot in the center of the grass where home plate had always been, a solitary figure stood looking out toward the development. At first Tom thought it was Maggie, mooning about, but the posture was wrong, the shoulders a little too soft and irresolute, the arms cradling the midsection not angular or awkward enough. It was his wife.

A couple stumbling from the development, a pair of teenagers who lived a few blocks away, nearly ran into her, quiet and small as she was, but they veered off at the last moment, clutching each other's waists, the boy's eyes as blind as a night animal's, his shirttail a crumpled rag outside his chino pants. Connie followed them with her eyes, and then she threw back her head and stared at the stars. Tommy felt afraid.

He went back to the television, back to the armchair, and when she came into the room with a glass of iced tea he pretended she had been with him all the time, just a little out of his line of sight. And she pretended, too. He had told his brother James that she was odd this time, mercurial and withdrawn, even from the children, although as soon as he'd said it he realized she had been that way for some time. Once he'd found her sitting on the floor, just looking at her good china. He couldn't believe that was normal.

"Women have these strange fancies when they're expecting, Tom," James had said, shaking his big handsome head and smiling, and they had left it at that. James had never been the kind of brother to whom

Tommy could confess that he feared his wife's strange fancy was for some guinea with big forearms from the old neighborhood.

He could not believe that she missed that portion of her life. She rarely went to see her father, sending Maggie instead, and he had not found this peculiar. He remembered going for the first time to her parents' home, those two old people, this one lovely, lonely child, and thinking that she was out of the world there, as though she lived in one of those little crystal balls with falling snow inside. He had been amazed that she had even learned to dance, had learned the melody to "Moonlight Serenade," until later, when he had gone to Celeste's house and seen Connie's connection to a normal life. He had always felt a touch of pride at having taken her away from all that, the heavy silent mother with the V cut into one front tooth from biting off thread at the sewing machine, the father who took all his affection outdoors and massaged it into the ground around his beloved plants. Once he had found her, pregnant with their second child, planting tomato plants in the backyard, before one of his sisters-in-law had made a comment about how well Italians did such things, and he had seen tears fall down upon her dirty hands. "I miss my father," she had said, although the old man was only twenty minutes away by car. "Go over and see him," Tom had replied, but she just shook her head. "You don't understand," she had said, sobbing. "Sometimes people are near but they might as well be on the moon." He thought he understood now what she had been saying then.

"How's everything else?" he finally said to his brother to break the silence.

"Come into the business, Tom," Mark said, looking up at him.

"Oh Jesus, not this again."

"Maybe I've been going about it the wrong way. I know your wife is pissed that I've been bothering you—"

"Says who?" Tommy said.

"She told Gail to tell me to lay off."

"Go on," Tommy said.

"But I need your help. Things are changing. There's a lot to be done." Mark stared at his hands. "I've been going over the books,

Tommy. They're not good. The old man moved a lot of money around in strange ways. I don't think we're as solid as he always pretended. Some of the construction companies aren't making money. He mortgaged two of the apartment buildings for that new equipment we got a couple years ago. It's going to take some doing to make things right."

"What do you mean, to make them right?"

"I think the business is in trouble, Tom. I need your help."

"Jesus," Tommy said.

"Jack and Joe are all right, but they're not so smart. I say do something and they do it. But I need a real partner."

"You're exaggerating," Tommy said. "You just want someone to argue with until Pop comes back."

"I need your help. I need someone to work with. It'd be good."

"I have a job," Tommy said, wiping his mouth. "I have a family, I have a house, I have a job."

"The cement company can run itself. Besides, he told me he's thinking of selling it off."

Tommy smiled sourly. "Oh yeah?" he said.

"I figured you knew."

"He'd go that far?" Tommy said.

"He says it's never been a big moneymaker."

"He's full of shit, Mark," Tommy said. "The other day at the hospital he told me he was going to have me fired so that I wouldn't be able to make my mortgage payments and would have to move into that house he bought. He was going to have me fired so that I'd have to work with you to keep food in my kids' mouths. He's got a little chessboard in his head and he's been able to move every piece on the goddamn board except two of them. The last two. Me and my wife. And he won't rest until the game is over, and he's won."

"Jesus, that's a horrible thing to say," Mark said. "Jesus, Tommy, I'm ashamed of you."

"What'd he tell you about me coming into the business?"

The question lay between them as Sal brought coffee and took their empty plates away. Mark took a long time putting milk and sugar in his cup. Finally he said, "The old man told me October first you start as vice president of operations. He says you make five thousand a year more than me."

Tommy laughed. "And you're ashamed of me?" he said, leaning across the table until his forehead almost touched his brother's. "God, Markey, I don't want to piss on your life, but look at you. You're a lackey for him. You don't even have kids because he said adoption was no good. Do you hold it when he takes a piss, too? He's got you just where he wants you. I thought he gave up on me a long time ago, because of Concetta, because I stepped out of line. Now I think he just waited until he knew I thought that, and then he came in for the kill."

"Do you hear yourself? You make your own father sound like a monster."

"You remember when we were kids and Sister Ann Elizabeth asked us to make a drawing of God? You remember? You made him tall and you made his hair yellow and his eyes blue. And so did I. She got such a kick out of that, that our pictures of God looked like the same person. That wasn't just a coincidence, Mark."

"I don't know what you're talking about," Mark said. "I just want you to come into the business with me. You'd be good. We'd be good together. The old man doesn't accept reality. The world is changing. The Church is changing. He's not far off on his jokes about the kaiser rolls. What if they decide to go to using plain pieces of bread at communion? That's a million bucks right down the toilet."

"You're talking to the wrong person about this. Go back to the hospital and talk to the owner of the company."

"He's not coming back, Tom," Mark said.

Tommy felt a chill in his chest and, almost reflexively, his shoulders hunched in, like little wings. "Get out," he said, but his voice was low.

"He's in bad shape. He's much worse than anyone thinks. James says the old man will never really be the same."

"Get out," Tommy said, his voice lower still.

"You come into the business with me, Tom. Take the house. It's a nice house, much nicer than any of those development houses.

Move your wife away from there. It's not good for her. It's not good for you."

"She's fine, Mark. I'm fine."

"No you're not," Mark said.

"Yeah, we are."

"Yeah? Where is your wife right now? Right at this very moment? I can tell you that Gail is at a white sale with Mom and that after that she's going to play bridge with some of her friends and after that she's having dinner with me. Where is Connie right now?"

"She's home taking care of her kids," Tommy said.

"If you're sure of that, fine. If you're sure of that I got nothing further to say. If you're sure of that."

14

MAGGIE LIT THE FIFTH FIRE HERSELF. She felt as though the match jumped from her hand to the big wet spot where the lighter fluid had collected on the plywood wall of the garage. The house was in the back of the development, up a little rise from the old creek, and its lumber was still orangy-yellow. It was the spot on the wall and the fresh look of the wood, she thought when she was finally alone, that made her think the flames would not spread, even as they covered the walls like a dazzling cape.

"Isn't it incredible?" said Debbie, who was standing just behind her.

Maggie was struck by several things at once: by the damp smell of the night, by a persistent trickle of sweat down the back of her head and into the hollow at the base of her skull, by how hot the flames became so quickly. It crossed her mind that she was making a memory, and that she would never in her life be able to communicate the sick feeling that afflicted her the moment the fire began to leap around her, the nausea that rose up in her throat as she heard the three people behind her breathing heavily in the still air. She wondered if this was the way her mother felt when she was expecting a baby. If it was, she would never ever have children.

They were out in the development, in a two-car garage. The big square empty space was filled with boxes: a No-Frost refrigerator, a No-Rinse dishwasher, a host of other appliances and fixtures in corrugated brown cardboard. The younger kids had been having a field day, turning empty boxes into tunnels, caves, houses, hauling them out of the big refuse pile to one side of the development and dragging them home as their mothers screamed from the kitchen windows "You take that right back where you found it." Damien had started collecting scraps of Formica, little punched-out circles and half moons where the kitchen installers had carved out holes for plumbing pipes or planed the edge of a counter into a curve. He had a big box full in his room, amid his butterflies and cacti, and sometimes he would take them out and look at them, feeling the smooth surfaces, even sniffing them, and smiling. "You're nuts," Terence said.

Maggie had gone to get Debbie after dinner, but Mrs. Malone had said she was not at home. "Did you two girls have a fight?" she added, frowning.

"Not exactly," said Maggie.

"You come inside and have a Popsicle and tell me about it," Mrs. Malone said, but Maggie had gone off by herself to the development. She knew exactly where to find Debbie and the others. She could smell them now, like a tracking dog; she could smell the accelerant and the sulfur.

The second fire had, like the first, flared and died. The third and fourth had happened when she was not there; one had leveled the walls of a closet, the other had left a black hole the size of the gym's center court mark on the bedroom floor of a house that was barely a frame. She had become accustomed now to not being able to find Debbie when she wanted her, to discovering her at the pool, giggling behind her hand with Bridget Hearn. They would fall silent, their faces flat, as soon as Maggie appeared. It was halfway through the summer, and Maggie felt that the structure of her life had tumbled down around her, her safe haven at the cemetery somehow strange and unsatisfactory now, her invincible grandfather wasting away amid the white of his hospital bed, her parents absent in spirit and sometimes in fact, her best friend a stranger. She had only found out about the third and fourth fires because Joey Martinelli had told her mother one afternoon when the two of them were in the kitchen having coffee and didn't realize that Maggie was in the house. When Maggie had come downstairs for lemonade, quiet in bare feet, her mother had leapt from her chair like a mouse caught in a spring trap, and Mr. Martinelli had been so discomfited that he had asked her how school was. Maggie had felt like an intruder in her own kitchen, and, lying on her bed afterward, had wondered if she would ever belong anywhere again.

She had gone over to the Malones' that same afternoon, and found Debbie in her room, lying on the bed, still pink from a day at the club. Maggie had lain down on Aggie's bed, too, and they had talked in a desultory fashion for a few minutes before lapsing into silence. Finally Debbie had cleared her throat. "I think before you come over you should call and see whether I'm here," she finally said. "And make sure I'm here alone and not already with somebody else."

Maggie had continued to stare at the ceiling. There was a crack that ran across one corner that she knew as well as she knew her own face in the mirror. She traced it with her eyes, back and forth, back and forth.

"Sometimes I might be with other people," Debbie added. "There are things that I'm interested in now that you're not that interested in."

"Like what?" Maggie said.

"How should I know?" Debbie shot back. "Maybe we're maturing at different rates. Bridget says she was friends with Gigi McMenamin for years and years and then they stopped being friends because Gigi just wasn't interested in doing anything. All she wanted to do was hang around the house and read."

"I know what you're interested in," Maggie said. "You're my best friend."

"Maybe I'm interested in other things now. Maybe I'm changing. Bridget says that being out of Helen's shadow has changed me. She says I act more like I'm in high school than most people my age."

"Bridget's a bitch," said Maggie, getting up and walking out.

That was when she had known that the next time there was a fire, she would be there.

But she never suspected that she would strike the match and start the fire. Richard had handed her the box of kitchen matches, his eyes flat, and when he had said, "Your move, Maria Goretti," she knew there was no way back to the way things had been before, to the times of Indian clay in the creek and Ouija boards. She sniffed the air and thought that the scent was an amalgam of what had been and what was still to come, of the old smells of cut grass and plastic toys and stew cooking and the faint ripe odor of standing water, and the new smells of plaster and linoleum, cement and concrete, all nice smells somehow. Sometimes she tried to close her eyes and imagine the field the way it had been only two months before, its reeds hiding the earth and the field mice and the occasional discarded soda can. And when she did, she could envision a field, but it was her imagined idea of one, like an illustration in a book, perfect arcs of gray-green laid on a bias, and not what had really been there at all. She wondered sometimes whether she was doing the same thing to her memories of her own life.

"Your turn," Debbie said.

Maggie knew why Debbie was angry. The day before, they had visited Helen in the city. They had put on summer dresses, because they always wore dresses when they went to the city, and they slipped out of the Malones' front door, which was only used by salesmen and for important parties, while Mrs. Malone was busy warming a bottle for the new baby. Maggie carried an umbrella. It was still wet from the day before, and the day before that. It had been one of the rainiest summers on record, Mrs. Malone said. The weather was making all the mothers feel that perhaps they would lose their minds. "I'll make you a deal," Mrs. Malone had said to the children one morning at breakfast, after Maggie had spent the night. "I'll stay out of your hair until Labor Day if you'll stay out of mine." No one stopped eating. The baby was in a corner, sucking noisily on his hand. He was a large boy, with no hair and an enormous mottled face. It often occurred to

Maggie that what passed as an offhand remark from Mrs. Malone would have been a turning point for either of her own parents.

For days at a time there had been no work on the development, and water ran down the raw brown slopes that stood for lawns in great streams, until ridges were worn into them and piles of silt lay in front of all the new houses. The ones that were only framed in turned a henna color, and the water in the basements grew stagnant on those rare afternoons when the sun shone. Even the negligible little creek, which Maggie and Debbie had been able to negotiate with one good broad jump since second grade, rose and covered its steppingstones, sloshing aggressively up over its banks and whirring around the stanchions of the railroad trestle. After the fifth day, three workmen from the county public works department had come and stared silently at the foot of one of the stanchions, where a narrow groove of earth had been worn away to a depth of three feet. They brought a dump truck full of gravel and filled it in. Maggie was so bored that she went outside to watch; she had put on her yellow slicker, and her wrists poked like sticks from the wide sleeves. She had outgrown it in three months, and outgrown, too, watching workmen shovel stones. Sometimes she took the nail Bruce had given her out of her jewelry box, placed it in the palm of her hand and looked at it, as though at any moment it would turn into something else. When Connie was home, Maggie tried to stay out of her way. When her mother was gone, Maggie stayed in her bedroom, peering out through the window, looking for fires in the rain.

Maggie and Debbie had taken the subway to Helen's building, walking three blocks from the station beneath one umbrella, and by the time they reached the apartment house, an ugly brick rectangle with a keyhole of an air shaft excised from the middle of the yellow-brown façade, their skirts were wet almost to the waist. "Nasty day, ladies," the man mopping the marble floors of the lobby had said pleasantly, eyeing their shiny, skinny legs.

Maggie had assumed that Debbie had asked her to come along because she had realized that Bridget Hearn was a jerk, and that Maggie was a much more suitable companion for such an important excursion.

This was not true. Debbie had told Helen that she might come by, and Helen had said that if Debbie brought Bridget she would not let them into the apartment. "Maggie saves you from yourself," she had said.

Debbie had been to visit Helen three times before, each time with Aggie, and she was affecting an air of great nonchalance, although she was terrified. Nearly every apartment in Helen's building was occupied by the widow of a Columbia professor, and the ladies all bore a great resemblance to one another, all small, slightly humpbacked elderly women with round hats like toadstools and pronounced foreign accents. When they spoke to one another in the elevators, they talked mainly of the price of produce, which they purchased in small quantities each day as part of their daily routine. When they shared the elevator with Helen or her roommate, they usually kept silent, their mouths as tight as the snap closures on their handbags.

One of them, who had herself been an anthropologist in Germany before her marriage, had written several letters in her ornate, rather spindly handwriting to determine how the girls had come in possession of the apartment, and whether they were old enough to be legally permitted to live alone. She was the one who entered the elevator with Maggie and Debbie now, staring down at the puddle on the floor their skirts made. Maggie noticed that the woman was wearing the same sort of shoes and boots that the nuns at school wore, low-heeled, black lace-up shoes with perforated uppers and translucent plastic boots that fitted the contours of the shoes exactly. Maggie's aunt Margaret had once told her that she had found those shoes the greatest impediment to remaining in the convent.

The elderly woman looked at Maggie. "Alone?" she suddenly spat out.

"Excuse me?" Maggie had said.

Debbie giggled.

"You are alone?"

"We're going to visit my sister," Debbie said. "Eight-B."

The elevator door opened. "Ah," the woman said, and stepped off.

"Oh God," said Debbie, when the door had closed.

Helen's apartment was silent. The peephole shone in the yellowish rainy-day glow from the airshaft window. Maggie stood on tiptoe to look inside, but she saw only her own distorted face, her nose as splayed as a bloodhound's. "We came all this way for nothing," Debbie said, pressing on the bell with her thumb. Maggie could hear it ringing faintly inside. Finally Debbie started back toward the elevator. "Come on," she said irritably. "They probably went out to lunch."

Maggie leaned on the bell again, staring back at herself through the peephole. As she walked away, the door opened. A girl with long brown hair and a flowered kimono that barely covered her behind stood there looking down at Maggie. She was holding a cup of coffee in one hand and a cigarette in the other.

"Yes?" she said a little grandly, with a hint of an English accent. Then she saw Debbie skittering down the hall. "Oh, Christ," she said. "Come on in. Helen, it's your little sister."

"Debbie," said Debbie.

"Debbie," the girl called to the back of the apartment.

Maggie walked in and sat down on the daybed, which was something like the sofa in her grandfather Mazzo's house, brown and shiny, its shabbiness accented by an embroidered shawl arranged over the back. The fabric was worn away from both arms. There was no other furniture in the room except for a record player and a set of bookshelves made from bricks and planks. Atop the bookshelves was a plastic version of the *Pietà*, with a rosary hanging around the Blessed Mother's neck. A Rolling Stones album cover was pinned to the wall.

Next to it was a professional black-and-white photograph of Helen. She was wearing a lot of obvious eyeliner and looked older and very beautiful. Her shoulders were bare. Maggie stood up to look at the picture closely as Helen's roommate exhaled and said, "Her Theda Bara look. Wonderful, isn't it?" Maggie nodded. She had no idea what the girl meant.

When Helen came in she was wearing the same kind of kimono as the other girl's, but in a bright salmon color, and her part was lost in the thicket of her unbrushed hair. Maggie thought she looked more beautiful than in the picture, the pale skin of her heart-shaped face pink at the cheeks and chin, her legs jutting out from her robe. "Didn't anyone ever teach you to call first?" she said.

"You don't have a phone," Debbie said, her eyes down, her arms crossed over her chest.

"Sure we do," said the roommate. "We got it last week."

"Don't you tell Mom," Helen said sharply, looking suddenly like her old self as she swept into the kitchen. "Do you want coffee?" she called over her shoulder, but neither of the girls answered.

When she came back into the room, a cup cradled in her hands, Maggie felt as though Helen had been gone a long time. She realized it was only a month since Helen had moved out, and she thought perhaps the other feeling was only because she had never belonged at home, had always seemed about to leave. She did not look at home in this apartment either, although her roommate did, yawning and stretching like a toddler just up from an afternoon nap.

"Mom won't let anybody move into your room," Debbie said, uncrossing her arms. "Aggie begged and begged. She sent in the money to hold your place at Marymount."

Helen laughed, not sarcastically, but with real happiness, her blue eyes alight. "That's all right," she said. "I knew she would. I'll come some day next week for dinner and talk to her after. How's Charles?"

"Okay. He sleeps all the time. Not like Jennifer was."

"Did you tell them about the part?" the roommate said, putting her cigarette out in the milky dregs of her coffee.

Helen smiled.

"Your sister got a part in a revue at a club downtown. It's called *A New World*. Sort of a folk-music thing. I swear she's going to be famous."

"Really?" Maggie said.

Helen shrugged again. "Don't tell Mom," she said.

"You're going to sing in a show?" Debbie asked.

"Don't look so shocked," Helen said. "I have a good voice."

"The face didn't hurt, either," her roommate said.

From the hallway came the explosive sound of someone laboring to clear his throat. Then there was the sound of spitting, and of the toilet flushing. Maggie and Debbie stared, transfixed, as a tall man with awry red hair walked into the living room, his chest and his feet bare, his blue jeans hanging so low on his hips that a small cloud of pubic hair stood out above the waistband. He was scratching his stomach and still clearing his throat. When he saw the girls he looked at them sleepily. "Sorry, wrong number," he said, and walked back down the hall. They heard a door close.

"Ooops," the roommate said.

"I've got to go to work," Helen said.

"The play is during the day?" Debbie asked.

"I'm still waiting tables. The play pays three dollars a performance. I can't buy shampoo with what the play pays."

Maggie was afraid to use the bathroom, but she had to go so badly she was afraid she wouldn't make it home if she didn't do it then. She looked quickly around the corner of the door, but the man with the red hair was not there. The seat on the toilet was up, and the inside of the shower curtain was wet. Maggie wanted to look in the medicine cabinet, but she was afraid someone would see or hear her. She ran the water, and pinched her cheeks to try to make them pink.

"Could you give me a hand with this?" she heard Helen call from a room down the hall, and she waited for a minute to see if the man would respond and then went into the bedroom herself.

It was an odd mixture of things, with Helen's old powder-blue spread on the bed and a silky New York City souvenir scarf thrown over the bedside lamp. There was a poster on the wall of a painting that looked like a pocket watch melting into the sidewalk, and a photograph of a young man who reminded Maggie a little of Richard. "Dali," said Helen. "James Dean." Maggie could think of no possible reply; it was as though everyone in the apartment spoke in code. Helen pointed down her back to a row of little buttons. "I can't reach the middle ones," she said, and Maggie bent over them, scowling.

"You've grown," said Helen. "You'll be as tall as I am soon."

"I'm already taller than my mother," Maggie said.

"But not taller than Richard Joseph. Is he still the *idée fixe*?"

Maggie felt as if they were back to code again. She shrugged. "He's not as great as everyone thinks he is," Maggie said, trying to coax another button through its loop and wondering how Helen would ever get into this dress if no one was around.

"Bravo," Helen said. "I know that kind of boy. All talk and no substance. He's cute, but he's a little too full of himself."

"Debbie still really likes him."

"That's no surprise. You and Debbie are like oil and water." Maggie frowned. She was finished with the buttons, but she fiddled around with the back of the dress to prolong the conversation. "I can tell you exactly what Debbie'll be doing in twenty years," Helen added.

"What?"

"She'll have three kids. She'll live in Kenwood or a place just like it. She'll be married to somebody she met in high school and married halfway through college. She'll say she's going to finish college when the kids are in school. If you ask her if she's happy, she'll say 'Of course I'm happy' and she'll be telling the truth."

"What's wrong with that?" Maggie said.

"There's nothing wrong with it, if that's what you want. It's just that most people don't decide, it just sort of happens to them. That's not what my life will be like twenty years from now."

"Tell me yours," said Maggie, and she stopped trying to pretend she was still buttoning and sat down on the bed.

"I haven't the foggiest. Maybe I'll be an actress. Maybe a dancer. Maybe I won't be good enough to be either and I'll wind up with three kids and a house in Kenwood." She laughed, and Maggie frowned again. "You're right, Maggie, that's pushing it a little. The point is, I haven't done anything yet that will force me in any particular direction. Somebody like my sister, she's already on her way to a decision. In two or three years she'll start dating some guy, and she'll get used to him and he'll get used to her. They'll go a little further each time they park, until they don't have any further to go. And their families will get to know each other and everyone will expect them to get engaged and pretty soon they will. And then they'll be married and the kids will show up and so on and so forth 'til the end of time. How old are you guys again?"

"Almost thirteen," said Maggie, liking the sound of it much better than twelve.

"The decisions you make when you're thirteen can decide who you will be for the rest of your life."

"But can't you change?"

"Sometimes. You can break up with the guy. You can marry somebody else. But after a while, you can't change a thing. Like my parents. Can you imagine one of my parents waking up someday and deciding they wanted to ditch seven kids, or move to a place where they don't know a soul?"

"That's what Debbie said."

"Wait a minute. You've lost me. My sister said these same things?"

"She said parents have no future, that their lives are over."

"Ah. No. That's not the same thing. Your life is over when you're dead. But the *kind* of life you have—that's settled early, sometimes by accident. Sometimes by character. Like Monica Scanlan. What will she be doing twenty years from now?"

"She'll be married," Maggie said.

"Kids?"

"Only two. Enough to make her seem like an all-right person but not enough to be too much trouble or make her get fat."

Helen grinned. "Kenwood?"

"No," said Maggie. "Someplace with bigger houses."

"California!" cried Helen.

"California?" said Maggie.

"And will she live happily ever after?" Helen asked.

Maggie stopped laughing. "No," she said quietly. "Monica will never be happy, no matter what."

"You're good at this," Helen said. "What will you be doing in twenty years, Maggie?"

"I don't know."

"Husband?"

Maggie thought of her parents dancing, and her parents fighting while her grandfather lay half dead, and of John Scanlan telling Mary Frances he was going to marry her whether she liked it or not, and of the nail in her jewelry box, and the mark of Richard's fingers on her arm. She was wearing a dress with sleeves today so that the bruise marks, a brownish-yellow now, would not show. "I don't know," she finally said.

"Kids?"

"I don't know."

"Kenwood?"

"I don't know."

"I think that's a good sign," Helen said. "Most of the people you know would answer yes to every one of those questions. Just remember that sometimes you drift into things, and then you can't get out of them. Not to decide is to decide."

"Not to decide is to decide?"

"Exactly." Then, in an uncanny imitation of the voice of Mother Ann Bernadette, the Mother Superior of Sacred Heart, Helen added, "I'm so glad we had this little talk, Miss Scanlan." She picked up her purse. "I'm going to be late for work."

"Thanks, Helen," Maggie said.

Helen smiled, her face as clear as though it had just been carved from some pale stone. "Thanks for buttoning me up. Be good. Have you been wearing my bathing suit?"

"It doesn't fit," Maggie said.

"Soon, Maggie. Soon it will."

Out in the living room, Debbie was sitting talking to Helen's roommate. "We have to go," Debbie said. "We have stuff to do." Maggie looked down at her dress. The hem was still a darker color than the rest, and occasionally it clung to her legs. The man had come into the living room again. "Anybody remember where I put my shoes?" he said.

" 'Bye," said Debbie.

" 'Bye," Helen replied.

"*Arrivederci*," said the man with the red hair, from the floor. He was peering under the couch. Maggie was surprised to see him do this; that was where her saddle shoes always turned up when she couldn't find them in the mornings, but she had never known a grownup to lose shoes.

The two girls had ridden down in the elevator in silence. Their train was already on the platform, and they rushed down the subway steps, their damp shoes making slapping noises on the concrete. For a moment as they sat on the plastic seats they were out of breath. Maggie held her umbrella between her knees.

"What were you and Helen talking about?" Debbie finally asked.

"The future."

"Did you tell her what the Ouija said?"

"No," said Maggie, pulling at a cuticle. She did not want to tell Debbie about what would happen to her in twenty years, just as she had not wanted to tell her about the bathing suit. They were silent again as the train rocked back and forth, lulling them into sluggishness.

"Do you think he slept there?" Maggie finally asked, looking up at the advertisements for wrinkle cream and continuing education just above the dirty subway windows.

"That's a stupid question," Debbie had answered, but Maggie didn't know if she meant stupid yes or stupid no. They sped through the tunnel, the air warm and smelling of grease. In the Bronx the train came suddenly aboveground, into the kind of clear white sunlight that Maggie felt she had not seen for weeks. She turned in her seat to watch the tops of tenement buildings go by, squinting into apartment windows, faintly seeing women in light clothing moving around behind the curtains. On a fire escape just opposite one of the stations two boys sat in shorts, chewing gum, and as they saw Maggie watching them they both gave her the finger. She turned around. The two girls were alone in the car.

"Do you really think Helen will be famous?" Debbie said.

"I do," said Maggie.

"I don't think that guy was sleeping there," Debbie said.

"Neither do I."

"Don't tell my mom."

"I won't."

"Don't tell your mom either."

"Don't worry."

They had not spoken again until they reached Maggie's house. It seemed deserted, as it did so often these days. Maggie came back from the bathroom to find Debbie holding the California bathing suit, turning it in her hands as though wondering what it was.

"You stole my sister's bathing suit," she said.

"You went in my drawers," Maggie replied. And suddenly she sucked in her breath, because she realized that Debbie had gone in her drawers a hundred times before, and she had never minded until then.

As though she had read her mind, Debbie said, "I always go in your drawers. But I never stole."

"I didn't steal it. She gave it to me. The day she moved out."

"Liar."

"It's true," Maggie said. "You can ask her."

Debbie looked at her and then threw the suit onto the bed. Maggie wondered whether it would have been better to pretend that she had taken it. She had never really understood, until that moment, how hard it must be to be Helen Malone's sister.

"I'm going over to Bridget's," Debbie said, shoving past Maggie. In the doorway she turned. "I'm getting to be somebody, too," she said, and then she added, "I hope you *do* move."

Maggie had known she would pay—for the time with Helen, for the bathing suit, for Debbie's feeling that Maggie had taken something that should belong to her. Every time she thought about that moment in her bedroom she felt sick, but not as sick as she felt when she found Debbie out in the development that night, daring her to strike a match, her eyes mean, with no vestige of friendship in them. Behind Debbie she could see Bruce, his face pink, and she knew that if he could speak he would say "Don't do it. You don't have to." She wondered why he was there. He didn't seem to shadow Richard so much anymore.

"Do it," Richard said, and the silence was so overpowering that the scrape of the match along the side of the box sounded like an alarm in the room. A tiny flame leapt up in the darkness.

"I saw your mom with that guy today at the high school, Maggie," Debbie said, and there was an edge to her voice. "They were parked in the parking lot. Bridget says—" Before Maggie could hear what Bridget Hearn had said about her mother and Joey Martinelli, she had tossed the match away from her like an unwelcome thought. The corner of the garage burst like fireworks, and a roar swallowed up the echo of the scratch of the match. And they all turned and ran into the darkness.

Maggie came around the corner of one of the raw new roads and thought she heard sneakers behind her, but after a minute the sound faded and was gone. There was gravel on the ground, waiting for asphalt to be poured, and her shoes suddenly skidded sideways, and she fell onto the road; she felt a sharp sting in the side of her calf and on one of her palms. She heard another sound behind her, and then headlights swept the gravel, a car traveling slowly by. She felt caught in the lights, and closed her eyes, afraid the headlights would pick up the pale green of her eyes in the darkness. But the car crept past. In the light from the dashboard, she could see Joey Martinelli behind the wheel. He looked strange, and it was not until he was gone and she had gotten to her feet, blood running down one leg and onto her white sneakers, that she finally figured out that it had looked as if he was wearing a clover chain on his head.

When she got inside her own kitchen she washed her leg and wrapped it with gauze. "Mom?" she called softly, and then a little louder, "Mom?" Finally she heard her father's voice in the darkened living room. When she went in, the ball game was on the television, and the only light in the room was the white light from the screen. "She's not here, Maggie," he said. "She's at Celeste's. Or someplace." There was such an air of quiet acceptance in his voice, and his eyes were fixed on the screen so completely, that Maggie asked no more questions. She went upstairs and cried, using Helen's old bathing suit, limp on her pillow, to wipe her swollen face.

15

HEN THE TELEPHONE RANG, CONNIE gathered Joseph up off the floor, holding him close as she walked across the hall to the bedroom. She distrusted the telephone, had never been able to see it as anything other than the bearer of bad news. Her parents had agreed to have one installed only after her mother had had a fainting spell one day, but even when it was put in, it sat there silently, like a big black toad, gathering dust on an occasional table, an outsider amid the cheap china figures. When the phone did ring, all three of them had stared at it with amazement, and it was always left to Connie to answer. Tommy had never understood why she liked to make dates with him at the end of the evening, instead of talking later in the week, and she did not know how to explain. What could she tell him: that she lived in a house where they preferred to keep communication at a minimum?

She put Joseph down on her bed and picked up the receiver. The baby stared at the ceiling, fingering the bridge of his nose and rubbing the ear of his old brown bear across his cheek and chin. "Bear," he said.

"Hello," Connie said, rubbing his warm stomach and smiling at him.

"Hello, Connie. It's Monica. Is Maggie there?"

The Scanlan grandchildren did not get away with calling their aunts and uncles by their first names. Connie did not know exactly what to say. Finally she said, "No."

"No, no, NO," said Joseph loudly, talking to the bear.

"I beg your pardon?" said Monica.

"I said *no*," Connie repeated.

Joseph was still babbling, making it hard for Connie to hear. "Would you tell her I called to ask her to be a junior bridesmaid at my wedding?" Monica said.

"I beg your pardon?"

Monica repeated herself, as though she had been practicing the sentence for some time.

"I'm confused," Connie said. "You're getting married?"

"You'll get the invitation this week. The wedding is at the end of the month."

"The end of the *month*? Who's the guy?"

"You don't know him. He goes to Fordham. His name is Donald Syzmanski. His father is a police officer." There was a silence. "A sergeant," Monica added coldly, as though the silence had implied criticism.

Connie did not know what to say. This was the longest conversation she had ever had with her niece. Monica had always reminded her of Gigi Romano, a beautiful girl she had known in high school, who had had an impossibly tiny nose and numerous matching cashmere sweater sets, and whose father was said to be a member of organized crime. She had married an older Italian man and moved to Las Vegas the summer after graduation. There had been 700 people at Gigi Romano's wedding, and her gown had been hand-beaded at a convent in Italy. In high school Gigi Romano had always referred to Connie as "deadbeat" because of the cemetery, and she had always gotten a good laugh out of it. Connie couldn't imagine why she was thinking of that now.

"Have you gotten a dress yet?" Connie finally asked, groping for something to say, and as soon as she said it she realized it was such a non sequitur that she laughed.

"Yesterday," Monica answered coolly.

Connie still did not know what to say. Finally, in the silence, Monica said, her voice cracking, "I assumed that you of all people would understand this. Please just give Maggie my message."

"I think you should call back and ask her yourself."

"No thank you," Monica said.

Connie paused. "I'm sorry, Monica," she finally said.

"Everything is fine," Monica said. "Thank you very much." And she hung up.

"Bear," Joseph said.

Connie lay down on the bed beside him, her hands cradling her lower abdomen. It was only slightly rounded, but it no longer flattened out when she lay prone. Three months pregnant and she had lost three pounds from the nausea, so that her ribs made her naked torso looked like a striped shirt. She knew that it would not make any difference. The baby would be large and healthy. They always were. She had worn a size-four dress the day of her wedding, and yet Maggie had weighed ten pounds. Who could tell what was inside you until it came out?

She felt tiny fingers on her arm. Joseph was patting her softly with one hand while he held his bear in the other. He put his thumb in his mouth and she buried her face in the nape of his neck. He was the only one she could love like this now. The two oldest children always pulled away from her, although it had been years since she had tried to kiss Maggie, both of them squeamish in the face of their shared femininity. And she was wary of Damien, who would climb all over her like an overanxious boy in the back seat after a high school dance. But Joseph was passive and pleased with the attention, and she lay there for a long time.

She felt sorry for Monica, not because she obviously was getting married because she had to, but because she knew the girl would let that fact simmer below the surface of her life, a boil of discontent forever. She would always feel as if she had been trapped, even though she would likely wind up with the same life she would have had whether she had gotten pregnant or not. Connie tried to remember when she herself had realized that, but she did not think she had ever needed to realize it. She had been happy on her wedding day; as she watched the little Tudor cottage surrounded by flowers and tombstones recede through the window of the limousine, she had thought to herself, "Now my real life can begin." She suspected that Monica's real life had been the one she had led up to now, and Connie supposed it would be hard to give that up.

She thought of Gigi Romano again: Celeste had once told Connie that Gigi had no children, only poodles and a midget chauffeur who took her everywhere, moving through the dry warm Las Vegas air in an air-conditioned car. Connie did not think it was going to be easy being Monica Scanlan's child. No, she thought, from now on it will be Monica Syzmanski. She knew it was unkind, that it was true that she of all people should understand, but she couldn't help herself: she began to giggle. Joseph giggled too.

She ran one of her hands up and down the bedspread, a quilted flowered spread made out of some sort of synthetic that was supposed to look like silk. Even in the heat it was slightly cool. She knew it was not a Scanlan spread, that she was supposed to have plain chenille, but she hated chenille, felt whenever she saw the spreads in the Scanlan house that she was looking at spare rooms in a convent or a hotel.

She caressed the spread, up and down, up and down. She loved to run her hands over things, to let sand filter through her fingers or to stroke the tiny fur collar of her winter coat. She supposed that that was what she liked about the babies, too, that for a year or so she could run her hands over their bodies, pale pink as the inside of a conch shell, and feel the thrill of their real silk skins. At a certain point she began to feel bad about it, and she stopped. Perhaps it was the memory of that moment in the cemetery years ago with Celeste and her own father, when she had seen into the sexual chasm that opened up, almost overnight, between parent and child. Or perhaps, Connie thought, it was that for a time touching your babies was like touching the best part of yourself. Connie, raised in isolation amid the dead, had never learned to touch others easily, except for her husband, who wanted to feel her just the way she felt her small children, proprietary and sure in the knowledge that he was stroking an extension of himself. She liked the feel of Tommy, too, but not casually, not out of the blue, only when they were actually determined to touch, in bed at night, which happened rarely when she was pregnant and not at all now. He was sleeping on one side of the bed, and muttering when he did sleep. Feeling her belly, she sighed. The phone rang again. When she answered there was a long silence, and the sound of breathing. "Hello," Connie repeated irritably.

"Oh, I'm sorry," she heard her mother-in-law say. "Is Tom there, dear?"

"He's at work."

"Oh, dear. Has he talked to James?"

"I don't know. I just talked to Monica."

"You did?" said Mary Frances, her voice trembling. "How did she sound?"

"Haughty."

"I beg your pardon?"

"She sounded fine," Connie said, lying back on the bed. Joseph began to chew the telephone cord.

"I don't understand what's going on anymore," Mary Frances said, and to Connie she sounded pitiful.

"I know exactly what you mean," Connie said, and meant it.

"Do you? Oh, good. Oh dear . . . well, I suppose I'd better call Tommy. Is he still at the cement company, or has he started working with Mark already? I don't know; your father-in-law told me he was starting in the business, but he didn't tell me when."

There was a long silence, and finally Connie said slowly, "I don't know exactly where he is. He doesn't know anything about this."

"I know, dear. It's just a help to talk to him. He's a good boy." There was another long silence, filled by the labored breathing, and then Mary Frances said in a rush, "Of course, the boys do marry, and then what have you got? 'A son's yours till he takes a wife, but a daughter's a daughter the rest of her life.' I've heard that many times and the other day it was in Dear Abby, can you imagine, so it must be true. 'A daughter's a daughter the rest of her life.' You should remember that."

Connie felt as though she had walked in on Mary Frances naked, as though for the first time she was seeing beneath the pale bouclé coats and the hats with the little veils. She could remember John Scanlan joking about what a flibbertigibbet his wife had been when he first met her—"diarrhea of the mouth," he once had said, and both James and Connie had winced—but Connie had never known that girl, only the woman who sometimes watched her family with bright, apprehensive eyes as she passed around the cocktail franks.

Finally Mary Frances said again, "Tom was a good boy."

"He still is," Connie replied, her empathy evaporating.

"Of course, dear," Mary Frances said, her voice a little firmer, more like her old self. "I'll call him now."

When she hung up Connie put her hands back down on the spread and stroked it again, up and down. Joseph was beginning to breathe regularly; his black eyes were only slits in his chubby pink face. From below the window came the honk of a horn, then another. The baby's eyes opened slowly.

"Oh, good," Connie said to herself, jumping up and brushing her hair. "Want to go for a ride, Jojo?"

"Ride," Joseph said as she scooped him up.

"Go bye bye," said Connie.

"Bye bye," said Joseph, waving at the bed.

Joey Martinelli was sitting in the car in the driveway, and as she came out he moved over to give her the driver's seat. She put Joseph in the back, where he curled up and began to suck his thumb. "I've never been so glad to see anyone in my life," Connie said, and they drove in silence until they reached the empty parking lot of the public high school, a squat building tinted aquamarine after the misguided architectural style of public buildings of the 1950s. Connie felt that by now she knew the big rectangle of asphalt by heart. She'd done sixty miles an hour on it, stomping on the brakes just short of the grass; she'd learned to accelerate coming out of a curve and had practiced doing a K-turn over and over again. The skid marks in one corner were hers from two weeks before. Now she was working on parallel parking.

Joey got out of the car, took two sawhorses from the trunk and placed them a good distance apart at the end of the lot, just in from the grass. Getting back in, he said quietly, "I'm glad to see you, too." Connie thought his voice sounded strange, but when she looked at him his face was turned away, toward the athletic field and the stand of trees at its edge.

"Could you go and direct me, like the other times?" Connie said.

He looked at her and smiled. "Nope. Your test is next week. Today you do it yourself."

"What if I scratch your car?"

"You won't scratch my car," he said.

The only sound was the breathy snoring of the baby in the back seat. Connie pulled forward, backed up, cut the wheel, pulled in, straightened the car. Then she did it again. Each time she imagined the crunchy sound of the back wheels running over a sawhorse, like the sound a Fifth Avenue candy bar made when you bit into it. She was sure parallel parking was like algebra; she knew she would never need it, but she had to do it to pass the test. After half an hour her arms hurt. "I need a break," she said, opening her door, looking down, and seeing with pleasure that she was only six inches from the grass and that the car was perfectly parallel with the edge of the blacktop. She let her head fall back against the seat, and lifted her hair up off the sides of her face. She could feel her thighs sticking to the leatherette upholstery.

"My niece calls to say she's getting married in a hurry, which means she's pregnant," she said. "Then my mother-in-law calls and starts talking about what she's read in Dear Abby. What an afternoon." She did not add that Mary Frances had suggested that Tommy was taking a new job, a job Connie knew nothing about, a job that filled her with fear and rage. She somehow felt that discussing Tommy with Joey would be disloyal.

Joey laughed. "That doesn't sound like the Scanlan family to me," he said.

"I know. But who knows what really goes on with other people? My father-in-law, who's Superman, is in the hospital. My mother-in-law,

Emily Post, is reading Dear Abby. Tommy's brother's daughter, who has never been seen in public with a spot on her dress or her hair uncurled, turns up pregnant. And my own daughter, who seemed as if she'd stay a kid forever, has two fancy grown-up bathing suits in the bottom of her underwear drawer and goes out at night to talk to boys in those damn houses you're building."

"She does?"

"They all do."

"Ask her if she knows who's setting these fires. They burned down an entire garage last night. If there'd been a breeze, it would have taken half a block with it."

Connie sighed. "My God, what a summer. Will we live through it? I feel like all hell started to break loose as soon as you showed up."

"Hey," Joey said, "don't blame me."

"I don't blame anyone for anything. People just believe what they want. That if you're a kid, you'll stay that way forever. That if you look like a Shirley Temple doll, you're a good girl. You live in a big house, everything's fine." Connie shrugged. "You know who my husband's family thought I was going to be like? Doris Delgaudio."

Connie and Joey both began to laugh. Doris Delgaudio had lived down the block from the Martinellis. She had worn red lipstick as thick as her ankles, crystal costume jewelry, and Capri pants. When she walked, her bottom swayed from one side of the sidewalk to the other, and she made a noise like Oriental wind chimes from the sound of all the crystal knocking together.

"I swear," Connie said, gasping for air, "the Scanlans were all waiting for me to fill the house with crushed velvet and red curtains, waiting to see if I'd stamp grapes with my bare feet in the backyard. I think what bothers them as much as anything else is that I didn't turn out to be what they expected. Their son married a guinea, she ought to at least *act* like a guinea. I think it drives them crazy, that I'm not one thing or another."

"Yeah, you are," Joey said, "you're terrific."

For just a moment, before it happened, Connie could see what was coming, but in the same way she was always convinced people who were hit by a bus froze in the middle of the street, she found herself incapable of doing anything about it. She saw his face move, then his arm and his shoulder, and then he had his arm around her and he was kissing her. Her mouth opened in amazement and she could feel his teeth.

It was the oddest feeling, being kissed by someone who wasn't Tommy. She kissed him back, and her body warmed and she shifted a little in her seat so she was turned toward him. She put her hand on the back of his neck and felt the short hairs, and try as she might, all she could think, while pleasure welled within her, was: This is different from Tommy. And this. And this. He put one hand on her bare knee and she felt a throb inside her groin, and then in her stomach.

"Oh, my God," he groaned, "you are so beautiful."

She imagined this was what she had read about in *Reader's Digest*, an out-of-body experience. She felt that she was looking at herself from somewhere near the inside light of the car, and thinking: Why, it's true. I look wonderful, all white whites and black blacks. Joey ran his thumb over one of her nipples, and the her that was still inside her body felt her joints grow warm. She whimpered softly. She had forgotten all about the baby in the back seat. When he put his hand between her legs she started to slide down, her shoulders jammed between the steering wheel and the seat, and the woman watching it all, the other woman she was, thought to herself, "This is exactly the spot I was in when I got pregnant the first time." She did not know whether it was the power of that suggestion, or the prone position, or the hormones that flooded her body as her excitement rose, but she suddenly realized she was going to be sick.

She opened the door of the car with one hand over her head and lurched out somehow onto the grass. She gagged a little, and the ground beneath her felt liquid.

When she got back into the car she left her door open because of the sharp vinegar scent of her mouth. Joey was sitting with his head in his hands, and she felt so sorry for what had happened that she started to reach out to stroke his hair and then stopped in midair. She wondered what would have happened if her stomach had not betrayed—or saved—her. When he finally looked up, she could see herself again in his dark eyes; her hair was ruffled and she looked seventeen, and beautiful.

"My being sick had nothing to do with you," she said. "From what I remember about kissing, you're a good kisser." She tried to laugh but no sound came out and he kept his head down. "I always feel sick like that when I'm going to have a baby."

"You're pregnant?" he said, and when she saw how dead his eyes looked she knew that she had been careless and mean without even suspecting it. Marriage had done that to her, she thought. Marriage had made her feel so safe and inviolate that she had felt free to let some man drive her around without ever thinking about how *he* might feel. It had made her secure enough to be surly with her husband and to ridicule his family. Once she had thought being married would make her part of a group, but instead it seemed to have made her a person so complete that she could refuse to look outside her own borders. Or maybe this was how she had become whole, by doing something selfish and wrong, just for herself, just so she could see herself in the mirror for the first time in her life and say: Ah. There you are.

"I thought you knew," she said. "I'm sorry."

She supposed that was how it looked to someone from the outside when you complained about your life, when you were lonely and confused. It looked as if you were ready to leave, as if you were looking for something else. She knew that was how Monica would think of her own marriage, would think that something you were forced to do, something that you hated sometimes, could not be something you might want. But she would be wrong to think that.

In the back seat the baby started making the wet sucking noises that meant he was waking up. Connie closed the door on her side. "I need to get home," she said softly, and she smiled at him.

"You drive," he said, and he looked out the window again, his chin in his hand.

When they pulled into the driveway, Maggie was sitting on the front steps. When she saw her mother she went inside. Connie thought again about how marriage could make you feel safe enough to hurt people without even knowing it.

"I'll come and get you for the test next week," Joey said.

"I don't think so," Connie said. "I think I'll go myself."

"You can't do that. You can't drive without a licensed driver."

"I'll get Celeste," Connie said. "Or Tommy."

"I'm sorry," Joey said. "I really feel like a jerk."

"No, no, no, no, no," Connie said.

"Yeah."

Connie lifted Joseph out of the back seat. "You're not a jerk," she said. "You're a great guy. I meant what I said about being a good kisser, too. You're going to make somebody a terrific husband."

His face hardened, and for the first time that afternoon, he looked mean. "You sound like my mother," he said, and there was no humor in his voice.

"That's a good way to think of me."

"No. I meant what I said. I don't care about the other thing. About the baby."

"It's a pretty major problem," said Connie with a tight smile.

"It didn't feel like a major problem back there," Joey replied, and Connie felt that warmth again.

"I'm a married woman." Connie could hear the quaver in her voice.

"You didn't feel so married back there. Admit it, Connie; you made a mistake. You and I, we're the same kind of person."

"I'm not sure what kind of person I am," Connie said.

"You're the kind of person who should be appreciated. You're not the kind of person who should be treated like some kind of outsider."

"Maybe I'll always be some kind of an outsider," she said. "Maybe that's the kind of person I am." She turned and began to walk into the house. When she looked back over her shoulder, he was staring at her. "Thanks for teaching me to drive," she said.

"That's not enough," he said, starting the engine. He leaned out of the window.

"I'm coming back," he said.

"We forgot the sawhorses."

"I'm not coming back for any sawhorses. I'm coming back for you. I'd worry about taking you away from the Scanlans, but they never had you in the first place."

Connie looked at him levelly. "I'm a married woman," she repeated.

"*Arrivederci*, Concetta Mazza," Joey said, and he peeled out of the driveway, leaving two heavy black stripes of rubber tread behind him.

16

HE FRONT HALLWAY OF THE HOUSE HAD a faint odor, a pleasant mixture of wax, cut grass, and what Tommy supposed was the smell of emptiness, a musky smell that was a bit like the smell of the classrooms in the Catholic boys' high school he'd gone to. Everything he did echoed: closing the heavy oak door, walking across the parquet floor, placing the freshly cut key, its edges still a little sharp, on the white wooden mantel in the living room. The only thing in the house was a bottle of window cleaner on the kitchen counter, left there by the black woman who took the train up from the Bronx to clean his mother's house once a week.

The living room was long and cool even in the summer heat, with four big windows along the outside wall and the brick fireplace across from them, with small flowered tiles laid on the hearth and cabinets built in on either side. Across the hall was a dining room with wood paneling halfway up the walls. The kitchen was enormous, with room for a big table and lots of chairs. Beyond it was a screened porch, and a yard with grass so smooth and green it looked like a golf course.

Tommy had gone to Sal's for lunch and hadn't had the heart to go back to the office, where Buddy Phelan kept looking at him sideways, wondering when he was going to say that he was leaving. He'd had lunch alone at Sal's, a roast-beef sandwich and a draft beer. He liked to eat alone, although he never admitted it. It seemed an eccentric kind of thing, like something you heard murderers had liked to do before anyone found out they were murderers. But after years of sharing a table, first with his four brothers and his sister, then with his wife and children, he found it soothing to sit with the *Daily News* propped between his plate and his cup and eat his sandwich without having to talk to anyone.

Sometimes, while he had his coffee, he and Sal would talk. He thought that Sal must be lonely, living upstairs above the bar in two rooms, alone since his mother died three years before. Sal was an only child, and now an orphan. Whenever Tommy tried to think about that, it was like imagining a man from Mars. Tommy thought how quiet it must be upstairs, and how Sal must have all night to read the papers, even the box scores for teams not in New York.

That morning Sal had just looked at him. Finally he said, "Word is you're getting a promotion."

"Word is sometimes wrong," Tommy said.

"I'd miss you," Sal said, wiping the bar with his rag. "But don't cut off your nose to spite your dad, Tom."

Perhaps that was why he had driven out here. He had parked his car down the street and walked up, so that none of his brothers would see the station wagon and report back that Tommy had given in. Or perhaps it was that he thought he might discover here how he felt about everything that was going on in his life, and what that everything was. Two nights ago he had gone upstairs to bed and heard his daughter crying behind the closed door of her bedroom, a high and lonely sound, like the sound the house made when it creaked in a high wind. He had stood outside for a minute, and then gone into his own room. For an hour he had strained to hear that sound, sometimes thinking he heard it, other times that it had stopped. Then Connie slid into bed beside him, and he fell asleep.

"Connie," he said aloud, as he went upstairs in this big house, and the word came bouncing back from the clean white walls.

Upstairs there were six bedrooms and four bathrooms. The bathroom off the biggest bedroom had a glass shower stall and a dressing room with big red roses climbing up the papered walls. In the ceiling of the dressing room there was a pull-down door and steps to the attic. As Tommy hoisted himself up he heard tiny footsteps, like fingers drumming on a tabletop, and he thought to himself, "We need an exterminator." He wondered if that thought meant that he was going to live here. For a moment he looked down below him, at the luminous oak beneath his feet, at the edge of one florid rose where the wall met the molding. He wondered if he was looking at the rest of his life.

The attic was surprisingly clean, and empty except for a big trunk, wood banded with metal. He lifted the lid slowly, afraid he'd hear the little feet again. The trunk was full. On top was a manila envelope, and beneath it a welter of lace and satin the color of tea. He could tell it was a wedding dress without even lifting it. Some dried flowers lay to one side.

He slid the contents of the envelope out and sat crosslegged on the unfinished pine floor. There was an old wedding picture, the bride wearing the sort of shapeless veil and straight, midcalf-length dress his own mother wore in her wedding pictures. There was a marriage certificate—Jean Flaherty to Harold Ryan, April 8, 1924, in Most Blessed Sacrament Church, Brooklyn, N.Y. There was a faded white ribbon, a scrap of material, and a postcard from Niagara Falls. Tommy could feel something small and hard in the bottom of the envelope. He shook it and into his palm fell a tiny tooth.

The attic seemed to have been cleaned, and the trunk stood in the center of the floor as though it had been abandoned. Did people think so little of the past? Tommy thought again of eating at Sal's, of a lunch he'd had the week before. A shaft of sunlight had been shooting through the cheap stained-glass fleur-de-lis in Sal's front window, so that bars of red and green and blue fell right across the plate placed in front of the third stool in from the end. Some of the men said that it was enough to give you indigestion, this big spot of color atop your corned beef and slaw, but Tommy liked it. He supposed it reminded him of church, perhaps of serving Mass when he was an altar boy, when he had felt solemn and important as he poured the water from the cruet over the priest's consecrated fingers—his father's cruets, his father's chalice. As he had taken the seat, he thought of what a creature of habit he was, and it made him afraid.

"Penny for your thoughts," Sal had said, and Tommy had found, to his great amazement and shame, that at the words tears welled in his eyes. It was dim in the bar at all hours of the day, and he hoped that Sal could not see.

"Your dad worse?" Sal asked, putting the cream in front of him, making Tommy suspect that the light was better than he thought.

"Ah, who knows," Tommy said, playing with his teaspoon. "The doctors never tell you anything. I don't think they know anything. Half the time he's full of piss and vinegar and the other half he's talking like a baby."

Sal wiped the bar and emptied an ashtray.

"My brother's daughter is getting married," Tom went on, "my niece, very pretty girl, very smart, all the best things. And suddenly my mother calls and says Monica's getting married, three weeks' notice, with her grandfather in the hospital. I understand these things, it happens every day, but jeez, I don't know, maybe it's better that my father can't come. She's marrying a Polish boy, my brother says he's a nice enough boy, but my father thinks that anybody who's not Irish should get out of town, you know?"

Sal nodded. He'd heard about Mr. Scanlan from the Italian guys who worked for First Concrete.

"I guess I figured these things didn't happen anymore, that girls were smarter, that guys were smarter. My brother was figuring on her finishing college, becoming a nurse or something. Now the boy will have to leave school, get a job." It flashed through Tommy's mind that the job would probably wind up being at Scanlan & Co., and that the news of the Polish grandson-in-law was going to be even more horrible for his father than he had at first imagined.

"Remember after the war," Tommy said, "how everybody talked about how tough the changes were going to be? I didn't fight, I was just a little kid, but I can remember everyone saying there would be changes, and there were changes, but they were all good. The wives stopped worrying, everybody bought houses, had a couple of kids, they were damn glad to be home. Now there's no war but there's changes, and they're all bad. You go to Mass, the kids are fooling around, no hats, they're changing the prayers, they're changing the music, the rules. I go downtown the other day for a meeting, and there's two young girls crossing Broadway in front of me, they're wearing dresses as long as one of my shirts. No stockings. No underwear, for all I know." He didn't say that one of the girls was Helen Malone, that he had leaned forward and peered through the windshield incredulously, that when a stray summer breeze had lifted the corner of her short Indian sack dress he had begun to feel very warm indeed and had looked down to see the fabric at his crotch straining visibly, until a car behind him had honked to let him know the light was green. It reminded him of the new bookkeeper in his office, the one with the bleached hair flipped up on her shoulders and the little-girl dresses with the collars and cuffs and the low waists, the one who always rubbed up against him when she passed behind his desk.

Sal reached beneath the bar and brought out the coffee pot. He poured a cup for himself, and a second cup for Tommy.

"You know my sister who's in the convent? I don't know what's going on with her, either. She's reading *Jane Eyre*. A nun! It's a book my daughter read in school. I never read it—I had to read *Moby Dick*—so I asked my daughter what it's about. Some woman is a governess and winds up marrying the man of the house. My sister the nun is reading this? The other day she went to buy a bathing suit. A bathing suit! My sister told me I was behind the times. Maybe that's it. I'm behind the times. I'm still back in the good times."

The two men stared at each other. "Jesus Christ," Tommy whispered, as though he was witnessing a miracle, "that's the voice of John Scanlan, coming right out of my mouth."

"It always has, Tom," Sal said with a smile. "You just never noticed it before. I think that's what parents are for. You need to learn to talk. They give you the voice." In the silence Tommy could hear the television, could hear some woman on one of the soaps say stridently, "Doctor, will I ever be a whole person again?"

"I don't know, Tom," Sal added, pouring himself another cup of coffee. "Nothing ever changes much around here. My mother died. I put the pinball by the door. I got a new TV. On St. Patrick's Day I have corned beef and cabbage on the menu and put food coloring in the beer. Girls get knocked up, old men die. Excuse me, nothing personal. I don't know about nuns. Your sister can't stop being a nun, can she?"

"Who knows anymore?"

"No, forget it, I don't think you can stop being a nun without a whole lot of rigamarole from the pope. But your father—I don't know. It sounds like he's pretty bad."

Tommy looked into his coffee cup again. The sun was moving and he had to move his cup to make it change colors. He wanted to tell Sal that his father was not the trouble. In some strange way he liked talking like his father, thinking like his father. When he thought about running the company with Mark, all he could think of was reining his brother in, telling him to watch it with the crazy ideas. As he watched his father's life ebb, day after day, he began to feel as if his father was flowing into him.

Now he sat on the attic floor and all he could think of was changes, how he hated them, how he wanted them to stop, how he sounded like the old man wasting away in his hospital bed. He looked at the wedding picture in his hand and wondered whether the people in that picture had intentionally left it in the dust, whether they had soured on their old dreams or simply had new ones. Tommy felt his own old dreams slipping away, but he was not sure what the new ones would be. He only knew that they would revolve around his wife. He walked to the edge of the ladder and looked down. He could see his wife in that dressing room, black and white and beautiful amid the roses, in her black bra and black half slip, fixing her hair in front of a mirror that would hang on the one wall.

This house felt too grand for him, like the house of an adult, not the house of an overgrown boy, but he knew she would seem at home here, small and elegant in the large, well-proportioned rooms. He remembered leaving Sal's the other day, driving aimlessly, his eyes clouded by tears, through the Bronx to Westchester, where he was to see about giving an estimate for the foundation for a new wing of the high school. As he turned into the entrance, a sedan had almost sideswiped him, driving too close to the center of the road, and he had yelled "Jesus Christ" and raised his middle finger to the driver before he saw that it was Connie, hunched over the wheel, her lower lip tight between her teeth, with that Martinelli guy in the seat beside her. He had pulled the car over in the parking lot, next to some sawhorses, and rested his head on the wheel until the sick feeling in his stomach had passed.

For hours after that he had driven around, listening to Sinatra on the radio. The day had faded quietly into night, the way it did on these hot August days, and the back of his shirt was drenched with perspiration, but still he drove around, until finally he took a right-hand turn and found himself in the parking lot of the hospital.

"Good evening, Mr. Scanlan," the youngest of the nurses said when he approached his father's room. Dorothy O'Haire was sitting in a plastic chair outside, working on some dun-colored piece of knitting. Seeing her there, Tommy assumed that his father was up and around, raising hell, but when he sat down by the bed he could tell that the old man was in a deep sleep; his eyes were still beneath the blue-veined lids, and his breathing seemed to stop between each inhalation, so that Tommy thought each breath was the last. On the bedside table there was an envelope with "Ryan house" written on it in the old man's florid handwriting, the pride of the nuns at St. Aloysius School; it had been there for weeks, and for the first time Tommy picked it up. As though the gesture had reached deep inside his failing consciousness, John Scanlan's eyes opened slowly, and he stared at his son.

"Something important," he said dully.

"I know," Tommy said.

"You do it for your mother," the old man said, breathing hard on each word.

"Yes."

"Move."

"We'll talk about it when you're a little bit better, Pop," Tommy said, holding the envelope.

John Scanlan shook his head and fell deeper into the pillows.

"No," he said. And then his eyes closed and the slow, measured cadence of his breathing began again.

Tommy had ripped open the envelope and slid the key, shiny as a new penny, into his palm. The one his father had tossed into Connie's lap, that Sunday that now seemed so long ago, had lain on their dresser, untouched, all this time. The freshly cut end of this other one had left a scratch just below Tommy's thumb. He had put it into his pocket, among the small change, and had left it there until this afternoon, when he used it to unlock the door.

Now, coming downstairs, the manila envelope from the trunk under his arm, he took the key from the mantel in the living room and held it again in his palm. Then he took out his key ring and slid it next to the keys to the car, the keys to his house in Kenwood, and the keys to his office. He expected to hear those tiny feet again, but there was only silence, and then the echo of his footsteps as he let himself out and locked the door behind him.

17

HE BRIDAL SALON WAS NOT EXACTLY what Maggie had expected. She had never really thought about getting married, although they had all discussed it enough at school. "If you could marry Paul or John, or any of the boys in class, which would it be?" JoAnne Jessup would suddenly ask her and Debbie at lunch. But that was just fooling around, and actually being married was not, at least as far as Maggie could see. Actually being married seemed so crowded with unspoken rules and odd secrets and unfathomable responsibilities that it had no more occurred to her to imagine being married herself than it had to imagine driving a motorcycle or having a job. She had, however, thought about being a bride, which had more to do with being the center of attention and looking inexplicably, temporarily beautiful than it did with sharing a double bed with someone with hairy legs and a drawer full of boxer shorts. Once she had tried on her mother's veil in the bathroom, a Juliet cap pocked with pearls, its long tail of net beige and tattered. She had locked the door, and placed the little dome on her head, then stood back to survey the effect. But she could not grasp the magic. Perhaps it required the entire outfit. She could not grasp it in the salon either, although she got glimpses of what she was searching for every now and then, in the racks of white dresses, misty as ghosts, hanging along one wall in plastic bags, or in the scratchy sound of one of them being carried across the floor in a saleswoman's arms. Monica had already gotten her dress, and they were there for the bridesmaids—Maggie, two friends of Monica's from Sacred Heart, and the groom's sister, who was unfortunately, as Aunt Cass had confided after Mass on Sunday, "quite large." Neither the fat sister nor Maggie wanted to take off their clothes in front of the others.

Monica sat slouched in a chair in a pale-blue blouse and skirt, her hair in a ponytail, acquiescing to her mother's wishes. If the bridal salon was not quite what Maggie had expected, Monica was not acting a bit like her idea of a bride. She seemed bored and anxious to get on with it.

"What about pink?" Aunt Cass said, and Monica replied, "Fine" in a tone that suggested the answer to What about yellow? Or green? Or blue? would have been "fine" too. The saleswoman brought out pinks of all shades and styles, and finally it was decided that the dresses would be high-waisted, like Monica's, and made from some fabric Maggie had never heard of before called silk shantung. There were little pillbox hats with veils, and the dresses were rather plain, so that the bridesmaids looked very sophisticated, except for the fat sister, who looked enormous.

"Now for the little one," said the saleswoman, a tiny woman dressed all in black, perhaps to better point up the colors of her wares. She spoke with a faint accent and had a bodice dotted with safety pins and needles trailing white and pastel wisps of thread. Maggie realized that the saleswoman was referring to her, and she followed the woman into the dressing room. But she saw at once that the dress there was different, puffed sleeves instead of cap, a big bow at the high waist in the back, even a different hat, like the straw sailors she had always had for Easter, except that it was pink, with a pink ribbon and a gauzy brim.

"Off with the clothes," the saleswoman said brightly, and Maggie turned her back, crimson. She was wearing her slip, the closest thing she had to a bra. She had stuffed the nylon skirt into her shorts, so that she had had lumpy legs all morning. The saleslady clicked her tongue. "You will need foundation garments with this," she said, unzipping the dress. "For the hose. And to give the line to it." But the dress, when it was on, had no line. It fell straight down Maggie's angular body. A carpenter's dream, she thought. Her hair hung in big hanks where her breasts should be.

"It needs *something*," said Aunt Cass, who had slipped in between the dressing-room curtains.

The saleswoman shrugged. "She is a little girl," she said, although Maggie was taller than she was. "It is not the same here"—she grabbed a handful of the bodice—"or here," lifting the skirt and dropping it with another shrug.

"What if we put her hair up?"

"Not with the hat. The hair, besides, is very fashionable today, for the young girls. But it has no style. Perhaps a little lipstick, some rouge." A picture flashed through Maggie's mind of herself on Halloween, when her mother wedged her on the vanity bench in the bathroom and expertly, seriously, her tongue snagged between her lips in concentration, made Maggie's face up. She was good at it, and Maggie always thought she looked wonderful, her lips fuller, deep red, her cheeks flushed with the powdered rouge, her lashes spiky with the mascara, coaxed from its red plastic case with a little brush and some drops of water. But she did not look the way the older girls did, their lips disappearing into their faces in their coats of white-pink lipstick, their cheeks pale, luminous as the moon.

Aunt Cass looked at Maggie in the mirror. Maggie looked back. Her face was hot. "You look fine, honey," her aunt said. She moved the curtains aside and the older girls crowded in. "You look so cute," one of them said, a buxom blonde whose chest had peeked out of the neckline of the dress she had tried on. "God, you're so thin," the fat sister said.

Monica stayed in the chair, playing with a piece of her honey-colored hair, wrapping it around one long finger. Her engagement ring glittered. Her mother moved aside so that Monica could see Maggie, and for the first time that day Monica smiled. "It's you,"

Monica said, narrowing her eyes. "It's really you." Maggie's eyes dropped until she could no longer see Monica's reflection in the mirror, except for one long tanned leg swinging back and forth restlessly over the silken upholstery of the green-and-pink striped chair. Then, with a great effort, she looked up again and stared her cousin straight in the eye. The smile was still there. "I think it's fine," Maggie said, determined to be agreeable. "Besides, no one will care what I'm wearing. Everybody will be staring at Monica. Everyone will be interested in her dress. No one will be able to take their eyes off her."

"It is the bride's day, certainly," said the saleswoman brightly, lifting the hat from Maggie's hair.

Monica rose from the chair and came over to the mirror, and Maggie noticed that she seemed a little clumsy. She looked Maggie up and down and then she went back to her purse and Maggie heard a scraping sound. Her cousin came up behind her, a smile on her face, and held up a lighted match.

"There is no smoking in the salon, miss," said the saleswoman primly.

"Tell my cousin," said Monica as she stared at Maggie in the mirror. Then she blew out the match.

"So I say to my soon-to-be-father-in-law, the New York City police officer," Monica began, circling Maggie, still holding the stub of the match, "I say, Sergeant, what if you had a lovely young girl who had never been in any trouble before and suddenly she joins a band of arsonists. Arsonists! And this is what he says."

One of the bridesmaids giggled nervously. "Monica, you are strange," she said.

"Shut up, Cheryl," Monica said pleasantly. Then she continued, "He says, Monica, my dear, if the local authorities were given such information, the girl in question would go to the local juvenile detention center. In other words, reform school. And I said, my, my, my. If I had such information, should I divulge it? And my soon-to-be-father-in-law said, it is your duty as a citizen. Well, you can imagine how upset I was. I hate to tell tales on people. I think anyone who tells tales on people is a rat." Monica caught Maggie's eyes in the mirror. "Especially about something important. Something that could ruin their whole life."

Maggie had wheeled around, but the saleswoman was kneeling at her feet, pinning the hem of the dress, and she was caught halfway between the mirror and her cousin. She finally managed to turn completely. With a smile, Monica held out the match.

"What is it like to be like you?" Maggie said, staring into her cousin's amber eyes, looking for something inside them.

"Don't play with fire," Monica said.

"I mean it. How can you stand yourself?"

"Maggie," said Aunt Cass, her voice trembling.

"Liar, liar, your pants are on fire," said Monica in an even voice. "Just a warning, Maria Goretti. Anything you can do I can do better. You may think it's Monica, zero, Maggie, one. But you're wrong. We're even now."

"That's not how I am," Maggie said.

"Oh," Monica said in a squeaky little voice. "That's not how I am. I'm a good girl."

"You are a witch, Monica," Maggie said.

"Now, Maggie," said Aunt Cass.

"My, my, my," Monica repeated, her smile tight.

"And you don't fool me one bit," Maggie added.

"I don't fool you," said Monica, and though her voice was low it somehow felt as if she was screaming. "I don't fool you. God! With your family? With your birthday six months after your parents' anniversary? Don't talk to me about fooling. Don't talk to me, Maria Goretti. All I have to do is open my mouth and you'll be in so much trouble you'll never know what happened. Good little Maggie Scanlan. God, if they only knew. You're worse than everyone else because you pretend to be so good."

"Monica, this will stop," Aunt Cass said.

"Can I believe my ears?" said Monica shrilly. "We're defending Maggie? How many times have I heard you talk about how her mother is not our sort, dear? How many times have I heard my father complain that she sucks up to Grandpop so she'll get more of the money? God,

Mother, one night when you were drunk you even called her a wop. Why are we standing up for her now?"

"Monica, you are not yourself," said Aunt Cass, her face crimson, her voice shaking.

"Oh, cut the Mary Frances routine," Monica said, falling back into the chair. "This is myself. This is it. This is me, the real me." She pointed a narrow foot at Maggie. "Who knows who she really is." Maggie looked down at her fingers holding the charred piece of cardboard as though they were strange to her. She threw the match on the floor. "You'd better learn the facts of life before it's too late, Maria Goretti," said Monica. "Or you'll wind up like your mother."

"I'd rather wind up like my mother than wind up like you," Maggie said.

"Same difference," said Monica.

"No," said Maggie.

"May we finish fitting the dress now, ladies?" the saleswoman said.

"I don't think I'm going to need the dress," Maggie said.

"You'll probably be in jail," said Monica.

"No, no, absolutely not, I will not allow this," said Aunt Cass, who seemed close to tears. "You must be in the wedding. It will seem strange to everyone if you're not."

"It will seem strange to me if I am," Maggie said.

"Maggie, please. I cannot cope if you make trouble."

Maggie turned back to the mirror. Her face was white and her eyes were glowing. The salon was completely silent, and in the silence she could hear herself breathing. "What do you think you'll be doing in twenty years, Monica?" Maggie said in a low voice, and she could tell by the look on her cousin's face that the question was first unexpected, then unpleasant.

"I haven't the faintest idea," Monica said.

"I do," said Maggie.

"You can tell the future now, Maria Goretti?"

"I can tell yours."

"Now let us take the dress off," said the saleswoman, and she drew the curtains and left Maggie alone again.

18

T WAS BECAUSE OF THE PARKING LOT that Connie almost turned back, not because of the hospital. She still found parallel parking a problem. She had driven right past her aunt Rose's house one afternoon because her uncle Frank's car was in the pitched driveway and she would have had to parallel park at the curb. The hospital lot had head-in spaces: she had tried them at shopping centers twice and found that if she cleared the car on the right, she wound up with her front bumper heading straight at the side of the car on the left, and if she started successfully toward the back of the space, she was sure to see that one side of the car was in danger of being pleated by the back bumper of another. Before Connie had known how to drive she had thought it was a silly adolescent thing, much overrated. She realized now that she had made herself think that about all the things she could not do, like swimming and riding a bicycle, and that there were difficult and elaborate skills the rest of the world had that she lacked. In a way the knowledge had been soothing; the thought of some essential inferiority made her feel more at home with others than her belief in her superiority had.

She had found herself frantic as she drove to the hospital, and she had thought at first that it was because this was only her second time out alone. But then she realized it was about Joey, about what had happened in the parking lot. Staring at her bedroom ceiling the night before, she had replayed it all in her head and felt herself flush all over again, flush and burn. And for the first time she had admitted to herself that the baby within her had saved her from committing adultery. She would have done it, in daylight, with Joseph in the back seat, if some combination of hormones and nerves had not forced nausea to triumph over lust.

She had hung around the kitchen all morning, finding odd jobs for herself, and it was not until she jumped at the sound of a truck door slamming that she realized she had been waiting for a visitor, waiting for the visit that would ruin her life.

She had gotten into Tommy's car, then; he had left it in the driveway while he went off with one of the cement-truck drivers, but somehow she saw the fact that it was there as an omen, a sign, and an opportunity to save herself. She did not know why she was here, at the hospital, except that in some odd way she equated her fall from grace with John Scanlan. Just for a moment, on the way there, she had wondered if her father-in-law had planned this, had somehow arranged for Joey Martinelli to be the foreman at the project for this very reason. "I'm off my trolley," she muttered to herself in the quiet of the car.

She found a space all the way at the back of the lot, where there were no other cars, and pulled in, straddling one of the painted white dividing lines. She walked toward the building, its big brick smokestack sending a plume of gray-black up toward the sky. In her straw bag was the *Daily News*, and an airline bottle of Four Roses she had found in the back of the liquor cabinet.

Her heart was throbbing so violently as she crossed the parking lot that she wondered if, beneath her blouse, it looked like a painting of the Sacred Heart, a red oval, fiery like a bull's-eye on her body. All night she had rehearsed what she would say, how she would try to persuade John Scanlan to give up the idea of moving them into that new house, how she would try to talk him out of forcing Tommy into Scanlan & Co. Tommy hadn't told her a thing, but she had known what was happening when she saw the new key on his key ring, and heard from Joey that the word was out that the old man was selling

First Concrete. She had thought at first that she would try to talk to Tommy, but then she had realized that it was useless to discuss the matter with anyone but John Scanlan himself. When she recognized this, she knew some part of her life was over, that she had grown up, and that it was not the liberation she had always thought it would be, but an acceptance of her own powerlessness.

She was relieved, at the visitor's desk, to find that no one else had a pass to be in John Scanlan's room. No one would demand an explanation of why she was stopping by for the first time in her father-in-law's month-long illness, and how she had arrived at the hospital. Standing in the doorway of the room, listening to John Scanlan snore hoarsely, she knew that her carefully rehearsed speech had been a waste of time. Looking across at his beaky profile, the hair slipping over his high forehead, she felt a frisson of fear and dislike, but she knew that he would never again be the power that ruled all their lives. His chest was too sunken, his breathing too tenuous. With a kind of sympathy she looked at the tubes running to and from the bed and realized that he was catheterized, and thought what a humiliating thing that was for a man.

When she stepped to the side of the bed she saw that someone else was there, too, asleep in a chair. It was John's secretary, Dorothy. Connie had only met her once, at a horrid party for John's sixtieth birthday, but she recognized her because something about her stolid face and figure had reminded Connie of her aunt Rose. Tommy had told her that Dorothy was helping out, although the table her father-in-law had been using as a desk was empty now except for a stack of blank Scanlan & Co. stationery.

"Dorothy," Connie whispered, touching her arm lightly.

The other woman slowly raised her head and looked at the bed, then up at Connie. Half asleep, she stared, and then her eyes widened with panic.

"It's okay," Connie said. "You must have fallen asleep. It's kind of stuffy in here."

"We were working," said Dorothy, her fingers, with their big knuckles, twisting round one another like a tangled ball of yarn.

Connie looked down at John Scanlan. It was clear that he was barely capable of consciousness, much less work. She tried to search Dorothy's face for some sign of guilt or fear, but the woman was staring at her hands in her lap. All Connie could see were the big tortoiseshell pins that held Dorothy's hair in an old-fashioned roll at the base of her neck.

"That was nice of you," Connie said.

"I have to go," Dorothy said. "I have to pick up my daughter." Her hands twisted again. "You have a daughter, too," she added.

"Yes."

"Mr. Scanlan likes her. Your daughter, I mean."

"I know."

Dorothy rose heavily. She wore a cameo at the throat of her white cotton blouse. Connie thought she looked out of time, like a visitor from the last century. Her eyes were red. She picked up her purse from the floor, and a paperback book. At the door she turned and looked at John Scanlan.

"He's dying," she said.

"Yes," said Connie.

"I'm glad," said Dorothy, and for just a moment there was a blaze of savagery in her eyes and an acrimony in her voice that made her seem half mad. Then she turned and left.

"Jesus Christ," whispered Connie, sitting down, repelled by the warmth still lingering from Dorothy's body. "What did he do to *her*? How many others are there? Jesus Christ, what a life this man has led." For a long time she sat there and watched him sleep. Twice a nurse came in, glanced briefly at the blue cardboard visitor's pass and at the patient, then left again. The level in the IV ebbed slowly. Connie read the *Daily News*. She left the little bottle of Four Roses in the top drawer of the bedside table. The light outside deepened slightly, from a white to a pale, pale yellow. Finally Connie came to accept that if the key to a prison were on her husband's key ring, he had put it there himself.

She had nearly made up her mind to leave when John Scanlan turned his head on the pillow and opened his eyes. The deep blue was masked by a rheumy film, like the shadow a dog's eyes develop when old age has set in. For the first time that she could remember Connie looked him in the face, eye to eye, and did not flinch, did not look away.

He stretched out his big hand, soft and dry as a snake's skin. The veins on the back were enormous, and by some trick of the light or because of his illness, they seemed to be throbbing.

"Franny," he said hoarsely, reaching for her.

Connie drew back, but he pulled her arm closer and threaded his fingers through hers, engulfing her palm in his own. "Don't be angry, sweetheart," he said, almost as though he was talking to himself. "You're prettier when you smile." And he grinned, a kind of rictus now that his face had been pared down to bone and sinew. Connie thought she had never heard his brogue so thick, even when he was telling stories at parties and had had too much to drink. His grip made the stone on her engagement ring cut into her finger.

For a long time he said nothing, just stared and breathed heavily, as though he had been running. "The children are in bed," he said once. "Good riddance." A few minutes later he winked at her, and said "You're my girl." Connie was pink with embarrassment, although she knew that it was not her he was seeing; she was afraid, too, afraid that he would somehow suddenly snap out of it and be enraged at so revealing himself, be enraged at being duped, even if he had done the duping himself. His lids drooped and he began to breathe more evenly; then they snapped up, like shades that had been pulled at the bottom, and he began to talk as though there was not enough time to get out all the words.

"I'm sorry you lost the baby, Franny," he said groggily, his voice catching on every consonant. "It was the blood that did it. The doctor said it happens sometimes, but there was no blood with the boys. She was a beautiful little thing, but the doctor said 'She won't live, Mr. Scanlan,' and you wanting a daughter so bad, after the three sons, wanting someone you could put in little dresses with the ribbons and things." He fell silent but his breathing was loud. "I remember when you said 'I'm not having any more to break my heart. You have all your boys.' And you didn't want to let me come near, but that kind of thing can't be allowed to last." Connie could hear the sounds of the hospital out in the corridor, the rattling of the gurneys, the footsteps of the nurses. Finally he added, "You can't deny your husband, Franny. That's God's law."

He turned his head away from her and breathed so heavily that Connie was terrified and thought for a moment she should call the nurse. It was a horrible noise, and she wanted it to stop, but she was afraid that if it did he would begin to speak again. She did not want to hear any more.

Finally he turned his head back to her, and Connie saw that the tears were running down his face. He looked at their two hands, linked at the edge of the mattress, and then he looked up, and his face was contorted with grief, his lower lip shaking as though he had palsy, the tears dripping off his chin onto his pajamas, darkening the thin cotton. He pressed the back of her hand to his lips, and Connie recoiled, but he pulled her toward him again, with all the strength of a young man. Connie thought his tears must clear away his blindness and he would see her for who she was, but when he looked up again he only whispered "Please," and she felt the kind of sympathy for him that she always felt for her husband, the sort you feel for a small child, although she never felt it for her own children.

"It's all right, John," she said softly, pressing his fingers. "Everything is all right."

"Say you forgive me," he said.

"I forgive you."

He turned his head away and looked at the ceiling. Then his eyes closed. He dropped her hand, and the snoring began again.

She sat there for a while, and then picked up her purse and left. It was cooler out in the parking lot, and the sky seemed a deeper blue. She knew it must be past dinnertime. She wished she had taken the bottle of whiskey with her; she thought she could use a drink. Driving home, hunched slightly over the wheel, she knew she had learned one thing that afternoon: she would never be alone with Joey Martinelli again. She thought of the old man lying in the bed, of all the business deals and the machinations, and of him saying, last of all, "Say you forgive me." She didn't want to need forgiveness at the end.

That night when her husband came home from the hospital he told her that his father had fallen into a coma and that the doctors did not expect him to come out of it again. "My mother's all upset," said Tommy, sitting at the red Formica table in the kitchen, sipping his beer and staring into space, "because she says the last words he ever said to her were 'This is the toughest goddamn roast beef I've ever tasted in my life' when she brought him a sandwich for lunch yesterday."

"It would be in character," Connie said, knowing that if she did not tell him now she could never tell him, yet knowing that for some reason she could not tell him now. She looked into his face, trying to find the man she thought, so many years ago, would save her. And she realized, without regret, that it had been the other way around, and that she would have to live with that responsibility, even embrace it, for the rest of her life. She realized that for years she had wanted to sit by John Scanlan's side and say "To hell with you." But she had moved beyond the desires of that woman now. She had become a person who could sit there, hand in hand with that awful man, and forgive him his trespasses, whatever they might be. And if her husband knew that, he would know something that would ruin his life even more decisively than his father had tried to do. He would know that his wife was stronger than he was.

"She thought he was going to get better," Tommy said sadly. "She thought he would be all right."

19

N ONE CORNER OF THE BLACK, A TINY zigzag of lightning leapt like a tic in the eye of the sky. Maggie could see it from her bedroom window, just beyond the sweep of gingham below the curtain rod. She was alone in the house. The lights were out. A thunderstorm was coming. Maggie's mouth was dry and full of an awful taste.

The adults were gone again. Maggie often came home in the late afternoons from riding her bicycle aimlessly on the back roads and found the house empty and airless, like a house in a horror movie after The Thing has passed through town and gone. She would go up to her room and soon would hear the idling of a car in the driveway, like dogs growling, and then the heavy sound of the car door and the lighter one of the storm door downstairs. Then the sounds of pots and pans from below, the preparation of dinner.

It seemed to her that all the adults were acting more like children than they had before. The bickering on Sundays, usually the purview of Maggie and Monica and a handful of the younger cousins, was now between Tommy and James, or Margaret and Mark. Mary Frances wept. Old patterns and alliances had surfaced and reasserted themselves, so that her grandmother was dependent upon Margaret, meek with James, and clinging and loving with Tommy. For some reason Mary Frances had decided to reupholster her entire living room in blue damask, and half the furniture was missing. The grandchildren sat on the floor, their patent-leather pumps and saddle shoes making spots of light on the carpet. The atmosphere made them silent and watchful. Monica especially was quiet. She sat at the mahogany dining-room table and read *Life* magazine, her face as white and shiny as the surface of the pages. "God, I wish he'd die and get it over with," she had said last Sunday, fanning herself with a magazine, her honey-colored hair waving wet on her temples. Then she had disappeared into the bathroom, the water running from behind the closed door. Maggie suspected that Monica was crying in there, and this, more than anything else, made her feel everything was off-center. The two of them had not spoken since their encounter at the bridal salon. Maggie was surprised to find herself feeling sorry for the bride, so drawn, so hard-eyed, so brittle in her descriptions of tea sets and china patterns, so joyless two weeks before what Maggie had always thought was supposed to be the happiest day of your life.

The development was quiet. Some of the kids had given up on it, bored and put off by the finished quality of the model houses. Others were worried about trouble. The fires had been in the local newspaper, and the mothers had started to sniff their children's shirts for the scent of smoke. The construction company had hired guards to patrol three times a night; on their first trip out they had picked up some ninth graders in the basement of a split-level house and brought them home while the neighbors watched from beneath their hall lights. A coffee-colored mongrel that had wandered into one of the model homes and become stuck in a crawl space, howling like a mourner at an Irish wake, had been taken to the pound by one of the guards and put to sleep before his owners had figured out where he was. The younger kids swore that his shaggy ghost haunted the house in the middle of the night, howling from below the kitchen linoleum. From Maggie's bedroom window she could see the guards in their tan uniforms, pale shadows with flashlight beams moving at an angle ahead of them. They passed through at nine and again at eleven and, she supposed, at some later time, too, when she was already asleep. In between they checked the doors and windows of the A & P in the next town, the two churches in Kenwood, and the Kenwoodie Club to make sure that no one had scaled the fence to go skinny dipping.

She had spent the day at her grandfather's cemetery, but she and Angelo hardly spoke now. More and more, Damien helped him out with his gardening, and Maggie had lost the knack for being happy there. Until this horrible sweaty season, lines had been drawn, in her house, her neighborhood, her relationships. Some of them were boundaries—good and bad, us and them—and some of them were lines that connected people—mother and father, friend to friend. They had all been rubbed out as surely as if they had been written in chalk, not stone, and Maggie knew she could not live without them. Sometimes she sat for hours with her back against the rough bark of a tree, blowing on a blade of grass between her fingers, wondering what would happen next. Often she cried.

When she got home, she had walked out to the development. She knew Debbie would be there. She had gone to the Malone house the day before because Mrs. Malone had invited her. Charles Malone had been in a bassinet in the kitchen, sucking loudly on the neckband of his T-shirt, little beads of prickly-heat ranged like a necklace around the crease in his fat neck. "That baby is more like a potato than a human being," Mrs. Malone had said, not at all regretfully, as she chopped onions at the kitchen counter. "He just lies there all day sucking on whatever he can get into his mouth. He'll want a beer by the time he's three."

"Aren't most babies like that?" said Maggie, who was sitting at the table while Debbie was upstairs getting dressed. Her long wet hair was dripping onto the seat of her shorts, and even though Mrs. Malone was all the way across the room, Maggie's eyes were tearing from the onions.

"Lord, no," Mrs. Malone said, dabbing at her face with a paper towel. "That Aggie didn't settle down until she was two. Crying all the time unless you carried her around the room on your shoulder. Lifting those little legs and passing gas so loud you could hear her all through the house. It was all I could do not to pitch her out the window." She lifted a corner of her apron and wiped her eyes. "Damn," she said. The baby lost his piece of T-shirt, let out a momentary yell, and had found his middle fingers by the time Maggie got to the bassinet. He had a funny egg-shaped head, like a cartoon character.

The entire house was in a tizzy because Helen was coming home for dinner. It was difficult to imagine what a difference six weeks could make. Helen had become a visiting dignitary from another world, Monica had become engaged and Maggie's mother had become a wraith who evaporated and reappeared without warning in her own home. Mrs. Malone, whose idea of a balanced meal was tuna on toast with a slice of tomato, had planned scalloped potatoes and Salisbury steak for the occasion, bending over cookbooks that had been shower gifts many years ago, their bindings still cracking when they were opened because they had so rarely been used.

Debbie found it all incredibly annoying: her mother dressed in fresh Bermudas and a pressed shirt, her father home early, a cloth on the dining-room table, which was usually reserved for family holidays, and Maggie invited without her permission and against her will. She had wanted to have Bridget Hearn there, too, but Mrs. Malone had said no. "She's not family," she had said in front of Maggie, who had flushed when Debbie said, with an abrupt gesture, "Neither is she." Debbie had gone upstairs to change without asking Maggie to go along, but Maggie had followed anyhow, listening as Debbie railed to herself as she dressed. "Does she think my sister is going to think she turned into a good cook in one month? Does she think my sister will all of a sudden think we eat in the dining room every night?" Maggie suspected that Debbie kept referring to Helen as her sister in an attempt to cut her down to size, but it was all in vain.

Aggie and Debbie had gone downtown with a friend of Helen's from Sacred Heart to see Helen in the revue. While Debbie had said it was "okay," Aggie had been more specific. "She had on this thing like a leotard, you know?" she said, leaning forward, her eyes bright in the beam of a flashlight they had turned on on the floor of the development house. "It was white and it had her heart painted on it like it was bleeding, with drops running down her stomach. And she sang this great song called 'Loving One Another.' And this guy behind us with a beard? He said to this other guy who was with him, 'That's the one I told you about.' And the other guy said, 'You weren't kidding.' " She looked really beautiful. It was really quiet when she sang."

"You could see through her costume," Debbie said.

"You could, a little bit," Aggie said. "Like you can see through my white suit right after I go in the pool? But I think people thought it was just shadows."

"Sure," said Debbie, snorting.

Debbie snorted now as she stood in the doorway of the kitchen. "An apron?" she said. "Oh, hush," Mrs. Malone said, trying to get the smell of onions off her hands.

"You use a lemon," Maggie said. "You rub it on your hands and then rinse them off with cold water."

Mrs. Malone looked over her shoulder in surprise. "Forty years old last month and I've never heard that," she said. "Does it work?"

"My mom does it."

Mrs. Malone opened the refrigerator. "I'll try it next time," she said. "I'll buy a lemon."

Debbie snorted. "Listen to Maggie," she said. "She knows everything." Mrs. Malone had looked from one girl to another and then turned back to the sink when there was a noise behind them. It was Helen, dropping some shopping bags and a big purse shaped like a shopping bag into a chair. She smiled at Maggie, put her finger to her lips and glided across the kitchen. She was wearing pink ballet slippers and a white dress that looked like a slip with pink flowers embroidered on it. Maggie could see that beneath the dress she wore no underwear except for tiny underpants. She had never seen such tiny underpants before.

"Guess who?" Helen said, putting her hands over her mother's eyes.

Mrs. Malone jumped and whirled around. She looked as wiry as an old man next to her soft, slightly rounded daughter. But a resemblance was there, in the clean planes of their faces, in the delighted, dazzled look they both wore.

"You're early!" Mrs. Malone said.

"Early?" Helen said, falling back a bit. "I live here!"

"Not anymore," said Debbie.

Helen whirled around and studied Debbie narrowly. Then she grinned. "You're right, Deb," she said lightly. Her hair was growing longer, and a heavy line of blue beneath her lower lashes made her eyes look even bluer. She stooped over the bassinet and ran one finger along the side of the baby's face. "He looks like a water balloon," she said.

The kitchen had begun to be crowded with Malones. Aggie was asking Helen about her show, and trying not to look down the front of her sister's dress. Some of the younger children were begging to open the shopping bags. Mrs. Malone leaned back against the sink, her arms folded, and stared at Helen. From behind Maggie, Debbie snorted. She went out of the house onto the front steps and Maggie followed her, although she wanted to stay with everyone else.

"You're going to get the back of your dress really dirty," Maggie said, as Debbie sank down on the dusty concrete stoop.

"Who cares?"

"Why are you so mad at me?"

"Don't flatter yourself."

"I'm going to leave," Maggie said. "I'm sorry your mother invited me if it makes you so mad."

Debbie acted as if she had not heard. "She's just like your cousin," she said. "She gets away with stuff because she's pretty. I don't even think she's that pretty. Her nose is really pointy. She used to try to squish it up with her fingers, but it still points."

Maggie sat down, too.

"I hate it when I go to school and somebody goes, 'Are you Helen Malone's sister?' "

"People always ask me if I'm John Scanlan's granddaughter," Maggie said.

"That's completely different."

From where they sat they could hear voices in the living room. The street was very quiet except for the sound of a truck on the next block spraying what was left of the vacant lot for mosquitoes. Small clouds of insecticide rose above the roofs across the street, and a sweet smell drifted toward them. "Certainly not," they heard Mrs. Malone say, and then Helen said with a laugh, "All right, then Coke. I thought you really *meant* 'Would you like anything to drink?' " Then there was a murmur from Mr. Malone.

"I got my dress for the wedding," Maggie said. "It's really nice. I have to get a garter belt to wear under it."

"Bridget says that I'm better-looking than Helen. She says that Helen's eyes are too close together."

"Bridget's a moron."

"Oh, I forgot," said Debbie. "You're Helen's best friend. Who would have figured that out?"

"I used to be your best friend."

"Things used to be different."

Maggie felt her eyes water and hoped it was only the insecticide. She thought she could hear hammering, very faintly.

Behind them the door opened and Helen stepped out onto the steps. "You're going to get your dress dirty," she said to Debbie.

"Who cares?" Debbie said.

Helen looked at Maggie and shrugged. "So do you guys want your presents or not?" Debbie could not help herself; she turned and looked up. From behind her back Helen produced two small boxes. Inside were silver hoop earrings, like little rings.

Maggie held hers in the palm of her hand and touched them with her index finger. "Thank you," she said.

"We don't have pierced ears," Debbie said sullenly.

"Not yet you don't."

The two girls were very still. Finally Debbie said, "They'll kill us."

Helen smiled. "Maggie, if I pierce your ears, what will happen?" she said, in exactly the tone of voice she had used to ask Maggie what she would be doing twenty years from now.

"My mother will yell at me."

"And then?"

"I'll probably get punished. Maybe I won't be able to go to the club for a week."

"It's almost September. The club will close on Labor Day. So what else can happen?"

"Nothing, I guess."

"So you'll get yelled at, maybe punished. But then you'll have pierced ears and new earrings."

Maggie smiled and looked down at the hoops. "Does it hurt?" she asked.

"Only for a minute," said Helen.

"I'll do it," said Maggie, and Debbie looked at her, her eyes wide. "Oh, this is unbelievable," she said harshly. "Maggie Scanlan, who's afraid to do anything wrong?"

"What's with you?" Helen said.

"Forget it," said Debbie. "I know you think she's great, but she's a big chicken. She won't do anything that will get her in trouble. Bridget says she's nun material."

Helen looked thoughtful. "There's trouble, and then there's trouble," she said. She turned and started upstairs, and Maggie and then Debbie followed her. Helen pulled them into the bathroom. There was a needle threaded with white cotton and a bottle of alcohol on the edge of the sink. "Stay away from Bridget Hearn," Helen said as she rubbed Maggie's lobes with alcohol. "She's a jerk." Maggie had smiled, and as the needle went in she did not make a sound. But as they went downstairs, their earlobes tingling, their hair carefully combed forward, Debbie had turned to her and said, "I dare you to come out tonight."

Now, from her window, Maggie watched the guard's car pull away, the pale beige glowing in the half light from the houses. The lightning leapt again, brighter this time, and there was the dim timpani of thunder far away. The lightning flashed and then remained, and as she narrowed her eyes she could see fire pluming from the roof of the house where she and Debbie had once taken up residence. Even at that distance she could see that this one, the eighth one, would be the one that would count, and she understood Debbie's valedictory remark. I won't go, she told herself. I won't go. Afterward, she wondered whether she had gone because of Debbie's dare, because she was worried about her friend, or because she was just as hypnotized by trouble as the rest of them.

She could smell the blaze as soon as she left the house, sharp and bitter, a chemical edge to the natural musk of smoke, a perversion of the autumn smell she'd loved all her life and would never be able to bear again. Trotting among the houses, she began to glimpse the fire, throwing the edges of the building into sharp relief. The house looked much as usual, except that in each of its windows there was a glimpse of waving, gaudy orange, like tattered curtains blowing. The lightning throbbed again, and after the thunder she heard a scream. She went in the front door and saw flames filling the back of the house, turning the walls to nothing, and she saw Richard and Debbie leaping about, laughing. Then Debbie gave a little scream again as the fire moved forward with a roar. "We did it," she cried, her voice shrill. "We finally did it!"

Maggie could see that in minutes the entire building would be alight, and perhaps the ones next to it, too. On the floor there was an empty bottle of Four Roses, its cap filled with cigarette butts, and Maggie wondered for a moment why they'd chosen that to feed the flames. Then she looked at Debbie, who was leaping up and down as though she was on a pogo stick, her hair corkscrewing into little curls in the heat, and realized she was drunk. Her blouse was unbuttoned almost to the waist, and a big bruise purpled her neck just where it met her collarbone. Maggie felt herself flush. She looked over at Richard, and he gave her a slow, sleepy smile and ran his tongue along his lips. He stumbled over and put his mouth against her earlobe, touching his lips to the string Helen had put there until Maggie was ready to wear earrings. Maggie smelled the liquor, a hospital kind of smell, and tried to pull away, but he kept his hand on her shoulder hard, like a vise.

"Hi, sexy," he said. And he looked over at Debbie and then laughed and turned back to Maggie. He was leaning on her, and Maggie suspected that if she stepped aside he would fall over. "You're the coolest-looking girl I know. I love your eyes. Your eyes are so cool."

Maggie shivered. The flames suddenly blazed toward them, leaping toward the ceiling, turning the fresh paint to a pale curdled mess. Debbie yelped and then looked over and said to Richard, "I wouldn't waste my time."

"This is bad," Maggie said. "You guys better get out of here. This is going to burn down the whole house."

"Good thinking," said Richard, who did not move. "Watch it burn with me. You'll like it. Relax. Just for once. You'd be so cool if you'd relax."

"You're crazy. The police will come now. We could all get arrested for this. Look at her. How are you going to get her home like that? What if her mother smells her?"

"She smells good," Richard said, and he ran his hand inside the back of Maggie's shirt. "So what if we get in trouble? Who cares?" He turned his face to her, streaked with soot, smelling of gasoline. "What difference does it make?"

"Deb, don't stay here," Maggie said. "They'll be here soon. You guys are going to get in so much trouble." But Debbie just stood there, staring. "Look at it," Richard said, and he moved toward the burning wall. And then as though the fire had reached out to throw its arms around him, a flame leapt out and flared on his sleeve, played around his hair. Debbie screamed and finally ran from the house, stumbling, and Richard ran behind her, panting, coughing, falling. Maggie knelt down beside him, and by the light of the fire she could see the shriveled red flesh of his hand and arm, and his singed hair and eyelashes.

"Ah, shit, Maggie," he said evenly. And then he began to sob with great wrenching heaves. "I think I blew it."

A few steps away, Debbie was sitting on the ground, her head turned to one side, being sick all over her hair. Maggie went over to her. "You have to get up," she said. "They'll be here soon."

Debbie lay back and stared straight up at the stars. "You tried to take my boyfriend, too," she said, slurring her words.

"Shut up. They could put you in jail for this. Come on." She pulled Debbie into a sitting position and then hooked her arms beneath her armpits. Richard was starting to wail.

"Go away," Debbie said as Maggie pulled her to her feet.

She went limp in Maggie's arms and Maggie dragged her to a house across the street that was almost finished. Gently she lowered her onto the linoleum of the kitchen floor. "Stay here," she said, looking down, but in the dimness she could tell that Debbie had passed out. Maggie buttoned up her friend's blouse and then ran between the houses, leaping over pieces of lumber and discarded cardboard, trying to keep from falling. Her own house was still dark. She saw a light in the window of the construction trailer, and veered toward it. She knew someone was there; she had watched Joey Martinelli's car pull up an hour before, moving with a series of little jerks like hiccups. Maggie had laughed out loud because it reminded her of the way her aunt Celeste drove, swearing at the clutch and the gear shift as she stalled in intersections, her middle finger stuck out the window as other drivers blew their horns and pulled around her. Then the lights had gone on in the trailer, yellow squares reflecting down on the dirt, picking up the little silver trajectories of moths dazzled by the beams. Maggie disliked Joey Martinelli, even though she knew in her heart that he was probably a nice person; it seemed that he was always hanging around, the edges of his mustache wet, half-moons of dirt beneath his square nails. She hated it when he asked about her grandfather. She knew that if her grandfather ever met Joey Martinelli, the man would barely be out of earshot before John Scanlon would start calling him a guinea. One afternoon he had come over to talk to her. "You're almost done over there," Maggie had said to be polite, pointing to the row of model homes.

He nodded. "Shelley Lane," he said.

"You're calling a street Shelley? Like Shelley Winters?"

"Like Shelley the poet," Joey said, his hands in his pockets. "Every street is going to be named after some famous writer. There's a Dickens Street, a Wordsworth Street. The models are called the Emily Dickinson, the Lord Byron, and the Edgar Allan Poe."

"Which one's the Edgar Allan Poe?"

"The ranch."

Maggie shook her head. "I hope no one who comes to see it has ever read Edgar Allan Poe," she said.

"The guy wanted to be an English professor," Joey continued, "but instead he went into construction with his father. He says it shows the best-laid plans of mice and men do something or other. I can never follow half of what he says."

"Weird," Maggie had said.

Now she ran along the tamped-down dirt of the sidewalk until she came to the end of what would be Shelley Lane and knew she had to ask for help whether she liked Joey Martinelli or not. The construction trailer lay across a wide swatch of untouched land, a boundary of grass the developers had planned in the mistaken belief that it would placate the residents of Kenwood, when all it did was to make Tennyson Park seem like another country, like a raw-looking mirage floating over their backyards, distant and unsubstantial, somehow hostile. Maggie could hear music from inside the trailer, the Beatles in harmony, Paul's strained soprano, John's lower, thicker voice as the backdrop. "Things We Said Today." There was a window in the door, and she pulled herself up until she could see through it.

Inside, her mother was standing at a gray table, and as Maggie watched she pushed back her hair with her fingers and looked up at Joey Martinelli, a look of such intensity on her face that Maggie drew back. When she looked again Connie had her head down and Maggie could see that the man was arguing, using his hands, finally putting them on Connie's shoulders. Maggie thought of the feeling of Richard's hand moving softly over her collarbone. On the table was a magazine, the same issue of *Life* Monica had been reading on Sunday, the one with Paul Newman on the cover in an undershirt. Next to it was a half-eaten Three Musketeers bar. As Maggie watched, Joey Martinelli let his hands drop, and Connie looked up again. She took his big fist in her small hand, opened it, and placed something in the palm. For a moment it lay there, under the fluorescent light, and Maggie saw that it was a key. She wondered whether it was the key she had seen on the kitchen table that day she had found out her mother was learning to drive, or the key her grandfather had tossed into her mother's lap, the key to the new house in which they were all meant to live happily ever after.

Joey Martinelli's fist closed around it.

Somehow Maggie was not surprised at what she was seeing, only a little sickened, as she had been the time she had found the dress that was to be her Christmas present on the top shelf of the closet and tried it on, smoothing the skirt until she looked into the mirror and saw her mother standing behind her, her face soft and dark with betrayal and disappointment.

Slowly she backed down the steps and went around to the end of the trailer. The car was parked there, a dark-blue Plymouth sedan, like the company cars that her grandfather's salesmen used on their rounds, anonymous, undistinguished. Her grandfather always said you could pick out plainclothes cops in the city because they always drove cars like this; plainclothes city cops and the priests in the neighborhoods the cops patrolled. "Show me a priest in a Cadillac," said John Scanlon, "and I'll show you a priest who is doing things he shouldn't." Maggie could see in the light from the trailer that the car was empty. She peered in the window on the driver's side. On the seat there was a pink cardigan sweater with little pearl buttons up the front, and another Three Musketeers bar.

She heard the door to the trailer open, and for a moment she was still; then she loped around behind the trailer and made for her own backyard. As she reached the edge of the development, she tripped over a stray cinder block and went sprawling in the dirt, her knees and chin stinging. Turning, she looked back and saw the orange rectangle of the burning development house, and all around began to see lights go on in other houses. From far away she heard screams, and then she realized they were sirens, getting louder and louder. She ran inside the house, upstairs to her own room, and crouched by the window again and watched as the fire engines pulled in, the men shouting to one another to hook up hose after hose to reach the hydrant outside Maggie's house that had been base for tag for as long as she could remember. "We're going to need an ambulance," one of them shouted, and then she knew she no longer had to worry about Richard. Someone stood in her backyard, watching, and then she heard the screen door slam, and footsteps running up the stairs.

"Maggie?" her mother called in the dark. Connie moved to the bed and felt the smooth cover. Then she turned on the overhead light. Maggie was facing the window, and her mother said "Maggie?" again and then stood beside her and looked down at her face.

"Oh no," Connie said. "Not you. Oh Jesus. Not you." Maggie raised her hand to her own hot face and when she brought it away it was black with soot, and even she could smell the gasoline on her fingers.

"How could you do this? How could you? Look what you've done. And you stink of booze."

"Me?" said Maggie. "Me? What have I done? What about you? What about what you've done? You've done worse than I have tonight." Her head dropped onto her knobby knees and the tears streamed down her legs, but instead of cooling her face they only made it hotter. She felt as if she could not breathe and then she raised her head and wiped it with her arm.

"There are rules," she said in a treble voice like Damien's. "There are rules. And if you break the rules you hurt people."

"I haven't done what you seem to think I've done," Connie said softly, and Maggie saw that her mother was wearing a clover chain on her head, and with one movement she rose and snatched it off and held it broken in her hand. Connie didn't move.

"There are rules you can break like that," said Maggie, gesturing out the window at the orange glow. "And then there are the rules that are, are—" She began to sob and the flowers fell from her hand to the floor.

"I wouldn't break those rules," Connie said. "That's not the kind of person I am."

"What kind of person are you?" Maggie said, looking up, and then suddenly she saw herself, and it was as if it was the first time, as if she'd never passed a mirror, never seen a photograph, never looked into her own eyes, and she realized that no matter what she might do with her life, no matter how she might twist or turn or move away, it would be for nothing, that she could never escape, not just who she was, but what she had come from.

"I don't know," Connie finally said, and the two of them stood in silence for a long time, watching as the water leapt through the air, putting the fire out, leaving an empty space in the row of new houses.

The noise from the incongruous nighttime crowd—men in black slickers, police with their buttons glinting in the light of the fire, people from the surrounding houses standing in their backyards, barely visible, like a ring of ghosts defending Kenwood—gave way to the faint, unmistakable sound of the last pockets of heat popping into oblivion and the water falling from what was left of the wreckage to the blackened earth. The two women watched in silence. They did not touch or speak or look at each other.

"That's over, the fires," Maggie said finally, her shoulders sagging beneath her white shirt. "I don't want to tell you who, but I promise you it wasn't me. Not this one. I promise you this one wasn't me, and I promise it's over. I promise."

She looked up at Connie and her face was wiped clean, and Maggie knew that her mother did not believe her, although she wanted to.

"I promise you too," said her mother, and Maggie saw that in some sense she might never understand, she had been right to have the suspicions and the fears she had had, and that this day, this night, was the end of a part of her life as surely as it was the end of the new house, now a tumble of glowing debris framed by the square of her window. Silently Connie turned and left the bedroom, turning the light off as she went, and Maggie lay down on her bed in her clothes. When she woke in the morning she was still in her shorts and shirt, but her sneakers had been placed side by side under her bed, and one of Joseph's crib quilts had been wrapped around her.

20

HEN TOMMY CAME HOME ON THURSDAY night it was already dusk. His dinner was in the oven, the plate covered with foil, and his wife was sitting on a collapsible lawn chair on the back patio, smoking a cigarette and giggling with her cousin Celeste. Tom stood in the kitchen, watching the moths flail against the screens, the fluorescent tube above the counter blinding him, so that when he looked out he could see the bugs and nothing more. He picked at the chicken and beans on the plate, licking his fingers and absently shaking salt over everything. He was not hungry.

After work he had played one-on-one for almost an hour with one of the mixer drivers, running up and down the asphalt court until perspiration falling into his eyes turned him blind and clumsy. Then he had gone to the hospital and driven his mother to church, to a novena to St. Jude, the patron saint of lost causes. Even with the sun down, it was near ninety degrees outside, and Tom felt as if all his energy and hunger and fight had melted into a puddle on the car floor, right between the acceleration pedal and the brake. When he looked at himself in the mirror in the men's room at the plant, a gray room with a persistent smell of Lysol, he thought of the old trick of holding a buttercup beneath your chin to see if you liked butter. Almost always there would be a pale yellow shadow cast by the flower, pale yellow like the color his skin was now, the whites of his eyes, the wet circles on his shirt beneath the armpits.

Down in the basement, below his feet, he could hear the washer going. It seemed as if the washer was always going in his house. He smelled a faint odor of burning and wondered if the vent on the dryer needed replacing again. Then he remembered the fire the night before, already doused and dead by the time he came home from his mother's house. He wished someone would burn the whole damn development down. Outside he could hear more laughter, and looking inside the refrigerator saw that four of his Miller High Lifes were missing.

He did not like it when women drank beer. He even thought it was inappropriate for his mother to have Scotch on Sundays. Whenever they went out to dinner he always ordered a whiskey sour for Connie, and one for himself to keep her company, although he could never taste the liquor in those things. Sal said fancy restaurants didn't use any liquor in drinks like that, only vanilla. He stood inside, drinking his beer, pressing it against his cheek. He did not like it when Celeste spent a lot of time with Connie. The rest of the time he could think of Connie as only his, his wife, nothing more or less. When Celeste came, he felt as though his Connie disappeared, in the way she had taken to doing. He put the bottle down on the counter.

"Tommy?" Connie called, hearing the clink of the glass. Her voice was high and a little giddy.

He walked to the back door, his hands in his pockets, and stood behind the screen like a shadow.

"Come on out," Connie said.

"Hi, Tom," said Celeste, holding the beer bottle by the neck.

"Come out," his wife repeated, and he slid around the screen door, trying to keep the moths from coming in. He knew he looked out of place in his dress shirt, his tie slack around his open collar, his lace-up shoes black and heavy in the heat. Even the lightning bugs were sluggish, blinking on and off in one spot for a long time. Connie's beer bottle was turned on its side on the ground, either spilt or empty.

"We're celebrating," Connie said. "Have a beer."

"Celebrating what?"

"Celeste got married. Today."

Tommy stared at Celeste, who nodded. "At City Hall," she said, with an Ethel Merman laugh. "On my lunch hour. Actually, I took two hours and had lunch anyway."

"To who?" said Tom.

"His name is Sol Markowitz. You don't know him. He runs a hat company on 37th Street. Mr. Mark's Hats. I met him at the deli on Broadway. He's very nice. Fiftyish."

Tommy knew this meant the guy was in his sixties. The last time Celeste had dated someone "fiftyish" he had died of a cerebral hemorrhage when they were at the track together and his horse had won.

Celeste was wearing white toreador pants and a black sleeveless blouse, her hair in an upsweep. "You didn't get married like that?" said Tommy.

The two women started to laugh. "I asked her the same thing," Connie said.

"I wore a dress, for your information," Celeste said.

"Red," said Connie, bursting into laughter and groping on the ground for her beer bottle.

"So?" Celeste said. "I'm not a kid. Besides, he already had the big wedding, the hall, the flowers, the whole bit. Thirty-five years ago. Who needs it?"

"That doesn't make him fiftyish," Tommy said.

"Picky, picky, picky."

"It's not like she wants to have children," Connie said, folding her hands lightly over her stomach.

Celeste shrugged. "Sometimes it's just time, you know? It's time to settle down, get on with your life, act your age."

"Act your age?" Connie said, giggling. "You? Give me a break. Tell me another."

"How many beers have you had?" Tommy asked.

"The enforcer," Celeste said in a deep voice, picking up her bottle and taking a mouthful. Tommy flushed bright red.

"Where's your car, Celeste?" he asked.

"The enforcer," Connie said.

"He's sending a car for me," Celeste said. "Sol is. He had business and I'm going to meet him at home."

"Where's he live?" Tommy said.

"Up in Connecticut. You two will have to come up for a barbeque with the kids. He has a pool. We have a pool. That has a nice ring to it, doesn't it? We have a pool. Seven bedrooms. It's nice."

"Celeste Markowitz," said Connie.

"Oh Jesus," said Celeste to Tommy, "your mom and dad will love that. Don't say anything, okay?"

"Tell you the truth, Celeste," said Tommy, pitching his beer bottle onto the grass, the faint beer buzz he got after a long hot day beginning right behind his eyes, "at this point in their lives I don't think my parents would care."

"Get out," Celeste said. "Your old man would care unless he was half dead."

"He is half dead," Tommy said.

"Tom," said Connie, turning to look him in the face, telling him he was spoiling the party.

"Your father will outlive us all, Tom," Celeste said.

"I think you'll outlive us all, Celeste," Tommy said, and suddenly he smiled. "Let me see your ring."

Celeste held out her left hand so he could see the heart-shaped diamond perched above her big knuckle. It was twice the size of the ring she'd had before. Even in the half-light, Tom could see that it was pale yellow, and he thought again of the shadow a buttercup made beneath your chin.

"That's great," Tommy said. "Beautiful. It must have cost a fortune."

Celeste smiled. Faintly, from the front of the house, a car horn sounded twice. "That's for me," she said, getting slowly to her feet.

"Bring him in," Connie said. "I have cake in the house."

"Sometime," Celeste said. "You can't rush these things." She turned to Tommy and laid one hand, the nails as slick as patent leather, along his hot cheek. "Be nice to your wife," she said, in a throaty, intense sort of voice, and Tommy had a heady feeling of *déjà vu*. Instead of having to root around for it for days, the memory came back to him instantly: Celeste at his wedding reception, shiny in bright blue, dancing with him, looking up to say, her eyes filled with tears, "Be nice to my cousin."

"I'm always nice to my wife," he replied now. "When I can find her."

"Be extra nice to her," said Celeste, and before Tommy could get the last word she had kissed him, and was gone, a cloud of L'Air du Temps lingering over the lawn chair in which she'd sat. Tommy realized it was a new scent for Celeste, perhaps in honor of the new husband. He leaned over and picked up her beer bottle. The top was red with lipstick. He carried the bottle into the kitchen.

Connie followed him. "Tom," she said. When he turned she was standing by the stove, smiling, a misty look in her eyes. It was the booze, he told himself, but still he was excited.

"I have another surprise for you."

"What's that?" he said, running his hands up and down her arms, his fingers encircling her tiny wrists. She pushed her hands into his pockets and his breathing changed, but she only took out his car keys and held them in front of his nose.

"Ta da," she said, and he could tell now that the beer had really affected her. The last time he remembered hearing her say "ta da" was when she came out of the bathroom the first night of their honeymoon in her negligee. He wondered for a moment how she was keeping the beer down in her condition.

Connie walked out the front door, the keys still held in front of her like a carrot on a stick, and he followed. She opened the passenger door of the station wagon and said, "Get in." Then she slid in on the other side and turned the key in the ignition.

"Where's the thing that makes the seat go closer?" she said impatiently, slurring her words a little.

"Are you nuts?" Tommy said. "What do you think you're doing?"

The seat slid forward with a jerk, and Tommy's knees were pinned against the glove compartment. When the lights came on, he saw the grass edging the driveway all sharp-edged and clean, like one of those arty nature photographs. Connie put the car into reverse and backed down the driveway. The bumper hit the street solidly.

"Why does it do that?" she asked, jamming on the brake and adjusting the rear-view mirror.

"This is not funny," Tommy said. "You're going to kill us both. It's bad enough that you don't know how to drive, but you're drunk to top it all off. Just stop."

Connie dug in the pocket of her shorts and handed him a square of cardboard. It was a temporary license from the Motor Vehicle Bureau. It said that Concetta M. Scanlan had brown hair and eyes, did not need corrective lenses, was five feet tall and weighed 103 pounds. Tommy thought she was probably a little heavier than that by now.

Connie was cruising silently down Park Street, holding a little too far to the right, staring a little too intently out the windshield, the way Tommy remembered doing when he had first learned how to drive. At the corner she turned left and went around the block. She went around the block again, and then a third time, before pulling back into the driveway. Part of Tommy noticed that she cut it a little too wide on the turns, but he thought that would iron itself out in time. The other part was so enraged that he could taste the metallic tang of adrenaline on his tongue.

"Ta da," she said again, as she turned off the engine. Without a word he walked back into the house and took another beer out of the refrigerator. He sat down in the living room in his chair and switched on the television. She came and stood in front of it, her arms crossed on her chest.

"Aren't you going to say anything?"

"What do you want me to say?"

"Congratulations would be nice."

There was a long silence. Finally he said, "Where are the kids?"

"Joseph is upstairs asleep. Damien is at my father's. Terence is spending the night at O'Brien's after his game, and I think Maggie is with Debbie."

"Oh, that's convenient," he said sarcastically.

"What's that supposed to mean?" said Connie, turning around to switch off the television.

Tommy just looked at her, his eyes cold, his heart pounding. He looked down and imagined he could see it pulsing beneath his damp dress shirt. The beer was making him feel tired.

"Do you have something going with that guinea?" Tommy finally said.

"You sound exactly like your father," Connie replied.

It was not, he thought, the way he had planned to bring this up. But it was the sight of her behind the wheel that had set him off, so small that it seemed scarcely possible that she could see over the dashboard or reach the brake pedal, like a little girl playing at being grownup. She was exactly the same, and yet she was entirely different. There was no need for her to be able to do this. He could take her anywhere she wanted to go. He went into the kitchen and uncapped another beer, wondering how he could have finished the last one so quickly, but when he came back she was in the same place, with the same hard look around her onyx eyes. Her face and throat were dewy with the heat, and she had faint dark circles just beneath her eyes where her mascara was smudging onto her skin.

"The answer is no," she said finally, breaking the silence, and there was a certain something in her voice that told him that the question had been neither unexpected nor unreasonable.

But it never occurred to Tommy that she might not be telling the truth. She was that sort of person, black and white, who would not lie about what she had done simply because facts were facts and you had to acknowledge them. "I never would have thought this of you," he said slowly. He could think of nothing else but clichés, and he drank his beer to stop from talking.

"Thought what of me, Tommy?" she said, raising her hands in the air. "That I would get tired of not fitting in? That I would want to do the things that other people do? I don't always want to be the strange one. I want to be happy."

"What's happy?" he said.

"I don't know," she said, dropping her hands. "But I know I haven't been it, whatever it is."

Oddly enough, he felt happy now, with just the two of them in their own living room, with his stomach full of beer. He remembered how, one evening in the hospital, his father had asked him to play a game of pinochle, beating Tom as he did all his sons. Then he had fallen back into the pillows, his collarbone like a wooden yoke beneath his pajamas, and said, "There's nothing like a game of cards to make you feel alive."

Tommy looked at his wife now and he loved her, loved how the veins showed blue around her neck just above the little collar of her shirt, how her hair fuzzed out uncontrollably in the heat, how she had joined him to make a life of their own, however flawed, however constraining. He loved all the little things. He did not want her to be like other people. He would never have loved her if she had been. He thought of her pulling into the driveway with such assumed competence, but with her bottom lip caught between her front teeth as she turned the wheel. He began to cry.

"No, Tom, no," she whispered, going to kneel in front of him and cradling his head on her shoulder. "No, no, no. It's all right. It's all going to be all right." Tommy started to choke on it, the hot salt, the booze, the grief, the loss of the father he wished he had had, the death of the world he loved.

"I was afraid . . ." he began, but she didn't let him finish.

"I know," Connie said. "I know. But there was nothing to be afraid of."

Tommy pulled away and looked at her and she smiled, inscrutable and wise. He couldn't tell her that somehow the driving seemed like a great infidelity all by itself, the separation, the pulling away. There was nothing to be done about that now, and he couldn't afford to lose her. He realized that she was the closest he would ever get to not being alone. His parents would die, and the children would change and leave, and there the two of them would be, in their living room, perspiring and talking in fragments.

"I love you," he said, and he started to cry again.

"Yes, honey. Yes, I know."

"Don't go away."

"Where would I go?" Connie said, and she held him for a long time. Slowly, almost in a dream, he began to undress her, there in the living room. It made him remember the first Friday night they had spent in this house, after they had moved from her aunt Rose's. Maggie and Terence were babies, and they had stayed behind in the Bronx while he and Connie came to arrange the furniture, put away the dishes, make up the bare beds. They had had dinner that night on the floor, on a blanket, with a bottle of Rose's Chianti for a kind of celebration, and by the time it was dark they were both drunk. They had pushed everything to one side—he could still feel the scratch of the wool blanket on his bare skin—and fell on each other right next to the dirty plates. Connie's bra had stayed looped around her neck throughout, as if she were a corpse in a *Daily News* rape-and-murder story. There were no curtains on the windows and Tommy had averted his eyes, afraid to see someone peeking in. But when they were finished they walked around brazenly, their clothes on the floor, staying up way past midnight as though they both knew it would be a long time before they would have this kind of freedom again. Tommy remembered walking through the half-empty rooms with one word going through his head: Mine. Mine. He had meant his wife, too. He said it again, now, as he pulled impatiently at her shorts. Their skins stuck together in the heat, and made sucking noises when they pulled apart. As they lay side by side on the carpet afterward, Tommy realized that he had forgotten, for once, that she was pregnant. She, he realized from her response, simply did not care.

"We have to get dressed," she said after a few minutes. "One of the children might come in."

But he was already half-asleep by that time, and he only pulled on his pants and fell into his chair, his head thrown back, his mouth open. She covered him with one of Joseph's blankets, a small square over the middle of his long body, and then she went upstairs to sleep by herself. In the middle of the night he woke up once, his head buzzing with a swarm of hangover gnats, filling his ears with noise and his eyes with little white lights, and he thought suddenly that he had been had once again. This was what his entire married life had been like: long stretches of tedium illuminated by moments, unexpected, when he knew that without her he would be lost. For weeks or months they moved through their separate lives and slept side by side as though they were two strangers who had mistakenly been assigned the same hotel room. And then something would happen and he would find himself staring at her as though he could see the soul of her, looking for an end to his troubles inside the loop of her arms, and he would be snagged with the fishhook of herself, with the barbed hook of his powerless infatuation with something that she seemed to have, some answer that she seemed to offer. She was the one, really, who had always had the power over him, and who always would; his father's bluster was nothing compared to it. He tried to remember all this as he lay there, the aftertaste of liquor awful in his mouth. He wished he had a pen and could write it down, but instead he vowed—perhaps aloud, he thought he heard some muttering in the room—to remember it the next morning.

When he woke again the watery blue of the sky told him that it was dawn. The pressure behind his eyes was enormous. The buzzing had reawakened him, and he pressed his hands over his ears. After a moment he realized that the noise was not inside his head, but in the kitchen, and as he took his hands away Connie appeared at the top of the stairs, her face very pale above the white of her nightgown. He felt embarrassed to look at her.

"Tommy, James is on the phone," she said. When he got up from the chair the room tilted a little. He picked up the kitchen phone and it was only when he actually said "Hello" that he realized he had never received a call this early in the morning, and even before James spoke Tommy knew what he would say.

"He's dead," his brother said.

21

GATES OF HEAVEN CEMETERY WAS NICE, Maggie thought, but not as nice as her grandfather Mazza's cemetery. It had a slight rise and fall to it, little hills and valleys crisscrossed with wide roads. Whole areas were empty, the grass stretching bright green and unbroken for a long way. There were no trees. They took good care of the lawns. Just inside the entrance there was a sign:

NO: PLANTING AT GRAVESITES
FLAGS
MILITARY MEDALLIONS

GRAVE BLANKETS PERMITTED ON CHRISTMAS, EASTER, AND MOTHER'S DAY.

NO UNAUTHORIZED VISITORS. PLEASE RESPECT THIS PLACE OF REST.

Maggie thought the last sentence was sort of nice, but the rest of the rules seemed harsh. Strangers strolled around Angelo Mazza's cemetery all the time, and no one thought anything of it. Mrs. Martini left photographs of the grandchildren on her husband's grave, weighted down with small stones. Women were always coming with pots of hyacinths or gardenias. They would kneel with their trowels in front of the headstones and dig a little hole and put the flowers in and then pat the earth around the roots gently, as though they were patting the person beneath. They never worried about the plants dying. Angelo took care of them once they were in the ground. It would have been nicer if her grandfather Scanlan could have been buried at Calvary Cemetery, but Maggie knew he never would have allowed it. She could picture him lying under his shirred white satin blanket, his black rosaries twined around his fingers in the stagy position that would never allow you to say the rosary in real life, thinking to himself, "Jesus, Mary, and Joseph, I'm surrounded by guineas." She laughed a little to herself, and her father frowned at her.

She knew that she should feel sadder than she did, but the fact was that she did not believe that her grandfather was dead, although she had knelt before the coffin and looked down at the waxy hands, still so big and powerful looking. He had made her recite the seven deadly sins just two weeks before. She had forgotten one. "Sloth," John Scanlan had thundered, the violence of the sound bringing two nurses to the door of his room. "And don't you forget it, little girl." Her grandfather had looked better, his mouth less elastic, his eyelids matching, both at half-mast. Sometimes when she would arrive at the hospital he would be sleeping, his breath rippling through his lips like that of an old horse, and when she left he would still be sleeping, even though she had sat there for an hour or two, watching the white light of the sun lay bright rectangles on the linoleum floor. Sometimes they played Parcheesi, and most of the time he told her stories about his childhood, about beating up Billy Boylan behind the garage on Lexington Avenue or being taken into the precinct house by the cops after he stole penny candy from the Greek's place around the corner from the tenement building where his family lived. Some of the stories had been new. Some Maggie had heard before, but they were transformed. For the first time Billy Boylan got some punches of his own in, and was not simply decimated by John Scanlan's invincible right hook; for the first time it turned out that some lemon balls had indeed been stolen from the Greek's. "The cops took 'em, and ate 'em!" her grandfather said loudly, as though consumption was the real crime. Occasionally the stories would be interrupted by her grandfather's doctor, a man named Levine who was ugly and very kind, and who disliked John Scanlan very much but was always cheerful around him. When Maggie first came to the hospital, Dr. Levine and some other doctors would often enter and make her move outside, pulling the white curtains hanging from the ceiling tight around the bed. Their shoes moved at the bottom of the curtain, their shadows made a kind of mime show. But after a few weeks Dr. Levine just felt for her grandfather's pulse, and then left. Maggie had imagined this was because her grandfather was getting better. Now, of course, she knew it had been because he was dying.

"What?" she had said, when her father told her. Tommy was sitting at the kitchen table drinking a glass of Pepto-Bismol, his face gray. "What? Are you sure?" She had gone upstairs to her room to think, looking out over the asphalt shingles of the new roofs to the place where the house that had burned had stood. For some reason she had thought of the picture in the Baltimore Catechism of mortal and venial sin: first the milk bottle with the little flecks of black in it, then the milk bottle dark as a moonless night, and then the bottle pure white again after confession. In some way she felt pure white.

She had not talked to Debbie since that night. She had barely talked to her mother, only watched her walk around the house with the wary eyes of the guilty. Now her grandfather was dead. She felt as though she was bereft of any connections at all. As she lay on her bed, she felt as though she was floating, the motion in her body like the motion of Cap'n Jim's big tug as it plied the Jersey coastline. She looked at the blackened supports of the burned house from her bedroom window, and although she couldn't explain why, she felt that the worst was over. Down in the kitchen, she had watched her mother making macaroni and cheese, to be heated in between visits to the funeral home, and she realized that it was the first proper meal Connie had made in weeks. Maggie wondered if that meant that Connie had come back to them.

The next three days had passed in a welter of small details: the boxes of tissues on every table at the funeral home, the black mantillas laid on the chair in the hallway at her grandmother's house, the holy card with the Sacred Heart on one side and her grandfather's name and the prayer of resurrection on the other. "Accept our prayer that the Gates of Paradise might be opened for your servant," it said. Her grandmother kept changing her mind about whether her husband should wear his blue or his gray suit, as though he was going to a communion breakfast. "For Christ's sakes, Mother," Tommy finally said, "if it matters so much to you we'll dress him in the gray the first night and the blue the next. Can we drop it now?" Mary Frances had started to cry, and been helped up to her room by Margaret. Looking back over her shoulder, Margaret had said quietly to her brother, "Displacement, Tom honey. Thinking about the small things so you won't have to think about the big ones." Maggie had watched with a great full feeling in her throat as tears rose in her father's eyes. For three days, she thought, they were all displacing. She had learned a new word. The only time any of it felt like real life was driving home in the car from the funeral home one night, stretched out on the back seat, her hot cheek against the cool vinyl of the seats. Frank Sinatra was on the radio, and her father was singing while her mother hummed and beat time with the toe of one patent-leather pump. "No, no, they can't take that away from me," Tommy roared happily. When the last few notes died away, he reached across for Connie's hand. Maggie could see their twined fingers in the space between the seats, the lights of the dashboard making blue stars in her mother's engagement ring. Then her father said, "Did they get whoever torched that house?"

"I think one of the boys did it. Mary Joseph's son. He was badly burned. They say he may lose a couple of fingers, and some of the use of his hand."

Tommy whistled. "Police?"

"I think they're handling it privately. The father has a bundle, and he's going to need it. The construction people want $25,000."

Maggie saw her father look over at her mother, his profile sharp against the windshield. "Yeah?"

"I get that from your sister-in-law," Connie said with a wary look. "That's where I heard it. I don't know if it's true."

Tommy grunted, satisfied. "The kid set these fires all by himself?" he added.

"He was the ringleader," Connie had answered.

Maggie stared again at her mother in the limousine stopped in front of the Gates of Heaven sign. Connie's eyes looked clear, her face smooth. This was how she always looked after the baby had settled in, once the bad part was over. The lines of her mantilla melted into the black of her hair. Everyone was stopped behind them, the cars with their headlights on, dim in the sunshine, snaking out onto Westchester Avenue. There were 111 cars in the procession: John's children, grandchildren, brothers and sisters, the workers from Scanlan & Co., the leaders of the unions that represented those workers, the leaders of the dioceses that bought what they made, a great long chain of procreation and commerce. There was one friend, a man named McAlevy who said he'd gone to high school with John Scanlan and had read his obituary in the newspaper. "A helluva pitching arm," the man had told Maggie's father at the funeral home. "Jesus, I'll never forget it. A helluva pitching arm." Maggie had seen the Malone car in the parking lot as she got into the limousine, but she knew she shouldn't wave. She saw it again now, as the limousine inched forward and the family slid from the cars and gathered under the tent that sheltered the old man's bronze casket from the noonday sun.

"I am the resurrection and the life," said the archbishop's representative, a monsignor with a deep, powerful, effortlessly dramatic voice, which alone had ensured his elevation in the church. Uncle James had implored him to say the words in Latin, had hinted at free vestments for the cathedral. The priest had reluctantly refused. The new order was inviolate.

Maggie could not concentrate on the words. A piece of green grasscloth was draped around the base of the casket, but it gapped near her feet and she could see the hole beneath. She knew that they would wait until everyone was gone and then the cemetery workers would lower the straps that let the box down into another box made of some kind of cement. And then they would fill the hole in and place the flowers on top. And by next year the grass would have covered it, and the scar would be gone. There was a largish headstone that said only SCANLAN. The stonecutter would come in a few weeks to finish it. Maggie was struck by the difference between knowing the routine and having it happen to someone she loved.

There was a movement behind her, and she turned to see her cousin Monica, her hand clapped over her mouth, retreat to the lead car, the one in which her grandmother and her uncle James had been riding. Monica seemed somehow to have lost her power, too. At the funeral home they had stood side by side in the ladies' room, and Monica had asked her coldly if she was bringing a date to the wedding. "Elvis Presley," Maggie had said in a monotone. "Paul McCartney. Marlon Brando. James Dean." Monica had smiled. "A comedian," she said. "A real ball of fire."

"Stuff it, Monica," Maggie said. "I'm tired of being afraid of you."

"Remember man . . ." the priest was saying, and Maggie finished the sentence in her mind, just as she would have done for her grandfather if they had been in his living room. Her lips moved: "that thou art dust and unto dust thou shalt return." It was a good feeling, to be able to do that, like knowing the answer in a spelling bee. Maggie suddenly remembered the doorstop her grandparents had kept against the door to the house in summertime. It was a three-dimensional octagon, like a faceted ball, made of milky green stone. Maggie had loved to play with it when she was small, to turn it from side to side to side. One day she had asked her grandmother which was the top and which was the bottom, and Mary Frances had tried to explain that all the sides were the same. "There really is no top or bottom to it, dear," she said softly, not noticing that John Scanlan was standing behind her until he reached clear over her shoulder and took the thing away. He turned it and turned it in his big hand, the hairs on the back catching the light so that they glinted silver and gold, and finally he hit on one side, identical to all the others except that there was a small nick at one edge. He crouched next to Maggie.

"This is the top, little girl," he said, and then he turned to the opposite side. "And this is the bottom. Top. Bottom. Bottom. Top."

Mary Frances had faded away, and Maggie had been happy. She liked answers. When they went to her grandparents' house, after this was over, she would look for the nick. She knew now that her grandfather had been making a point, not telling the truth, but she agreed that the first was more important than the second.

It was nearly time to go. The heat was drying the drops of holy water the priest had sprinkled on the metal lid of the casket. Her grandmother stood with her arm through Uncle James's. The monsignor had turned to speak to her, and she blinked at him as though she could not quite place him.

Maggie followed her parents back to the car. Mrs. Malone stopped to talk to Connie, and Debbie hung back, she and Maggie standing awkward and silent in their black patent-leather shoes, their Teenform garter belts itchy above their pelvic bones. Debbie was wearing her Easter hat, white with black daisies, and a black piqué dress that had once been Helen's and was still too big on her.

"I'm sorry about your grandfather," she said to Maggie softly.

"That's all you have to say to me?" Maggie said. "I saved your life."

"You're nuts," Debbie said. "You got me in a lot of trouble. I fell asleep and didn't get up till two o'clock. I had to go sleep at Bridget's house. Now I'm not allowed to go anywhere. And my mother says you and I can't be friends anymore."

Maggie looked over at Mrs. Malone. For a moment Debbie's mother looked at her, and then she tilted her chin up in a way she had when she was angry, and stared past her. Maggie could not imagine why Mrs. Malone would be angry at her.

"How am I in trouble with your mom for what you did? What did you say?"

"You should have taken me home, Mag."

"You shouldn't have had anything to drink. We're only thirteen. I could see right down the front of your blouse." Maggie stared at her friend's neck. There was a very faint purple mark, ineptly concealed with what looked like Max Factor pancake.

"Oh, grow up," Debbie said. "What are you, my conscience? If you think you can handle everything, then do it. But don't do it halfway. If you're going to save somebody's life, then save it *all* the way."

There was a long silence. The two girls looked down at their shoes, hazy with dust.

"My mother said Richard's father is paying for everything," said Maggie finally, not looking up.

"He's okay," Debbie said. "Bridget says they're sending him to military school. He's going to need plastic surgery on his arm, Bridget said, and one of his fingers was burned off. That's pretty disgusting, but at least it wasn't his face. God, that would have been bad. It didn't even touch his face, just his arm. And it was the arm he doesn't use to write or throw, Bridget said. He'll write and tell me soon. I don't know how I'm going to see him at military school."

Maggie said nothing, only fingered the tissue in her hand. She looked at Debbie, her hair frizzing in the heat, and knew that she would always think of her as her best friend. She looked at Mrs. Malone, who still avoided her eyes, and knew that that was over, too, and she thought that maybe it was Mrs. Malone she would miss most. She would miss having a mother she didn't have to push away, having a mother nothing like herself, having a family with no complications. Her eyes swam with tears, until the sunlight broke into little pink particles and she saw everything as a blur. She had known her grandfather would die. She had gotten used to the idea, little by little over the summer, that he was not invincible. But she knew that she had still believed that some things lasted forever.

" 'Bye Deb," she said.

"God, you're always so dramatic," Debbie said. "That's what Bridget says."

Maggie looked away and saw that now her grandmother had the monsignor on one side of her and Mr. O'Neal on the other. Suddenly her grandmother crouched down and lifted one side of the grasscloth. "Oh, God," Maggie heard Connie say, and the two of them moved away from the Malones and stood behind Mary Frances.

"Could you get your father, sweetheart?" said Mr. O'Neal, wiping his forehead with his handkerchief.

Mary Frances wheeled and brightened. "Maggie, these gentlemen are confused. Go get your uncle James and your father." And suddenly all the boys were there, in their dark suits, looking so alike, so flushed and full of blood. For the first time Maggie saw the family resemblance, and saw it in herself, too.

"I just wanted to know on which side the baby was buried," Mary Frances said, her voice loud enough that people began to look over. "He is under the mistaken impression that there is nobody else in the Scanlan plot." The five men, their hands folded in front of them, turned as one to Mr. O'Neal, who wiped his forehead again.

"Perhaps one of you could show your mother to the car," he said.

"Is there another casket there or not?" Tommy said.

Mr. O'Neal looked at Mary Frances, and then his narrow nostrils flared. "Absolutely not," he said. "And I can assure you that I had a number of conversations with your father about these arrangements over the years and it was understood—twelve places. He and your mother. You five and your wives."

Tommy grimaced. "What about my sister?" he said.

"The sisters make their own arrangements," said Mr. O'Neal, as though that settled everything.

"My parents had a child who passed away at birth," Tommy began. "A little girl."

"My understanding was that at the time she was buried at a cemetery in the Bronx," Mr. O'Neal said.

"And he promised to move her," Mary Frances said, and Maggie could see that her face was beginning to fall, as though the pouchy cheeks were melting just a little. "He promised to bring her up here so that we could all be together." Mary Frances looked imploringly at Mr. O'Neal. Then she took Tommy's arm. He looked around at his brothers, but they were staring down at their clasped hands. Maggie heard her father say, very softly, "He didn't do it, Ma. Maybe he forgot."

He put his arm around Mary Frances's shoulder. A path opened for them through the people who were left, and he guided her to a car and climbed in after her; his long arm was the last Maggie saw of him, pulling the door closed with a loud *thunk*.

"This is not my fault," Mr. O'Neal was saying as Maggie and Connie walked to another limousine. Margaret was already inside, and in silence they drove to the big fieldstone house. There were plates of cold cuts, and Swedish meatballs in a chafing dish with a little candle underneath to keep them warm, and fried chicken and potato and macaroni salad. But Mary Frances never came downstairs. Maggie spent most of the afternoon fetching Mr. McAlevy a fresh drink and listening to him tell a long story about a policeman, a bar in Brooklyn, a colored man, and an Irish gang that seemed to have no point and certainly nothing to do with John Scanlan. She excused herself when she saw Margaret climbing the stairs with a plate of food, and followed her to the door of the girls' room. Across the hall she could see her grandparents' room, neat and empty, her grandfather's gray suit laid out on the bed.

"Have you seen the stone doorstop?" Maggie asked.

"What, sweetie?" her aunt said, balancing the plate of chicken and potato salad on one hand and pushing a piece of hair under her wimple.

"Remember the doorstop? The big round ball with the flat sides that always held the door back?"

"I haven't seen that for years, Maggie," Margaret said impatiently. "Would you go get me a 7-Up with just a splash of Canadian Club in it and bring it here?"

"A cherry?" Maggie said.

"Not necessary," Margaret said, opening the door and taking the food inside.

When Maggie came back, her grandmother was sitting up in bed, eating chicken and patting her face with a tissue. Somehow it was the sight of Mary Frances in the single bed, Elizabeth Ann's bed, that finally got to Maggie, so that when she handed her the drink she began to cry, wiping the tears from her cheeks with the back of her hand until Margaret handed her one of her big plain white cotton handkerchiefs.

"You were his favorite," Mary Frances said, and as Maggie looked at her grandmother, so small and raddled-looking, lying in the small bedroom with the two Scanlan & Co. crucifixes over the two beds, she knew that their lives would never be the same again. On the table next to the bed was a copy of *Wuthering Heights*.

"It's really good," said Maggie, picking the book up and sniffling. "There's some boring stuff at the beginning and end but the main story is great."

"As good as *Jane Eyre?*" Margaret said.

"Better."

"What?" said Mary Frances querulously, eyeing them over the edge of her glass.

"Maggie was asking about the doorstop for some reason," Margaret said loudly, as though her mother was deaf.

"The what?"

"That big stone doorstop we used to have downstairs."

Mary Frances beamed. "You may have it, dear," she said to Maggie.

"But where is it, Mother?" Margaret said.

Mary Frances thought for a moment. "It's in the cabinet to the left of the stove, on the bottom shelf near the back. I put it there last year after your grandfather threatened to throw it out the window. He'd stubbed his toe on it in the dark." Mary Frances patted her face with the tissue again. "I know he'd want you to have it, dear," Mary Frances added.

"Although maybe some time you'll explain to me why you want it," Margaret added, eating potato salad from her mother's plate.

Maggie thought for a moment. "I think it's displacement," she said.

Her aunt Margaret narrowed her eyes, and Maggie could tell that she was trying to decide whether Maggie was being smart or not. Margaret leaned back on the bed, the skirt of her habit hiked up to her knees, her black legs crossed at the ankle. "This family has a future," she said finally.

"What?" asked Mary Frances.

"Nothing, Mother," Margaret said, and she winked at Maggie.

22

IT WAS CONNIE, OF ALL PEOPLE, WHO had taken her mother-in-law to the grave of her daughter, back in one corner of the cemetery where Connie had grown up. Connie had called Angelo Mazza the morning after the funeral, and then she had called Mary Frances, and picked her up in Tommy's station wagon. Mary Frances slid into the passenger seat, clutching her black handbag as though this excursion was the most natural thing in the world. There was no conversation. Mary Frances took out her rosary and said it soundlessly, the silence punctuated by the clicks of her crystal beads on their silver chain. When they drove through the gates to Angelo's little house she let them slither back into the blue velvet pouch in which she kept them.

"This place is very pleasant, Concetta," Mary Frances said as she emerged from the car.

Connie actually thought the flowers looked tired at this time of year, a little florid in their color, like a woman wearing too much makeup to disguise her age. The rose of Sharon and the hollyhocks were ragged, and the daisies had gotten leggy and fell over in untidy clumps. Most of the day lilies were gone, and the handsomest parts of the cemetery were those that had turned a deep green, in a final burst of good health before the early frosts defoliated them. As though he had been thinking the same thing, Angelo emerged from his house carrying a small pair of clippers. He looked neat and elegant in his gray pants and white shirt.

Connie felt as tired as she'd ever been in her life. Part of it was the pregnancy, and part was the heat, and part were the events of the last few days. That morning two police officers had arrived at the front door. They were young, boys really, ten years younger than she was, and they wanted to talk to Maggie.

"I understood that the builders would not be pressing any charges, that they had agreed to receive restitution from the family of the boy responsible," Connie said.

"We have to do our own investigation, ma'am," one of the officers said quietly, and Connie flinched at that last word, and felt very old. She was glad Tommy had gone over to Scanlan & Co. for the day. She called Maggie down from her bedroom. Maggie was barefoot, her hair wet from the shower, and she froze at the bottom of the stairs as she saw the blue uniforms.

"We're particularly interested in the last fire," the officer said.

They sat on the couch and Maggie sat on the floor cross-legged, her shoulders slumped, her arms limp. "Why are you talking to me?" she said.

Connie started to speak, but before she could the officer, flipping through a spiral notebook, answered, "We talked to a Miss Hearn, who said she had no association with the fires. She sent us to a Miss Malone, who said the same. She sent us to you."

Connie could see Maggie only in profile. She had always known that the day would come when her daughter's transformation would be complete, when she would not only be separate but equal, when she would become adult. Connie knew that this could take a long time; she felt that for herself it had happened just the other day, in the parking lot at the high school and in John Scanlan's hospital room. She had expected it to happen when Maggie got her first period, developed breasts, fell in love. But it was happening here, now, horribly. There was a tightness around the square jaw, a hard glint in the eye, that was the look of a woman. It was like that just for a moment, and then it was replaced by the soft vulnerable look of a child who has been mistreated. Maggie's mouth was open, but nothing came out. Then Connie had said, "My daughter was here with me that night. She couldn't have had anything to do with it."

The older of the two cops had looked at her for a long time. Connie was quite sure that they'd heard such a story from a mother a hundred times before. Finally he said, "We're happy to know that, ma'am," as he slapped his notebook shut and rose.

On the ride with Mary Frances to the cemetery, Connie thought of that moment, and of the moment when she saw Maggie's face change and watched the end of innocence right before her eyes. She still did not know how much of it was knowing that Debbie had betrayed her, and how much was what Maggie had seen the night of the fire, the things she had meant when she had said, her eyes blazing, "You've done worse than I have tonight." She did not know whether her daughter had seen Joey Martinelli kissing her in the car, trying to undress her in the construction trailer, or arguing with her when Connie finally had pulled away, empowered by knowledge and not this time by nausea.

Connie wondered, too, what Joey had seen in her own face when she handed him the key to the trailer, what had made him finally crumble and grow still after hours of argument. She knew what she had seen in his: it was that same glaze her daughter had had beneath the watchful eyes of the police, the awareness of the world the way it truly was.

"Life is a terrible thing," she said matter-of-factly.

"Yes, dear," said Mary Frances. "But then, what else is there?" And she slid out of the car as Angelo Mazza came forward to greet her.

Connie realized it was only the third time her mother-in-law and her father had met. Mary Frances seemed to have regained some of her aristocratic manner now that her husband's illness was over, but it was a little weary and worn, like something familiar she had fallen back on purely from fatigue.

"Good morning," Mary Frances said to Angelo quietly. "This is very kind."

Angelo gave a slight bow and then held out his arm. "Shouldn't we drive, Pop?" Connie said, but Mary Frances said, "I would rather walk."

In silence, under a lowered, pale gray sky, the thick air smelling of rain, they trod the asphalt, springy beneath their feet, until they came to a freshly cleared spot by the wall. Connie could see that her father had cut back the wisteria, sinuous and predatory here in the old section, and that some years ago he had planted violets around this stone, their heart-shaped leaves large and plentiful now, the little facelike flowers gone this late in the season. A small square headstone bore only the word SCANLAN, with the disembodied head and wings of a cherub above it. Time's grime, the decades of snow and rain, summer and winter, had left black rubbed deep into the design and the letters. Mary Frances stood with her head down, still holding on to Angelo Mazza's arm.

"I have kept it very good," he said quietly. "Very nice. In the springtime it is always purple, first with the wisteria, then the violets. Very sweet."

"Yes," Mary Frances said. "Thank you."

Connie was sure that there was something strange about this, about the fact that Tommy's sister had been in her own backyard, as it were, even before she first set eyes on Tommy. But it seemed no stranger than anything else she could think of, no stranger than the fact that two people sometimes cleaved together their whole lives long because of something they'd done in the back seat of a car, no stranger than the fact that two people could cleave together their whole lives long, while one thought she'd been made a promise and another that the promise didn't matter much. Or that people could have hard feelings for so long and have them evaporate overnight. Connie put a hand on her mother-in-law's shoulder. "You can have her moved as soon as you want," she said.

"No," Mary Frances said. "This is fine. I just wanted to know where to come. It would be a shame to disturb this."

"Maybe that's what John thought," Connie said.

"No," said Mary Frances sadly, slipping her rosary beads out of her bag. "He just couldn't be bothered. He thought it was a whim. God rest him," she added reflexively.

Connie stepped away from the corner, to give her mother-in-law privacy, and she and her father walked out to the road. Damien was back by the rosebushes, doing the fall fertilization. He had waved to her across the expanse of bushes and headstones, but he had not gotten up from his work. Once she saw his lips move and thought he was talking to a bug.

There were no funerals today, although somewhere across the way Connie could see the garish display of color upon one mound that showed where a grave had been recently filled and all the funeral baskets and wreaths laid atop it. The gladiolus had always repelled her just as they had her father, but she minded them less because they were dead than that they had always been such a symbol of death itself. She remembered shuddering at her wedding when she saw those frilly spears, so unnaturally tall, standing on the altar. Between two rows of headstones she saw Leonard Fogarty running the hand mower, the skin of his flat head pale white beneath the stubble of his brush cut. He would be pleased when he turned and saw her, would come running over with his awkward gait, smiling all over his face, calling "Hi Hi Hi." She remembered him on her wedding day, too, and the sound he had made, like a calling bird: *oooooooh*, as she came out of the house in her pale cream dress, the color of eggnog.

The cemetery was a beautiful place, although she had had enough of the accoutrements of death during the past week to last her a lifetime. It shamed her to know that she was thinking of a new life as well; not the one inside her, but the one around her. They all were. Even Mr. O'Neal had been happy at John Scanlan's wake, although he had done his best to hide it. The family had taken the heaviest, most expensive bronze casket he had for what he knew would be the largest funeral he would handle all year. The Scanlan family had printed up a thousand holy cards in anticipation of the crowd. When all of the nuns from Margaret's convent entered at once, Mark had turned to Tommy and whispered, "Call and get more cards."

"Get the sewing machines converted quick for blouses and table runners," Tommy whispered back, and Connie, overhearing, had had to stifle a laugh. Tommy turned and grinned at her, and then, very softly, he ran his hand over the down of her upper arm. She had shivered and then slowly smiled.

For part of the evening she had found herself alone in one corner with her sister-in-law Gail, who had never become accustomed to the lively air of Catholic funerary rites, particularly the position of the departed at the front of the room like a table centerpiece. Nevertheless she had tried to join in. "He looks good, doesn't he?" Gail had said to Connie.

"He looks dead, Gail."

"You two are certainly taking this hard," Gail said. "Tommy has seemed so moody. It wasn't like him to snap at Mother the way he did."

Connie sighed. "He loved his father," she said, thinking of how little nuance the sentence contained.

"Yes," said Gail piously, adjusting the lapels of her black suit. She looked down at Connie's belly, draped in black wool. "Aren't you hot?"

"It's the only black maternity dress I have," Connie said. "Tomorrow I'll have to wear a blue one."

Gail looked down at her hands in her lap and twisted her wedding ring. "We're going to adopt a baby," she said.

"That's wonderful, Gail," said Connie, feeling a surge of pity for her sister-in-law, her hair so carefully barretted back, her fingers turning, turning her ring. "That's great. You'll love it. It's the most wonderful thing in the world, being a mother." She wondered what it was about this situation that made her say so many things that sounded right but felt suspect. She was afraid that if she stayed here much longer, among the liverish pink and pale green brocades, she would find herself, like the head of the carpenters union now standing behind her, talking of what a good man John Scanlan was, and how much he loved his sons.

"We couldn't have done it while he was alive," Gail said, her voice still lowered as though she was afraid her father-in-law would hear. It was a testimonial to John Scanlan's vivid personality that even Connie, who had no illusions about death, had looked up several times during the evening and momentarily expected him to leap from his prone position and throttle someone who had done him dirty over the years.

"How do you feel about all this?" Gail said suddenly, in what sounded like an accusatory tone.

"Do you mean am I glad he's dead?" Connie asked, and without waiting for an answer she went on, "Not really. I thought I would be, but I think it will probably upset things more than it will help them. And it will be hard to be happy at the wedding on Saturday. But I'm glad for you about the baby."

"Mark can do what he wants," Gail said. "I can do what I want. So can you."

Connie was silent for a minute. She could see John Scanlan's nose, beaklike and fierce, and then two more visitors knelt in front of the casket and blocked her view.

"No one can do what they want," she said, thinking of the look on Joey Martinelli's face when she had given him back the key to the construction trailer.

"I guess I can understand if you're sad," Gail went on as though she hadn't heard. "The way he talked about you—how Tommy was the only one to marry a girl with looks, how the rest of the grandchildren, even Monica, were washed-out from too much Irish inbreeding and your children were the only ones who were halfway decent-looking or had half a brain. If I had had to hear one more word about what great legs you had, I would have screamed."

Connie looked at her sister-in-law for a long time, and suddenly, to her surprise, she felt tears fill her eyes. She felt great pity for John Scanlan, and anger at him, too. "Well, Gail, that's the first I've ever heard of the high regard my father-in-law had for me," she said.

"It would have killed him to say anything nice about anyone to their face. He didn't even kiss me at our wedding. I never heard him say a kind word to Mother. I don't even believe he loved her. I think she was just a baby machine. Excuse me. I didn't mean anything by that."

The man and woman kneeling in front of the body rose, and Connie could see that the woman was crying. She was wiping her face with a tissue, wiping away her rouge so that one cheek was a gray-white, the other a gay pink. It was one of John Scanlan's sisters, the one he always called Fat Marge.

"Who knows how he really felt about anything?" Connie had said, and then she had looked across the room to a corner where Dorothy O'Haire sat lost in the shadows. She was wearing a cheap black suit, clutching a black patent purse. Earlier in the evening, before anyone else had arrived, Connie had come in to make a list of the people who had sent flowers so that Mary Frances could send thank-you notes, and Dorothy had been kneeling at the casket with a little girl at her side. The child wore a beautiful navy blue dress, some gauzy stuff over linen, and a big sailor hat. When she had turned away from the casket, Connie could see that the girl had her mother's dullish yellow hair, but her eyes were of a clear and translucent blue. They were Scanlan eyes.

"Oh, Dorothy," Connie had said.

"Mrs. Scanlan, this is my daughter," Dorothy had said primly. "Her name is Beth." The girl curtsied. "How do you do?" she said, like a little girl in an old movie. On the bosom of her dress her initials were monogrammed in white: EAO. Connie knew that the O stood for O'Haire, and she was just as sure, as sure as if the name had been spoken aloud, that the E and the A stood for Elizabeth Ann. She wondered whether the girl's mother had chosen the name, to stake her claim, or the girl's father, to try to make amends or to live life over. After a few minutes, Dorothy had taken the child outside and put her into a car with someone, Connie could not see who, and then had come back inside alone. "I wanted her to pay her respects," she said to Connie, finding herself that same seat in the corner, and every time during the evening Connie looked over, she had wondered if John had provided enough money for both of them. And she realized she knew another thing she would never tell her husband, and she felt weary with the weight of all the secrets it required to protect those you loved.

Now in the sunlight Connie looked over at her own father and wondered if that's what he had done for her, all these years, if his silence was really protection from a world he found too terrible to live in. He stood silently studying the cemetery, making sure it was perfectly groomed, everything in place. His flawless world, Connie thought, where none of the people are mean or dishonest or careless because none of them are alive. Angelo left her for a moment to say something to Leonard, and then walked back slowly, his shirt glowing in the sun. She was glad she had worn a skirt, even a flimsy cotton wrap one, its ties strained by her thickened waist; her father was offended by women in pants. Her hand went to her hair to smooth it off her forehead.

"Mr. Scanlan is buried," Angelo said.

"Finally," said Connie.

"He was supposed to have the child buried with him?"

Connie nodded. "That's what his wife thought. I don't know whether it was a misunderstanding, or he just ignored her."

"Different things are important to different people," Angelo said. "Most people hate the bugs—your son loves them. Most people talk too much—your daughter listens."

"My daughter is a woman now."

"Of course," said Angelo. "This summer it happened. Anybody could see. When your mother was her age, she was already married. One baby on the way, one baby to come. Children grow fast. Except if they are here." And he looked around him again. Mary Frances joined them, her rosary in her hand, and Angelo escorted her in his courtly fashion back to the car.

Connie was quiet on the drive home, overwhelmed by events. She and Mary Frances fell back on their old ways for much of the drive, the older woman talking in a desultory fashion about Monica's wedding. Connie thought it would be an interesting affair, judging from the fact that the groom's family had wanted his name on the invitations to read Donald "Duck" Syzmanski. As they neared Mary Frances's house there was a long silence, and then the older woman began to speak, almost to herself, so low that Connie had to bend her head to listen.

"No one ever understands what it's like unless they're in it themselves," Mary Frances said. "People look at your children and they see them all in a lump. Even their father, calling them "the brood," herding them into the car for Mass every Sunday morning, making rules to fit them all, about staying out late, about homework, about spankings if they got into trouble, even for Margaret, with her little fanny in white cotton pants, her skirt pulled up. But their mother never sees them that way. Even now, all standing together, men in their suits, too big to hug, you see them all as themselves, clear—Jimmy with his everlasting questions, following you around the house: Why does this happen, Mama, why does that happen? Why does the sun rise and set? And Mark, walking him around the living room in that little row house we had, walking him every night with the colic while he screamed and screamed, the sky so black outside that it was like the end of the world. And Tommy curling like a little shrimp next to me on the beach, pulling a towel over his little shoulders so he wouldn't burn. "Be a man!" John would yell at him, and he'd try to lie still, so still that no one would notice him."

Mary Frances looked over at her. "Do you understand what I'm saying?" she said. "The baby was stillborn and they came at me with a needle to put me to sleep and I said, damn you, give me that child. And I baptized her right there, and she was so pretty, with pink skin like flowers. And I kissed her face and she was real to me, as real as any of the others, even now. More real, maybe. Because you think of what they'll become, and you're always disappointed. Though they're all good boys, all fine, they're never exactly what you dream they're going to be. Only she, only she never disappointed. Even today I dream the same dreams about her as when I kissed her face." She bent her head over her hands, and then lifted it and stared out the windshield. "I kissed her, and then I let them give me the shot."

Connie pulled into the driveway slowly because she found it hard to see through the tears in her eyes, and because she was so overcome to hear Mary Frances put into words Connie's own feelings, the feelings about her children that she had believed were twisted and peculiar and hers alone. She felt the weight of all the wasted years, of the playacting that all of them had done while they lived with that great central figure, that star now dead. Connie supposed that that was the sin for which they would all have to forgive John Scanlan, the sin of forcing them all to play their thankless roles. Her mother-in-law climbed out of the car and then turned back and leaned through the window.

"Tomorrow at the wedding I will tell my son that I want to sell that house his father bought. I will tell him I want the money and he won't be able to argue with me about it. It's not that I mind people trying to arrange other people's lives, but if they do it, they have to do it right." She drew a deep breath and her voice wavered as she added, "The boys say that I can't live here alone, and it could be that they're right. If I had my druthers, I would prefer it be you and Tommy who move in here. Any of the others would drive me crazy. That's not why I'm having him sell the house. I'm not making a deal with you. I just want you to know what I think. I'm tired of keeping my mouth shut. At least you and I wouldn't have to pretend. You could have your ways and I'd have mine." She stopped for a moment. "And I love my son," she added, as though she only had the one.

They looked at each other for a long moment and then Mary Frances began to speak again, and this time her voice was hard and clear. "There are two spaces in that plot in your father's cemetery," she said. "I want the other one. I am telling you and I will tell Tommy, because everyone else will think I'm crazy and they will do what they want in any event. But I'm telling you that it will be your responsibility to see that this time I get my way. The rest of them will want to do what is proper, but you will make them do what is right." Connie leaned over toward her. She wanted to call her something but she couldn't think what and so she simply began, "John said to me in the hospital—" But Mary Frances cut her off. "He did the best he could, dear," she said, sounding more like herself. "A man can't be what he isn't. He did the best he could with what he had. That's something for you to remember. Tommy does the best he knows how."

"I know," Connie said, her eyes filling again. Mary Frances turned and walked into the house and Connie wondered if she should try to tell her more, should try to tell her how sorry her husband had been, although whether it was for the death, for failing to move the baby's body, or for something even more unforgivable she was still not sure. She supposed "He did the best he could" was the best benediction anyone could hope for.

23

MAGGIE SAT ON THE BENCH IN FRONT OF her aunt's old dressing table, her long legs hidden beneath the ruffled skirt. Her bridesmaid's dress hung on the back of the closet door. Connie stood behind her brushing Maggie's hair over and over again as though she was painting, coat after coat. Connie was so small that her head just barely topped Maggie's when she stood behind her, so that in the mirror they looked like some strange Indian goddess, one dark head above the other, one set of arms resting in the lap, another rising and falling, holding a brush.

"You two look like sisters," Aunt Cass said.

Monica was in the bathroom putting on her makeup. She looked like the centerfold in one of the *Playboy* magazines the boys had hidden beneath the floorboards of the development houses. She was wearing something called a merry widow, a one-piece lace garment like a very fancy swimsuit, which pushed her bust up and whittled her waist to nothing. "Should she be wearing that?" Connie had said with some concern, but Aunt Cass said that Uncle James said it was fine. Maggie could not imagine Monica modeling such a thing for her father, but she was not inclined to ask questions on this particular day.

Behind her, her mother was humming tunelessly. She was wearing a new dress, a simple red drape in some satiny material. Her lipstick matched. Her hair was in loose, shiny waves over her shoulders. It seemed incredible that she had been so recently to a funeral, but Uncle James and Mary Frances had insisted that the wedding go on as planned, with no sign, even in their clothes, that there had been a death in the family except that the five priests concelebrating the Mass would make mention of John Scanlan during the prayers for the dead. "My father would have wanted it that way," James told several of the mourners at the funeral, who nodded solemnly.

Maggie knew this was not true. John Scanlan would have wanted them to cancel the whole thing, deposit or no deposit. (Actually, Maggie knew, he would have wanted Uncle James to demand that the deposit be returned and to threaten legal action if it was not.) "Give the devil his due," Maggie thought he would say, but she could not quite conjure him up, with his broad white grin and his glittering blue eyes, saying it. She could barely remember his face; she could only remember his hands, big, the hairs on them like a web.

In the mirror her own eyes seemed dead, too, looking inside, and then they came alive as she looked up at her mother. Connie had drawn Maggie's long tail of hair up onto the back of her head, and she was separating it into sections, smiling to herself, as though she had a secret. She picked a thin piece of pink ribbon off the dressing table and began to braid it through one section, her hands quick and sure. Maggie sat silently until her mother had made six narrow braids and pinned them into long loops, chestnut shot through with pink. When Connie was finished she picked up a silver mirror from the dressing table, glancing first at the engraving on the back. "From your aunt Margaret's hope chest," she said, and handed the mirror to Maggie so she could see how her hair looked from behind.

With her hair pulled back, her forehead and cheeks pink, her eyes bright without their dark frame, Maggie felt suddenly shy. "It feels strange," she said, returning the mirror. But then she thought that sounded ungrateful and she added, "It looks nice."

Monica emerged from the bathroom in her merry widow and white stockings, her hair still in rollers, Mary Frances's good pearls around her neck. She had lent Maggie her add-a-pearl necklace; she had not wanted to, but Aunt Cass had insisted. "As a peace offering," she had said, and at that moment Maggie had heard her grandfather's voice loud and clear, saying, "Peace offering my ass." Monica was holding a mascara wand. "Well, well," she said, tilting her head. "The ugly duckling turns into a swan."

"You look lovely, Maggie," said Aunt Cass.

"When you're old enough to wear makeup you just might look like a real girl," Monica said, rearranging her bosom in the boned bodice of white lace.

"She's wearing makeup today," said Connie, "or this pink will wash her right out." Connie opened her purse and began to remove a bottle of foundation, a compact, and a pat of pink rouge. "I'll take that mascara when you're done with it, Monica," she said.

Connie held Maggie's chin in her hand and began to smooth creams onto her face, turning it this way and that and occasionally rubbing something off with a finger she'd touched to her tongue. It seemed to take a long time, with Connie humming and looking at Maggie dispassionately as though she was a piece of furniture being refinished. Finally she let go of her chin, and kissed the top of her head. Maggie almost jumped out of her skin.

"What are you going to do about these?" said Connie, and with her index finger she flicked the limp circle of dingy thread hanging from one of Maggie's earlobes. Maggie inhaled. She had kept her ears hidden beneath her hair for a week. Connie went into her purse again and removed a square of tissue. Inside were a pair of earrings, teardrop-shaped stones, purple-red, dangling from small curving pieces of gold.

"This is going to hurt," Connie said, snipping the strings with a nail scissors and pulling them out. It took her a minute to get the earrings in, and Maggie kept very still, looking into her own eyes again. Her mother stepped back to look at her.

"Ta da," she said.

"Where did you get those?" Maggie said.

"They were my mother's. I found them after she died. It was so strange to see them, because I don't think she wore a pretty thing her whole life, at least when I knew her. Your grandfather couldn't tell me where they came from either. And I wasn't interested in wearing them. They've been sitting at the back of one of my drawers for years."

"You couldn't have worn them anyway," said Maggie, moving her head from side to side.

"Sure I could have. Aunt Rose pierced my ears when I was a baby. I just stopped wearing earrings when I got married. Now the holes are closed up."

"Why did you stop?"

"It used to be something that only girls right off the boat did. Girls like your aunt Margaret didn't have pierced ears."

"And you were a girl like Aunt Margaret?"

Connie grinned. "I tried to be," she said. "I don't think I was very good at it."

"Oh, Connie, what a beautiful job you've done," Aunt Cass said. "Will her hat fit over that hairdo?"

"No," Connie said. "I don't think she'll wear the hat. It's not really her, Cass. And the other girls are wearing hats and dresses that are entirely different."

Aunt Cass narrowed her lips, but she looked again at Maggie's hair, and then she sighed. "Maybe God will count the ribbons as a hat," she finally said.

"Go into the bathroom and see if there's any Vaseline," Connie said to Maggie. "Put a little on your lips and blot it off."

Her mother moved aside and Maggie saw herself in the mirror. She could not believe what her mother had done, how she had managed, with her Touch 'n' Glo creamy ivory and her Autumn Roses cake rouge and her eyebrow pencil, to turn Maggie into a shadow of Connie herself, a manufactured double. She leaned forward but try as she might she could not make the resemblance go away, and it suddenly occurred to her that this was the only difference between the two of them—a little color, a little pressed powder, a few years.

"Thank you," she said to Connie's reflection.

"It was my pleasure," Connie replied, as though the two of them were partners in some antiquated dance.

Maggie drew one of Mary Frances's housecoats tight around her lanky body and staggered into the bathroom in her new dyed-to-match damask pumps. Monica was leaning into her own reflection in the medicine cabinet mirror. The bathroom was strewn with curlers, bobby pins, pots of cream and foundation, bottles of perfume.

"Excuse me," Maggie said, moving past her cousin to reach for the Vaseline on top of the toilet tank. Monica recoiled, and Maggie thought she was about to get nasty again when suddenly she moved toward the toilet and fell to her knees. The retching was painful to hear, as if Monica had a fishbone in her throat; a roller fell from the front of her hair onto the floor. Maggie leaned forward, picked it up, and held back the long curl so it would not get in Monica's way.

The vomiting seemed to go on and on, and Maggie felt stupid standing there, bent over, holding a piece of hair, afraid to move. She had seen the same thing happen too many times to her mother to misunderstand, and this made her feel stupid, too. She remembered saying to her cousin, "You don't fool me one bit," in the bridal salon, and she knew everyone had thought she meant more than she was saying. Perhaps, she thought, her grandfather would in fact have wanted the wedding to take place today, funeral or no funeral. She could see the red welt on Monica's tanned back where the merry widow had pressed into her flesh, and when her cousin finally rose, using the toilet to hoist herself from her knees like an old woman, Maggie saw that her mascara had run in gray rivulets all over her face, making little rivers in the pink of her makeup. Her eyes were bloodshot, her lips swollen, the veins on the part of her breasts spilling from the top of her fancy underpinnings blue and swollen too.

Maggie watched Monica in the mirror as she methodically began to apply cold cream to take off her ruined makeup. When Monica's face was bare, she put out her hand peremptorily, her polished nails pearly, and retrieved the roller. She twisted the long lock of hair back up and began to redo her face, first blotting a single tear that ran down the side of her nose.

"Monica," said Maggie, "I'm really sorry. I'm really sorry it turned out like this."

She knew she had said the wrong thing when she saw the usually implacable face contort. Her cousin whirled round to face her, so close that they were almost touching. "You just don't get it, do you, Maria Goretti," Monica said, her eyes wild. "This is the way it is. This is the way everything is. It's one screw job after another, and then you die. You really think it's going to be like some goddamn little story, but this is what it's like when you grow up. One bad thing after another, and you just have to say 'To hell with it' and go on to something else. But not you. You're going to walk around with that little sad face and those little sad eyes and go, oh, oh, I'm really sorry, you didn't live happily ever after, you—"

"Shut up, Monica," Connie said, standing in the doorway.

"You should be able to fill her in, Aunt Concetta," Monica said after a moment's silence. "I'm going downstairs for my prenuptial crackers, so I don't throw up on Father Hanlon's best vestments."

"You do that," Connie said as Monica put on a robe.

When she was gone Maggie sat back down at the dressing table. "I feel stupid," she said.

"Your cousin is the one who's stupid," Connie said.

"You know what I'm talking about. I didn't even figure out why she was getting married. They probably all thought I was an idiot when we went for our dresses. They were all making little comments about whether Monica's could be let out, and I just sat there listening. You should have told me."

Connie knelt on the floor, lightly, as though there was no belly under the red tent of her dress. She looked up into Maggie's face, her eyes blazing. "Maggie," she said, "there are some things that aren't that important. There are things that seem tremendously important at the time and then years later you look back and think you can't believe you ever worried so much about them."

"You sound like Monica. Everything's silly."

"No," Connie said, smoothing her daughter's hair. "That's not what I mean. It's just that whether you're getting married because you're having a baby isn't as important as getting married and having the baby. Monica's wrong. She's one of those people who sees everything bad. And there are other people who see everything good."

"Like who?"

"I think deep down inside your father is one of them. Your aunt Margaret, too, probably, in a different way."

"What about you?"

"Not good or bad. Things just are."

"And me?"

"I think you'll probably be like me."

The two of them looked at each other for a moment. Finally Maggie said, "Monica said something else to me, too. When we were getting our dresses." She watched her mother's face, but it was very still. "About when you got married. And when I was born."

Connie smiled slowly, but she didn't show her teeth, and her eyes were cold. "She's going to have a hard life, that girl," she finally said, as though she was talking to herself. Then she looked at Maggie and said, "What did I just tell you? There are things that seem important to some people that just aren't important at all."

"You should have told me," Maggie said.

"I wouldn't have known what to say. We got married. We had a baby. I wouldn't change a thing."

"Can I ask you a question?"

"Yes."

"Were you going to have a baby and that's why you got married?"

"That's one way of looking at it."

"That's wrong, isn't it?"

Connie sighed. "What's wrong is if I was angry about it for the rest of my life. Or if you were ashamed." Connie rose and took Maggie's dress down from its hanger. She cradled it in her arms and then she looked Maggie in the eye and said, "It's wrong to light a fire. It's worse to enjoy it."

"I didn't enjoy it."

"I know."

"You don't believe me about not doing it."

Connie was quiet, her face blank.

"It's complicated. I sort of did it, but I sort of didn't. Does that make any sense?"

"Yes," Connie said. "I know exactly what you mean."

"It was hard to think about it while it was happening."

"I know that too."

"Why did you tell the police I wasn't there?" Maggie said.

"Because that seemed closest to the truth."

"Did they believe you?"

"I don't know," she said. "Probably not. Raise your arms." Connie slipped the dress over Maggie's head. She zipped it, and stepped back. "You look beautiful, Maggie," Connie said, and then she corrected herself. "You are beautiful. That's the truth, the whole truth, and nothing but the truth, so help me God."

Maggie looked at herself in the mirror. She stood up and her mother's head behind her disappeared, so that now she only saw herself, and she knew that it was true. "I still feel stupid," she said. She looked at herself again, and behind the mask of the makeup she could see the Maggie Scanlan she used to be, and around her eyes she could see someone else, someone harder to know, harder to understand. She couldn't figure out which of them was worth being, or whether it was possible, just for today, to be both at once.

But later, in church, as she stood to one side of Monica, who was serene and lovely in her high-waisted white organdy, without a hint of belly, she knew that she had learned something. It somehow came as no surprise to her as she came up the aisle to look over and see Bruce in one of the pews with his father, staring at her with his mouth slightly open. It seemed perfectly natural to smile slightly at him and then bow her head to sniff the roses in her nosegay, although she could feel the color rising in her cheeks beneath the artificial pink of the rouge. And when it was time for the vows, Maggie's head came round with a snap as the groom recited his, and she realized that when she had envisioned this moment, thinking about the wedding, she had taken for granted that he would say "I do" in the same voice she had heard say "Oh God" that night on the beach. But his voice was unmistakably the voice of an entirely different person, and after that first swift swivel of her head, she was somehow not at all surprised.

24

TOMMY WAS NOT DRUNK. NEITHER WAS he sober. Dessert had been taken away—it was, as was customary, ice cream and a slice of wedding cake that tasted like sweetened cotton balls—and now a gnarled little man with a cart filled with liqueurs had stopped by his table. Tommy looked at the candy-colored bottles and almost sent him on, then thought better of it and, feeling vaguely English, asked for a brandy. Connie shot him a sidelong look, and he laughed. He was having a good time.

Monica's wedding reception was being held at a country club just north of Kenwood and several rungs above the Kenwoodie Club. The banquet room was paneled in knotty pine, and the chairs and restroom walls were covered with green-and-red tartan. It was what John Scanlan always referred to disdainfully as "high Episcopal," and the fact was that James was the first Catholic they'd ever admitted. The membership committee had postponed a decision on his application until after the Kennedy-Nixon presidential election to see which way the wind blew. James had certainly planned a high Episcopalian reception, with meager food and a bad band, all overpriced, but his plans had gone awry. For one thing, the groom's family had persuaded the band, Jimmy Jones and the Lamplighters, to play a number of polkas, which had been received with much screaming, whooping, and lifting of women old enough to know better into the air. For another, the groom's father had taken off his cutaway jacket early in the evening, exposing his service revolver, which, he explained to Tommy, he always wore off duty, "just in case."

"Jesus, in this world, Tom, you never know," he said feelingly.

"The God's truth," Tommy said, having the time of his life and his second Scotch.

Finally, there were John Scanlan's brothers and sisters, all eleven of them. James spent most of the cocktail hour trying to lay blame—and Tommy suspected that he was prime suspect—for it turned out that after the funeral, someone had mentioned to all of them that they were welcome at Monica's wedding. Coming down the aisle to take her seat on the arm of one of the ushers, and already concerned that her daughter was going to be sick at the very sight of Communion, poor Cass had been astounded to see almost two dozen people she had not invited sitting in pews very near the front of the church. She had called the country club from the vestry after the service, and asked that two more tables be set up. It was a tight fit.

Tommy spent most of the cocktail hour talking to his aunts and uncles, whom he had never seen very often. None seemed remotely put out that their brother had given them the back of his hand, except for one cut-rate party a year, for the last forty years. "A prince," John Scanlan's brother Brian, a sanitation dispatcher in the Bronx, kept repeating with tears in his eyes. "If he had been born twenty years later, he would have been the first Catholic president, mark my words, Tom. That smart he was. Our mother used to tell us, 'Boys, when your brother's elected pope, don't do anything to embarrass him.' Little did she know about his way with the ladies. But president he could have had, Tom, if the time had been right."

"He would have made an interesting president, Uncle Brian. We probably would have gone to war with the British."

Brian narrowed his eyes, and then grinned. "You're a great one for joshing, son," he said. "It's a grand affair, isn't it?"

"I'm going to go dance with my wife," Tommy said.

"Bless her," Brian said, staring into the depths of his drink.

"Ten thousand if it's a penny," Tommy said to Connie as they danced to "Strangers in the Night" sung by as bad a Sinatra imitator as Tommy had ever heard. "Country club, open bar, prime rib, six-piece band. For something they threw together in a month, my brother did some job on this wedding."

Connie hummed along with the music, and Tommy pulled her closer. Her stomach felt like a Tupperware bowl placed between the two of them. Suddenly Tommy remembered how the priests had made them slow dance at high school sock hops with a dictionary wedged between their pelvises. If anything, it had increased the consciousness of the near occasion of sin.

"Love was just a glance away, a warm embracing dance away," sang Tommy so loudly that couples near them heard him over the electric din of the overeager organist, and several of them smiled.

"Maggie looked beautiful coming down the aisle," said Connie. "But somebody should have told her to hold her bouquet up around her waist."

"She did fine," said Tommy. "Who did her hair? You?"

Connie smiled up at him.

"It's the first time I've seen her face in three years," he said as the music ended.

Now, adrift in that happy haze somewhere between sobriety and the point at which he started to cry uncontrollably at things like "Danny Boy," Tommy saw his daughter across the room, laughing with a boy in a blue sports coat. The kid was skinny, with dishwater-blond hair that stuck up at the crown and a big mobile mouth full of teeth; he ducked his head whenever Maggie turned to look at him, but as soon as she turned away he would stare at her profile as though it was a crucifix and he a new seminarian. He reminded Tommy of someone, but he could not tell who. Maggie looked strangely grownup, perhaps because he was indeed seeing her face, seeing the lines of her square jaw, sharp now as the baby fat disappeared. "Still flat as a board," he muttered to himself, sipping at his brandy, not meaning to speak aloud. "What?" said Mark, dropping into an empty chair next to him.

Another polka was ending, and suddenly, as if in some primitive hostile response, his aunts and uncles had risen to their feet at their tables, wedged in by the swinging kitchen door, and commenced an a cappella version of "When Irish Eyes Are Smiling." They all had fine voices, and had been well trained in the choir of St. Aloysius School; the singing was so loud that men playing golf on the 11th hole, not far from the huge plate-glass picture window of the banquet room, turned, perplexed, looking for the source of some melodious buzzing that had reached their ears. Tommy could not contain his glee and joined in at the end, hoping the groom's family would not offer some folk song as a rejoinder. But instead the groom's father leapt to his feet with a cheer. "Erin go Bragh!" he cried, clapping his big slab hands.

There was much clapping, and the singers took bows, laughing and hitting one another on the back. "Jesus," said Mark. "Oh, relax," Tommy said, grinning as the band started on "Danny Boy," the Lamplighters recognizing a good thing when they saw one.

"Tom, I need you to help me out," Mark said, lighting a cigar.

"Not now," Tommy said. Mark had been pressing him about Scanlan & Co. since the night of the wake. He thought it was the perfect plan for him to take over John's job and have Tommy take over his own. "I'm thinking about it," Tommy added, as his brother continued to stare at him. "I am giving it serious consideration. Honest to God."

"I need you to look at the books," Mark said.

"I've looked at them."

"What!" Mark said, and Tommy loved the look on his face so much he threw back his head and laughed.

"It's not as bad as you think," Tommy said. "He was careless about some things, but the bottom line isn't as bad as you think. On the other hand, it's nowhere near as good as they think." And he motioned to John Scanlan's brothers and sisters, who were singing "Danny Boy" and sobbing happily.

"How the hell—"

"I took the keys from his dresser and let myself into the office one night after I went to the hospital."

"And it's okay? Everything's there?"

Tommy laughed again, this time without pleasure. "Jesus, Mark, what did you think? That Dad cooked the books? That we were bankrupt? That John Scanlan had been playing the ponies on the side and buying fur coats for his secretary?"

Mark tightened his lips and looked away.

"Holy God!" Tommy said. "You really did. You're incredible. Goddamn incredible."

"Things looked suspicious to me," Mark said.

"So he moved money around a little bit more than he should have. So on some things he robbed Peter to pay Paul. But more than that—forget it. Only in books, Mark. You don't wake up one day and find out that Saint John of the all-cotton cassocks is leading a double life." Both men looked toward the bandstand. Their aunt Marge had just poured a beer all over one of her brothers. James got up from the dais and hurried toward her. Monica's nostrils were flaring. The bridegroom was laughing and she gave him a look that Tommy imagined could turn a man to stone. Something about its intensity reminded him of his father, and he pitied the young man in his rented tuxedo sitting, chastened, next to his niece. "I did always wonder about him and Dorothy," Tommy said absently.

"Jesus!" said Mark. "You think he was doing Dorothy?"

"Ah, who cares now?" Tommy said, watching Marge wave her finger in his oldest brother's distinguished face, knowing as surely as if he could hear her that she was reminding James Scanlan that she had once changed his diapers.

It was the wrong time to tell Mark that the company had been paying Dorothy $1000 a month for years, putting her on the books as a paraffin supplier. Tommy had been oddly unsurprised. Mary Frances already knew. Tommy had been sure of it when he watched his mother seat Dorothy in the third row at the funeral Mass. Connie had met the little girl at the funeral home, and when Tommy saw she was not at the Mass he had asked his wife what the child looked like. "What's her name again?" he asked, and Connie had replied quietly, "Beth." Then she had added, "I think she's like Maggie, a combination of her mother and her father." And Tommy let it go at that. He would keep the checks to the bogus paraffin supplier coming, and he would try not to think about the rest. He had known what his father was really like all those years, but he had never had to stare it in the eye until that moment in the hospital when the old man had tried to suck the soul out of his body as his dying act. Tommy would never choose to look that in the eye again, and he would never expose it to the eyes of anyone else. He looked at Mark and added quietly, "The point is that people are different than you think, but they're not that different. Dad wasn't Dr. Jekyll and Mr. Hyde. He was just the guy you saw, and then the real guy. And they're never the same thing. He did good work. But he wasn't the Second Coming of Christ, like he wanted us all to believe. You'll have some cleaning up to do, some loans to consolidate, some changes to make. But things are good."

"So you'll come?"

"I didn't say that. Besides, maybe I want the top job." His brother's eyes grew big, and Tommy laughed again. "Just kidding you, brother. We'll talk about it soon. But not today." The two of them sat silently as couples whirled around the dance floor. Tommy's uncle Brian and aunt Maureen danced by, both with tears in their eyes. Tommy remembered that even his father, that most unsentimental of men, had sometimes teared up over "Danny Boy." Tommy himself had never liked it; it was difficult to sing along with. James went by, dancing with Margaret, his face red from fighting with his aunt. Margaret was still light on her feet, even in her heavy black Cuban heels, her horrid nun shoes. "Dad's turning over in his grave at that sight," Mark said, but his brother had already moved away from him. Tommy tapped James on the shoulder and cut in, grabbing his sister with a grin. "Oh, good," Margaret said. "You're a much better dancer."

Tommy and Margaret had learned to dance together, in the basement of the big house, with Tommy Dorsey on the radio. Lightly they circled the room. "Are you all right?" he finally said.

Margaret frowned. "I think so," she said. "I think I was going through a little temporary insanity this summer. Or puberty."

"I thought we already had puberty," Tommy said.

Margaret looked up into his flushed and boyish face. "I think our whole lives are puberty," she said. "I think we all have to grow up again and again. Isn't' that depressing?"

"It's crazy, is what it is." Tommy dipped her so her veil hung straight to the floor as the last notes died away. "Leave the convent. Come back and be my sister again."

"You're drunk, Tom," Margaret said, laughing. "Beside, you just want me to move in with Mother. Go dance with your wife." But when the band began to play again, Tommy recognized the song after the first few notes, and shook his head. He kissed his sister, smoothed his hair with his hand, and crossed the room to his daughter. He was just drunk enough to feel like Douglas Fairbanks, Jr.

"They're playing our song," he said to Maggie.

She flushed an unbecoming red and turned to the boy, who ducked his head again. Tommy was surprised when the kid looked up suddenly, his lip with its fuzz of facial hair working, and thrust out his hand. "Hello, Mr. Scanlan," he said. "I understand you are a fine basketball player. Maybe some day we can have a game." Without waiting for a response he turned and walked away, disappearing into the great expanse of tables, chairs, flower arrangements, and drunken Irishmen. Once he looked back over his shoulder at Maggie. "Jesus, what the hell was that all about?" Tommy asked. And turning to Maggie he said, "Isn't that the kid whose mother died two years ago?"

"His name is Bruce," Maggie said.

"Can he really play decent ball?" said Tommy. Then he remembered why he had gone to her and he held out his arms. Monica and her father were already dancing, the bride's train thrown over her arm, a little soiled where it had dragged on the ground on her way into church. Monica looked over her father's shoulder, and he looked over hers. They looked like an illustration in a woman's magazine: That Special Day.

Tommy turned to Maggie and gathered her up, gliding around the floor, circling the other couple with long, graceful steps. Every fourth step he would spin, holding Maggie's fingers in his lightly. He felt good, covering the polished parquet, his shoulders squared. He looked down at Maggie, whose pink dress belled out behind her slightly, but she was looking down at her feet.

"Don't look at your feet," he said.

"I can't follow if I don't," she said.

"Stand on mine," Tommy said. "I can take it."

"Daddy, I'm wearing high heels. I'm too big to stand on your feet."

"Then close your eyes," he said. "Close your eyes and don't think about it."

Maggie tilted her head back and shut her eyes; the lights made copper spots on her hair, and little sparks shone from the amethysts dangling from her earlobes. Tommy kept his arm tight around her waist and turned again, and now she was finally following him. She could not dance like her mother, but she was making a creditable show. As his eyes passed, only half-seeing, over the tables ringing the dance floor, he could tell that people were watching them. He dipped her once, spun, dipped her again, and still she kept her eyes tightly closed and her torso limp and pliable. Tommy began to sing along with the band:

> You're the spirit of Christmas,
> My star on the tree,
> You're the Easter Bunny to mommy and me,
> You're sugar,
> You're spice,
> You're everything nice,
> And you're Daddy's little girl.

He sang all the way through to the end of the song, and when it was over James and Monica walked away from each other and Maggie and Tommy just stood there for a moment. Even after the music ended, she waited a full minute before she opened her eyes.

"You did good," Tommy said.

"I liked it," said Maggie. "Why didn't you ever tell me that before, just to close my eyes and not try so hard?"

"I never thought of it before," Tommy said. Suddenly there was a loud crash, the drummer giving his cymbals a good whack. "It's hokey-pokey time," the lead singer called. "Go dance," said Tommy, and when he got back to his table he saw that the boy had claimed her again, standing opposite her in the hokey-pokey line. He tried to figure out who the boy looked like, but he could not. Tommy turned to look at his wife, who was watching the dancers with a small smile on her face, and then he glanced over at Maggie, who had the fixed and exhausted smile of someone who has been having a wonderful time for hours. "I'm a lucky man," he said out loud, and he finished his brandy, took Connie's hand and led her onto the floor.

25

HEN MAGGIE WOKE UP THE DAY AFTER the wedding, she could hear voices coming faintly from the back patio. From her bedroom window she could see her aunt Celeste and her mother outside, sitting in lawn chairs, coffee cups on the cement at their feet. The clock said noon. Maggie had missed Mass for the first time since she had had the mumps three years ago. She noticed that the earrings, which she'd taken off and put on her bureau, were gone. She put on a pair of old pink shorts to match the ribbons in her hair and went downstairs.

"Hi," she said softly, stepping out into the backyard.

Celeste grinned. "Boy, were you right," she said to Connie, and then to Maggie, "Honey, you look like a million bucks with your hair like that. I can't wait to see the pictures of you yesterday."

Maggie went out the sliding door and sat crosslegged at Cece's feet, her head down. Her aunt was wearing a hot-pink dress that consisted of one tier of ruffles atop another. She had on hot pink plastic earrings and her engagement ring winked at Maggie. "Happy birthday," she said to Maggie. "Your present's inside. It's a diary."

"Celeste!" Connie said. "You couldn't wait and let her open it?"

"What the hell."

Connie went into the kitchen and returned with a small box in her hand, wrapped in silver paper with a pink bow. "Happy birthday," she said, handing it to Maggie.

"God, I remember it like it was yesterday," Celeste said with a grin. "Remember the size of you, Con? I mean, people died when they saw you coming down the street. And then Tommy calling us from the hospital and telling me, 'Celeste, she's the biggest goddamn baby in the hospital.' He said that to everyone. 'Bigger than any of the boys, too.' God he was excited. I just kept trying to imagine ten pounds of baby getting out of your body. Maybe that's what put me off having kids. I remember when you brought her home. I've never seen two human beings look so goddamn happy. You had such a smile on your face, I'll never forget."

Connie looked down at Maggie and smiled. Maggie had finished unwrapping her gift. It was a heartshaped locket with her initials engraved on its face in curly script. "Your first real piece of jewelry," Connie said, taking it from her and leaning over to put it around her neck."

"It's really, really nice," Maggie said quietly, and she didn't say any more. But she fingered the locket as she sat on the ground and each time she felt the little grooves of the engraving beneath her fingertips she smiled.

"Monica just called you," Connie said.

"How? She left for Bermuda this morning."

"She called from the airport," Connie said. "She wants to make sure that you don't throw her bouquet away. She gave me instructions about how to preserve it until she gets back."

"That little witch," said Celeste. "You keep that bouquet longer than two weeks, it'll outlast the marriage."

"I think you're jumping to conclusions," said Connie with a small smile.

"Not because she's expecting," said Celeste. "God, if every marriage that started that way broke up, nobody would be married." Maggie raised her head and listened carefully. "But a man can only take so much and so much of Monica is about two weeks' worth."

"Maybe marriage will change her."

"Ha," said Celeste, and Maggie laughed. "So," her aunt added, "you caught the bouquet. You know what that means."

"She didn't mean me to catch it," Maggie said. "She threw it right at one of her friends but it bounced off somebody's elbow and just landed in my hands. I wasn't even trying."

"It's okay," Celeste said. "I caught the bouquet at your mom's wedding and I was already married. Maybe if you're married and catch it it means you're next to be divorced."

The three of them sat looking over the fields behind them. There were twenty-four houses now: four complete, the rest in various stages of framing and finishing. The remains of the charred house had been razed, and another had already been framed in. For a moment Maggie remembered what the fields had once looked like, and then the memory was gone, and she thought that in a few months she would not even be able to remember what Kenwood had been like before the development started.

"It really looks different back here," said Celeste, who had always been able to read Maggie's mind.

"It's going to change the whole place," said Connie. "They're going to build twenty-four more after these. Some builder has plans for a shopping center just down the road. We'll be surrounded."

"I saw your friend Joe on the avenue yesterday when I was picking up groceries for my mother," said Celeste. "I told him he missed his chance with me. I haven't seen him around here too much lately." Celeste squinted at her cousin in the bright sunlight. She'd always been able to read Connie's mind, too.

"He's busier now."

"Have you finished your driving lessons?" Celeste asked.

"I have my temporary license. My permanent one comes any day now. I drove my mother-in-law over to Calvary Cemetery the other day all by myself. And now at least I have ID if someone in a bar doesn't think I'm twenty-one."

"No small accomplishment," said Celeste, and she arched one penciled eyebrow.

"Give it a break, Ce," Connie said.

"Are you moving?" Celeste asked.

"I think so. It's funny how I just lost all my upset about it. My mother-in-law needs us over there. The question is whether to move into her house or the one down the street. Tommy says they may need to sell the other one to pay some of the bills from the business."

"We really might move?" Maggie said.

"I don't know," Connie replied. "Let's wait and see how your grandmother does."

"Grandmother, Schmandmother," said Celeste. "You'll have five kids soon, and you've got four bedrooms. You'll have to start hanging them from the chandeliers. That's a nice big house the old lady's got."

"Give it a break," Connie repeated.

"How's being married, Aunt Celeste?" Maggie asked.

"It's better this time," Celeste said thoughtfully. "But still it's the same. It's not natural, having someone else telling you what to do all the time. But at least we're not arguing about how much I spend on my clothes. When I was married to your Uncle Charlie, one little blouse and—pow! He broke my nose once over a winter coat."

"Don't tell her things like that, Cece," Connie said. "It'll make her think all marriages are like that."

Celeste lifted her eyebrow again.

"They're not. Look at my mother-in-law. She's a changed person since her husband got sick."

"Probably dancing in the aisles," said Celeste, lighting a cigarette.

"You know that's not true. That man was her whole life. That's the thing the kids don't understand. I was looking at Monica yesterday and thinking, *she has no idea*. It's not just a man. It's your house, your kids, your family, your time, everything. Everything in your life is who you marry."

"That's the longest speech I've ever heard you make, Con," said Celeste somberly.

Connie stared across the fields, her lips still red with a trace of lipstick from the day before. "Somebody moved into one of those houses yesterday," she finally said. "I saw the truck from the upstairs window when I was getting ready to go out."

Celeste shrugged. "Big deal. You know what Sol always says. The more things are different, the more they're the same."

"That doesn't make any sense," Maggie said.

"Yeah it does," said her aunt. "Think about it."

Upstairs a screen was lifted with a sound like fingernails on a blackboard. "Connie," came Tommy's tortured voice. "I need tomato juice."

Celeste laughed. "I'll come in with you," she said as Connie rose. "Put some vodka in it. That'll make him feel better."

Maggie stayed out on the patio and thought about what her aunt had said. The more she thought about it, the more she thought it was ridiculous. She thought about life with her grandfather gone, her grandmother alone, perhaps her entire family living in the big stone house and hanging out in the gazebo. She thought of Monica with a baby and a husband, never again to go to a dance with one boy and dump him halfway through the evening for someone better looking, and of Helen perhaps getting a part on Broadway and having strange men spend the night at her apartment. She thought of Debbie being Bridget Hearn's best friend, or maybe thinking she was until Bridget dumped her, and she tried to think they deserved each other, but instead she got a feeling in her chest as though a rib was broken.

She thought of her mother driving her around during the winter months, while the dark outside and the dashboard lights within made a little oasis of the front seat of the car. She knew that even a week from now things would be different. School would start, and she would spend her days in her green uniform blazer and her plaid skirt, her saddle shoes raising blisters on the joints of her toes and the back of her heels after three months in sneakers and flip-flops. On Tuesday they would shop for school supplies, copy books with their spines still closed tight and pencil boxes that smelled as freshly plastic as Christmas morning. There would be no more nights in the development because she wasn't allowed out on school nights. Soon all the windows of the new houses would be filled with yellow light and the spindly saplings they were planting along Shelley Lane and Dickens Street would grow up to be trees. And soon it would seem as if Tennyson Acres had always been there, and only the older kids would say "Do you remember before they built the development?" and would know what was inside each of those walls. Maggie wondered if someday the people in the last house by the woods would rip up their wall-to-wall carpeting and find the old *Playboys* beneath the floor.

The gold of her locket was warm beneath her fingers. She took a letter from the pocket of her shorts. "Dear Maggie," she read, "I am really glad you are willing to write to me even though we are in the same place and school is starting. I have a lot of things to ask you which are easier to write in a letter than to say to your face. Your face is great but my conversation is not. (HA HA!)" Even now, after reading the letter at least six times, Maggie's breathing felt funny when she got to that part: your face is great. She wondered if Bruce could dance. He had never asked her for anything but the silly line dances at the wedding, perhaps because his father was there. Each time she had looked at him he had looked away and cracked his knuckles. When his father told him it was time to go, he had pressed the letter into her hand, but before he moved away, he had squeezed it hard.

Inside the house she could hear her aunt and her mother laughing. She wasn't sure whether her aunt Celeste was wrong about things changing and staying the same, or whether it was one of those differences between children and adults, like the way they were always saying that time went by so quickly when just to get from June to September seemed to take a lifetime.

Maggie walked through her own backyard to the beginning of the development. The soft ground sagged beneath her feet, and she could see in the cement of the curbs that Terence and his friends had been there, putting in hand and footprints, and leaving their initials: TSS, KAK, RVQ. The asphalt for the roads had not been laid yet, and she could feel the pebbles through the soft thin soles of her sneakers. Up ahead of her was the first house to be finished, a ranch house with sliding picture windows in almost every room. Maggie remembered that Richard and Bruce had written their names inside the doors of the kitchen cabinets the day they'd been installed.

Maggie approached soundlessly, close enough to see into the living-room window. A man and a woman sat on a couch against one wall. He was bald, with his shirt sleeves rolled to the elbow, and she had a short cap of black hair, like a bathing cap, and tiny black eyes. They held round glasses, almost like bowls, filled with dark amber liqueur, and they sipped at it as they looked around them. Their furniture looked as if it had elbows, it was so angular, and on the wall above the couch was what Maggie was sure must be modern art, a soaring splash of fuschia dotted with black and gray. It was pretty, really, and the gray matched the couch. The man rose and Maggie leapt back, her heart pounding, but when she looked in again she could see that he was only adjusting the picture, and she imagined they had just hung it, hung it before they unpacked any of the cardboard boxes stacked at the far end of the room, before they began putting away their dishes and discovering names written in pencil inside their brand-new cabinet doors.

The woman rose and stared at the picture, a hand on her hip, and then she said something to the man and stood tapping her foot while he made the smallest adjustment. A voice in Maggie's head said stridently, "I'd bet my bottom dollar they're Jews," even though Maggie herself was thinking that they looked mostly Italian, and Maggie recognized it as her grandfather's voice. And she knew that for the rest of her life, from time to time she would hear that voice within her head.

She wondered if this was what it was like to be haunted. Or perhaps that was what heaven was, the eternal life of your own point of view fired off, every now and then, inside the skulls of unsuspecting friends and relatives. Maggie thought that her grandfather would live that way in her mind, until the day when she died herself, when there would be other people around to remember her. She looked back at the houses of Kenwood, old and familiar, and she looked around her at Tennyson Acres, and the two seemed to her to be the past and the future. She heard her grandfather's voice again, saying, "There's the here, and then there's the hereafter." That was how it looked to her, the two parts of the neighborhood, like here and hereafter, like what had been and what was to come. Her grandfather was finally having his hereafter, but he was here, too, inside her head, and she was glad of that.

It wasn't only the dead that lived with you that way. When she closed her eyes she could hear Helen say "Not to decide is to decide," and her mother saying, with a great throb in her quiet voice, "Not good or bad. Things just are." She knew that twenty years from now she would still hear all those voices in her head, and she knew that as long as they stayed there she would be able to do all the things she had to do, to make all the choices she had to make. But yesterday, as she had walked down the aisle, looking into the curled heart of the pink rose at the center of her bouquet, she had heard another voice, telling her to lift her chin, to keep her shoulders square, to walk slowly. And suddenly it had come to her, as she was dancing with her father, the stars of darkness exploding inside her closed lids, that the voice she was hearing was her own, for the first time in her life.

About the Author

ANNA QUINDLEN's nationally syndicated opinion column, "Public and Private," appears in *The New York Times* and in many other newspapers around the country. She was a reporter and editor with the *Times* from 1977 until 1986, when she created the column "Life in the 30's," which appeared in the *Times* and other papers for the following three years. *Living Out Loud*, a collection of these columns, was published by Random House in 1988. Anna Quindlen is married, and is the mother of two sons and a daughter. This is her first novel.

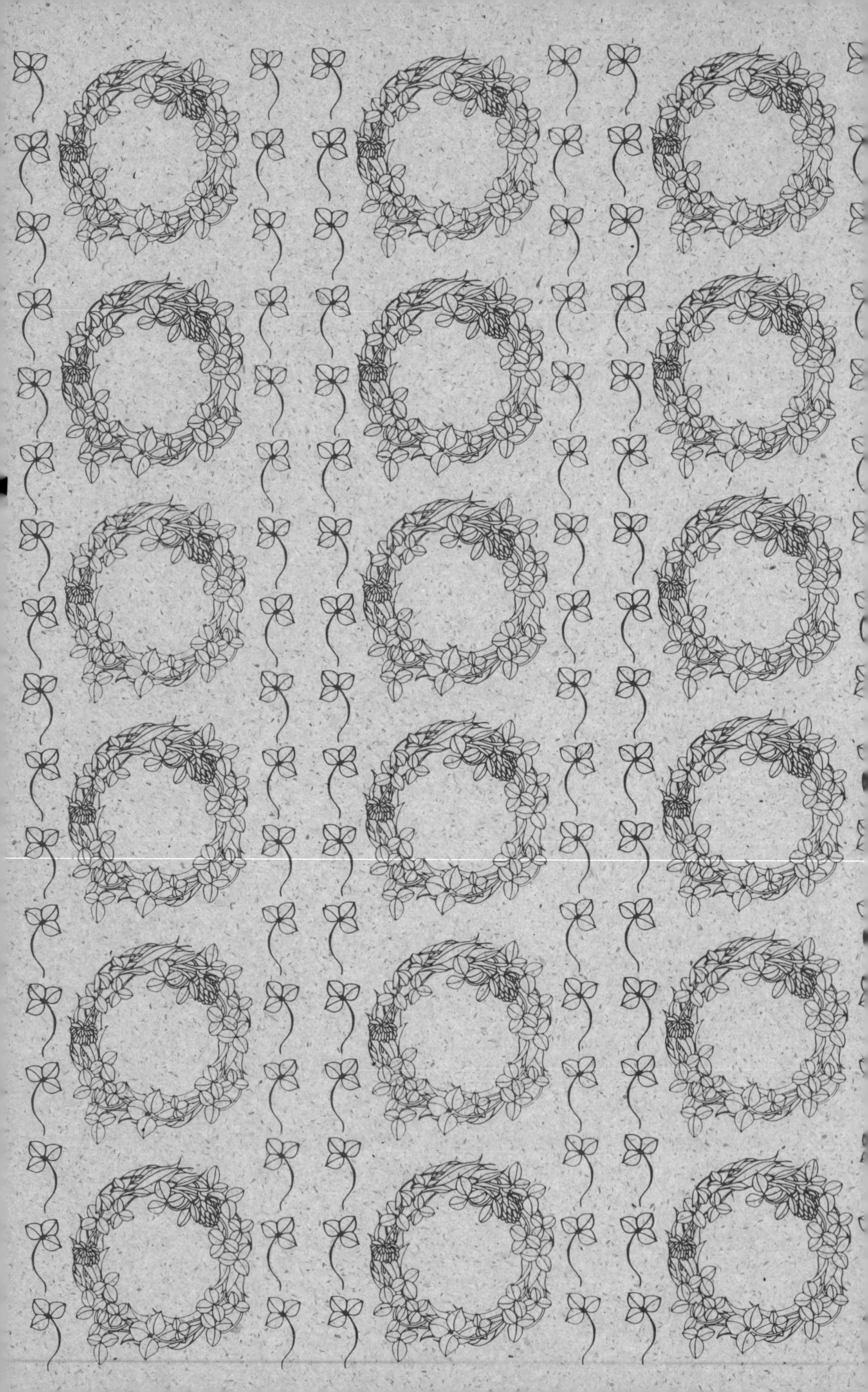